Praise for Jacquelyn Frank . . .

"Jacquelyn Frank's *Nightwalker* series depicts an engrossing alternate world, drawn in prose that is lush and lyrical."
—Linda Howard

"Jacquelyn Frank knows how to write an intense, rip-roaring good read!"—Cathy Maxwell

"Jacquelyn Frank is a fresh new voice, a stunning new talent. I look forward to the next book."—Sherrilyn Kenyon

"An astonishing, fresh, captivating voice—paranormal fans will devour this book!"—Lori Foster

"I cannot say enough good things about this new series. Ms. Frank has created an intriguing alternate universe populated with some fascinating people."—www.aromancereview.com

. . . and her enchanting first novel, *Jacob: The Nightwalkers*

"Jacki Frank's *Jacob: The Nightwalkers* is filled with mesmerizing, breathtaking, scorching sex—and filled with unforgettable characters."—Christine Feehan

"Like the most delicious chocolate, *Jacob: The Nightwalkers* is rich, dark, and satisfies every craving."—Joann Ross

"The pantheon of hot paranormal authors just expanded to include a bright new talent in the form of Frank. Exploding onto the scene with a fresh voice and an original viewpoint, this debut author is a huge find. Her vivid alternate reality centers on a brand-new culture that is absorbing and filled with highly intriguing characters. Keep your eye on this author and this series, they are both going places."—*Romantic Times* (4½ stars, Top Pick)

"*Jacob* by Jacquelyn Frank is highly intense and extremely action packed. Thrown for a loop from page one, I could not put this book down until I finished."—www.romancejunkies.com

Also by Jacquelyn Frank

Jacob: The Nightwalkers

Elijah: The Nightwalkers

Published by Zebra Books

GIDEON
THE NIGHTWALKERS

JACQUELYN FRANK

ZEBRA BOOKS
Kensington Pubishing Corp.
www.kensingtonbooks.com

ZEBRA BOOKS are published by

Kensington Publishing Corp.
119 West 40th Street
New York, NY 10018

All Kensington titles, imprints, and distributed lines are
available at special quantity discounts for bulk purchases for
sales promotion, premiums, fund-raising, educational, or insti-
tutional use.

Special book excerpts or customized printings can also be
created to fit specific needs. For details, write or phone the
office of the Kensington Special Sales Manager: Attn. Special
Sales Department. Kensington Publishing Corp., 119 West
40th Street, New York, NY 10018. Phone: 1-800-221-2647.

Zebra and the Z logo Reg. U.S. Pat. & TM Off.

ISBN-13: 978-1-4201-2483-5
ISBN-10: 1-4201-2483-8

First Printing: June 2007
10   9

Printed in the United States of America

ACKNOWLEDGMENTS

*This time there is only one entity upon which I would
like to focus all my gratitude:*

To Kensington Publishing

*For all that you have done, for every single sector or
group or individual who has had anything and
everything to do with the creation of the Nightwalkers
series as it stands on the shelves today and in the future.*

*My special thanks to the sales force who made a first-time
author come out with an astounding first-time print
run with Jacob. You people are incredible and I dedicate
this book, its beauty, and its successes to you. Every
time you see it or Jacob on a shelf in the store, you
should feel the outrageous pride that comes from a
job not just well done, but done in splendor.*

To the art department, I LOVE THIS COVER!

*And Kate: You are a goddess, my ultimate cheerleader,
and the driving force behind everything that is
happening for this series. You baby me, spoil me,
and scold me as necessary but you never,
never once, lost faith in me or this series.*

*Just so you know that I am aware I am the
luckiest lady in the world.*

Thanks to all of you.

Prologue

"We must enforce ourselves more strictly as the time approaches. In the age of the rebellion of the Earth and Sky, when Fire and Water break like havoc upon all the lands, the Eldest of the old will return, will take his mate, and the first child of the element of Space will be born, playmate to the first child of Time, born to the Enforcers . . ."
—*The Lost Demon Prophecy*

The Vampire eyed the Demon before him with a lengthy, contemplative gaze of midnight blue. The black centers of his eyes were slightly oval in shape, the contour just enough of an oddity to incite one's curiosity, beckoning one to lean in closer, to gaze and study them just a little deeper, to stumble into them like a well-spun web. Since such temptations could not lure the Demon, the Vampire's only intention of close study was strictly for scrutiny as he tried to decipher the silent figure's purpose.

With uncharacteristic patience and largesse, the Vampire leaned back in his chair and casually hooked an ankle over one knee as he did so. As usual, the Demon was biding his time before he began to speak about whatever it was that was on his mind, whatever it was that had brought the Ancient to the Vampire's lair. It was always good that he put so much care of thought into his speech, the Vampire mused to himself, because when this Demon spoke it was often to lay brutal truths at the feet of whomever he was conversing with. As admirable a trait as that was, it was not so refreshing as one might expect it to be, particularly when it heralded pivotal occurrences in the lives of the Nightwalker races.

Since time had begun, ages before the mortals had spread across this earth like an intemperate pandemic, there had been the Nightwalkers. The Dark Cultures. Those who basked in the moon for their daylight, and slept or hid from the sun when its acidic rays would try to touch their susceptible skins or minds. The clans had run with the wild beasts of Nature, their special gifts rooted in Her ways, keeping them connected to the soil, the free creatures, and the pulsing, magmatic center of Her heart. And though in the modern age the mortals were the dominant population by a dramatic percentage, the Nightwalkers yet lived. The Dark Cultures were preserved, each with its separate ways and traditions, and each had carved out niches in those places that remained isolative and usually too inhospitable for humans. Some had adapted and now lived on the fringes of human societies, emulating or enjoying mortal ways . . . or a careful facsimile. Almost every clan had carefully laid laws and beliefs about how far its members could go when it came to dealings with human beings.

Time had not cut the Nightwalkers' links with either moon or sun. Errors and enemies had severely thinned out the ranks of all of the different clans in one way or another, and yet they survived—quiet, unknown to mortals for the most part, and searching for ways to find harmony in a rapidly changing world. But the world had changed before, and would change again, and there would always be the Nightwalkers to dance beneath the moon and sleep behind the sun.

"You have not come to visit in a great while, Gideon," the

Vampire observed in the capricious way of his people, no longer wishing to wait for the Demon to come around on his own time. "I had not expected to see you."

Gideon lifted his cool, silver eyes from the delicacy of the rare zebra's milk he had been swirling idly in his glass. The exotic milk, and others like it, was a Demon's alcohol. It was proof that though Nightwalkers greatly resembled humans, usually very handsome and appreciable ones, there were distinct differences in their chemistries and physiologies. These distinctive differences would set them apart as supernatural beings to the common eye, should they decide to flaunt them.

But the Nightwalkers used great care here. Human beings could become overzealous at even the smallest hint of myth or mystery. It was in their nature to fear that which was more powerful than themselves, a failing that would not change until they matured as a species.

Regardless of the fact that he himself boasted unusually riveting features, the Vampire was struck, as he always was, with the drilling effect of the Demon's molten mercury eyes. Gideon's facial appearance, agelessly aristocratic, showed nothing of his having existed for a more than a millennium, but those eyes most certainly did. Since Demons also tended toward a swarthy complexion, looking perpetually tanned, it magnified the startling effect of Gideon's gaze.

The Ancient Demon also had hair of incredibly pristine silver, long enough to touch his collarbone and tied back with a thin strip of tanned leather. In humans, this coloring would be a sign of age, but the Vampire knew Gideon had been born with his hair color, and, in spite of it, would never look a day over the age of thirty-five. Perhaps a little closer to forty when one took those aged eyes into account.

"If you have felt slighted in any way, Damien, I extend my apologies," the Demon said with distant manners, his rich voice filling the echoing places of the large room.

Damien dismissed the idea with a click of his tongue and the brushing wave of an elegant, long-fingered hand.

"We are creatures of the ages, Gideon. We have long since learned to not feel slighted when one or the other of us goes into seclusion for whatever reason." Damien's indigo eyes narrowed on the Demon seated across from him. "But I admit that I am curious as to the motivation for your visit after all this time."

"I am afraid it is not as social as I might have wished it to be," Gideon said. "I am here to serve you warning."

"Warn me?" Damien cocked a gracefully arched brow at the Demon.

"Yes. As the most Ancient of my race, to the most Ancient of yours."

Damien acknowledged the reverence of Gideon's distinction with a graceful inclination of his head.

"Despite the vast differences in our races, Gideon, you and I have always found much in common with one another."

"And it is a commonality that brings me to your door now. A common enemy."

This revelation made the Vampire's spine straighten with sudden tension.

"Necromancers." It wasn't a question. They had both been alive too long not to know what was of import to one another. "Damn," Damien hissed, suddenly standing and pacing the floor of his cavernous parlor. "I should have known. I should have sensed something was amiss!"

"How do you see that?" Gideon asked, one brow lifting inquisitively.

"Gerard has gone missing. I had thought he might have just gone to ground, as my people do from time to time, but Gerard had just roused from a century-long sleep, so I thought it odd he would return so quickly."

"It is still possible that is all that has happened."

"Possible," the Vampire agreed, "but he is not the only one to go missing, and you know as well as I do that it is unlikely to be coincidence. Have you any idea how many we are to contend with this time?" The ancient Vampire stilled his stride, his hands curling into fists and his fierce eyes flaring with his obvious contempt for the odious human magic-users who had plagued the Nightwalker races for centuries. "How foolish I was to hope that, since there had been no necromancers for this last century, we had seen the last of them. It is embarrassing to my intelligence to speak of it even now."

"You have been no more or less foolish than the rest of us," Gideon said darkly. "I am the most ridiculous of them all."

The Demon was silent for a long heartbeat, and Damien's supernatural senses hummed sharply with subconscious awareness of the Demon's disturbed thoughts. Out of respect, however, Damien would never think of scanning Gideon in order to obtain those thoughts.

"Along with the return of these necromancers," Gideon continued, his perfectly pitched voice as even and unaffected by emotions as ever, "we have discovered that Druids are yet in existence."

"Druids?"

Now *that* truly surprised Damien. There had been no Druids for the space of an entire millennium. Their reemergence would have been thought a thousand times less likely than this distressing news of necromancers. Damien was well aware that the Demons and the Druids had once, long ago, been engaged in a terrible war, with history recording that the Demons had eradicated the entire Druid race.

"How do you come by this information?" Damien asked curiously.

"I have met them. They are hybrids, partially of Druidic descent, partially human. Apparently Druids hid themselves among humans all those centuries ago, in order to escape their Demon hunters."

"And bred with them," Damien added in sudden

understanding. "And they are pure enough to have Druidic abilities, even after all this time?"

"Purity . . ." Gideon's lips twisted with the sensation of irony that flooded him. "Apparently, purity is less powerful than this particular fusion of races. There are only two active Druids at this time, both of whom are under Demon protection, and they are greatly coveted." The Demon inclined his head slightly. "For the most part."

"I have yet to find a culture of perfect uniformity in any matter. It is to be expected. At least they are not met with hostility."

"The war is long forgotten. The oldest of us who might hold grudges are all perished, save myself, and I have grown well beyond such childish impulses."

"No doubt," Damien agreed without wit.

"The first Druid is the mate of our Enforcer, the other the mate of the Enforcer's youngest brother. The first female . . . She is powerful in unexpected ways. Ways that I am not at liberty to discuss at this time. Her sibling is awakening to her abilities much more slowly, but I have reason to expect that she will be just as unique. It is also clear they are only the beginning."

Damien returned to his seat, sitting down very slowly, taking the time to brush his dark, stylish clothes into place so he could think on Gideon's information. He always listened very carefully to the way others spoke, to the way they worded phrases. Gideon had confessed already that he was intentionally withholding information, but the Vampire Prince sensed other depths to the story that promised to be fascinating and dangerous.

"I trust that you are guiding these . . . hybrids? I do not relish the idea of unregulated beings of power in our world. The misguidance of necromancers is sinister enough, not to mention the less seemly Nightwalkers amongst us already."

"I find it odd that you would voice such an unnecessary question," Gideon remarked serenely, sipping his beverage and rolling the bouquet of it over his tongue for a moment.

"At times I find comfort in voicing a concern just to hear the verbal assurance. I know you will do what you can and must do. More so, I suspect, considering the history you share with the Druids." Damien lifted his own glass, inspecting the ruby liquid within for a thoughtful moment. "I had always thought the eradication of the Druids was an ill-decided action, Gideon. But that was a time, as I recall, when we Vampires were avaricious enough to enjoy the idea of Demons and Druids eliminating one another, leaving us to become more powerful. Even though I was young then, I do remember that the popular way of thinking at the time was that it was no more our place to interfere in the actions of your race than it was yours to interfere in the actions of ours."

"Perhaps if there had been such an intervention in this instance, we might have saved a great many beings a tremendous amount of grief," Gideon speculated.

The Ancient Demon spoke matter-of-factly, but Damien was too old and too wise not to know the weight those words carried on the Ancient's soul.

"War rests heavy on everyone's memory, Gideon," the Vampire said quietly. "I myself, in my youthful boredom and impulsiveness, warred my people against yours those four centuries ago."

"I appreciate your attempts at my absolution, Damien; however, your energy is best spent in other ways." The Demon placed his glass on the table at his elbow, the sound of the crystal contacting the ornate glass a resonating warning that Gideon was not feeling so detached and level as he projected to others around him. "I am highly aware of my part in the atrocities of our war with the Druids, and cognizant of the price Demons have paid for it. It may be that a small part of my absolution rests in the hands of the others who will come in the footsteps of the two female Druids, but my sins are far too great to be so easily forgiven."

"No sin that weighs on a soul for a thousand years is too great for forgiveness, Gideon." His indigo eyes darkened a fraction more. "At least, that is my own personal hope."

Gideon did not rebuke the Vampire again. They both held a fair share of sin on their shoulders, and neither could bring himself to dash even the slightest part of the other's hope. Strange, that after so long, they held any hope at all. Gideon had always suspected, though, that it was some sort of defense mechanism, this thing called hope. He was a cynical creature, from tip to toe, and no one who knew him in any degree would argue that, but they would perhaps be a little shocked to know that there might be a part of the Demon that still held out for a glimmer of absolution. Gideon was not a man used to giving explanation or apologies for his actions. He was the oldest and most powerful of his kind, and with that distinction came the privilege of doing pretty much whatever suited him. In order to reach such an advanced age, he was considered to have learned enough to know best.

A prime example would be his presence in the lair of the Vampire Prince who was seated across from him. Within his own race, Damien was the mirror of Gideon's position and power. Though the Vampires and the Demons were not enemies, they were not great friends either. There were those on both sides of their races who held little tolerance for the other, and others still who actively sought to antagonize one another. But this had been true between differing societies since time was time. There was no such thing as a perfect peace so long as there was free will and obstinate ignorance in the world, even in races so long lived, so powerful, and so renowned for great intelligence and sophisticated reasoning.

They were failings that the two of them had dryly referred to as their more "human" aspects.

"And as to your earlier question, Damien, it is unknown exactly how many necromancers we are contending with this time. However, recent experiences and interrogations with them indicate to me that their ranks have been growing quietly for some time now. It is their recent activities that have only just made them visible to us."

"Have there been Summonings?" Damien asked edgily. The act of Summoning, when a necromancer stole a Demon and held it captive, was the most horrible fate known to Demonkind. Once captured in such a way, a Demon, no matter how intelligent, how refined, powerful, and controlled, would, after being bombarded by the vile, blackest arts that had captured him, transform into a hideous, practically mindless monster—into the very image of a Demon that was more widely accepted by the human race. No doubt it was this effect witnessed by necromancers over the centuries that had imprinted the image in human legend in the first place. In all myth, there was sometimes more than a grain of fact.

The Nightwalker races were living proof of that.

"Several," Gideon continued grimly. "I cannot even begin to explain the ramifications this has caused within my race."

"You do not need to explain. Necromancers rarely stick to the Demon race, as you know. No doubt we will begin finding the ashes of my kind staked out in the sun soon enough, not to mention the gory remains of Lycanthropes and the other Nightwalkers."

"The only consolation I can give you at the moment is that since the kidnapping and retrieval of our King's sister, there have been no other instances of Summoning," Gideon said. "The necromancers have been silent."

"Silence can be as threatening as action," Damien mused, his ringed hand sounding the rim of the crystal glass he held like a high-pitched instrument.

"I agree. They are an arrogant species, these human, dark-magic users. They do not remain quiet for long.

Only long enough to regroup. That is why I am here giving you fair warning, Damien. I know they will be returning, and we must all be prepared."

"It is appreciated. I will be certain to alert my people."

Chapter 1

"*Siddah! Siddah* Legna!"

Magdelegna turned when the high-pitched voice called to her, barely able to glance over her shoulder in time to see a young body hurtling into her legs from behind, nearly knocking her to her knees. She laughed as she twisted around to see the little creature clinging for his life to her gossamer skirts.

"Daniel! You are pulling your aunt's hair," she scolded him, gently extricating the softly curled tresses out from under his grasp on her knees. She gathered the coffee-colored mass in her hands and then pulled it over her shoulder to further protect it from her nephew's enthusiastic greeting.

"Mummy is awful mad at me. Please don't let her spank me!"

Legna sighed with her exasperation, prying her nephew off her legs so she could lower her impressive height down to his significantly smaller perspective.

"Your mum is my sister, dearest heart, but that does not give me the right to gainsay her punishment of you when you have been naughty. In truth, when I was a young girl, since your mother is my eldest sister, she used to punish me when I was naughty." Legna tried to suppress her smile when the young boy's face took on a horrified and hopeless expression. Her heart went out to him as she remembered all too well how strict her sister could be. "Anyway, I seem to recall you begging for asylum not two days ago. Are you in so much trouble again so soon?"

"But, Aunt Legna, you are my *Siddah*. You can tell her not to spank me."

"Daniel, it is because I am your *Siddah* that I should encourage your mum to discipline you. When it comes time for your *Siddah* to foster you, she will be very strict with you. I promise you, dearest heart, that I will be a very stern teacher. And my first lesson to you is that you must face up to the ramifications of your mistakes. All good men do."

"But I am not a man. I am a little boy. I am only six years old."

"True," Legna acquiesced with a nod, "you are just a boy. But how often have you told me that you wish to be a man as brave and strong as your uncle? You claim that one day you will be King of all Demons, like your uncle Noah. Correct?" She waited for his reluctant nod. "Now, what kind of King would you be if you cowered away from your own wrongdoings?"

"I don't suppose I would be a very good one," Daniel said, lowering his huge blue eyes to the floor so his aunt could not see the tears in them that matched the quaver of his voice. "But I did not mean to be a naughty child on purpose."

Legna sighed once more, taking pity on her precocious nephew.

"I know that. I truly believe that you wish to be a good child in your heart."

"One can only hope that my son will learn to follow his heart one day," came a dry observation from the entrance of the arboretum.

Legna stood up to her full height, smiling at her sister Hannah as the other woman moved into the room to scoop her errant youngster from the floor, setting him high on her shoulder.

"For now, though, as long as he insists on giving in to mischievous impulses, such as hiding under the Great Council table during session, he must take his punishment."

"Oh, Daniel, you didn't." Legna tsked at the child, making his chubby cheeks turn a brilliant scarlet color.

"I didn't mean to. I was just playing hide and seek with Uncle Noah."

"Yes, well, next time perhaps you ought to begin the game by actually informing your uncle he is part of it instead of having him find out the hard way, eh? For now, it is home and to bed with you, where you will think about your behavior until your father returns. Then you will discuss the matter with him, because it is clear that my discussions with you have no effect." Hannah set her child onto his feet and gave him a light whack on the bottom to propel him in the right direction. "Off with you. Find your *li-li-ni* and travel home." Hannah reached out with her powerful senses for a moment, searching for the location of the child's nanny. "She is in the nursery with your sisters. Perhaps if you are in bed and quiet by the time I come home, I will rethink telling your father how naughty you have been."

"Yes, Mummy," Daniel promised, his head and voice as low and contrite as a young boy could possibly manage. He shuffled out of the arboretum, casting his aunt one last pleading look before he meandered across the Great Hall, clearly hoping to put off his confinement for as long as possible.

"Daniel, I have seen snails move faster," Hannah scolded, having not even turned around and still knowing what her progeny was attempting to do.

Hannah's mothering instincts were a marvel to Legna. Her sister's seemingly unending patience was even more of a miracle considering Daniel was the second youngest of six siblings. Hannah and Legna waited until Daniel had gone up the main stairs to their brother's castle, well on his way to finding his *li-li-ni*, before exchanging amused looks.

"He is quite a handful, my sister," Legna remarked, laughing softly as she turned back to the small bonsai tree she had been pruning so patiently. "I hope you plan to wait some time before adding to your brood as you repeatedly insist on doing. I do not think I could be *Siddah* to any more of your children."

"I would never do such a thing, sister." Hannah laughed in return. "I fear that Daniel and Eve will be quite enough for you to manage in the coming century. Take solace in the fact that they are a good seven years apart in age. Also, Noah is *Siddah* as well to them both. You will not be alone in their training. No one is."

"That will make it easier, provided I am still under our brother's roof when the time comes for you to foster them to us."

That got Hannah's attention, and the tall woman, her black sheet of hair with its red highlights so much like their brother's, went to touch her sister's shoulder.

"Legna, are you trying to tell me you are considering leaving our brother's household? Are you unhappy here?"

"Unhappy? Noah is King, most revered of all Demons, as well as one of the most powerful Fire Demons in all our history. You know well enough that in spite of the volatility of his root element, he is most loving and attentive, his power and responsibility making him incredibly sensitive to the needs of those around him. I am busy here, as both his chatelaine and an invaluable diplomat of his court. I could never be unhappy under my brother's roof."

"Very well, not unhappy, then. But perhaps . . . wanting?" Hannah queried, touching her sister under the chin to encourage her to look into her eyes. "Legna, I may not be a Demon of the Mind and a great empath, as you are, but I know my sister well enough to know when her emotions are troubled."

"Truly, you are mistaken, Hannah," Legna insisted, leaving her sister's touch to concentrate once more on the plant she kept studying but had yet to prune since the conversation with her sibling had begun. "I lack for nothing here, and I have no tremendous desire to leave. But it will be five years, give or take, before Eve reaches the age of Fostering, and longer still before it is Daniel's turn. A great deal can occur even in that short span of time. I was only musing aloud. It is nothing for you to make a fuss over."

The indelicate sound Hannah made broadcast the likelihood of her believing her little sister's claims, but at that moment Noah entered the arboretum.

"Hannah, I swear to you if you do not take that little scoundrel of yours in hand, I will do it myself."

"Noah, please, you know Daniel does not mean any harm. He is just a boy," the mother argued for her child, waving off the matter as if it meant nothing to any of them, quickly forgetting that she had been just as perturbed with him.

"Hannah . . ." Noah warned, his tone as close to scolding as he dared, knowing his sister, as a female Demon of Fire, had the temper to match his own.

Legna turned to glance from one sibling to the other, as usual wondering which of the two Demons who boasted connection with so hot-blooded an element would be the first to lose their temper, as they often did when they came head to head with one another. Luckily, Fire Demons were rare. Unluckily, it was quite volatile to have two in the same family.

It often fell to Legna, the empath and consummate diplomat, to discern who was getting hot under the proverbial and literal collar quickly enough to defuse the situation. Hannah and Noah dearly loved one another, but often the love was strongest when they were not too close to each other and definitely stronger when they were not arguing opposite sides in a contest of wills.

"Hannah, the boy may have heard things that will disturb him," Noah said, his tactic changing to a gentle warning that appealed to Hannah's strongest instinct, that of a mother.

"What is it, Noah?" Hannah asked quickly, her hand lifting to her throat, where she nervously tugged on the lovely ruby choker her husband had given her on their wedding night. She was not one to get rattled easily, but the habitual fingering of the jeweled choker was a dead giveaway that she was disturbed.

Each of the three Demons standing in the flourishing arboretum was well aware of the recent troubles that had begun to plague the Nightwalker races. Legna herself had become a victim of these happenings when she had been Summoned by four necromancers intent on stealing her powers and those of her fellow Demons for their own ends and uses. If not for Providence's divine intervention and the newly birthed skills of a befriended Druid, Legna would be dead. Or worse. Hannah's fear was well founded under these circumstances.

"There is no new news for you to feel threatened by at this time, Hannah, so do not fret overmuch. However," Noah continued, "we were discussing methods of dealing with necromancers should we encounter them in the future. I do not need to tell you that listening to the Enforcers and warriors debate the best tactics to rid us of this threat was not the thing for six-year-old ears."

"Yes, you are right, my brother. I am sorry. I will go to Daniel at once."

"Hannah." Noah took his sister's arm as she went to hurry past him, turning her gently to him so he could brush a fond finger down her cheek and kiss her forehead warmly. "I love my nephew, you know that. I am worried for him. I do not mean to be harsh."

"You are King, Noah. It is your duty to worry for us all. And I know that, at this time, it is a heavy burden. I will see to Daniel."

"And in the future, I will look under the Council table before we begin our meetings," Noah added, winking at her with humor so that she laughed. Hannah kissed her brother's cheek and then, with a sudden blurring of the lines of her statuesque figure, spun herself in a collection of smoke that promptly funneled out of the castle via an open space in one of the high stained glass windows of the Great Hall.

Noah turned to face his younger sister, arching one brow to a fairly smug height. Legna lifted a brow back at him, giving him a delicate smattering of applause.

"And I was afraid you would never learn the art of diplomacy," she remarked, her lips twitching with her humor. "It merely took you the entire two and a half centuries of my life. Longer, actually. You had a few centuries' head start."

"Funny how you seem to recall the fact that I am far older than you only when it suits your arguments, my sister," he taunted her, reaching to tug on her hair as he had been doing since her childhood.

"Well, I can say with all honesty that this is the first time I have ever seen you forgo a good argument with Hannah, opting for peace instead. I was beginning to wonder if you were my brother at all. Perhaps some imposter . . ."

"Legna, be careful. You are speaking words of treason," he teased her, tugging her hair once more, making her turn around to swat at his hand.

"I don't know how you convinced the entire Council that you were mature enough to be King, Noah! You are such a child!" She twisted her body so he couldn't grab at her hair again. "And I swear, if you pull my hair once more like some sort of schoolyard bully, I am going to put you to sleep and shave you bald!"

Noah immediately raised his hands in acquiescence,

laughing as Legna flushed in exasperation. For all her grace and ladylike ways, Noah's little sister was quite capable of making good on any threat she made.

"I mean really, Noah. You are just about seven hundred years old. One would think you could at least act like it."

"Legna, these past months I have been doing nothing but act my age. You are the only one who relieves that for me. It is my belief that we should never completely give up that part of us which is childlike, fun loving, and mischievous. And," he said, moving close enough to brush back a strand of hair that had become mussed by his abuse, his affection for her shining clearly in his eyes, "so long as you continue to keep me young at heart, I will never let you forget to stay that way as well, little sister."

Legna smiled softly at him, reaching to kiss his cheek warmly in a return show of tenderness and support. She had been teasing him, but she suddenly regretted it, knowing he had been heavily burdened for a very long time with the crying needs of their race. She would let him tease every last hair from her head if it gave him some peace and happiness to balance out his stresses and duties.

"You tell me this and other things like it on a daily basis, my brother." She paused long enough to take his hand from her face in order to wrap it between her own. "In fact, you have been most attentive for these past five months."

"There is no harm in a brother showing his beloved sister the measure of his affection," he countered, following her lead as she led him out of the misty greenhouse.

"True. And you have always been quite attentive to me over the years," she agreed. "However, Noah, since the Summoning—"

Noah stopped short, pulling his hand free of hers abruptly.

"I do not wish to discuss it." His voice dropped several

dark octaves, a chill of rage lacing behind the low tones. "It is over. The monsters who dared to steal you from me are dead. You are safe and that is the end of the matter."

"Who is it you are thinking to protect by refusing to discuss this?" Legna confronted him suddenly, finally feeling as if she had dodged the topic for long enough. "Me? As you say, I am safe now, so what does it matter? Do you still think to hide behind Isabella, the one who saved me from becoming Transformed? We must protect Isabella. Isabella is a precious commodity. Isabella, the Enforcer, and her special Druid/human hybrid powers! Oh, let us not reveal how she saved me, or it will give others false hope, possibly put our Bella in danger." Legna's tone had gone way past sarcasm at this point, her gray-green eyes flashing with her frustration. "Noah, no one is here but you and me. No one! I want you to turn and look at me and talk to me about why you are avoiding this discussion when there is no one here but *me*."

"Legna." Noah paused, holding his silence while some sort of internal struggle went on behind the green and gray eyes that matched hers in expressivities as well as color. "Words will never satisfactorily describe the profundity of the loss I felt that day you dissolved into nothingness right before my eyes. I swore in that moment that if by some miracle I had you safe in my reach once more, I would never allow anything to put your existence in jeopardy ever again. If I do not discuss these things with you it is because I cannot bear to relive the pain of that moment, nor can I entertain the fear of it happening again without it paralyzing me." He finally looked up at her, meeting her wide eyes. "This family, as well as this kingdom, cannot function beneath a King paralyzed with fear and pain of such magnitude. I beg you to let this topic rest from now on, Magdelegna. If not for the safety of you and others involved, then for my peace of mind."

Legna remained still for a moment, her natural senses picking up on Noah's keen distress, her heart pounding in rhythm with the slightly panicked beating of his. His fear was palpable, and so alien. Noah was the bravest and most steadfast male she had ever known, and it shook her to sense the debilitating emotion from him. But what endangered her feelings more was the realization that he was keeping something from her.

In effect, it was like lying to her. Even if she had not been able to empathize with his feelings, the way his eyes dilated slightly, accompanied by the spike in his pulse and blood pressure, would have given him away. Add to it the fact that she very easily could feel a strong anxiety lying beneath his fear, and Legna was certain of her perception.

She took no offense that Noah was lying or hiding something in addition to the issues he had mentioned, because he had always felt that brotherly need to protect her no matter how old or how powerful she might become. He was well aware that she was more than strong enough to penetrate even his formidable attempts to shield his emotions from her. He was merely hoping that she would overlook this minor shadowing of the truth, out of her love for him. Or possibly out of his love for her.

"Noah," she said softly, her beautiful voice designed to soothe the minds and emotions of those she used it on.

She reached out to touch her brother's hair where it curled over his forehead, the contact helping her connect to the firing synapses of his brain where too many thoughts were crowding in his mind. She sent herself into him, her spirit and power coating him in a soothing sensation, toning down his fear for her safety, building up the stoic confidence in his ability to protect those he served that had been the norm five months ago.

Noah let her comfort invade him, let her soothe him. He had resisted her attempts to do so in the recent past, feeling far too guilty for the danger she had been exposed to, to be willing to allow himself to feel better. He had wanted to be ridden by his fear and his guilt, hoping that somehow it would drive him to find the solution to their vulnerability to Summonings, a search that had been in progress almost as long as the Earth had existed. But all it had managed to do was exhaust him and fray his temper. He was ready now to be soothed, to be forgiven. He was ready for Legna's absolution.

"You are so much like Father," she murmured softly, her voice threading through his soul like a powerful balm. "I was so young, but I never forgot how . . . how much larger than life he always seemed to me. So strong, so protective. I was never afraid when he was there. I know you say I was too little, but between both of our memories, I feel it with all of my soul."

Noah was so overwhelmed by the emotion she drew to the surface that he reached for her, dragged her into a tight hug that broadcast his gratitude. It was the perfect thing for her to say to him, and even though he knew such things were part of her special talents as a Demon who had mastered the inner workings of the Mind, he was happy for it nonetheless.

"Legna," he sighed feelingly, "how I wish Mother could see you, how beautiful you have become, how strong."

Legna's eyes misted over with emotion, her arms hugging Noah as tightly as he held her. She had been too young to remember much of either of her parents, but she had always recalled their father more powerfully than their mother, who was but a ghost in her mind. Noah had known her for centuries, long enough to be able to fill Legna with stories of her. He had done equal service to their father as he had raised her after their father had been Summoned within the following year of their mother's death. The Enforcer had been forced to destroy him in his Transformed state, but Noah had never once held Jacob liable for that painful necessity. As with many things that cut him far too deeply, though, Noah would not discuss either of their parents' deaths.

Demons were immortal, which mostly meant long lived. They were also quite difficult to kill, which added to an already extensive life span. So when Demons lost their siblings or parents or other family, it was usually to some great violence, and it left its mark on the sensitive souls of those left behind. Noah had always refused to tell Legna how her mother had died when Legna was little more than a toddler, and all other potential sources around her knew of his wishes and remained equally steadfast in their silence.

She did, however, remember quite well the day her father had been Summoned by an accursed human necromancer. She knew Noah remembered it, too. It was no doubt why the trauma of last Samhain had marked him so heavily. She did not need to read his emotional memories of having watched her body dissolve into nothingness to know how that moment must have scarred him. It had scarred her as well. She would never forget the pain and terror of that instant for as long as she lived.

But as she urged him to exchange memories of emotion using her empathic abilities—she of how she remembered their father, and carefully selecting and sharing what he held within him of their mother—they realized how very much like their parents they had become. It was comforting, healing, and uplifting to know.

"You were Father's angel," he told her.

"And you were Mother's. I can feel in your heart how much she made you feel special."

"She swore the day I was born I would be King. Father used to laugh at her. What mother does not have the grandest dreams for her child?" Noah moved his head back to look down into his sister's pretty face. "But I think she truly knew. I also think she knew she would not live to raise you. She made me swear to protect you above all else. At least once a week she would tell me how I must keep that promise."

"And you have," Legna insisted. "I do not just say that to comfort you, so stop thinking it. It was you who saw the importance of Jacob's connection to Isabella when she first arrived among us, even though she seemed nothing more than a human with only an honest wish to help us at the time. It was you who allowed her access to the library, skirting the outrage of the Council by doing so. Because of that access, she found the lost Demon prophecy. We discovered that Druid/human hybrids were in existence and were necessary for our survival as a species. Because of you, Jacob allowed himself to fall in love with her, to want to marry her.

"*Because of you*, beloved brother, generously offering to join them in the ceremony yourself, I had my hands on her the night of the full moon those five months ago when I was Summoned. If not for that connection, Isabella would never have been dragged with me into the prison of the pentagram, allowing her powers to dampen its effect and prevent my transformation into a monster that Jacob would have been forced to hunt down and destroy."

"Do not," he murmured, pulling her forehead to his lips, his desperation communicated through the hands that enfolded her head. "Do not speak of it. It shatters my soul to even think about it."

It would have destroyed him.

Legna, his graceful, precious sister, caught in the dark, twisted magic of a pentagram that would have destroyed her beauty, her very soul, twisting her into a likeness of a demon humans would have expected to see. She would have become a monster who would have been hunted and destroyed in order to protect vulnerable humans and Demons alike. It would have been enough to embitter him for the rest of his life, and that was a frightening prospect for a man who ruled an entire species. He knew there was a huge difference between normal humans and the mortals from that species who dabbled in black arts and became necromancers, but if he had lost Magdelegna, he was not certain he would have been able to maintain the distinction.

"But all has turned out well," Legna insisted to him, squeezing his hands in comfort. "You must stop thinking such dark things, Noah, and live in the comfort of the moment. I am well," she reiterated, giving him another little squeeze to make him absorb the impact of her statement.

Noah nodded, smiling finally, his eyes lighting to a soft ash and jade color as he accepted her comfort.

"Yes. You are well. And healthy." He took her hands in his, spreading her arms wide and perusing her. "I wonder sometimes why no one has come to my door demanding to make you his mate. Perhaps it is because, like Bella and Jacob, it is a Druid who must win your heart and soul. The chance of you being matched in an Imprinting has suddenly become a tangible thing. An amazing thing. You can see it now for yourself, just as I saw it when Mother and Father were alive. No one who has ever spent time in Bella and Jacob's presence could possibly ignore the miracle such love can be, how rewarding that deeply spiritual connection is. Jacob is a changed man. I have never seen him so happy or content, and Bella is glowing with love as well as her pregnancy. I find myself envious."

"I know." Legna smiled softly at the mention of her new friend's name and the good fortune Bella had found in her love for Jacob the Enforcer. "There has not been an Imprinting in our society in almost . . . well, frankly, I do not think I can remember when. I, for one, always used to think it was a fairy tale little girls were told. This was before I understood Mother and Father were Imprinted. I wish I had . . . I wish I could remember what you do. I wish I could remember the depths with which they loved one another. You make it sound so beautiful, and now that I watch Jacob and Isabella, how passionately they love, I wish it even more."

"Well," Noah chuckled, "little boys were told these fairy tales as well, but I think we tended to concentrate on the part about it being the most outstanding sexual experience known to exist in the world."

"Noah!" Legna gave him a little shove as she scolded him. But she broke into giggles in spite of herself. "I think I might have thought about that once or twice myself. Take heart. Two Imprintings in a single week last October bodes well for you, my brother."

"One can only hope," Noah said with a lecherous wink that compelled his sister to cluck her tongue at him and roll her eyes in exasperation.

"You are incorrigible! And you wonder where your nieces and nephews get it from?"

Noah laughed, shaking his head. He realized then that Legna had once more found a way to turn the conversation away from herself and onto something entirely different. It had been her habit for as long as he could remember. Legna never discussed herself, her empathic nature always urging her to put her needs and emotions aside in order to assist others.

"Your point is well taken, sweet. I am beyond redemption and it is no wonder none will have me. In any event, I myself am far too busy to run around trying to find a Demon or Druid who suits me, no matter how tempting the rewards. Besides, all the courting nonsense, the emotions and sensitivity . . . We shall leave such things to the Enforcers. Simpering and sonnets suit them far better than they do me."

Legna elbowed her brother in the ribs as punishment for his irreverent referral to Jacob and Isabella. Before Isabella, Jacob had been a lonely man, his soul aching to be accepted and cared for to balance out the stigma of his position as the one who enforced the laws on his own kind. So used to being held in contempt, as a necessary evil, Jacob had only discovered true happiness the day he had literally caught his Isabella up in his arms. Noah liked to tease Jacob for being "ruined" and "besotted," but Legna knew her brother was happy for the Enforcers. Happier still, now that they would provide an addition to their race within a year, the first child born of a Druid and Demon mating in over a millennium.

Sometimes, though, Legna could not escape the feeling that Noah teased too brightly and tried too hard for wit with his disparagements of the Imprinting. She was an empath, she was his sister, and she had eyes in her head. Legna could see what he did not think she did, what he thought he guarded so carefully from her. She had seen the many times when the Enforcers were guests in their home, when Bella and Jacob sat with their dark heads bent together with so much love and sensuality of need for each other, and how gray-green eyes so like her own had watched them covetously.

"Well, I for one would be well pleased to see you so 'afflicted' as Jacob is," she teased with warm neutrality, giving him a classic smile of beautiful mischief. "But for now, you have reminded me of an appointment I am late for." Legna stood on her toes to buss her brother on the cheek. "You look tired and ought to nap."

"I am not an old man in need of naps in the middle of the night," Noah retorted indignantly. "The moon is only just come high."

"Suit yourself, Noah. It was only a suggestion. Forgive me for bruising your delicate ego." She was mocking him, stepping several feet back and spreading her arms wide as she curtsied low and reverently, with all the grace she had earned through her Demon genetics. The next moment, with a flourish of a wrist, she exploded into a soft cloud of smoke and sulfur, teleporting away before Noah had any hope of retorting to her impish behavior.

"Brat!" he shouted to the high ceilings after her, even though he was pretty certain she couldn't hear him.

He stepped toward the fireplace, starting a blaze within it with the merest whisper of thought, and sat down in his favorite chair.

"A nap indeed," he muttered under his breath. "I can give or take energy with the snap of a finger!" he announced proudly to the empty room. "I do not require sleep in the middle of the night like some babe. I will teach that girl a lesson in respect one of these days."

The thought was interrupted when he yawned ferociously. Catching himself doing so, he loosed a sheepish laugh. Glancing around quickly, sealing off his home with a few spare thoughts, he settled back deeper into his chair and allowed himself the luxury of closing his eyes.

Chapter 2

Isabella turned and looked over her shoulder when she felt the air pressure in the room change with a distinct pop. She instantly knew who her guest was, even before the smoke had cleared. Bella cried out happily, dropping her watering can onto the window shelf and flinging herself through the remaining mist of sulfur to hug her newly arrived friend.

"Legna!"

"Bella, it is so good to see you," Legna greeted her happily, hugging the petite Druid carefully in order to avoid squashing her rounded belly. They were acting as though they had not seen each other in ages, rather than a week. It was probably because Bella was so happy to see another woman that she was projecting it enough to affect the sensitive empath. Sometimes Legna got swept up in others' enthusiasms, and she did not mind. It was one of the better emotions to get caught up in.

Isabella laughed, pulling back to look at her friend, tossing back her heavy head of pitch-black hair, the tresses gleaming like raven's feathers as they immediately snaked down the length of the Druid's spine. Isabella barely reached Legna's shoulder, so petite compared to the empath, who was very close to being six feet tall. All Demons were tall. Bella often complained that talking to them gave her a crick in her neck, but Legna had noticed Bella's neck never seemed to hurt when she had to reach for her mate's kiss.

"You are such a liar," Bella accused without zeal. "I look like I am carrying a small basketball under my dress. I'm only five months pregnant and I'm already tired of waddling around."

"Well, far be it from me to remind you, but that baby is half Demon. Five months is only a little bit over first trimester, by Demon standards."

"Okay, just for reminding me of that, you are no longer my friend. Poof yourself out of here right this minute," Isabella commanded, her hands on her hips in mock indignity as she glared at the beautiful woman across from her. Magdelegna chuckled, moving with her fluid grace in order to circle the little Druid's shoulders with a comforting arm. "And," Bella sighed wistfully as her arm circled Legna's waist, "you have to go and have a perfect figure on top of it."

"Now, now," Legna soothed and scolded her. "How is Jacob?" she asked, guiding Bella to a comfortable couch in a cozy conversation area near a beautiful window of stained glass picturing the wilds and wildlife of a forest. The empath felt the care that had gone into the piece, saw the detail, and it was all very breathtaking. Moonlight struck through it, sending silvered colors over them as they sat on couches close to but opposite one another.

"Busy." Isabella exhaled hard, trying to shove her heavy hair behind her ear with impatient fingers. "I should be helping him. I am supposed to be his partner. It says so in black and white . . . or . . . well, actually it's kind of a grayish beige scroll with little red—" Bella gasped, then growled in frustration at herself because she had found a tangent. "The point is, I am destined by this wondrous lost Demon prophecy I discovered to be the one that changes all of Demon destiny by working at his side. Instead, I'm stuck here, sitting on the couch, watching and feeling everything that happens to him from a distance. It really bites." Bella pulled up her legs, crossing them in a meditation position. "I'll tell you this, if he gives me one more order with that *W* word again, I'm going to divorce him before we even finish the wedding."

"The *W* . . . ? Okay, Bella, as usual you have lost me. *W* word?"

"Yeah. *W*, . . . as in Wife. Ugh! He's always saying or thinking things in this high and mighty way and tacking the word 'wife' onto the end like it's some kind of password that lets him order me around." Bella noted her friend's still perplexed expression, so she screwed up her face, attitude, and voice into an uncanny approximation of Jacob. "'I do not want you hunting in your condition, *wife*. It is too dangerous for you and the babe to accompany me, *wife*. I have told Elijah that there are to be no more training lessons until after the birth, and do not argue with me about this, *wife*, because my mind is set.'" Isabella sagged back with a frustrated sigh. "Oy! It's just so obnoxious and so . . . high-handed! You know the honeymoon is over when you go from 'my love,' 'my little flower,' and 'my heart' and become simply '*wife*.'"

Legna smothered the urge to chuckle. Her little friend's famous sarcasm always tickled her, and it was meant to tickle. Bella had a way of hiding behind her wit and humor. She was stating things that clearly disturbed her, but she mocked them in such a way that anyone who did not know her would treat it as little more than a comedy routine.

Legna knew her better.

"Now, Bella, you know Jacob adores you. He naturally wants to protect you. He literally worships the ground you walk on."

"Ha ha," Bella said dryly. "Earth Demon. Worship the ground. Cute. Really cute."

"Well, come on now. Seriously. As a Demon of the Earth,

Jacob has a great affinity with nature. Of all of us, he is the one who knows the most about life and death and the way nature replenishes and selects her perpetuation. He has a respect for it that transcends every feeling he has with perhaps the exception of his love for you. But he is also a hunter, born with the ability to capture any prey by using the senses of the most skilled predatory animals. Knowing the nature of such beasts, carrying their insight with him always, it is part of him to understand the dangers that lurk in the tall grasses.

"Like it or not, Bella, you are vulnerable right now. I know you are powerful and becoming quite skilled in your own right, but what position would Jacob be in if in the course of your work, in a dire circumstance, you should come into danger, be held hostage, or even become mortally injured? I can come up with dozens of scenarios, and Jacob can imagine far more with four centuries of experience as Enforcer to draw on. You have been Enforcer for five months; he has four hundred years behind him of this, the Vampire wars for a century, the Lycanthropes for three . . . There is unusual peace now, save for the necromancers, but there are many variables and you are very precious to him.

"And anyway, what self-respecting male would not be anxious for a beloved mate who is carrying his child—a child who by being born will represent the first of its kind? Human and Demon DNA have never combined in any way before. Yes, you are half Druid as well, but still . . . I could understand why Jacob would be a little concerned . . . and a little overcautious."

"Well." Isabella nibbled on a nail, a sure sign of her own state of nerves. "Maybe I wouldn't mind so much if I were really his wife." She laughed wryly because she knew that the Imprinting went far deeper than ceremonial words could reach. She knew that Legna was aware of this as well. "We still have about a month to go before we can finish our rudely interrupted wedding ceremony.

If my sister teases me one more time about being the 'out-of-wedlock, impregnated tramp' of the family, I am going to have to murder her and dump her body in a cornfield somewhere."

"Bella," Legna scolded, giggling softly at her friend's pique. "Your sister Corrine is no paragon of virtue since she and Kane Imprinted, I assure you. She and Kane came to our home for a meditation training session with me, and I was occupied a few minutes longer than I expected. Well, by the time I got to the parlor, I could sense . . ." Legna's head dipped and she blushed softly. "Let us say it would have been imprudent of me to walk in."

"You're kidding!" Bella gaped at the empath for a moment. "In Noah's home? A governing seat where Demons come and go all day long?"

"At least they closed the parlor doors." Legna chuckled. "She's chafing at the bit for Beltane just as much as you are, believe me." Legna rubbed her friend's knee in a very effective gesture of comfort. "Besides, you know that you are Jacob's lifetime partner in all the ways that matter. To him, you were his wife the moment you first touched."

"Well, I'm thinking someone is going to have to do something about that Demon law about weddings only taking place on Beltane and Samhain," the Druid groused. "It is seriously cramping my reputation. Say"— she snapped her fingers in inspiration, her violet eyes sparkling with mischief—"I seem to recall you being the King's . . . uh . . . cousin? No, no, that's not it." Bella made a great show of tapping a finger to her chin in thought. "Um, oh yes! His sister!" she said, as if she hadn't remembered all along. "Surely *you* could encourage him to discuss the matter with the Great Council."

"Bella, you goose." Legna laughed. "I wish I had that kind of power over my dear brother. However, I do not. No more than you have over Mother Nature and her plans for the duration of your pregnancy."

"You mentioned it again!" Bella scolded with a dramatic screech of exasperation, making Legna sigh and smile with amused patience. "Well, at this point I would be happy if we ended up with an average between the time required for a human gestation and the Demon gestation of thirteen months. *Anything* is better than thirteen months."

"What has Gideon told you?" Legna asked, unable to resist avoiding Bella's violet gaze as she mentioned the powerful medic's name. She turned her attention to smoothing out the aqua silk of her gown's long skirt, her fingers tracing the rich golden embroidery swirling over it in a repetitive pattern. "Is he still personally monitoring you?"

"Yes, he is. Actually, that alone is enough to make me a little nervous." Bella exhaled a little shakily. "I was talking to Hannah and she said that in all six of her pregnancies, she was never monitored so closely. And certainly not by the most Ancient and highly skilled medic in all of Demon history. They say that Gideon has forgotten more about healing than all the other medics combined will *ever* know."

"Well, perhaps Gideon is merely making an extra effort because it has been so long since a Druid and a Demon have mated. And yes, I am sure the fact that you are half human does make your case unique, but I am also certain he only means to be cautious. You know how direct he is. If there were something to worry about, he is not one to keep you uninformed."

"True. He would at the very least inform Jacob if there were something to be concerned about, wouldn't you say? Jacob and I have very few secrets between us, what with our ability to share one another's thoughts."

"I must admit, Bella," Legna confessed, "that even though I am a Mind Demon, I am quite grateful I can only read emotions, unlike my male counterparts who can trade thoughts as you and Jacob do. I am positive that I would not want to know everything someone was thinking. Trust me, knowing everything they are feeling can be quite troublesome enough. And as for Jacob being able to read your thoughts, I do not know how you bear it. I am not so certain I would enjoy someone else having access to my most private ruminations. I suppose the closest I come to that is with Hannah and Noah. We have always had a strong sense of one another's needs, desires . . . pain. But I promise you, there are things that have crossed my mind that I hope Noah *never* finds out about."

Legna gave an impish wiggle of her brows, making Bella laugh.

"I'm familiar with that particular desire," Bella said with a nod. "Still, there's something comforting about the vast openness of the sharing and honesty between Jacob and me. And . . ." She paused, her face softening with a warm, beautiful thought, her skin, like pale satin, flushing with a gentle glow. "My love, my mate, lives within me always, Legna. I'm never completely alone, even when he tries to give me solitude. And I don't even mind. Part of me realizes that, for the rest of my life, I will never be alone again. Better still, I will never be lonely. It's compelling in a way I can't possibly describe. My sister is only just beginning to learn this for herself. I have tried to help her, but I always fail to describe it to her adequately."

"Your description lacks nothing, Bella," the empath confessed quietly, a catch of emotion in her throat and a shine of bittersweet happiness in her eyes for her friend.

"Corrine's power acquisition is taking much longer than mine did. Gideon believes it's delayed because of how close she came to dying."

Bella shuddered as she remembered the image of her sister lying close to death in her bed, gray and gaunt from the energy drain she had suffered. A Druid only came into power when his or her Demon mate came into contact with them for the first time. At the time Corrine and Kane had encountered each other, no one had realized she was a Druid, destined to be with Kane and destined to wither away without his nearness and energy to replenish her.

"It has been taking time, Gideon says, for her connection with Kane to rebuild and repair itself. He likened it to having brain damage, where the brain has to reroute function in other ways to compensate for the damage." Bella shook her head. "I watch her struggles and I am so frustrated for her. I want her to be as happy as I am. I want her power to come so she will know what we have inherited. As a logical person I know it will take time, but as a sister—a pregnant sister at that—I want to yell out to the Fates, 'C'mon already!' She's already been through so much."

"She has come very far already. She is looking healthy and does not become weak as quickly," Legna soothed her.

"Gideon said as much, but he also said she may have more setbacks and that we should be prepared for that. He explained that the damage has made her pathways to power fragile. But you know this. This is why you are teaching her meditation and focus techniques. It is by his prescription."

"It will never cease to amaze me, the extent of Gideon's knowledge. He is the only Demon in all the world who was alive during the time of the last Druids. In spite of it being over a millennium ago, he still remembers such details of the connections between Druid and Demon, and of the healing processes of a race he thought was obliterated. It boggles the mind to think he was only a fledgling himself at the time."

"Yes. It's quite remarkable." Isabella leaned forward, lowering her voice to a whisper. "But Gideon holds a great deal of weight on his soul over having been a part of the original massacre of the Druids. I believe he feels he should have known better, in spite of the fact that the entire world was fairly savage at the time and he was a mere fledgling following the orders of the Elders of the era."

"War never makes sense when the aftermath is studied a thousand years later. It is a testament to his strength that he has survived in spite of all the deaths, Summonings, and worldwide upheavals of a millennium. A thousand years." Legna shook her head with amazement. "Even those Demons who are past their fifth century have difficulty comprehending such a lifetime."

Isabella nodded, sitting back once more and absently rubbing her distended belly. "So you are certain he would tell me if he had concerns about the baby?"

"Positive," Legna affirmed with a curt nod. "There may be a great many things about Gideon I do not understand, or even like, to be honest, but his straightforwardness is admirable, even if somewhat harsh from time to time. Besides, Jacob would not tolerate anything less than total forthrightness, and Gideon would respect that. Their friendship is still much strained, in spite of Gideon's welcome return to mainstream Demon life and his Triumvirate seat on the Great Council. However, Jacob's latent hostility would not keep Gideon silent if speaking was called for."

"I know," Bella said softly. "I don't think that Jacob has quite come to terms with Gideon's rude behavior around me in the beginning of our relationship."

"But he would be foolish to turn away the most skilled medic in Demon history when that Demon offers to oversee the pregnancy of his beloved mate," Legna pointed out. "And Jacob is no fool. No matter how deeply his Imprinted instincts have made him come to distrust other males who come too close to you, I believe your safety is paramount to him. He wouldn't let anything stand in the way of that, not even if it were Prince Charming himself who needed to tend you."

Isabella tossed back her head and laughed aloud at that, appreciating the mischievous sparkle in the other woman's eyes. Legna was impressively unmoved by the power of the male Demons who surrounded her night in and night out, century after century. Isabella had appreciated that from the moment she had met the female Demon.

This brave characteristic in her friend had served as a model for Bella, teaching her to put her foot down and stand up for her rights and perspective even before her own ability to absorb and use the powers of those around her had come into play. Other Demons had learned to respect her long before they had been forced to respect the magnitude of her awesome ability to render anyone from any Nightwalker race completely powerless.

Luckily, this was the same power that had forced Isabella into being included in Legna's terrifying Summoning during her and Jacob's aborted wedding ceremony. It was that same power that had nullified the damaging effects of the pentagram that had caged them together.

Even though the experience had been terribly harrowing, Isabella was constantly grateful to have had a hand in sparing her friend the fate of being Transformed. Among other things, it would have destroyed Jacob to be put in the position of hunting the sister of his King, forced to destroy her before she destroyed others. Jacob's relentless sense of duty and his respect and love for Noah would have made his course clear, but Jacob carried his failures hard, and he would have blamed himself for not doing more to save one so important to the man he looked on as a brother as well as monarch.

No one meant as much to Isabella as Jacob did. Perhaps not even her sister Corrine, whom she loved with all of her heart. Jacob was her heart *and* her soul, and she would be deeply affected if he were to ever suffer that magnitude of pain. Worse yet, the responsibility could have fallen to Isabella herself, destined by that newfound ancient prophecy to hunt the Transformed.

She had been born with the genetic code for her special abilities just for that purpose, unaware that they were lying dormant, waiting only for the day she and Jacob finally crossed paths.

Jacob had experienced the untenable situation of enforcing those he had once been friendly with. There had even been times when he had been required to destroy them after they had been perverted into the monsters a pentagram's black magic forced them to become. But Isabella was so much softer in the heart and so new to her Enforcer role; she had not yet been confronted with destroying a Transformed Demon she had once known and cared about.

It was her deepest fear that she wouldn't be able to do so when the time came, and Legna immediately became aware of the weight on her friend's heart as the expecting woman considered the possibility. She did not mean to intrude, but Legna's power was always "on" just like Bella's was, and the effort to control it came when trying to shut it off or lower its effect. She had allowed herself to relax too much during their conversation and had inadvertently picked up on Bella's serious emotions.

Legna kept her countenance, not sharing her knowledge with her friend about her fears. Isabella was half human and used to a more private lifestyle than that of Demonkind. Legna had come to realize that Bella was disturbed by the seemingly intrusive habits of those Jacob knew.

In fact, the biggest offender was Gideon. He would never wait to be given leave to come and go, no matter how many times Bella lost her temper with him. It was his nature to believe his way of thinking was correct and the ways of the human woman were utter nonsense. After all, he had survived ages and a great many threats more impressive than the temper of a hybrid Druid female.

Just then, as if bidden by Legna's thoughts, a strange

silver light sparkled into the room, winking instantly into the form of the great medic.

Instinctively, Legna surged to her feet. Whenever she and the Ancient occupied the same space, she could not fight the urge to go on the defensive. She and Gideon had a history of hostility, born out of a brief moment of foolishness and painful words. It was a moment that Legna could not allow herself to forget, for all her forgiving nature, and one that Gideon continually denied ever happened quite the way she remembered it.

It wasn't exactly Gideon in the room. It was an astral projection of him. This was the way a Body Demon traveled quickly. In this form, they were able to sense and feel everything around them. The only thing that limited a Body Demon's astral form was the inability to use their inborn powers of healing others. He was powerless, to an extent, in this form, but Legna had learned never to underestimate the eldest of her kind. It seemed the longer they lived, the more potent they became and the more tricks they learned. She wouldn't put any ability she could conceive of past the great Ancient.

"Legna," he greeted her coolly, nodding his silvery head with respect, his starlight-colored eyes flicking over her form briefly. "You are looking well."

"I am well, thank you," she returned just as cordially.

Gideon turned to Bella, giving her a slight bow as well.

"Enforcer. You are well, I trust?"

"Yes. I would be better, however, if you could somehow manage to squeeze the concept of knocking on the door into that vast intellect of yours," she remarked sardonically, clearly not expecting it to happen anytime soon.

"I do not recall Legna striking upon the door before her entrance," the Ancient noted offhandedly.

That caused both women to exchange startled looks and then face him with dual accusing stares.

"Just how long have you been here, Gideon?" Legna

snapped, her irritability escaping her control and eddying outward in a tangible ripple of emotion.

"Obviously long enough," he replied, clearly unperturbed, "to know you did not knock when you arrived."

It seemed to make perfect sense to him, while causing both women to seethe.

"You mean to tell me you were floating around my house all this time? Spying on us?"

"Hardly. I arrived only moments before Legna did, and when she appeared I thought I would be kind enough to allow you both some minutes to visit before I intruded."

"Gee, you're all heart," Bella said tartly. "Did it not occur to you for even one second that our conversation was a private one, and that it was *rude* to listen to it?"

"No."

Legna and Bella both exhaled large breaths of frustration at the male Demon's unconcerned shrug.

"There was nothing of an extremely private nature within the conversation that I can recall," Gideon added, his bright eyes glancing over both women as if he were trying to figure out an illogical puzzle. "Your obvious irritation is senseless."

"Yeah," Bella said dryly. "It would be . . . to you." She clearly gave up, waving the matter aside with a hand. "So, to what do I owe this pleasure?" she asked of the medic.

Legna didn't immediately hear his response. Her ears were ringing with her continued outrage. The last thing she would have ever wanted in a million millennia would be for Gideon to hear her defending him or his behavior, touting how skilled and majestically Ancient he was. He was already so infuriatingly arrogant! But he had flown around in his nonvisible astral form, listening to her reassure her friend about his abilities, no doubt basking in it and preening the whole time.

Gideon's eyes flicked over to her, the strange silver light within them giving her an eerie chill, almost as if he had just been privy to the rancor of her thoughts. *It is an illusion*, Legna argued with herself. It was a disarming trick he constantly used to maintain the upper hand and a position of advantage. He always seemed to have a bagful of these subtle psychological tricks at the ready, but she was a Mind Demon broaching Elder caliber come half a century or so, and she'd be a simpleton if she could not recognize them.

Legna turned her back on the implacable mercury stare, dismissing him and the entire conversation he was having with Isabella. She folded her arms across her slender stomach, moving with a soft whisper of silk and poise to gaze out of the window and down the cliffside, taking in the English coastline through a portal of colored glass. It was easy for her to move in and out of touch with much of her power, but in the end it was all innate, all reflex and instinct at the ready and seeking input. It required enormous effort to truly shut down all the depths of her extrasensory abilities, but she began to do so, using the crash of the surf on the sand and rocks as a metronome for the meditative process. Legna had no choice. She had to lock it all down, because whenever the medic was in her presence her senses were always overwhelmed. She knew he had powerful mental barriers. Anyone who watched his detached, emotionless manners could see that all of his essence and emotion was slammed in a protected prison that he had no interest in accessing in the slightest, even in the privacy of his own mind, it seemed.

With Legna being an empath, such a void should be disturbing yet quiet. But it was not. Instead, his energy seemed to grasp at her, tendrils of it reaching and clutching almost painfully before letting go. Every time a connection was made, impulses fired her mind with images and impressions she had no hope of comprehending. It was like an electrical overload, one she never felt with anyone else. Jacob, Noah, Elijah . . . other Council members . . . all so powerful in their own right, but none with this vibrating force of presence that made her psyche ring like tones through crystal. Crystal shattered when the pitch ringing through it reached a certain resonance. That was how she felt, as if she might shatter if she stayed too long in his company. So she never went near him if she could avoid it and she always escaped the room he was in as quickly as she could. She could not stomach the idea of his power touching her psyche in such ways.

This was one of those times, however, when she could not make a graceful exit. Isabella needed her there. The Druid's heart was beating fast with her worry and it was a clear, impassioned desire in her mind that Legna stay. So she did, keeping close enough to comfort Bella and focusing on the tide and sea to comfort herself.

Gideon watched as Legna stared out of the window and down at the coastline. He could see the heated changes in her body chemistry, the flush of her skin that intensified with what was obviously an irritable emotion. He knew he had offended her yet again, but he had long ago resigned himself to the fact that he always would. She was an overly headstrong female, persistently thinking and behaving in ways that made little or no sense to his more rational and logical mind. It had gotten worse, he had noted, since the Druid had come into their midst. Isabella had almost no reservations about saying whatever she felt aloud, with little thought to the respect his position or those of many others usually garnered. She was young, raised human, and it was expected for her to have immature and somewhat barbaric ways. Bella was also a stranger to their culture, so it was a somewhat excusable type of behavior. Legna had no such excuse. She had been raised in the Demon way, knowing all the protocols and societal expectations of her.

Gideon held up his simple conversation with Isabella as he continued to study the perturbed female Demon. In the eight years he had been in seclusion, she had grown astoundingly in her powers and abilities. Demons often went through great surges of development during their lifetime, a series of almost adolescent growth spurts, and she was young enough as an adult to experience these. Yet Gideon could not remember seeing such an unexpected leap in strength and ability in a Demon since . . . well, since her brother's youth. Their genetic stock was predisposed to such things, but Noah was of Fire. Fire had its own rules when it came to growth within because of the way the Demon could draw energy from outside sources. Demons of the Mind were a young breed, the eldest and first born of the ability only recently lost to them at the age of 405. Since Lucas's birth, Demons of the Mind had become a regular and frequent element for the young. The guidelines of their development were set down in expected patterns well before Legna's birth.

The medic also knew that Legna was aware enough of this growth and the peculiarity of it to make a pretense of being somewhat weaker than she really was. He wondered at that, curious as to why she would deny such remarkable aptitude. He had been observing her somewhat closely these past five months, since his reemergence and her Summoning. However, her continued hostility toward him kept him at a suitable enough distance to prevent him from making a complete diagnosis of her metabolic development. Just as she could read emotion, Legna used the powers of her mind to put up impenetrable barriers around herself, strong enough to keep even Gideon's formidable powers somewhat at bay.

That was only part of the obstacle, though. The other part was within Gideon himself. When it came to Legna, he found himself compelled to reserve any action that, should she sense it in any measure, she might take as an intrusion . . . a violation. He had made the mistake with her once in the past, and would be hard-pressed to ever repeat it. Despite what Isabella and Legna thought, he was quite capable of learning from his mistakes . . . when he chose to.

Gideon turned back to Isabella, noting the nervous way she was stroking the distended belly that housed her developing child. He had been aware of her fears and concerns even before overhearing her conversation with Magdelegna. However, contrary to what Legna believed, he was quite capable of holding his thoughts to himself when he thought it would be better for his patient. He was incapable of lying, even if he had seen use in it. The truth of his concerns over the hundreds of things that could go wrong with Isabella's pregnancy would give her little peace of mind and could potentially have ill-reaching ramifications. So he kept his counsel, offering no false comfort and no frightening truths. He would allow her to continue to draw her own conclusions, so long as it did not reach a pitch of worry that would be detrimental to her health. Unknowingly, Legna's affirmations of his straightforward nature had been advantageous to both him and the mother-to-be.

"I see no need to arrive in person this week," he informed Isabella. "However, if you should require anything or experience any concerns, you may contact me immediately."

Gideon took a moment to do a last visual check of the breeding woman, his fingertips touching her chin, turning her head to the side gently as he inspected her pulse and blood pressure with a momentary glance. He briefly ran a hand over the swell of her belly, and then he stepped away from her, dropping his touch from her before the male Enforcer sensed his mate had been touched by another male and showed up in an agitated swirl of dust. Jacob had made no secret of his possessiveness of Isabella. This sometimes occurred in an Imprinting, depending on the nature of the element the Demon came from and factors in personality. Jacob's affinity with nature made him very susceptible to surges of territoriality when it came to that which he held most precious. The Enforcer was capable of curbing the emotion when absolutely necessary, so it would not become overly detrimental or antagonistic. Bella herself did not even bat an eyelash worrying over things like jealousy. She was probably the most trusting soul Gideon had ever met, her hopeful youth and unblemished naïveté sometimes so pleasing, even while it made her vulnerable to the future pains that came with being a part of their species.

Gideon had just moved a significant distance away from the little Druid when a violent dust devil swept into the room, coalescing with a twist into the form of the Enforcer. Jacob was a male of awesome power, and though his was a lean, athletic build, he radiated that fact from every pore. The Earth Demon could manipulate mighty forces of nature, such as gravity itself, with a mere thought. Next to Fire Demons, Earth Demons were the most powerful of their kind. This was why he had been chosen to be the one to hunt the renegades of his own race. The implacable depths of his dark, warning gaze as he fixed it on the medic said much about what being forced to hunt down and sometimes even destroy those he had once called friends had made him capable of. Gideon and Jacob had done battle only once. It had been enough to give them both a healthy respect for each other's abilities, as well as creating an underlying tension between them that might never resolve itself.

"Gideon," Jacob greeted coolly, moving in the blink of an eye to enfold his beloved mate into the protection of his embrace. When he looked down into her face, he softened in that remarkable way Gideon didn't think he would ever get used to. It almost relieved him when Jacob's nearly hostile gaze returned to him. "I thought we had agreed you would warn me before you visited with Isabella," he said, his tone so even that it was every inch threatening.

"I had expected Isabella to warn you herself. After all, she is the one in constant mental contact with you. Not I."

"And you are capable of projecting yourself to me before you appear to her just as easily."

"You were hunting, Jacob. I decided to let you finish your task in peace. This was to be only a brief visit. And as you see, we are thoroughly chaperoned."

Gideon gestured to Legna, who, in a remarkable way he had begun to notice, had managed to make herself go completely overlooked. Even Isabella seemed to suddenly realize she had forgotten all about her friend's presence. But now the stately, graceful woman was turning a soothing smile on the tense people half a room away from her.

"Jacob, it is good to see you."

Jacob grinned at Legna, nodding his head. "How is Noah?"

Legna quirked a brow. "Did you not see him in the Council?" She glanced from one Enforcer to the other, then to Gideon. "I understood that Noah was in Council with you all this morning, discussing the necromancer threat."

"Yes, we were. But he was . . . unsettled, after discovering Daniel beneath the Council table," Jacob informed her.

"And he had words with Councillor Ruth, as usual," Isabella added, rolling her eyes in reflection of her feelings about the cantankerous Elder. "We all did. I swear, that woman gives me ulcers." Isabella hugged her mate to herself in comfort. "I believe she still blames Jacob for the death of her youngest daughter's mate. It's unfair. How could any of us have known any sooner than we did?"

Legna's spine straightened suddenly, the strong emotions that burst from Jacob forcing her to catch her breath as they pummeled her. She realized then that Jacob had never forgiven himself for that lost life.

Before Bella had come to them, Jacob's primary duty had been to keep Demons and humans apart, believing as they all had for thousands of years that humans were too fragile to withstand the seduction of a Demon. During the Hallowed moons, the full moons of Beltane in May and Samhain in October, Demons were compelled by a mystical explosion of sexual compulsion. It was believed that it was originally meant to perpetuate their species, but because of Demon foolhardiness, the Druids meant to be their ease and their mates were all murdered in war. So the madness of lust had grown out of proportion with time, and this lust could be directed in lawbreaking directions, no matter how strong the Demon's moral codes and self-control.

Even Gideon—powerful, invulnerable Gideon—had not been immune. So it had been the Enforcer's role to track down those who attempted to break that law, punishing them for it, keeping humans and even other Nightwalker species safe from this uncontrollable, animalistic nature that overcame his fellows. This past Samhain, the same time that Bella first was becoming revealed to them, Jacob had prevented Ruth's daughter Mary from seducing a human man, punishing her severely, as the infraction called for. All the while, the Enforcer had been unaware this human man was actually part Druid, destined by fate to be Imprinted with Mary. Jacob had had no inkling that their brief contact before the actual enforcing had triggered the dormant Druid genetics in the would-be victim. How could he? There had been only one Demon among them old enough to know the true nature of Druids, and Gideon had never expected that an exterminated Nightwalker population had actually become hybrids in the human population.

These alien genetics blossomed into dominance, overwriting existing DNA from that of a mere human into that of an awakening Druid. Once this happened, a Druid became mortally dependent on their Demon mate's elemental energy, just as the Demon became dependent on the Druid's love and ability to bring peace to them during the Hallowed moons. Once mated in the Imprinting, that Demon would never fear the Enforcer again. As a pair, they would grow as content and powerful as Jacob and Isabella were becoming.

Unfortunately, Mary's mate, kept away from the fledgling Demon as she was punished and held under watch until Samhain passed, had starved from the deprivation of his mate's energy, dying before Jacob could rectify the mistake.

There was no way Jacob could have known, and yet Ruth would not forgive him. Worse, Jacob refused to forgive himself. He could not bear to see crime or injustice go without rectification. It was what made him the miraculously capable Enforcer of Noah's laws that he was. He was invaluable to Legna's brother. But it was also what made him so unforgiving of himself when he felt he had failed.

Legna knew it would just take time before Isabella's sweet, loving emotions for him would heal him of his guilt. Even now she was sharing thoughts of comfort with him. Legna felt an oddly hollow pumping to her heart as she absorbed the eddy of the Enforcers' love for one another. She realized then that just as there had been truth behind Noah's joking about their relationship, there was truth for her as well. She envied them. It was a heartbreaking craving shadowed with a malevolent flutter of jealousy. She turned away once more, ashamed and inundated by her own emotions for a change, and guarded her face from prying eyes as inexplicable tears burned in her eyes.

She had to be tired, she excused herself, trying to shake off the ache that continued to beat through her. She felt foolish. She scolded herself for allowing things to affect her as if she were some green fledgling not yet trained in controlling her own powers and emotions.

Pressing harsh fingers into her damp eyes, she turned to the others.

"Isabella, we will visit again soon. There is something I have forgotten to take care of and I must hurry to complete it before dawn." She didn't even hug her friend good-bye or acknowledge the men in the room. With a familiar flourish of her elegant hand, she teleported away in a flash and a small cloud of sulfur.

"She is getting good at that," Jacob remarked, the peculiar exit making him forget his own thoughts. "She is not yet an Elder, but she leaves less and less of a display behind every time I see her teleport. She is strong for one so young."

"For those of us who can call being almost two hundred and fifty years old 'young.'" Bella laughed, cuddling up under Jacob's possessive arm even tighter. "Compared to you guys, I'm an infant!"

"Fledgling, little flower," Jacob corrected, giving her forehead an affectionate kiss to go with his endearment for her.

"I am afraid I must also take my leave," Gideon interjected, his mind fully on Legna's unusual departure. He had seen something. Something within the empath that was not quite clear to him, but it was potentially physiologically alarming. It had been an impression more than anything, his power weakened by his astral state. Still, it had his interest, and he was compelled by an urge to confront Legna. This impression troubled him. If Gideon had learned anything in his vast lifetime, it was that his instincts were rarely wrong.

"In the future, Jacob, I will exercise more care when approaching your mate. My apologies." With a curt bow, Gideon vanished in a brilliant flash of silver light.

Jacob and Isabella exchanged perplexed looks and thoughts. But after a moment, Bella's eyes began to drift over Jacob's body and the nature of her thoughts changed significantly, punctuated by a sexy, mischievous smile.

"Want to make love to a basketball?" she invited.

Jacob threw back his head and laughed, all painful memories banished in an instant, minimal feelings in the face of his beloved's wink and smile.

Chapter 3

Legna materialized in her bedroom, the familiar pop of displaced air the only announcement of her arrival. Still, Noah would know she had returned. Being her brother aside, Noah was always sensitive to the proximity of all sources of energy. Legna moved to her bed, sitting down slowly as she exhaled a deep, cleansing breath. There was comfort in the protection of her brother's house, although, at times, she did find herself agreeing with Bella's desire to have a little solace, a few precious moments of privacy.

She knew it was strange for her to feel this way. She was a Demon. Demons thought privacy was an outdated human concept. What use were secrets amongst creatures who, no matter what element their abilities were drawn from, always had some sort of innate sensory perception that almost immediately told them the nature of an encountered situation? Noah, for instance, could have the manor packed with guests on special occasions, a hundred or more, and he would be aware of every single energy signature, where it was, and what it was doing. Legna's sense of emotion was equally vast. She would know, even without purposely seeking it out, who was arguing, who was laughing, who was making love, and who was as drunk as the proverbial skunk. They had all lived long, seen it all, done things far more exposed to criticism or embarrassment. What difference did walls or knocking make? A philosophy Gideon clearly lived by. The part he forgot was the common respect of choosing his moments to suddenly cross certain boundaries.

Still, to be alone in her thoughts, in her actions. The idea had a certain appeal to it. Why it appealed to Legna at this particular time of her life, she did not know. It just did. It was a false ideal, she knew. Nightwalkers abounded throughout the world and the human concept of privacy was an illusion of ignorance being bliss.

Still . . .

She was restless, and she knew it was only a matter of time before others besides her intuitive sister and brother began to pick up on it even more than they already had. Traditionally, when Demons were perceived as dramatically restless or unhappy, they were guided into a group of mentors and bombarded with attentiveness and counseling. It was a common belief that Demons without a sure awareness of themselves and their goals could be led astray. They were too powerful a species to be allowed to give in to emotional whims and be left open to potentially negative influences. Demons felt that guiding one another was one of the most primary purposes of their lives.

Becoming Corrine's guide in meditation, for example. Young and confused, recovering from the terrible starvation sickness that had almost killed her as it had Mary's mate, who could allow such a lost one to go without guidance and support? It would be barbaric. *Siddah* were another example. Being the Demon version of what humans called a godparent was the duty of every Demon. All adults and Elders fostered the children of their loved ones, giving them the firmer hand of guidance that sometimes parents had difficulty doing themselves. Legna was of course *Siddah* to two of her sister's children. However, beyond that as-yet-unrealized role, she was also one of many Mind and Body Demons who became mentors to the dissatisfied souls of Demons who had lost their internal compasses.

Had she, too, fallen into this disturbing category? Or was she only just beginning a journey toward that disembodied state of being? Oddly enough, the nature of her feelings led her to suspect that all the attention and constant companionship that would follow any sort of confession of restlessness would be exactly the opposite of what she wanted.

She had felt this way ever since the Summoning. It had come on her gradually at first, almost unnoticed. Then she had begun to display short bursts of temper, something she had almost never done before. It had been excusable the first and second time it had happened, considering what she had gone through, but what about the third time? The fourth? It was so out of her character that it was a wonder she wasn't already in the midst of a mentored intervention. Then again, she had gone out of her way to hide the occurrences, smoothing them over in a way that probably only a skilled Mind Demon could get away with, using her mind and her ability to draw in those of any power with the enchantment of her soothing voice. But along with those soft manipulations of emotions and people's perceptions of her temper came guilt and remorse and the feeling that she was misusing her abilities. This only added to her confusion. Demons were rarely apologetic for the things they did with their abilities. What was the purpose of a power if it went unused? And she agreed with that. Usage of ability deserved no excuses, unless it betrayed the boundaries of the law or certain moral and professional ethics.

She would have been lying if she told herself these alterations in her perspectives and personality did not frighten her. There wasn't a night that went by that she didn't speculate that perhaps Bella's protection during the Summoning had not been as complete as they had all thought. Before Legna's rescue, there had been only one Demon to ever be retrieved quickly from a necromancer's pentagram. The result had been tragic, the pitiable creature rapidly going mad, attacking his brethren and behaving in manic and perverted ways. So the rescue had meant nothing, and Jacob had been forced to destroy the tormented soul after all.

What if that was slowly happening to her as well? Perhaps she was being foolish and arrogant to believe she would be the only Demon to ever escape a Summoning completely unscathed. If this was the case, did it make her a coward that she wasn't doing the right thing and letting someone know her fears?

Legna gained her feet again, rubbing her hands together as if they were chilled, pacing the ornate woven carpet that covered the stone floor, her silken slippers barely making a whisper of sound and the sheer outer panels of her gown fluttering in the breeze her movements created.

Realizing what she was doing, she stopped short, glancing heavenward and seeking strength for a moment. She moved to the window, pulling the drapes aside so she could see the vast lawns and gardens that stretched out before the grand castle. Noah's choice of a home was clearly a throwback to the time in which he had been born. Like him, she had always felt more comfortable in its environment than in the more modern choices that were available.

Dawn was starting its approach and she should be tired, preparing for bed, and getting ready to snuggle down in the warm sunlight-streamed room for the day. Legna glanced at the magnificent four-poster bed behind her, even going so far as moving to touch the heavy tapestry bed curtains she had made for it many decades past. The scenes depicted within reflected all those she had loved at the time, most of whom existed still. She touched the figure of a dark-haired, jovial male Demon who was prevalent in the artwork, his image repeated often.

Lucas.

Her *Siddah*, her mentor. The man who had become as much a father to her as her brother had become after their father's death. She had never been at a loss for strong males in her life, and she had adored every one of them. They had taught her so much, molded her into who she was, striking the perfect balance between guidance and freedom, discipline and contentment.

And now, along with her father and her mother, Lucas was dead. She closed her eyes, shaking her head to try and ward off the last images she had been given of Lucas. Darling Lucas, trapped in a pentagram across from her, spouting her most precious secret, her power name, for all to hear and use against her. And, the ultimate betrayal, his poor body and soul twisted into those of a demoralized monster.

That was the night Legna had learned what it truly meant to hate another creature. She had never thought herself capable of it, but she had felt it like a white and black poison burning through her every cell, scorching beneath her skin until she was certain her pores would ooze with the vileness of it. It had struck her in the moment she'd finally gotten her hands on one of the four human magic-users responsible for the travesty that had forced the end of Lucas's precious life. She had acted on her rage and, for the first time in all her years, Legna had learned what it meant to let loose her instinctual animal nature.

It was this nature within her that had wrapped her hands around the throat of the necromancer who had dared to be a party to caging Legna and her mentor. This living predator inside of Legna had refused to let go, encouraging the female Demon to plunge her mind into the psyche of the necromancer, visiting a relentless mental hell upon the offending creature until the reprehensible girl was dead from the horrors of her own twisted mind.

What had frightened Legna about the act was not the fact that she had discovered herself capable of taking a life, but that she had thrown her face and voice up into the night and enjoyed it so wildly. In that moment, it had seemed as though she had never known such delight, and it had taken hours until she had finally begun to come down from the rush of it. It had been days before the high had dissipated completely. To say that she had felt bereft afterward would have been an understatement. In fact, she wasn't certain she had ever gotten over the resulting emptiness. Had she so enjoyed being a killer? Or was it the idea of revenge she had soared upon? As a Demon, she had never been led to believe that self-defense and even retribution were things to be feared, so long as the laws of her people were followed closely. But still, this aftermath had disturbed her greatly, and five months later it showed no signs of being resolved.

A sudden prickling of the hairs on the back of her neck brought Legna's attention sharply from her soul-searching. Her head came up, her sensory abilities extending from her like a rippling blanket, seeking to identify the disturbance approaching her.

And it was an approach. She was certain of it.

No sooner had the thought crossed her mind then the air in the room displaced itself from the sudden occupation of Gideon's imposing figure in the center of the floor. There was no scent of sulfur, as she usually left behind in these instances, but that only told her that the Mind Demon who had transported the medic to this location had been an Elder, stronger and more skilled than an adult like her.

The Ancient's arrival at that particular moment had an extraordinarily disturbing effect. If there was anyone amongst her people who would be able to determine the meaning of the changes she was feeling within herself,

Gideon would probably be it. And, of course, she would have preferred to burn in hell before asking such a private thing of him. Yet now he was here, as if bidden by her thoughts, standing in that always so self-assured manner he had, and looking elegant and spotless in the old-world style of clothing he favored more often than he did the modern attire in his wardrobe. Right then, he wore white from head to toe, relieved only by silver embroidery that perfectly picked up his natural coloring. He wore breeches of a soft cottonlike material that fit him like a second skin and extended into leather boots of the softest tan color possible before it could be called beige. They reached up to just below his knee, so that he looked like he was going riding. As was his habit, he wore a silken shirt with long, piratical sleeves that rippled from his extremely broad shoulders to cuffs of soft lace, the delicate material resting along the backs of powerful hands, his long fingers finished elegantly in spotlessly manicured fingernails. He wore a single ring, a silver loop on his thumb shaped into the medics' signet.

Legna looked away from him before she found herself doing an overly accurate mental description of the way the laces of the shirt were neglected beneath his throat, allowing the material to gape haphazardly over his collarbone. Suffice it to say, Gideon wore the habits of his lifetime like an unapologetic statement, and he wore them very well. He blended the male fashions of the millennium in a way that was nothing less than a perfect reflection of who he was and how he had lived. This only served to beautify his distinctive and powerful presence with his incidental confidence.

"Gideon," she said evenly, inclining her head in sparse respect. "What brings you to my chambers so close to dawn?"

The riveting male before her remained silent, his silver eyes flicking over her slowly. Her heart nearly stopped with her sudden fear, and immediately she threw up every mental and physical barrier she could to prevent an unwelcome scan and analysis of her health.

"I would not scan you without your permission, Magdelegna. Body Demons who become healers have codes of ethics the same as any others."

"Funny," she remarked, "I would have thought you to believe yourself above such a trivial matter as permission."

His mercury gaze narrowed slightly, making Legna wish that she had the courage to dare a piratical scan of her own. She was quite talented at masking her travels through the emotions and psyches of others, but Gideon was like no other. She was barely a fledgling to one such as he.

Gideon had noted her more recent acerbic tendencies aloud once before, irritating the young female even more than usual, so he resisted the urge in that moment to scold her again and instead let her attitude pass.

"I have come to check on your well-being, Magdelegna. I am concerned."

Legna cocked a brow, twisting her lips into a cold, mocking little smile, hiding the sudden, anxious beating of her heart.

"And what would give you the impression that you need be concerned for me?" she asked haughtily.

Gideon once more took his time before responding, giving her one more of those implacable perusals in the interim. Legna exhaled with annoyance, crossing her arms beneath her breasts and coming just shy of tapping her foot in irritation.

"You are not at peace, young one," Gideon explained softly, the deep timbre of his voice resonating through her, once again giving her the feeling that she was but fragile crystal, awaiting the moment when he would strike the note of discord that would shatter her. Legna's breathing altered, quickening in spite of her effort to maintain an even keel. She did not want to give him the satisfaction of being right.

"You presume too much, Gideon. I have no need for your concern, nor have I ever solicited it. Now, if you do not mind, I should like to go to bed."

"For what purpose?"

Legna laughed, short and harsh. "To sleep, why else?"

"You have not slept for many days together, Legna. Why do you assume you might have success today?"

Legna turned around sharply, driving her gaze and attention out the window, trying to use the sprawling lawn as a slate with which to fill her mind. Mind Demon he was not, but she knew he was capable of seeing far enough into her emotional state by just monitoring her physiological reactions to his observations. Legna bit her lip hard, furious that she should feel like the child he always referred to her as in their conversations. Young one, indeed. How would he like it if she referred to him as a decrepit old buzzard?

The thought gave her a small, petty satisfaction. It did not matter that Gideon looked as vital and vibrant as any Demon male from thirty years to a thousand would look. Nor did it matter that his stunning coloring gave him a unique attractiveness and aura of power that no one else could equal. All that mattered was that he would never view her as an equal, and therefore, in her perspective, she had no responsibility to do so for him.

Gideon watched the young woman across from him closely, trying to make sense of the physiological changes that flashed through her rapidly, each as puzzling as the one before it. What was it about her, he wondered, that always kept him off his mark? She never reacted the way he logically expected her to, yet he knew her to be extraordinarily intelligent. She always treated him with a barely repressed contempt, though she never had a harsh word for anyone else. He had almost gotten used to that since their original falling-out, but this was different, far more complex than hard feelings. Gideon had not encountered a puzzle in a great many centuries, and perhaps that was why he was continually fascinated by her in spite of her marked disdain.

"It is not unusual," she said at last, "to have periods of insomnia in one's life. Surely that is not what has you rushing into my boudoir, oozing your high-handed version of concern."

"Magdelegna, I am continually puzzled by your insistence in treating me with hostility. Did Lucas teach you nothing about respecting your elders?"

Legna whirled around suddenly, outrage flaring from her so violently that Gideon felt the eddy of it push at him through the still air.

"Do not ever mention Lucas in such a disrespectful manner ever again! Do you understand me, Gideon? I will not tolerate it!" She moved to stand toe to toe with the medic, her emotions practically beating him back in their intensity. "You say respect my elders, but what you mean is respecting my betters, is that not right? Are you so full of your own arrogance that you need me to bow and kowtow to you like some throwback fledgling? Or perhaps we should reinstate the role of concubines in our society. Then you may have the pleasure of claiming me and forcing me to fall to my knees, bowing low in respect of your masculine eminence!"

Gideon watched as she did just that, her gown billowing around her as she gracefully kneeled before him, so close to him that her knees touched the tips of his boots. She swept her hands to her sides, bowing her head until her forehead brushed the leather, her hair spilling like reams of heavy silk around his ankles.

The Ancient found himself unusually speechless, the strangest sensation creeping through him as he looked down at the exposed nape of her neck, the elegant line of her back. Unable to curb the impulse, Gideon lowered himself into a crouch, reaching beneath the cloak

of coffee-colored hair to touch her flushed cheek. The
heat of her anger radiated against his touch and he recognized it long before she turned her face up to him.

"Does this satisfy you, my lord Gideon?" she whispered
fiercely, her eyes flashing like flinted steel and hard jade.

Gideon found himself searching her face intently, his
eyes roaming over the high, aristocratic curves of her
cheekbones, the amazingly full sculpture of her lips, the
wide, accusing eyes that lay behind extraordinarily thick
lashes. He cupped her chin between the thumb and
forefinger of his left hand, his fingertips fanning softly
over her angrily flushed cheek.

"You do enjoy mocking me," he murmured softly to
her, the breath of his words close enough to skim across
her face.

"No more than you seem to enjoy condescending to
me," she replied, her clipped words coming out on
quick, heated breaths.

Gideon absorbed this latest venom with a blink of
lengthy black lashes. They kept their gazes locked, each
seemingly waiting for the other to look away.

"You have never forgiven me," he said suddenly, softly.

"Forgiven you?" She laughed bitterly. "Gideon, you are
not important enough to earn my forgiveness."

"Is your ego so fragile, Legna, that a small slight to it
is irreparable?"

"Stop talking to me as if I were a temperamental
child!" Legna hissed, moving to jerk her head back but
finding his grip quite secure. "There was nothing slight
about the way you treated me. I will never forget it, and
I most certainly will never forgive it!"

Gideon reached out, taking her by both of her shoulders,
hauling her up with him as he regained his height. He un-
intentionally pulled her off balance, forcing her to sway into
his body slightly in order to prevent herself from teetering
further off center. Her soft curves skimmed against the
harder planes of his torso for all of a second. The Ancient

male felt a sensation shimmer through him that he couldn't immediately define, his silvery brows knitting with his momentary confusion. The situation was too volatile to waste time on a cursory sensation, however, so he put it aside as he put Legna at arm's length.

"Legna, I do not need to explain to you the difficulties we all experience during the Hallowed moons. Especially the Samhain moon. I never meant to cause you pain. I have always been disturbed by my lack of control that night."

"Oh, I am sure you have," Legna hissed, fighting back the embarrassing sting of tears that threatened to overwhelm her. "How awful it must have been for you to realize you had defiled your wondrous ancientness with the kiss of an infant."

Legna pulled herself out of his hold, turning her back on him violently as the back of her hand tried to press back the sound of pain brewing behind her trembling lips. She lost her battle with her tears, shamed to feel them skid down her flushed cheeks.

They had barely spoken of that night—a mere nine years back—mostly because Legna could hardly stay in the same room with Gideon for more than five minutes at a time. But much of their gap in communication was because Gideon had been in a self-imposed exile for the past eight years, driven there by his shame over having stalked a human female and being forced to face the humiliating justice of the Enforcer as a result. The incident with the human female had taken place the very next Samhain moon after the one that had caused the rift between Legna and Gideon. To Legna it had only served to add insult to injury, forcing a shameful pain upon her that magnified that of the original encounter.

And she remembered that night, that moon, the entire incident as keenly as if it had happened five minutes ago.

She had been restless that particular full moon, much

in the way she had been feeling only recently. But as expected, on that Hallowed night it was intensified a thousandfold. She had been pacing the gardens, chilled by the clouds that drifted over the bright moon, waiting impatiently for Noah to emerge from Council. She had been hoping he would somehow be able to distract her, keep her from going stir-crazy. But as she had wandered the distant mazes of sculpted bushes, it was Gideon she had stumbled across. She had been surprised, not having sensed him at all. What was more, Council was in session and he was one of the Triumvirate, one of the three most powerful voices at the Council table.

He had stood there, his face turned up to the moon, as if he were a wolf ready to bay in worship of it. His powerful body was locked rigidly in place, every muscle flexed, tensed to react to whatever came across his path. Legna's senses had suddenly flared to life, no longer unaware of his presence, and she was overwhelmed with the emotions abruptly radiating off the usually serene Ancient. He was holding a rash of wild impulses barely in check, his need crashing over her like a violent tide, making her gasp aloud in shock from the force of it.

Gideon had turned then, the speed of the movement barely perceptible to her vision. She suddenly, breathlessly, found herself being dwarfed by his presence, his power, and his remarkably vital body. She had no hope of erecting her usual safeguards against such a potent influence. It was far too late in any event. His raw emotions had long since taken over hers. She became a mirror for them, making them hers in a way she hadn't even thought herself capable of.

"Magdelegna."

He spoke her name with a low, predatory sound to his voice. She even heard the guttural growl of contemplation he loosed beneath his breath. It called to Legna's primitive restlessness of that night. She had narrowed her eyes, taking his measure very slowly, unaware of how inviting and sensual an act it was.

Gideon easily saw the rush of her blood as her pulse quickened. He saw her skin flush with awareness in her erogenous zones as she devoured his imposing frame with fearlessness and blatant curiosity. She had stepped closer to him, a soft undulation of her long, feminine body, making him realize that she was only about six inches shorter than he was. It placed her proportionately close to scale against him, and he knew instantly how well she would fit his body if only he closed the small gap that remained between them. Her scent had carried on the still night air, overwhelming the crisp autumn odors all around them with her special perfume of sweet spices and a nectar of ghosting feminine musk from her obviously provoked body.

Gideon had been enthralled by the uniqueness of that scent, his head lowering slightly as he drew a deep breath to bring the bouquet of her beauty deep into his lungs. In the blink of an eye, his hand shot out and seized her by the nape of her neck, jerking her forward toward him so hard that she felt their breastbones collide. She was tall, but Gideon had to lower his head to close the distance between their faces just the same. He held her still, not allowing her to turn her head in any direction he did not wish it to turn. He bent his silvered head until his nose brushed the curve of her swanlike neck.

Legna felt the rush of his breath against that sensitive portion of her skin, unable to resist the shiver that shuddered through her and the impulsive purr that vibrated over her vocal cords. Her senses were bludgeoned with the fierce sharpening of arousal that rocked through the powerful male who held her so possessively. It was safe to say that, as an empath, she had experienced much of this emotion over her centuries from others as they had indulged in passions of the flesh, but she had never felt anything like this in all of her life. She had never even conceived of such overwhelming intensity.

He had wrapped her hair up in his fist, bringing the silky mass to his lips and rubbing it against them slowly, all the while boring into her soul with the hot ice stare of his eyes.

"Magdelegna," Gideon said again, her name a command on his tongue.

She felt him move aggressively against her, making her very aware of his physical response to her closeness. She felt liquid heat slither throughout her entire body just from the understanding of her effect on him, the heated sap coiling into intriguing puddles of arousal in equally intriguing places.

"I could make you feel in ways no female has ever dreamed of feeling," he had promised her, his smooth voice so perfect and so hypnotic with its low, beckoning pitch, creating a whirlpool of desire deep in her soul as his free hand slid to the curve of her waist, moving boldly to the arch of her lower back. It was as if they already knew each other with perfect intimacy, from thought to movement, from feel to touch, from male to female.

Legna's breath came quicker as he aggressively appraised her, his gaze like melting wax, scalding her everywhere it touched her. His fingers came forward over her rib cage, fanning out until each had found a fit in the spaces between the flexible, curved ribs. His thumb slipped under the weight of her breast, slyly stroking the sensitive flesh in a way that shimmered right through her. She gasped softly, her head falling back until her throat was fully exposed to him. He released her hair immediately, his hand covering the alluring expanse she'd provided, his fingers greedily absorbing the vibrations of the low sounds of invitation she made. Then his fingers were moving aside and his lips touched her in their place. His breath was a potent heat against her skin, making her shiver as her flesh exploded in goose bumps all the way from her neck to her heels. His mouth was masculine magic, his lips stroking her in prelude to the damp questing of his tongue.

Her mouth began to ache with the desire to capture the taste and feel of him, her lips tingling and flushed full of blood in a broadcast to him of her need. His mouth came to hers suddenly, hovering above those thirsting lips as he drilled her with the intensity of his mercury gaze.

"*Neliss . . .*" he murmured, reverting to the elegance of their ancient language. "*Neliss ent desita.*"

Beauty of the ages.

His mouth touched on hers at last, and she welcomed him with an eager sound of encouragement. White lightning sensation bolted through her, making her taut and weak all at once, bending her back in his hold as he insistently sought her compliance. His lips were sensual against hers, exploring with purposeful tempo, gentle, searching yet not aggressive. Legna thought a little dazedly that she had expected him to be a little harsher in his impatience. She could feel tempestuous emotions radiating from him like the brilliant moonlight at his back. However, the thorough nature of the kiss was very much in character for him. Thoughtful, methodical, and full of supreme confidence as he slowly examined every fine detail of her lips alone. When his tongue touched her lips for the first time, it was a slow stroke along her bottom lip that was like the caress of moist, sensual velvet. Her mouth opened slightly to allow an erotic sound of feminine pleasure to escape on a softly exhaled breath.

For the first time, her eyes slid closed, sparing her the penetrating heat of molten silver, even if it had been from under half-mast lashes. He saw so deeply inside of her, wanted to see so deeply inside of her, and it was as if she were already naked beneath his command of her. His hand against her ribs burned with his body heat, just as the rest of him did, marking her with the intense impression along all the surfaces of her skin.

When she made that aching sound of pleasure, Gideon finally breached her mouth, his tongue slipping past her parted lips, tangling with hers instantly. Her hands came up, her slim fingers sliding along his back, up to his shoulders, finally holding him there with the strength of a butterfly but the power of a Titan. Her touch alone made him groan softly against her, but added to that was the taste of her, so warm and sweet, like sun-warmed nectar, and he was but a bee driven by instinct to drink deeply of her. She hardened him, like liquid metal plunged into water, and it was an eroticism and a weighted agony to feel it. It had been so long since he had craved a woman in any fashion at all, Hallowed moons be damned. Sexual need was one thing, a bodily thing, and a physiological function that he could control better than any other Demon since control of the Body had been his one true mastery for a millennium. Needing Legna was something else entirely, an entity not within his realm of puppeteering.

To Legna, his kiss was yet another perfect reflection of Gideon. Bold, unapologetic, and brutally honest. His entire being radiated his hunger into her, his aroused body moving purposefully against her flushed and pliant one. He allowed her to feel his cravings, to feel the way she expanded his need, and to feel the pleasurable pain of his heavily hardened body as his hips rubbed against her. Then the curiosity and method of his kiss began to stutter in its smooth, controlled feel. He was tripping over the aggressive demands of his Demon nature. She could feel it as he began to devour her with increasing intensity, the surge of the base, animal nature that was such an elemental part of them all. This was her craving. She could not bear a moment more of his gentleness. The burn of the moon was within her, begging for more. Demanding it.

So she played him, played his senses with every feminine trick in the book. She moaned, low and erotic, into his mouth, allowing her feelings to overwhelm her until the single sound duplicated, then chained into soft gasps of aching pleasure. Her hands pulled around to his chest, sliding up to his shoulders, finally diving deeply into the silver hair along the back of his head. She returned his kiss just as assertively as he gave it, refusing to be the only haven for their joined tongues. She reached for the back of his head, holding him to her as she delved deep into his mouth for a richer taste of him.

His response was volatile, his hands grasping the back of her rib cage and hauling her completely off her feet and further into him. Her sensitized breasts were crushed into the hard wall of his chest, her flat belly in completely flush contact with the ridges of his taut abdomen. Her hips were cradled against his, his poorly restrained erection pressing urgently against her. The world began to swing away from her in a dizzying vortex of feeling and she was completely lost to emotion and sensation. His kiss went on and on, bordering on brutality, as if he had crossed a desert bereft of physical contact and she had suddenly become his only oasis. Legna would not realize then how accurate the metaphor floating through her mind actually was.

It was in that moment, on the heels of that thought, that Gideon had suddenly broken away from her, shoving her back away from him so hard that she nearly fell onto her backside. He had cursed richly, using a term she wasn't sure she knew the full meaning of, but could certainly feel its intent. She had been too overwhelmed by her abruptly bereft feelings to make any sense of it. Confusion rushed through her as she tried to comprehend what he was doing.

He swore again, condemning himself, berating her.

"This is madness," he had uttered hoarsely, his hand striking through his hair in a rare expression of disturbed emotion. "You are a child! *A child!* I am stronger than this. I will not give in to this ridiculous impulse of madness. I refuse!"

And before she was finished hearing the words, he had turned and fled with the preternatural speed of a creature with perfect control over anything he wanted his body to do.

She had been left bereft, insulted, and humiliated beyond words. She had collapsed to the ground, too shocked to even cry, his words ringing brutally against her feminine pride, her delicate ego. And after that, the very next year, he had chased down a woman not even of the same species, stopping only because Jacob had battled him away from the unsuspecting creature.

So no, she had never forgiven him. And until this moment, she had never wept from the injury he had visited upon her.

Gideon watched her closely, knowing she was upset, unable to figure out how to proceed. He was not at all skilled in handling a woman's sensitive emotions. He was not a Mind Demon, after all. He was aware that he had handled the original situation poorly, but he had always been at a loss to figure out how to repair the damage, so he had hoped it would fade with time and things would revert to their normal state. It was an error in thinking that, faced with it as he was at that moment, felt almost as sharp to him as the acts he had committed so arrogantly during the Druidic war. He had made grievous mistakes then, and clearly had done so now as well. One would think that a thousand years would provide enough information to circumvent such errors, but apparently they had not.

Gideon moved closer to her, and Legna could feel his body heat against her back. It always amazed her that the Ancient Demon seemed to radiate an almost humanlike heat in spite of the fact that Demon body temperature was normally five degrees lower than that of the mortals.

She felt the intensity clearly, however, and it only served to unsettle her further.

"I wish for you to leave," she said tightly, not looking at anything but the artistry of the garden outside her window. The dawn had come, tingeing the sky rose and orange, its soft colors reflecting off every shiny leaf of every tree in sight. She should have been in bed, settling in for the day, relaxing and drifting into dreams that had nothing to do with pain or humiliating tears.

"I will not leave, Magdelegna."

Legna winced inwardly, wishing he would stop using her full call name as he did. It reminded her too clearly of the compelling timbre he had used to beckon her to him all those years ago.

"Fine," she said bitterly, "you can feel free to stay."

She lifted her hand, moving it in the familiar twist that helped her to focus on directing herself to her target. Before she could begin the teleport, the medic had hold of her wrist, locking it tightly in his grip. Legna glared at the elegant fingers circling her hand and finally turned to face the owner of the offending appendage.

"As usual, you are determined to have your way regardless of my feelings, Gideon," she accused sharply. "You are cruel and insensitive. You have no reason for detaining me, and I have no desire to be in your company. Remove yourself," she threatened coldly, "or I will call on my brother and the Enforcers to do it for you."

"Your suppositions are inaccurate, Legna. I have very good reason for detaining you." The Ancient relaxed his hold on her wrist a little, allowing their hands to fall, still linked, between them. Legna knew, however, that it would only take an instant for him to tighten his grasp should she even think about freeing herself. "Reasons, I suspect, you would not care to share widely with others, including your friends, the Enforcers."

"You are uttering nonsense," Legna snorted. "I have nothing to hide."

"Oh, no?" One silver brow lifted in warning, barely giving Legna a moment to step back from him, trying to press herself as far back into the stony window frame as she could. The Demon followed the retreat with ease, his body a mere whisper away from touching hers. "Legna," he murmured softly by her ear, his breath washing down her neck, giving her a heated chill. "I can see what you try to hide from us. I see the power within you that you pretend not to have. I see things that you probably do not even know about yourself. You have changed much in this one short decade, and yet you choose to perform below your aptitude. Perhaps," he murmured softly, an absent hand pushing her hair back gently from the ear he was engaging, "your brother might like to know why his sister behaves the way she does. I know I am quite curious."

"Have I ever mentioned how much I despise you?" Legna hissed out, trying not to notice the peculiar swirls of heat in her body that answered to the stimulation of his touch against her skin. "If you wish to extract intelligence, hire a detective."

"I have always preferred to get my information directly from the best source," he told her, his eyes traveling down the long length of her body once more. It unnerved her whenever he did that. She knew it was nothing more than an assessment, a medical scan, and that he was probably taking her measure in the purely biological ways of a medic, but the quicksilver weight of his gaze always left her feeling heavy and exposed in very feminine places.

"If I answer your questions," she relented at last, all fears put aside as the overwhelming desire to put him at a distance flared wildly into her consciousness, "will you leave me alone?"

"I am afraid that will depend upon the answers, Legna."

"But you will maintain my confidentiality?" she persisted, her eyes dark with suspicion.

"I had thought we had already discussed my bindings to my ethics."

"You never answer me directly!" she snapped at him. "You talk in obscurities so that you can later take an action and fit your words to suit your needs. You are bound to medic ethics, Gideon, but I know full well you are also bound to the Council's ethics. If a conflict should arise, it is the Council ethics you will honor above all else."

"Legna," Gideon said quietly, his voice deep and even, weighed with an eerie seriousness that made her become very still. "My primary concern is, and always has been, for the health of those I serve. No matter who they are, no matter what it takes for me to reach my goal of a cure." He placed a fingertip beneath her chin and raised it to make certain their gazes locked. "If it takes a clear promise that I will respect your confidentiality, no matter what, then you have it. Nothing you tell me will go beyond us."

"Not even to Noah?" she challenged.

"Look at me, Legna. Look at me with all of your power and you will see there are no lies or deceptions. I will not discuss you with anyone. Not to Noah, nor Jacob or anyone else. Not without your permission. I swear it to you, Legna, I will not speak of this to anyone else any more than I spoke of that night between us." He slowly searched her expression of surprise. "Whatever you think of me," he continued, "I have never, in all my vast lifetime, broken my word."

She believed him. Not only because he opened himself to her scan, inviting her to seek out any hidden motive, but because there was something so compelling in the honest concern for her well-being that swirled behind his silver eyes. There was true caring in the absent caress of his fingertips against her jaw. His promise was the purest of truths.

Legna looked away from his tirelessly penetrating

gaze, feeling suddenly exhausted, as worn out as she probably should have been after so many days without rest.

"Very well," she acquiesced at last.

Satisfied for the moment, Gideon released his hold on her, stepping back and giving her room to relax and breathe.

"I am compelled to warn you that I am a creature of direct tendencies," he said quietly. "I have heard you explain as much to Isabella, but given the history of your temperament toward me, I feel I should remind you of it so as to avoid you taking any further offense."

"Please," she laughed shortly, rolling her eyes, "I do not believe things can get any worse."

Gideon did not agree with her about that, but he took it as her indication of understanding.

"I have noticed you are trying to hide the true extent of your abilities," he said. "Why?"

"Because I . . ." Legna drew her bottom lip between her teeth for an anxious moment. "I believe it is abnormal for an adult Mind Demon to have such advanced skills. I am a good fifty years from becoming even a rudimentary Elder, and yet I have noticed some of my powers seem to have gotten ahead of themselves." She absently pulled the heavy cloak of her hair into her hands. "I did not wish to draw attention or curiosity to myself."

"So I am correct in assuming that you can teleport without leaving the display of smoke and sulfur behind, as accomplished Elders can?"

"Yes. How did you know that?"

"Because it clearly takes concentration for you to leave those traces of residue with which you are covering up the advanced ability. I have noticed that you have been taking a few seconds longer to teleport when, before this, your speed had increased. This indicated to me that you were taking slightly longer to think about what you were doing. Also, there is no reason why I should have been able to stop you just now. I may be fast and strong, Legna, but you have surpassed being easily distracted long ago. The motion of your wrist is little more than habit and, I believe, an attempt to remind yourself to take that one last step of adding camouflage before the actual teleport. I should also mention that I saw you teleport once in an urgent situation where you completely forgot to add the . . . smoke and mirrors."

Legna blushed and looked down at the carpet, sliding her slipper into a threadbare portion of it in consternation. She had thought she was being careful, and it bothered her to know she had been so transparent to Gideon.

"So, does this make me some sort of mutant?"

"It is far too soon to make a diagnosis of that accuracy," he chided, reaching to take her hand and guiding her into the center of the room. "I need to do an intensive scan, Legna, and for that I need your complete cooperation."

Legna sighed with impatience, her hands resting on her hips in a sign of pique she had clearly adopted from the Druid Isabella.

"I said I would, did I not?"

"There is no need for your acerbic remarks, Magdelegna. I warn everyone before I begin a scan of this nature because it is very intimate. I must touch you, for instance. It is very similar to a mind touch, but it is done both physically and with my power. I may project my astral self into you if necessary. You will have no secrets from me physically at that point."

Legna swallowed, her heart fluttering with anxiety at the idea of allowing herself to be so vulnerable to him. But she had grown weary of the act she had been putting on and the fear that was riding so heavily behind it.

"Well, so long as you do not poke around where you do not belong," she said. Gideon lifted a silver brow, making Legna realize the way what she had just said could be interpreted. Again, her tanned skin blushed a sharp hue of pink. "You know what I mean," she added, unable to look at him for some ridiculous reason. "Stay away from my mind. I know that you are powerful enough to decode brain synapses."

"That is something I do very rarely, for it takes a great deal of effort and can be a bit painful for me. Also, the intrusion of my power on those maps can affect memory patterns."

"My point exactly."

He made no reply. Instead, he began to walk a circle around her, his eyes visually assessing every inch of her body. Gideon noticed immediately that Legna had a tendency toward rapid respiration lately. He was aware of the training her type of Demon went through, and even more personally aware that Legna had always prided herself on her smooth, level nature, so similar to his own with its methodical thoughtfulness before action was spoken or taken. It was often the way of empaths and telepaths from their race to show a face of utter calm and serenity. Lately, whenever Gideon had encountered her, she seemed more emotional, or at least allowing emotion to show in ways she hadn't done since becoming an adult. The point that had compelled him, in fact, was the one they had just argued over. Why now, all of a sudden, was she letting him be aware of her wounded pride from that night that had passed between them? Oh, he had known his thoughtless behavior was very likely to evoke adverse emotions in her, but Legna would never have let them show.

He moved around to her back and stepped closer. He was aware of her closing her eyes and trying to settle her breathing, regulating her flighty pulse with a chosen meditation technique. The change that slid through her physiology was swift and remarkable. She had an impressive control over both her voluntary and involuntary systems, another indication of her skills having risen closer to Elder ability rather than adult.

Gideon reached out to gather her heavy hair in his hands, dropping the silky sheet of it over her shoulder. He then placed his hand on the back of her neck, encircling the warm, slender column as he stepped closer still. He closed his eyes, not a necessary action, but one that helped him focus. Immediately he began to extend his sensory abilities into her, beginning by slipping down the length of her spine and spreading throughout her nervous system.

He felt the electrical feedback sparking through him and he took its measure, finding her to be a little overstressed and hyperaware of her surroundings at that moment, but that was understandable considering her anxiety over the exam itself. He reached deeper into her nerves and synapses, measuring the chemicals within that regulated pain, reflex, and conduction. Unthinkingly, he touched his forehead to the back of her head, his deep, even breaths slipping over her neck and shoulders. He felt her shiver, but from the inside out, and the resulting feedback washed back through him and into his own body, forcing him to mimic the reaction. Startled, Gideon opened his eyes. That sort of response had not happened to him since his adult years. He had long ago learned to prevent himself from being affected by the nervous impulses of a patient he was examining. His brows lowered with puzzlement, but he returned to his task, once more embedding himself deeply into her nervous system, this time reaching cellular levels. He scanned one bundle of nerve structures at a time, picking through them from dendrite to DNA. At the same time, his hands moved over her shoulders, cupping them, curving around her arms.

He splayed his fingers as he came around to her collarbone, embedding himself into the structures and functions of her lungs and heart. He felt the beat of her heart flutter almost uncertainly, but then it began to trip a rapid cadence that was nowhere near what it had been moments ago. Again, Gideon felt a flashback of sensory input, his own heart suddenly speeding up to match hers in perfect syncopation. The medic inhaled sharply, resisting the urge to pull away, to shut himself off from these abnormalities. It was nothing too dramatic, really. Nothing that could be thought of as dangerous. It was simply a peculiar aberration. But the aberration continued to affect him in other ways. Her breath quickened once more, and his did as well. Her body heat blossomed above normal, sending swirls of heat spreading through his tissues.

Gideon pulled away from her suddenly, all of the reactions distracting him so much that he was forced to take a moment to regain his focus and concentration. He glanced down at his hands, shocked to realize they were shaking.

"Is something wrong?"

His eyes darted up. She had turned around to face him. Her skin was flushed, a beautiful coral pink that could have been part of the dawn breaking just outside her window. She was a remarkable work of feminine beauty. He had always thought so, but in that moment, there was more, a depth that he had not been previously aware of. It was a sort of magnetic allure, one that seemed to sing into him, feeling like a hum that vibrated over his nerves, heightening his already sharp awareness of her.

"No," he responded absently to her question. "I do not know," he corrected himself, taking one more step back away from her.

"Gideon, you are worrying me," she said in a soft pitch that was all but breathless.

"It is . . . unintentional, I assure you. Everything seems to be fine so far. I have only just begun the intensive scan."

"Then why did you stop?"

Why indeed? He could hardly explain to her what he did not understand himself. But he was an Ancient member of this mighty race, the only one of his kind. Certainly he could absorb or circumvent these minor anomalies until it was time to include them in his final analysis. He was more convinced than ever that there was more happening to Legna than met the immediate eye. The solution, however, would not be as easy to discern as he had originally thought.

"I needed a moment to refocus," he explained at last. "I am ready to resume."

"Okay," she said carefully, sounding as though she had not been completely convinced by his explanation. However, she obediently began to turn back around.

"No." He stopped her, a hand on her shoulder. "Remain facing me."

She complied, tossing her hair back over her shoulder so he would not have to move it for her. She did not close her eyes again, this time watching him closely. He flexed the fingers of both hands and then reached for her. This time his target was her waist. His palms slid over the silk of her gown, curving around her hips. Legna was not thin in any human sense of the word. She was a proud display of grand, graceful height and extremely feminine curves. She was fit, just muscular enough to make her quite strong, yet sculpted with a womanly definition. Humans who knew Demon females socially, not realizing they were of a differing species, often referred to them as goddesses or Amazons. Gideon was able to understand why quite easily. Legna would cast a shadow over any female of any race.

He realized he was allowing himself to be distracted and shook his head gently to refocus himself. He fixed his eyes on the track his hands were following, from hips into the distinct curve of her waist, up to the spread of her rib cage. Instantly, he could visualize her internal organs. He scanned them thoroughly, finding the anatomy to be as clean and healthy as those of any Demon of her youthful age. Apparently, though her abilities had aged before her time, her body had not joined them. There was an aberrant condition that struck the occasional Demon, causing them to age faster than they should. Gideon was grateful this was not the case with Legna. It was one of the few diseases that could kill a Demon. The medics had not been able to break down the causes of it, and so could not prepare a solution as yet. Luckily, there had not been a case of it in 103 years.

He slid his hands back down the path they had just traveled, moving closer to her as he spread his fingers and palms over her hips. Legna gasped softly, her body jerking unexpectedly. Instinctively, Gideon held her tightly, not wanting to break the deep connection he was forming.

"Be still," he murmured.

"Forgive me . . ." she said, the uneasiness of her voice lost on him.

Gideon was quickly checking through her muscular structure and then weaving very gently into the complexities of her reproductive system. Suddenly Legna cried out again, her hands hitting his chest and grabbing fistfuls of his shirt, her entire body trembling from head to toe. This time Gideon gave the reaction his full attention. He looked into her wide eyes, the pupils dilating as he watched. Her mouth formed a soft, silent circle of surprise.

"What are you doing?" she asked, her breath falling short and quick.

"Nothing," he insisted, his expression reflecting his baffled thoughts. "Merely continuing the exam. What are you feeling?"

Legna couldn't put the sensation into words. Her entire body felt as if it were pooling with liquid fire, like magma dripping through her, centering under the hand he had just splayed over her lower belly. So, being the empath she was, she described it the only way she could with any efficiency and effectiveness. She sent the sensations to him, deeply, firmly, without preparation or permission, exactly the way she had received them.

In an instant, Gideon went from being in control of a neutral examination to an internal thermonuclear flashpoint of arousal that literally took his breath away. His hand flexed on her belly, crushing the silk of her dress within his fist.

"Legna!" he cried hoarsely. "What are you doing?"

She didn't even seem aware of him, her eyes sliding closed and her head falling back as she tried to gulp in oxygen. His eyes slid down over her and he saw the flush and rigidity of erogenous heat building with incredible speed beneath her skin. And as it built in her, it built in him. She had created a loop between them, a locked cycle that started nowhere, ended nowhere. All it did was spill through and through them.

"Stop," he commanded, his voice rough and desperate as he tried to clear his mind and control the impulses surging through him. "Legna, stop this!"

Legna dropped her head forward, her eyes flicking open and upward until she was gazing at him from under her lashes with the volatile, predatory gaze of a cat.

A cat in heat.

Chapter 4

Gideon was riveted in place, the huntress's look in her eyes holding him more than her hands did in that moment. Suddenly, the nine years between that long-ago Samhain night and this one evaporated. Gideon remembered everything he had been feeling when she had accidentally stumbled upon him that particular full moon, the very same memories and feelings he had refused to examine ever since. Loneliness, pain, and a brutal hunger beyond the scope of all definition. He had been assaulted relentlessly by them all. It had been twisting through him, worse and worse, year after year, threatening his sanity. It had made him angry, feeling somehow weakened and cheated. He had spent a millennium learning how to control everything about and around himself. He was the most powerful Demon in their history. How could this petty, primal thing be affecting him as if he were some kind of cosmic tadpole flipping around mindlessly in a primordial ooze?

And then Legna had suddenly been standing before him, just as she was now, and everything had changed. It had become all about heat, and need, and the desire for a taboo youth and beauty he had always admired above all others. Not only that, but she had looked at him with that catlike intensity in that moment as well. It was so seductive, so powerful, and so clearly determined. Her will was a formidable thing, but he had never realized how formidable until she had turned it on him.

And now, it was burning into him again, her eyes hot with intent, flaring to a jeweled green color as she slowly, thoroughly, measured him as a male. That purposeful gaze sent flames licking over his skin. Arousal ten times more powerful than even the Hallowed moon had inspired went roaring through him. It had been centuries since he had last shown any real interest in a being of the opposite sex. With a life so long as his, one tended to transcend the physical needs of the body, either with more intellectual pursuits or just because no matter what the variety of partners, nothing new could come from the experience and a sensation of repetition set in.

At least, that had been what he had thought until the night he had lost himself to Legna's wicked eyes. He had blamed it on the moon, reaffirming the weakness to himself later on when he found himself stalking the halls of Noah's home far oftener than could be explained away, always watching as Legna floated from one room to another, seemingly oblivious to him, never remaining in his sight for more than a minute at a time.

He had struggled with himself the entire year, and as Samhain had loomed dangerously before him once more, he had purposely removed himself from her influence. He had known on some level that she would be too great a temptation to resist, and he did not want to find himself forcing his will upon her in the middle of a fit of passionate madness.

He had thought the distance would save him. Instead, it had destroyed him, leaving him vulnerable to any female that caught his slightest attention. And that female had unfortunately been a human. A simple, fragile human who would never have survived the nature of a Demon mating.

There was no describing the mortification that followed after he had been caught attempting to break that most sacred of all their laws. The only bearable recourse was to lock himself into deep isolation, exiling himself from everyone and everything, which he had done for the last eight years.

Gideon had reemerged, ironically enough, last Samhain, when Legna had put out a call to him, dragging him to her side with a thought. This was so that he could aid a critically wounded Jacob, the same Demon Enforcer who had punished him, and rightfully so. Gideon had thought that, if he could perform normally and with control amongst his people as he had during that recent volatile time, then his bout with the madness must be over. He had thought it safe to return to mainstream Demon life, his internal struggle overcome, defeated.

How wrong he had been.

He now knew that he had not learned how to resist Legna's allure after all. He never would. Not so long as Magdelegna had those luring eyes and the will of a brilliant, cunning huntress that flared behind them.

Gideon looked directly into her avaricious gaze, feeling the intent of it on a primitive level, the part of him that had been bred into his instincts at the beginning of time when the males of his kind had first come into being. Like males of many species, his task was to attract the female, but hers was to choose him if and only if he suited her above all others. It was then that he realized the scan had subconsciously taken on the ritualistic form of a mating dance, triggering action and reaction in them both in ways they had never expected.

She tilted her head slowly as his quicksilver eyes locked onto her face, her hair sweeping across her back and shoulders, curling over her hip and thigh like a living appendage. She reached for the hand he still held over her lower abdomen, pulling it away from her body and releasing it, a low, challenging sound erupting from her throat. Her lips twisted into an erotic smile, her tongue slipping out to wet them slowly as she stepped unhurriedly to her right. The movement was seductive poetry, rippling up along her supple form like a beckoning wave.

"You did this," she accused softly.

Gideon realized she was correct, to an extent. They had both been undeniably attracted to each other for a very long time, their minds and attitudes and pride the obstacles that had prevented them from exploring it. But when he had entered her healthy body with his power, he had unwittingly set a chain of events in motion, bypassing the mental barriers they had erected against one another, fusing them instead on a purely biological level. Then she had sent her power into him, completing the cycle, locking them one to another in an irresistible loop.

"I may have begun it, but you perpetuated it, Magdelegna," he told her, watching her closely as she moved one step, then another, slowly beginning to circle around him. Gideon held very still, a difficult thing to do considering his entire being was thrumming with awareness and arousal. Still, he never took his eyes off her.

She seemed to be contemplating his words, much as her eyes were contemplating his body. Gideon had never known such a primitive sensation in all his life. The power of it overcast any memory of sexual stimulation he'd ever felt in all his years.

She was remarkable.

She was a thing of primal beauty.

Legna moved closer to the male standing in the middle of her room, so aware of every nerve in her highly stimulated body that she wondered why she wasn't screaming from the overload. She was still so connected to Gideon both mentally and through their joined power that his realizations, feelings, and awareness had become a part of her. She knew what was happening to them, but she was not afraid of it. She thrummed with his ancient power, feeling it soaking into her like a high-amplitude electrical shock that was locked in a continuous feedback loop. It was divine. It was deadly.

She did not care, because she knew without a doubt that he was as much under her spell as she was under his. They each had a naturally dominant nature. He was familiar with his, and she was just discovering hers.

She smiled, her entire face slipping into an image of beautiful sin.

"You spurned me," she reminded him, moving close enough to him to touch his biceps, the muscle beneath the smooth silk of his shirt jumping tightly in response. Her fingertips slid up over his shoulder, changing from a ghostly touch to a bolder one as she crossed the broad width of his back and then followed the length of his spine. Her palm curved over his fit backside briefly before dropping away from the tension-tight musculature.

"I know," he said roughly, his eyes burning like starlight as he watched her come around to face him. "I was a fool. I was guilty of the arrogance you accused me of."

It satisfied her to hear that. The feeling was reflected in her expression as she drew up close to him so they were almost touching, breast to breast. He lowered his gaze to her mouth, the inviting shape of it making him thirsty for her taste. He remembered how exotic it was, remembered how it had flowed over his taste buds like refined honey. But she had made it very clear that she was dictating the moment, so he made no aggressive moves toward satisfying his desires.

Legna felt his need and the way he held himself in check, waiting for her to dictate the path and pace. It pleased her, made her interest in him spike off any measurable scale. His aroused state was sharp, his scent blanketing her like the aroma of an exotic rainfall. She closed her eyes, drawing in a deep, slow breath, filling her lungs with him. Gideon groaned under his breath, feeling her counterarousal as it was projected into him.

His hands curled into fists at his sides as he repressed the urge to seize her. She opened her eyes and he was shocked by the vivid silver they had become, an astounding reflection of his own. This he could not coherently explain. He was far too wrapped up in her dance of seduction to even want to try.

Legna lifted her hands to his chest, slipping two fingers down the strip of crisscrossed laces that held his shirt closed, freeing them with so quick and light a touch, he didn't realize her achievement until the moment both of her hands slid into the parted fabric, caressing the athletic contours of the muscles beneath, setting his skin on fire.

"Magdelegna," he whispered, "in all my life, I have never come close to any creature as beautiful as you are."

The compliment pleased her, her connection with him so firm that she knew he meant it. Gideon was a being of truth and fact, so long as it was not too close to his own faults for clarity. Now that he had admitted the truth to himself, he would see to it that she was fully aware of how he felt about this particular truth.

"You managed to resist me all these years," she mused.

"It was hell on earth," he insisted honestly.

She leaned close, whispering in his ear through the lightest clench of her teeth. "You hunted a human female rather than come to me."

"I was trying to protect you." He drew a deep breath, her aroma that of wild spices and, once again, that wraithlike touch of musk. "The human female was nothing but an instance of insanity and unfortunate timing. I did not want to use you for my sexual gratification in a moment of disrespectful madness. Your value is so far above so callous an act, Legna. I would have shamed us both if I had used you in such a way."

"You shamed me the moment you called me a child, Gideon," she told him sharply, her nails biting into his skin in reflection of the pain he had visited upon her.

"The words of a coward," he confessed hoarsely. "I was so afraid of the lack of control you inspired, Legna."

"And are you still afraid of what I inspire within you, Gideon?"

"Yes," he admitted, "I am." He reached up, his knuckles brushing up and over the curve of her elegant cheek. "I never once suspected such intensity could exist. It is humbling to live for over a millennium and realize there is still something to be learned . . . that there are still things capable of surprising you."

She smiled contentedly at that, her eyes closing as she turned into the warmth and affection of his touch. Gideon ached from head to toe for her, the whole of his body and mind feeling as if he contained energy too vast to remain withheld for long.

"Tell me now," he murmured, "what you will choose. Are you going to leave me, Indirianna?" he asked, her most precious secret, her power name, falling over her like the touch of a thousand fingertips, reaching deep into the most hidden parts of her, forcing a gasp of stunned pleasure from her slender throat.

"You know my name," she said with wonder, shocked to find it did not terrify her as it should have.

The common names the Demons knew one another by were merely call names, selected for convenience and as a nod of respect to those represented in the stories of the Christian Bible. Power names were something else entirely. Once someone knew a Demon's power name, they could exert their influence over them. A Demon's power name was the essential component in a Summoning. With it, a necromancer could force a captive Demon to do whatever he or she wanted it to do. This was why it was the most seriously protected secret each of them carried, none of them even daring to share it with their mate for fear they could come to harm for having the knowledge.

"Say my name," he countered, his hand wrapping

around the irresistible length of her neck. This time it was he who whispered into her ear. "Say it."

"I do not know what it is," she said, her breath rushing out of her in an astounding rhythm.

"Yes, you do. I feel it. You only have to search for it inside of us." "Us" was the appropriate term. It was almost impossible in that moment for them to discern whose thoughts belonged to whom.

Gideon was the oldest of them all. There was no one older, so no one who had once known his power name could possibly be alive. His parents were dead. His *Siddah* were dead. If Legna discovered his name, the ramifications were inconceivably serious. He would be putting his very existence into her hands. He would be placing all of his power at her fingertips, gifting her with the potential for his absolute submission. Legna tried to step back from him, the shock of what he was offering her too much to bear. But he had made sure to have his hands on her and now kept her tight and close within them.

"I cannot," she whispered, her body beginning to shake. "No one should know that. No one. I am not strong enough to keep it, Gideon. Any male Mind Demon could take it from me!"

"You are stronger than you think, *Neliss.*"

"Not strong enough. Please, do not ask this of me." She pushed at him, jerked herself backward, using the weight of her body to try and break free. He held her for a moment longer, looking deeply into her panic-stricken expression.

"One day," he said softly.

He opened his hands and released her.

She stumbled backward with her sudden freedom. One hand flew to her breastbone, pressing on it as if she were trying to physically restrain the laboring rise and fall of it. He moved closer to her one last time, tilting up her gaze with a coaxing fingertip beneath her chin.

"You have made your choice, have you not?"

She did not pretend to mistake his meaning. A large part of him still stirred within her awakened mind. She realized there was a name for what had just passed between them. He was Imprinted on her now, for all time, and she upon him. Though they had not come together in the most intimate physical sense, each had marked their territory upon the other. Legna could feel the changes within herself already. Her scent was changed, forever mingled with his. Her thoughts were filled with the images of his thoughts. His power was now becoming a part of hers.

"Did I ever have a choice?" she asked, her entire body shaking with the shock of her realization.

"Yes. You know very well that you did."

He was right. She did not want to admit it, but the choice had been hers to make, although nature and fate had made it an irresistible situation by rousing the feminine predator in her, bringing its very distinctive desires into the process.

"I have chosen you, Gideon," she murmured affirmatively. "And you have chosen me. But how is this possible?"

"It is rare, Legna, I know. This happens between two Demons maybe once in every couple of centuries. But you can feel how real it is, can you not? It is inside you, just as it is inside me. For all time."

"But . . . Isabella and Jacob . . . Corrine and Kane. I thought that the prophecy said our mates were meant to be found in Druids."

"Perhaps it is because we were always meant to find our counterparts in the Druids, and not each other, that it is so rare between two Demons to Imprint. But there are no absolutes, Legna. Demons have fallen deeply in love even without the Imprinting for centuries, only the most profoundly lucky ones having this experience. You were meant for me. I see that now with astounding clarity. Why I did not understand it sooner is beyond me."

Gideon realized now that he also knew the source of her

seemingly strange development. This exchange had actually begun nine years back. It was the parts of himself he had left behind within her, from that brief, torrid encounter, that had sped her maturity. He had made her stronger than she had been, her chemistry becoming flooded with the traits of his. That was why he had adapted to her autonomic functions during his scan. She had already begun to become a part of him, just as he had begun to become a part of her. They had been too lost in their clashing emotions to recognize it.

"Gideon, I am afraid."

Her confession was not wholly unexpected. He had felt as much. It was why he had let her break away from him. It was why he was going to ignore the strangling demands of his body and allow her time to accept him outside of the bewitching physical need they shared.

"I know you are," he said softly, his soothing touch on her cheek helping her to focus, to calm her violent emotions.

"You are so powerful, Gideon. You are the most revered Ancient in all of Demon society, past and present. How can I possibly . . . You were right," she blurted out. "Compared to you, I am a child. What can I possibly offer to you that would have this Imprinting make sense?"

"A powerful lineage. A fascinating and complex intelligence. Beauty of the ages." He leaned closer, his mouth hovering a breath away from hers. "An Imprinting does not need to make sense. It is what it is."

Gideon moved that breath forward, capturing her mouth for what felt like the first time in forever. He was instantly intoxicated by the heat, the texture, and the immediate passion of her kiss. She accepted him so readily, so without reservation of the body even though her mind feared him. Desire for her began to burn through his soul all over again, if indeed it had ever truly stopped. He shared the sensation with her, swallowing her startled gasp when the feelings made their impact on her. His mouth took from hers wildly, his hands coming to cradle her head as she swayed forward into him, deeper and deeper into the hot clash of taste and tongues. She was pristine ambrosia, food for the gods, and it sent spears of want plunging down through his body. Control? It was hers and hers alone. He suddenly understood what it might be like for those on the receiving end of his power. What he was receiving from her was electric, powerful, and a healing of his self-imposed solitude that was like a beneficent balm.

Legna felt soft impressions flowing into her thoughts. She felt Gideon's realization of what his age and isolationism had cost him in loneliness. She ached for him, in both need and sympathy, as he allowed himself to bathe in her presence, her touch, and her kiss. She heard words of passion, as old as time itself, swirling through her mind. His voice, even in her mind, was so rich and so darkly seductive as it drifted through her thoughts, encouraging her, reassuring her, telling her in both graphic and poetic detail what her kiss was doing to him.

When he finally broke away from her, they were both boasting eyes as magically bright as tinsel and gasping for an elusive, calming breath that would take far too long to come to either of them.

But Gideon forced himself to step back from her, although he never broke their intense eye contact.

"You have fears," he rasped quietly. "You need time. I will give it to you as best I can, *Neliss. Nelissuna.* My beautiful one." The romantic endearment made Legna's head spin with hundreds of emotions, both his and hers. "But," he continued, his tone clearly reluctant, "Beltane approaches rapidly, and I will not be able to maintain any semblance of chivalry on that ancient night. No Imprinted pair can resist the lure of that powerful night of fertility and rebirth."

"I know. I remember the stories," she whispered, her heart beating so fast that it ought to have exploded from her chest. "I am grateful for whatever time you give me,

Gideon. I . . . I can feel the pain you are in at this moment from your . . . your denial."

"It is our combined pain, Legna, just as it is our combined need. I can only be thankful that it is not the month of Samhain. That would be an unbearable torture. It has been for nearly this entire decade."

She nodded, reaching up to touch his handsome face, suddenly needing to, now that she was free to do so. His eyes closed and he took in a deep breath to try and center himself. She was aware that even so simple a touch had a profound influence on him. It amazed her. It fascinated her.

He opened his eyes then, white fire flaring hotly within them.

"Send me home, Legna," he commanded her, his voice hoarse with suppressed emotion.

She moved her head in affirmation even as she leaned toward him to catch his mouth once more in a brief, territorial kiss, her teeth scoring his bottom lip as she broke away. It was an incidental wound, one he could heal in the blink of an eye. But he wouldn't erase her mark on him, and they both knew it.

Finally, she stepped back, closed her eyes, and concentrated on picturing his home in her thoughts. She had been in his parlor dozens of times as a guest, always accompanied by Noah. His library, his kitchen, even the grounds of the isolated estate were well known to her. She could have sent him to any of those locations.

But as she began to focus, her mind's eye was filled with the image of a dark, elegant room she had never seen before. Hand-carved ebony-paneled walls soared up into a vast ceiling, enormous windows of intricate stained glass spilled colored light over the entire room as if a multitude of rainbows had taken up residence. It all centered around an enormous bed, the coverlet's color indistinguishable under the blanket of colorful dawn sunlight that streamed into the room. She could feel the sun's warmth, ready and waiting to cocoon any weary occupant who thrived on sleeping in the heat of the muted daylight sun. It was a beautiful room, and she knew without a doubt that it was Gideon's bedroom and that he had shared the image of it with her. If she sent him there, it would be the first time she had ever teleported someone to a place she had not first seen for herself. The ability to take images of places from others' minds for teleporting purposes was an advanced Elder ability.

"You can do it," he encouraged her softly, all of his thoughts and his will completely full of his belief in that statement.

Legna kept his gaze for one last long moment, and with a flick of a wrist sent him from the room with a soft pop of moving air. She exhaled in wonder, everything inside of her knowing without a doubt that he had appeared in his bedroom, safe and sound, that very next second. Legna turned to look at her own bed and wondered how she would ever be able to sleep.

Nelissuna . . . go to bed. I will help you sleep.

Gideon's voice washed through her, warming her, comforting her in a way she hadn't thought possible. This was the connection that Jacob and Isabella shared. For the rest of the time both of them lived, each would be privy to the other's innermost thoughts. She realized that because he was the more powerful, it was quite possible he would be able master parts of himself, probably even hide things from her awareness and keep them private—at least, until she learned how to work her new ability with better skill. After all, she was a Demon of the Mind. It was part of her innate state of being to figure the workings of their complex minds.

She removed her slippers and pushed the sleeves of her dress from her shoulders so that it sheeted off her in one smooth whisper of fabric. She closed her eyes, avoiding looking in the mirror or at herself, very aware of Gideon's eyes behind her own.

His masculine laughter vibrated through her, setting her skin to tingle.

So, you are both shy and bold . . . he said with amusement as she quickly slid beneath her covers. *You are a source of contradictions and surprises, Legna. My world has begun anew.*

As if living for over a millennium is not long enough? she asked him.

On the contrary. Without you, it was far, far too long. Go to sleep, Nelissuna.

And a moment after she received the thought, her eyes slid closed with a weight she could not have contradicted even if she had wanted to.

Her last thought, as she drifted off, was that she had to make a point of telling Isabella that she might have been wrong about what it meant to have another to share one's mind with.

It was well after dark by the time Legna roused herself from Gideon's highly effective sleep inducement. She stood in the dark of her room for a long time, leaning against the windowsill, her face turned up to the night lights in the darkened sky.

Somehow, everything seemed incredibly different. Scents, sounds, silence. It all felt more tangible, more real. It was an impressive sensation for one who had lived her entire life seeing deeply beneath the surfaces of things. She felt the cold night air sweeping over her bare skin, the sensuality of standing nude before it a stimulating experience. With a smile, she moved to her wardrobe to select something to wear.

Legna had always taken particular care in the way she dressed, her clothes and style quite distinctive, always feminine, always reflecting her special grace. Still, this day she was compelled to take even greater pains with her appearance. It did not take a genius to figure out why, and she could not help but laugh out loud at herself as she pivoted before her mirror to view the flow of her heavy satin skirt. The dress was full length, dropping over one shoulder in the Grecian style of a toga, then twisting and falling from her waist in the trailing folds of a train of ruby satin shot through with silver threads that reminded her of Gideon's eyes.

She blushed softly as she viewed herself in the mirror, suddenly aware that he was once more behind her eyes, seeing her just as she did.

"You could at least warn me," she said aloud, cocking a scolding brow at her reflection.

And deprive myself of this side of you? I would not dream of it.

Legna smiled, moving closer to her looking glass.

She gasped when she got a closer look at herself, her hand coming up to her cheek in shock as she looked into her eyes.

"My eyes!" she exclaimed.

My eyes, he said.

He couldn't have spoken a clearer truth. It was his mercury-colored irises that had become part of her reflection, the multicolored gray and green gone from their familiar place. She sighed with resignation, supposing to herself that since it wasn't likely she could do anything about it, she would have to get used to it.

"I do not suppose you will show up here suddenly sprouting coffee-colored hair?" she asked hopefully.

No, sweet, that is not likely.

"Well, this is a highly unfair situation!" she cried with exaggerated petulance. "An exchange historically indicates one thing being swapped for another. So far I only see you in me, but none of me in you. It feels terribly high-handed. How typical of you."

He did not respond, only a soft impression of laughter flitting through her mind. Odd, but she realized then that she had hardly ever heard him laugh before. She was surprised by how comfortable it sounded on him. He had always been so serious, so . . .

Self-possessed.

"If you do not mind, do refrain from editing my personal thoughts," she scolded, her arching tone taunting and haughty.

Gideon replied with silence, and flashing a triumphant grin into the mirror, she flipped the long braid of her hair over her shoulder and glided out of her room. She stepped rapidly down the white marble stairway that led directly into the Great Hall, the train of her dress a billowing, shining banner behind her. She flew off the last few steps, nearly running over Noah in her haste. Her brother caught her around her waist, swinging her into a safe balance at his side so she wouldn't fall for tripping over him.

"Noah!" she greeted breathlessly, her hands steadying herself on his arms. "I am sorry, I did not see you."

"That much is clear," he teased her in return, kissing her cheek in greeting as she kissed his. "You seem to be in a hurry. Oversleep, did we?"

"I . . . suppose. Yes." Legna lowered her eyes, avoiding his direct line of sight as she released him in order to fuss with her already perfect skirts.

Noah's head snapped up all of a sudden, his sensory abilities sparking like flint and steel around them.

"What is it?" Legna asked.

"I'm . . ." He hesitated a long minute. "I'm not sure. I had the strangest feeling that Gideon was here."

Legna couldn't help it, she had to turn her head away in order to hide the telltale flush that swept over her. The movement caught Noah's attention and he narrowed his eyes on his youngest sister.

"Legna? Is Gideon here?"

"Not that I know of. I just woke up, remember? I have to go." Legna flew up to kiss him quickly and then like a flash was out of Noah's reach and heading for the front entrance.

However, Noah was not above extending his reach. Legna was forced to come up short of her goal when a wall of heat, just hot enough to give her the equivalent of a sunburn, fell over the portal. Legna uttered a sound of consternation, her hands resting on her hips as she turned to face her brother.

"All right, what is this? House arrest?"

"If you choose to call it that," Noah remarked absently, moving to approach his sister to better scrutinize her. "What is going on, Legna? I get the funny feeling I am on the outside of some sort of cockamamy scheme you are engaged in. No doubt something my Enforcer's troublemaking wife has goaded you into."

"Funny feeling or not, brother dearest, you are going to have to do a *lot* better than this to keep me still enough to find out!"

And with a flick of her wrist, she was gone, the snap of the change in air pressure making Noah's sinuses twinge. *She did that on purpose,* he thought to himself, his internal voice sounding as petulant as he felt as he rubbed the bridge of his nose. Whoever had said that Fire Demons were the most powerful of their breed was a total moron. Sure, he was one of the most destructive of his brethren, but Legna had it all coming and going, and she knew it. She never had to sit still for anything she didn't want to. She could travel anywhere instantaneously. And to top it off, she was able to tell him what he was feeling long before he could tell it to himself. And those were merely her innate abilities. Her intelligence and simpatico ease when it came to deciphering psyches and societies put her even further out front.

"It is a good thing she is on our side, is it not?"

Noah started, turning to confront the Demon who had appeared at his back with flawless silence and concealment.

"Jacob! You just took ten years off my life," Noah hissed.

"Only ten? I must be losing my touch." Jacob looked from Noah to the last place Legna had been standing. He nodded his head in her former direction. "What was that all about?"

"I have no idea, but I am beginning to feel like I am the only one who does not know what the hell is happening in his own damn house."

"Sorry state of affairs, seeing as how you are King and all," Jacob said, his lips twitching with amusement as Noah glared at him. "That is only my opinion, though. Perhaps I will ask my troublemaking wife for hers."

Noah had the grace to openly wince.

"You heard that, hmm?"

"And therefore . . ." Jacob prompted.

"She heard it, too," Noah concluded with comical pain. "Forgive me, Bella. I think I am just in a foul mood."

"She says she will forgive you as soon as she needs a babysitter."

"You know, I think you better go out there and enforce some of my laws before I begin to think of how many ways I can set your ass on fire," the King said meanly, the glare of his gaze all business.

"I would, but I am in need of Gideon. Where is he?"

"How should I know?" Noah asked grumpily, moving to the fire and sinking down into the only thing in the room that wasn't giving him grief: his favorite chair.

Jacob followed the King, a perplexed look on his face.

"Wait a minute, Noah, are you saying Gideon is not here? Was not here?"

"No. Why would he be? There is no Council meeting today. And in spite of—" Noah broke off, his eyes snapping up to Jacob's. "Why did you think Gideon was here?"

"Because I know his scent. That and his presence are quite distinctive, as you are well aware."

"Yes, I know," Noah mused. "It's funny, but I could have sworn I felt his energy myself not five seconds ago. Perhaps he was in the area. Legna did not mention he had been here when I asked her." Noah settled back and shrugged. "Whatever the reason, it is probably not important."

Jacob murmured a sound of agreement even though he didn't look completely satisfied. "Well, I have to find him. I will visit with you later."

"Jacob, is something wrong? Is Isabella okay?"

"Probably. She is not well today. It could be a normal thing for a human female, but since she is usually as resistant to common ailments now as we are, she is nervous. I figured Gideon could ease her mind."

Noah missed the wince that crossed his friend's face that would have given away the indignant argument flying through the Enforcer's thoughts. Jacob's female counterpart huffily took umbrage to his claims of exactly who it was that was nervous and who had insisted on seeking Gideon, because it certainly had not been her.

"Tell her I hope she feels better," Noah said, his fondness for Bella quite clear in his tone. "Bear with her, old friend. She's breaking new ground. It can be pretty frightening to play Eve for an entire race."

"Do not worry. When it comes to my Bella, I would do anything to see to her happiness. That includes making others do anything to see to her happiness," Jacob said. He meant the words, of course, but he was hoping they'd help soothe someone's bristling pride.

"I'm sure Gideon is going to love that," Noah laughed.

Jacob grinned, altering gravity so that he began to float up from the floor.

"If you see Gideon before I do, will you tell him to come to Bella?"

"Of course. Tell her I said to start behaving like a real

Druid or I—" Noah was cut off by a sharp hand motion and a warning expression from the Enforcer. It came a little too late, however, if Jacob's pained expression was anything to judge by.

"There goes your invitation for our wedding," Jacob muttered. "And I think I am close behind you."

"I would believe that if I were not the one who is supposed to perform it and if you were not the father of her otherwise illegitimate child," Noah countered loudly, clearly talking to the person beyond his immediate perception.

"Ow! Damn it, Noah!" Jacob grumbled, rubbing his temples as Bella's scream of frustration echoed through him. "Do remember I am the one who has to go home to her, would you?"

"Sorry, my friend," Noah chuckled, not looking at all repentant. "Now get out of here, Enforcer. Find Gideon and tend to your beautiful and charming mate. Be sure to mention to her that I said she looks ravishing and that her pregnancy has made her shine like a precious jewel."

"Noah, if you were not my King, I would kill you for this."

"Yes, well, as your King I would have you arrested for treason just for saying that. Luckily for you, Jacob, you are the man who would arrest you, and the woman who also has the power to do so is sure to punish you far better than I can when you get home."

"You are all heart, my liege," Jacob said wryly.

"Thank you. Now leave, before I begin to expound on the disrespect that this mouthy little female of yours seems to have engendered amongst my formerly loyal subjects."

Jacob clearly had a retort for that, but he wisely held it behind sparkling eyes. A moment later, he turned into a twisting whirl of dust, floating out of a high castle window and leaving Noah alone.

Chapter 5

Bella stood up from the seat on the couch she had been commanded to remain in, rubbing her hands together anxiously as she paced the carpet. Joking and jibes aside, Jacob was trying to stay very close to her thoughts. Isabella would have been lying if she had said she wasn't comforted by his presence, even if he was currently lecturing her about her persistent inability to obey his commands. In this instance, to remain seated and to try and relax.

"It's just a headache and a little nausea, Jacob," she said aloud to the empty room. "I don't see why you feel the need to bother Gideon."

Better safe than sorry, Bella. And I can tell you need to put your mind to ease. Despite your claims otherwise.

Well, I don't know which makes me more nervous, feeling strange or watching you react to me feeling strange. If this is some sort of gas bubble or something, Gideon will massacre me. Correction, massacre us.

You feel how you feel, love. That is always allowed. I am going to be a while. Please sit down and rest?

Isabella nodded, and even though he couldn't see her do so, he got the impression of her agreement. She released him from the forefront of her mind, curling up in a corner of the sofa, wearily settling her head until her lids began to droop.

Just as she began to fall asleep, there was a knock at the door.

Legna appeared just outside of Jacob and Isabella's house, standing in front of the door. Bella was not expecting her today, so today she would use the courtesy of knocking. She made certain to reflect her well-mannered actions back at the male ghosting through her mind. Maybe now he would learn something about human protocol.

I would not count on it, Nelissuna.

Do you mind? I would like at least a little privacy while I talk to my friend.

Privacy is a human foible, Legna. You have been associating with the Druid too much and adopting her idiosyncrasies.

She is my friend. I love her dearly and owe her much. If you have a problem with that . . .

Do not threaten me, Legna. It is quite a waste of your time.

Are you going to remove yourself or not? she demanded.

Given a choice . . . not.

Very well, let me rephrase that . . . get out or I will put you out. And do not assume that I cannot or will not do so. Imprinting or no, I am a Mind Demon and I will figure out exactly how to do it. Also, I am still an individual despite this whole situation and I will have my freedoms.

I see. Well, if you intended to insist, I do not see why you bothered to ask me at all.

I did not ask. Well, not the first time. And the second one was just . . . oh, never mind! Are you always going to be this literal? Because let me tell you, it is a pain in the ass. And do not even think of saying anything else about Bella's influence on me!

Perish the thought. Enjoy your visit, Nelissuna.

As simply as that, she felt him drift away from her mind. There was so much of him becoming a part of her, weaving into her very make-up, that she couldn't be certain he was completely shut off from her thoughts. Was it even possible for Imprinted mates to block one another off from the inherent connection of their minds? Had it ever been tried? Had it ever been desired before? This was all still too new. It would take her some time to sort through everything she was feeling, not to mention what effect it would have on her abilities to be supercharged by the shared power of an Ancient of his caliber.

But there was a cunning part of Legna that was realizing open thoughts and silvery eyes were a very small price to pay for the power promising to come her way.

The mercenary sensation disturbed her with a shiver, but she shook it off and chose to ignore it. She wasn't going to let any part of this intimidate her.

Legna lifted her hand and knocked for Isabella.

Jacob reached Gideon's residence in record time, propelled to extraordinary speed by his concern for Isabella. He drifted into the manse through an open window, changing from dust to Demon with a quick twist of movement.

He glanced around the immediate room, scenting the strong presence of his prey of the moment. It had been many years since he had last been here, in the Ancient's domain. He was surprised to realize how familiar the place still felt in spite of the fact that he still felt uneasy with the medic himself, unable to fully dismiss some of the negative feelings that had arisen between him and his former friend. But Isabella's needs came well before his own, and Isabella needed Gideon.

"Jacob."

The Enforcer turned at his name, having already sensed the Ancient's arrival in the room.

"Gideon, I require some of your time."

"Of course. Is something wrong with your mate?"

"I do not believe it is anything serious, but she has these bouts of nervousness and I think she makes herself ill from it. She will not often or openly admit it, but she worries a great deal and, I admit, her imagination, which is so brilliant, can also be a curse for her in such times. She requires your reassurance. No other medic will serve the purpose. She trusts you and no one else as far as the pregnancy is concerned."

"Understandable. I have told her not to hesitate calling on me and I meant it. She is my highest priority."

Jacob was silent for a moment, absorbing how that made him feel and reconciling it with everything else he felt toward the medic.

"Then I am grateful," he said at last, inclining his head in brief respect to the Ancient.

"You are welcome to my help. Come, let us—"

Gideon!

The cry rang through Gideon's mind so loudly and so suddenly that he winced sharply, jerking his head to the side, a hand going to his forehead in irresistible reflex as pain blossomed over his left eye, cheek, and neck. He was mildly aware of Jacob reacting with surprise to the inconceivable picture it must have made, but he turned his thoughts to the urgent priority of Legna's call, come so soon after she'd ordered him away.

Is it Isabella? he asked, quickly reaching the conclusion from knowing where she was and the purpose of the Enforcer in front of him.

Yes. She is on the floor. Gideon, there is so much blood!

Gideon looked up at Jacob, and in that moment the Enforcer paled visibly beneath his natural tan. Apparently he had just become aware of Isabella's distress as well.

"Sweet Destiny," he whispered.

"Jacob, remain where you are," the Ancient commanded.

"I will not!" He exploded in instant fury. "She is my wife, Gideon, and you do not command me!"

"Jacob, Legna is with Bella," Gideon said firmly, "and she can teleport us both far faster than we could travel to her side by your means."

"Legna?" Jacob scoffed. "She is not strong enough to carry us both so far."

"Yes, she is. I beg you to trust me and stop arguing, as time is of the essence."

That silenced the distraught Enforcer, forcing him to nod in agreement and draw back from the aggressive stance he had taken in Gideon's space.

Legna, you can do this.

No! Not both at once! Not across such a distance!

Yes, you can. With me as part of you, you can do anything you set your mind to. Sweet, you are much stronger than you may ever realize. You always have been, even before I ever touched you. Destiny would not give me a weak companion.

She was silent and Gideon could feel her gathering her energy after turning her back on her doubting thoughts. Apparently, Bella's condition was serious enough to compel her to try, and Gideon was over-whelmed with a sense of pride at how well she shoul-dered her responsibilities and how she accepted his word on faith . . . and a whole lot of hope.

Jacob watched the world squeeze together before him, the visual phenomenon that the teleporter experienced when sent by a Mind Demon to another place. It was as if Legna was folding the two points in space together until they touched, making the exchange from point A to point B seemingly as easy as taking a step forward.

The pressure change shot through the sinuses of the arriving males, disorienting them for all of a second.

Gideon's first impulse was to look for his patient, but at the same time his new sensitivities for another woman demanded his attention. He felt the wave of nausea and faintness that rushed through Legna. He turned, finding her unerringly, and reached out to catch her in the nick of time, easing her to the floor in a gentle motion.

"See to Legna," he demanded of Jacob. "She needs to recover quickly."

Gideon knew nothing was wrong with Legna that some time to recharge her energy would not cure, so he felt no hesitation in leaving her to Jacob. The Enforcer, whose eyes had settled on his damaged mate, was not so rational. He ignored Gideon's command as every fiber of his being screamed to go to his woman, who lay sprawled at painful angles in the spreading warmth of her own blood. Jacob crossed the room in a beat, his boots crunching through broken glass and other debris as he did so. Neither male gave the chaotic alteration to their surroundings any other thought as they both reached for Isabella.

Gideon connected with the inert figure of the small Druid female and immediately recognized that the petite creature seemed even smaller without the vibrancy that normally accompanied her consciousness. She lay like a pitifully broken sparrow, as if somehow a car had come through the parlor and crushed her at full speed. The medic saw Jacob's impulse to catch up her hand in his, and his quick discarding of that need when he saw the burns and blood on both appendages. Though she was unconscious, the Enforcer could not tolerate causing his mate even the slightest of pain. So Jacob knelt on a single knee close to her side, the back of his fist resting against his lips as he seemed to press back the building rage that was turning his eyes a uniform black.

Gideon touched her forehead, his palm encompassing it entirely, going beyond the cold temperature of the grayed complexion of her face and sinking quickly and deeply into her body. Straight away he was filled with the alarms within her, her already active natural defenses and healing abilities drawing him to her wounds. But no matter how quickly Nightwalkers healed, they could never be able to compensate for a trauma such as this without outside intervention.

Clearly, someone had attacked the little Enforcer. She was battered and bruised from head to toe, apparently having been thrown about like a limp doll in some beast's mouth. She was scored with the marks of an electrical attack, burned at the places the blasts had struck through her as effectively as bullets. It was the signature attack of a necromancer. The scent of her scorched flesh filled the room, underscored by the rusty aroma of blood.

Even in her pregnant state, it was clear Isabella had put up a remarkable fight. She had ferocious defensive wounds on her hands and arms, and the room around them had been obliterated in the confrontation. The question was, if a necromancer or any being of power was responsible for this, how had her attacker circumvented her awesome dampening and power-theft abilities?

The query could wait. Gideon focused on his task. Most of the blood was coming from the fetus Isabella carried, or rather, the placenta that nourished the tiny being within her. Though she lay in a pool of the precious liquid, Gideon could better assess the loss of it from within Isabella rather than by visual survey. It was bad, and getting worse. He could repair the damage, but he could not replace the blood without help.

"Jacob," he said softly, his attention split between the beginnings of his healing and the import of filling in the Enforcer, "she is in critical need of blood."

"Give her mine," he said immediately, extending his arm quickly.

"No. You are Demon, Jacob. Your blood types are not compatible. Especially not with her being partially human."

"We are all Demon here, Gideon. Who can donate to her if not her husband?"

Gideon looked up, meeting Jacob's frantic eyes, realizing the fear he must be feeling.

"Her sister, Jacob. Corrine is the only other hybrid amongst us, and, luckily, her relative. It is enough to make her compatible. If she is not entirely so, I can help with that. But we must act quickly or we will lose her and the baby."

"You will *not* lose her!" Jacob roared suddenly, his rage and fear getting the better of him as he surged to his feet, his hands coiled into violent fists. "Do you understand me, medic?" he continued with hoarse violence and pain seething from him as he shook with his emotions. "If she dies . . ." Clearly the Enforcer couldn't even finish the thought. He fell to his knees again, his pain so extreme that he couldn't maintain any semblance of control.

Just then, Legna came to with a violent gasp, sitting up straight in one jerking movement. Jacob's emotions had bombarded her unprotected mind, shocking her into wakefulness like a dose of electric voltage. She struggled for breath, gasping and choking, tears and a single, agonizing sob wrenching from her exactly as they were forcing themselves out of Jacob. Legna had never known such all-consuming anguish in the whole of her life. It felt as though she were being stripped of her soul, as if she were watching her own spirit die a terrible death and there was nothing that she could do about it. Even the agony of being Summoned could not compare to this devastation.

Then there was a soft touch within her mind—gentle, soothing, and healing. Her eyes lifted to meet Gideon's, swimming with her sparkling tears as they trembled on her lashes. His gaze was strong, steady, and radiating his confidence in her. It was precisely the anchor she needed to begin to protect herself from Jacob's unwitting mental assault.

Gideon gave her several breaths to reorder her

thoughts and control. Her eyes cleared of pain and turned to calm, the steady protection of her safeguards flying up with awesome strength around her. He could tell by her slightly dazed expression that the power of them had amazed even her.

"Legna, I need you to fetch Corrine," he said softly, their connection to one another allowing the request to repeat simultaneously in her mind so he would not speak loudly over Jacob's grief.

Legna took the command in stride, this time only a moment of doubt wasting their precious time. She got quickly to her feet, drawing even Jacob's attention as she did so. The Enforcer ran a hand over his wet face, looking up at the beautiful Demon with shock and disbelief.

And then hope.

As powerful as Jacob was, he could only travel so fast. Corrine and Kane had taken to splitting their dwellings between England and New York. At the moment, Corrine was in New York, an entire ocean away. He never would have been able to bring her there in time to save his wife. Even finding another Mind Demon powerful enough to do so would have taken an endless amount of time. But as the empath closed her eyes, taking a deep breath so long and so full it captivated him for a long minute, he realized that Legna was about to attempt to do this remarkable feat . . . and it would be an endeavor that even an Elder would have difficulty accomplishing.

Jacob rose quickly to his feet once more when he saw her fingers curl into her palms, her entire body trembling with her exertion. He did not dare touch her and disrupt her concentration, but he stood close, ready to save her from what would no doubt be a harsh consequence should she succeed. A moment later, Jacob felt a sensation cross over his skin, causing every hair on his body to stand on end. The next he knew, a brutal burst of air exploded in the center of the room, blowing back his hair with a nearly hurricane force. It lasted for a second, and suddenly Corrine was standing before them, looking stunned and just shy of screaming. Demons were used to being plucked suddenly out of their lives for one reason or another; the former human clearly was not.

Legna swayed for a moment, then collapsed once more. Her skin tone went from tan to a sickly beige. She lost consciousness with a rattling exhale of breath that gave Jacob a chill as he caught her against himself and lowered her gently to the floor, kneeling over her. He was awash with questions, and with immeasurable gratitude, but put them both aside as he checked Legna's pulse and breathing. Drained power stores not only left a Demon vulnerable, but could potentially be damaging. As before, Legna was no longer protected from the emotions running rampant around the room and her mind could be injured or overrun by them. It was the kind of damage that could leave her completely comatose.

Realizing this, Jacob drew away from her. There was no controlling his state of distress in such a moment, but touching Legna made for a stronger pathway into her psyche.

Meanwhile, the moment Corrine saw Isabella lying on the floor in her own blood, she reacted with the speed only a loved one could manage. She skidded across the blood-soaked floor, kneeling in the sticky fluid as she heedlessly shoved Gideon aside, lifting up her sister's head in order to cradle it gently in her lap.

"Bella," the redhead sobbed softly, the long curls of her hair spilling over the unconscious woman like a protective curtain as Corrine bent to kiss her forehead. "Oh, sweetie, what have you gotten yourself into this time?" she asked in a combination of grief and exasperation.

"Corrine, I need your hand," Gideon said quietly, holding out his palm to her.

Since Corrine had been living in Demon society almost as long as her sister and knew exactly who Gideon was, she did not hesitate to obey. The medic had saved her life once; she had to be positive he would save Bella's as well. Gideon's fingers curled around the slender wrist she extended, his opposite hand doing the same to Isabella's. He began the needleless transfusion, rapidly gathering pockets of whole red blood cells from the one female and distributing them into the other. They were compatible enough that he only had to make minor adjustments to the life-giving cells. It was just as well. In her drastically weakened state, Isabella could not handle much more alteration of her internal body without causing distress to the already taxed fetus within her. Isabella's color began to return and Gideon heard Jacob breathe again for the first time since the transfer of blood had begun. Corrine was a bit paler for the experience, he noted as he released her wrist, allowing her to sit back into her brother-in-law.

The pressing emergency had been dealt with, and Gideon was able to sit back and take a breath. He took that moment to examine the extraordinary emotional pain Jacob was going through. Now that he had just become part of an Imprinted pair himself, he wondered if he would find himself feeling as strongly as this. He was not an emotional being, so it disturbed him to realize it might be a possibility. He prided himself on his level nature and thinking. Being slave to his emotions could severely debilitate his judgment.

Gideon put his thoughts aside, but he was unable to help glancing at Legna's prone form as he touched Isabella once more in order to continue the healing process. His destined mate was merely exhausted, a complete drain of her energy that could have been a bit dangerous if he had not been there. Even as he healed Isabella, a second level of his consciousness was loaning his personal energy to Legna, bringing her to a state of safe, deep sleep.

Turning his full attention to Bella, Gideon painstakingly

began the task of repairing every gaping wound, a chore that would have been a daunting expenditure of energy and skill had it been anyone other than him. He did not bother with asking for permission to touch her, letting Jacob deal with it himself, knowing his priorities. He moved into the best position for his task, a classic doctor-patient gynecological form where he slid between her legs, resting her thighs atop his own to support the broken appendages and reaching for a straight-on access to her baby. The manipulation straightened her entire body, relieving pressure and pain. His hands slid over her belly, peeling back her bloody shirt and revealing the vicious bruises and lashing cuts all over it.

"Oh my God," Corrine gasped with strangled horror.

It was clear what had been the target of this attack. As Jacob's black-ice eyes took in the sight, Bella's sister reached up to seize handfuls of his shirt, clearly holding him in place, keeping him from acting in rage while supporting him at the same time. Gideon closed his eyes and focused on Bella's worst injury, the reattachment of the placenta taking priority and requiring a great deal of attention and energy. Her jeans were saturated in blood, which seeped brightly into his white pants, somehow making the reality of it far more real to those who loved her as they watched. Corrine began to cry and Jacob now held her in return. There was nothing Gideon could do about their emotional distress, so he simply attended his chores. He would tell them later how bruised the baby was and how all of Bella's wounds were coming together in his mind. She had not fought. She had only protected. Every crushed bone, every laceration, even the position in which they had found her body told the story of a young mother who had lain curled into herself, protecting her child with every ounce of her will and consciousness as she had been kicked and beaten and bashed into this little heap of brokenness.

Gideon healed on. The fate of Destiny was perpetuity,

he thought with no little respect. Destiny, a woman Herself, had lent Her fate to the tiny Druid. By lending it to Bella, she was allowing him to be able to heal her and the bruised baby in time to save them both from irreparable harm.

Destiny . . . and Magdelegna.

If she had not arrived to find Bella at exactly that moment, it would have been far too late by the time he and Jacob arrived on their own. Gideon appreciated the fact that Destiny and outright luck were key elements to this rescue recipe, especially when taking into consideration that he and Legna had only been Imprinted for a few hours. Had he not pressed to examine Legna that morning, he would never have been able to hear her desperate summons tonight. She might not have even thought to summon him at all, her rancor toward him interfering with her judgment.

Gideon recognized that Legna had sacrificed much tonight, and all for her love of this pretty little woman who would not only forever be the first of her kind, but in Gideon's opinion, the most exceptional. How much of that opinion actually belonged to Legna he did not know, but their blending awareness was making him understand her perspective and respect for Bella much more clearly.

As powerful as he was, and though his abilities were ancient and refined, it still took well over an hour before he could sit back on his heels and take a breath that finally was not focused on directing healing energy into her.

"Jacob," he said at last, turning to meet the worried eyes of the other male, "she is sleeping now. I have healed her as far as needed. The bruises and minor cuts are up to her own healing system. I can do no more for her. Only rest and time will bring her the remainder of the way."

Gideon was tired, and Jacob could see it clearly in the

faded gray of his eyes. It reflected exactly how serious the situation had been that their most powerful healer found himself so taxed.

"Put her to bed," the Ancient instructed him. "All is well with her and the babe." Gideon paused to survey his surroundings for the first time. "It looks as though she was engaged in a very difficult battle," he remarked, noticing burns that scored the walls and the complete tossing of all the objects in the immediate area, "but it is a lie."

"How do you mean?" Jacob asked, watching Gideon gently ease away from Bella, laying her out gingerly and with infinite compassion in his every touch. It had always baffled Jacob how the medic could be so cold and detached in his personality, and yet when he healed or touched an injured being he transformed into the epitome of tenderness and seemingly emotional caring. It was almost as though he saved the power of his feelings so he could use it to heal.

"Here . . ."

He reached to touch Isabella's chin as her husband came closer. Her head rolled easily aside, her sleep unable to be disturbed even if he had been harsh, because she was under his compulsion to remain so until she was healed and replenished. Gideon brushed back the wild tangle of her black hair from where it covered her throat, revealing two widely spaced puncture wounds in her neck.

"What the hell is that?" Jacob demanded hotly, reaching to touch the wounds.

"It looks like a bite from a Vampire!" Corrine said, her emerald eyes distressed.

"No . . . I do not think . . ." Jacob looked up at Gideon helplessly.

"You fought the Vampire wars. Have you ever known a Vampire to take the blood of another Nightwalker?"

"No. It is taboo. And I have seen Vampire wounds. There are more than just two incisors in a Vampire's mouth, and you can usually see their entire set of dental impressions for several hours after the bite."

"And all of her blood is on the floor and in our clothes. No. This is some sort of weak attempt at deception." Gideon shook his silvered head in puzzlement. "Also, the marks are burned, and they end just below the dermis. As an attack, it seems fairly ineffective an injury."

"Oh!" Corrine's gasp drew their attention as she leaned to brush her fingers over the suspect wounds. "I know this! Every New York girl knows this! It's a stun gun!"

"A stun gun?" Gideon asked. Because the Demons lived without technology, and Gideon lived secluded from humans entirely, he had never heard of this weapon. But Jacob had.

"I think you are right, Corr."

"Not a common handheld, though," Corrine added. "One of those distance guns with dartlike barbs that shoot out and stick into the target as power is conducted through wire. They're used in prisons."

"But why would a necromancer—" Jacob halted himself, clearly answering his own question in his thoughts.

"To circumvent her abilities," Gideon agreed with his silent but obvious conclusion. "Once she is hit by the gun, she is incapacitated, and the injury of that much voltage going through her would nullify her power with pain. Bella cannot use her ability if she is overrun with pain." Gideon looked up at Jacob with a coldness added to his implacability. "You had best call Elijah and have him investigate this further. The capture of necromancers is his domain and responsibility, not yours, no matter how driven by your sense of retribution you are to take care of it yourself. Your place is with Bella. She needs your presence, your strength, and to know that you are safe from danger. It will take a while before she will be conscious enough to tell us what happened. A longer while still if you do not follow my instructions in this to the letter.

"When she does awaken, she is not to have visitors or arouse herself from her bed. You can question her for Elijah as needed. Her immune system is going to be very fragile for a while. Demons may not manifest many common ailments, but it does not mean they do not carry the pathogens for them around with them. She is still part human, and this incident will leave her both powerless and vulnerable for some time. It is little different than when you were ill, Corrine, only she will recover quicker.

"Take her to a safe haven. Make it a very short distance and do not alter her molecular structure, Jacob. I will attend her tomorrow and will be making frequent visits for the next week, so be prepared for that. She should be fine as long as a trauma of this magnitude does not reoccur. I suggest you have Elijah post warriors for her protection, especially when you have to hunt. And when I say complete bed rest, I mean it, Jacob. I know how stubborn she is. Make it clear to her. No lifting, no bending, no cleaning, no cooking, no exertion whatsoever until I say otherwise."

Gideon didn't spend another second to see if Jacob had understood or moved to obey his orders. He immediately stepped over to Legna and leaned over her. He picked up her limp hand, folding it into one of his as he brushed several stray hairs that had escaped her braid off of her forehead.

"*Nelissuna*," he murmured softly, leaning close to her. He sank his power into her quickly, assessing her current health once more just as a precaution that was no doubt overprotective. But she was becoming his other half, so it was to be expected that he would behave in such ways, he determined to himself rather clinically. She was exhausted, and the only thing he could do now was let her sleep.

He moved his position, carefully sliding his hands beneath her until he could lift her up into the cradle of his arms. He stood up in a simple movement, her weight nothing to him. He felt her head roll gently against his shoulder, her warm face resting against the side of his neck. There was an answering ache from inside of his chest, forcing him to realize he was a little more disturbed by her state than he had expected to be. It did not matter that with all of his expertise he knew she was fine. What mattered was that she had suffered great stress and discomfort, most of it by his urging.

Their Imprinting on one another was going to be a little more difficult than he had originally thought. He could probably manage his feelings of concern for her well-being and health eventually, but he sincerely hoped he would not be afflicted with the possessiveness Jacob struggled with. The hope extended to Legna's perspective, too. He did not think he could tolerate a possessive mate. Gideon could only take comfort in the idea that Legna was a professional at managing emotion and had studied how to do so almost all of her life. Nor did she seem to be the type to indulge in these kinds of jealous traits.

It was a terrible contradiction to Demon nature, this territorialism. Almost every Demon in existence used touch to share their abilities with one another. It wasn't always necessary, but they were instinctively compelled to do it, just as they were an instinctively affectionate race. Certainly, all Demons were possessive to a certain degree when mated, but the ability to control it should not be any different than any other irrational emotion. Gideon was also realizing that the possessiveness of Jacob toward Isabella was unique because of how Jacob's life had unfolded. It had been a difficult one, filled with the ostracism of his position in society. It was easy to see why he guarded his treasure so avidly.

"Gideon, I am going to take refuge at Noah's," Jacob

said, lifting Bella from her bed of debris and battle. "I can take Legna."

"I would prefer if you brought Legna and me to the manse," Gideon countered. "Isabella requires peace and rest, as does Legna. I do not think that will last long with the two of them across the hall from one another."

"Point taken," Jacob agreed. "Corrine, will you watch over her? Also, are you in contact with my brother at the moment?"

Corrine nodded.

"He's right here," she said, touching her temple to indicate Kane had been monitoring the entire situation with his telepathic abilities. This communication ability was the male counterpart of Legna's empathy. "He is very concerned for both you and Bella. He says . . ." Corrine paused to concentrate on the voice of her mate in her head. "He is about to teleport to Elijah's home in order to speak with him on your behalf about Bella's attack. He will also warn Noah of what is happening. After he speaks to Noah, he will come here to hold watch with me until you and the warriors arrive."

"Thank you, Corr. And thank my baby brother for me as well."

"Consider it done," she assured gently. "Now let's hurry and put Bella to bed. I'll sit with her until it's time to go to Noah's. Kane and I will remain in England to be with you until she's well."

Jacob put Isabella to bed upstairs, under Corrine's watchful eye, then came back down to Gideon. He stood before the Ancient for a long moment, his expression eloquent with his gratitude. Gideon nodded his head silently in acceptance. Jacob reached to touch the other two Demons, turning them both completely weightless and flying the three of them out of the door toward Gideon's household. Since he was completely preoccupied with his wife's condition, Jacob did not think twice about Gideon's request to take Legna to his home rather than her own. The Enforcer, normally so observant, had not even noticed the significance of Legna's increased abilities and change in eye color. Gideon was grateful for that. He wanted more time with his intended mate before others began to interject their feelings and opinions into the matter.

Chapter 6

Jacob's need to return to his wife overrode any desire he might have had to ask any further questions of Gideon, so he and Legna were left alone quickly after their arrival at the manse.

Gideon carefully carried his intended up the stairs, entering the very bedroom he had sent an image of to Legna that morning. It looked different in the dark, however. It was moonlight that struck the colors of the windows into the room, making them distinctively darker and more eerie than the fairylike comfort of the daylight refractions. But Gideon found it the more beautiful of the two, and so would Legna, he hoped.

Gideon had always indulged in his taste for uniquely beautiful things. His house was a museum of that particular facet of his make-up. Like most long-lived species, he had collected extraordinary art and antiquities over the centuries. His collection, however, was a rich display of one-of-a-kind beauty.

As he rested Magdelegna down in his bed, he could see all too clearly why she had been chosen to be his mate. Even in her exhausted state her repose was something to behold. He sat beside her gingerly, not wishing to disturb her natural sleep and, as a result, having to cast an inducement on her to replace it.

He reached to touch her cheek, the still-pale skin reflecting a star-shaped lavender design from the window opposite her. Of their own accord, his fingers moved to caress her throat. He allowed himself to feel the rush of need that coursed through him. It was a sharp, razor-bladed thing, and he knew that it would only become more honed over time.

But he had promised his incredibly brave mate time. She still feared him. He realized that he must keep that promise at all costs. He saw this need with extreme clarity. If a woman so courageous as to risk the unfeasible without any concern for herself found fear in something, then she deserved the luxury of as much time as he could sanely manage. He had known Legna all of her life, from the moment she had been born. Legna only knew what she had been raised to think about him. He had read it all in her mind these past few hours. He was the Ancient Demon, and no one truly knew the extent of his power. At the heart of his nature it was clear he was rooted in the old ways, when respect and obeisance had been not only expected but were deemed a divine right. He never asked, only demanded or stated, and he anticipated unquestioned results by doing so. His will was indomitable, impossible to fight, so she would be up for a pitched battle should she ever try.

Gideon was unlucky in one other way, a more serious way that would reflect a terrible representation of himself to her. Deeply within Legna's subconscious, she had a memory of him that she was utterly unaware of.

It was the memory of the day her mother had died.

She did not remember it consciously. The trauma had been so painful for the little girl who had witnessed the tragedy that those who had been there had decided to remove it from her accessible memory. One day she would grow strong enough to retrieve it despite the methods they had used to circumvent the memory. Perhaps one day very soon. It would be a hard day for her, and a terrible day for him. He had always suspected that on some level she had been aware of his part in that day. It was perhaps why she always resisted being near him. She would not understand the compulsion as anything other than an unexplainable fear or aversion. No doubt she had always attributed it to the warnings Lucas had filled her head with during her youth in an attempt to teach her to respect those of greater age and power, according to custom.

The only thing within her that was in his favor was her experiences watching him heal others, and the one time he had healed her and Noah after a horrible accident that had nearly killed them both. She remembered the former with feelings of awe and respect, but also with curiosity and contemplation as she witnessed the gentleness of nature he exhibited during these acts. And, though she didn't truly remember the healing during the latter incident, it was still a part of her, whispering positive impressions about him into her perpetually curious opinion of him.

It was on these slim images within her that he was basing all of his hope. All he could do otherwise was pray for the opportunity to win her trust and confidence in him—before she recalled the memory hidden so deep within her. If he could manage this, it would be so much less painful for her. If it happened too soon, it could cause incredible damage to them both.

He was racing the clock, and he knew it. He had wasted the past nine years and cursed himself for the fool he had been. Be it the ill memories to come, or be it Beltane, he needed to coax her to him first. He understood the odds were against him, and that encouraging her to stretch her strength and abilities as he had today could cost him dearly, making her develop in power more quickly than she would have otherwise. However, as he had explained to her, the curing of his patients always came first . . . even over the well-being of his own

heart and soul. He had done what he'd had to in order
to save Isabella and her child. It was not possible for him
to do otherwise.

Gideon stood up, moving back a step from his sleeping guest. She immediately turned onto her side, facing
him, her arm reaching across the bedspread in an attempt to reach him. An enormous ache of emptiness
tightened in his chest, the compulsion to return to her
side brutally overwhelming.

He turned and walked out of the bedroom, unable to
help feeling as though he had just left a part of himself
behind.

Legna's eyes opened slowly, blinking in the face of
fading daylight.

She felt disoriented and confused. The room was full
of extraordinary colors, all of them splashing across
structures and furniture that were familiar and alien all
at once. She took in a careful breath, almost as if she
wasn't sure she would be able to breathe in this strange
environment.

The scent that slowly threaded its way around her and
invaded her senses was also familiar, as well as extraordinarily stimulating. She released a soft sound of curiosity
and captivation. Legna stretched out slowly, the movement rippling through her like a sensual awakening.
The simple movement made her instantly aware of the
warmth of a body beside her, the body that owned that
distinctive and delicious scent.

She turned to him, so close already that when she made
the simple movement it brought her into snug contact
with him along his side. The breath that she had so carefully achieved a moment ago left her in a rush of haste and
amazement as she rose up on an elbow and took in the remarkable sight of Gideon beside her in bed. He was asleep
on his back, bare-chested and in a relaxed repose of

crossed ankles and a hand beneath his head. His other hand lay on his stomach, rising and falling with each deep breath he took. He wore silk pajama pants of a beautiful sky blue, the drawstring of which was draping off the edge of his left hip.

In that moment, Legna realized just how incredibly and beautifully *male* the Demon beside her was. Because he was always clothed and refined whenever she saw him, she had never truly appreciated the development of the physique he had been concealing beneath expensive silk and embroidery as well as movements of elegance and tightly wrapped control. Even that morning in her bedroom when she had touched him so boldly, she had not reconciled her touch to what she was now seeing with her eyes.

To begin with, he had unbelievably wide shoulders. As a Demon female of great height and sturdy build, she rarely felt dwarfed or shadowed by a male, but Gideon had always managed to do so. Now she could see how his arms were much larger around at the biceps than the span of both her hands. He also had a chest and stomach of artfully sculpted definition, without a single sign of a silver hair to mar the plane of it. His trim waist came to the enticing V that she had always enjoyed on a male, and though the pants he wore were somewhat loose, there was no mistaking the distinct power of his thighs or the strength in his calves.

She had known Gideon her entire life, yet she was realizing that she was seeing him with perfect clarity for perhaps the very first time. There was no childhood intimidation now, nor was there wounded feminine ego to stand in her way.

She was simply a woman, looking at a man, who was anything but simple.

His hair was longer than she had realized. He usually kept it in a tightly bound tail, as was the popular style among the males of her race. But now it was loose, streaming like a waterfall of pure shaved silver over his pillow. His brows were silver, his lashes purely black. His jaw was shadowed darkly with the beard that had grown in as he slept. Upon close inspection she realized it would be streaked both silver and black if he had let it continue to grow. For some reason, it made her smile.

It was strange, but he looked both younger and older as he slept. Younger because he was truly relaxed, having shed the rigidity of the flawless control he held over his poise and body during waking hours. Older because, somehow, seeing him strictly as a male only added to his presence and power in her mind. If she were not so fascinated she might have been a little intimidated.

Legna reached out impulsively to touch his hair. It was unexpectedly soft and smooth, nowhere near the brittle feel of metal it tricked her into expecting. It was clinging to her fingers as if caressing them on purpose, the eerie sensation giving her a shiver as she double-checked his state of sleep. Once she was satisfied she was getting away with her trespassing undetected, she grew bolder, leaning farther forward over him, her breasts pressing against the hard musculature of his arm as she did so. She touched his face so lightly she could barely feel him. Curiously, she followed the arches and curves of it, from wide forehead and aristocratic cheekbones to his strong, slightly cleft chin and the perfectly sculpted lines of his mouth.

Braver still, she traced her butterfly touch down the firm column of his throat, marveling at its complete antithesis to the slim shape of her own and how strange it was that she found that to be a sexy thing. She had not realized a man's neck could look so appealing.

She licked her lips slowly, her eyes riveted to the movement of her fingers, breaking her attention away only briefly now and then to check his breathing or his closed eyes to monitor the maintenance of his sleeping state. She touched the broad curvature of his collarbone, tracing it with single-minded fascination. She moved her exploration to his chest, noting the marks she had left on him had healed naturally, only the ghosted presence of the impressions of her nails remaining. It pleased her to realize he had not used his skills to heal them, and then it disappointed her that their bodies healed so damn quickly. She pressed her lips together to prevent a giggle from escaping her. It was a silly, clearly territorial thought, but she made no excuses to herself for it.

Her fingertips next drifted over his belly, softly weaving around his fingers, enjoying the increasing warmth of his skin as she traveled. She paused, her eyes scouting ahead of her touch, and nibbled on her lower lip as she considered whether or not to continue her secret tour of him.

Her question was answered when she suddenly felt his hand wrap around her fingers. She gasped, jerking back instinctively, her face flaring with heat while her neck prickled with chills. Nevertheless, he held tight, preventing her withdrawal, pressing her hand to his stomach beneath his own. She looked up into his eyes, vexed by the humor ghosting through them.

"How did you do that?" she demanded. Eyes and breathing aside, it was impossible to fake sleep with a Mind Demon. She should have picked up on the rise of his awareness as he awoke.

"You continually attempt to fit me into the molds of the men you are acquainted with," he said softly. "I am extremely different than anything you know, Magdelegna. It would help if you expected what you would least expect, and go from there."

"Gee, you are so wise," she said in a high, cooing voice, blinking her lashes with ridiculous speed. "I am so tremendously lucky! Most girls get stuck with an insufferable, devious, underhanded snake of a man."

The humor of her act drew a smile to one side of his mouth, and Legna couldn't ignore the way it turned her insides around when the smile glowed warmly in his eyes.

"You will never bore me, *Nelissuna*. I can see that fact straight to my soul."

"But I can clearly see you being easily capable of boring me to tears," she countered archly, trying to free her trapped hand with a determined tug. He was even stronger than he looked, she thought.

"How are you feeling?" he asked, noticing her struggle and insults about the same way he would notice a passing speck of dust.

"Why can you not tell me? You are the medic, are you not?" She exhaled sharply. "Will you please let go of me?"

"No."

Legna growled in frustration at him.

"You are so obnoxious!" she accused. "I hate it when you do that!"

"Do what? Answer a question? If it disturbs you, I will ignore your questions from now on."

"You know exactly what I mean. I hate it when you lay down the word no as if it were the last letter of the law. And do not think I do not know that you are doing it on purpose just to irritate me, because I do!"

"Then you should cease giving me the opportunity to say it," he told her, his tone so matter-of-fact that she almost screamed at him. "And you should be careful of those little growls you insist on making, *Neliss*. They are . . . very stimulating."

Suddenly Legna forgot all about trading barbs with him and became very aware of his warmth above and below her trapped hand, the solid strength she leaned up against so cozily, and the very clear hunger that was brewing under the humor he had been using to hide it.

Now that he had her full attention rather than her acerbic defenses, he slipped his hand out from under his head and reached to touch her soft, warm cheek with fingertips as light as the ones she had explored him with.

"You are so very lovely, Legna. I have always thought so. Even as a child, you were quite stunning."

"It took you long enough to tell me so," she said, but there was no true energy to the would-be sarcastic remark.

"Yes. I know. But I always felt it would be inappropriate. Noah is . . . I was his *Siddah*. I began fostering him from the time he was ten years, his abilities proving to be too powerful to wait until he was at the usual age. He was like a son to me . . . more so after your parents were gone. Noah treated you more like a daughter than a sister as he raised you in turn. It always felt like a barrier I ought not to cross. Even now, I do not welcome the time when he discovers what is happening between us. I can see you have the same concern."

"Yes," she agreed. "But in time . . ."

"Yes. Time. I am finding myself in great competition with time of late."

"He will resist at first, but if he thinks you will make me happy, he will eventually come around," Legna assured him.

"So then"—he picked up her hand from his stomach, lifting the palm to the kiss of his lips—"all that remains is for me to convince *you* that I will make you happy, so that you are able to convince him of it."

"A daunting task, to be sure," she murmured, looking at her arm to see if there were any visible signs of the sensation the touch of his mouth was causing to rush up the length of it. She blinked twice and shook her head slightly to clear it of the dangerous predatory sensation stirring within her thoughts. "I have not asked about Bella," she said, discreetly trying to clear the catch that had entered her voice. "Is all well?"

"Yes. Both she and the baby will survive and, eventually, regain their health."

"Thank goodness," she sighed. "If I ever complain about the changes going on inside me, remind me of how they saved my friend's life." She hesitated to catch her breath as his mouth brushed back across her sensitive palm.

"Legna, why are you so afraid of me at the moment?"

She met those penetrating eyes of his, feeling as if they were searching her very soul. It made her breathless and nervous.

"I am afraid of how easily you seem to . . . cause strong emotions within me with such a simple touch."

"And if I told you that you have the same power over me?" he asked, his rich voice hypnotically gentle.

Legna knew in an instant what that knowledge made her feel. She felt that baser side of herself stirring into awareness, threatening to overcome her as it had in her room so recently, in the garden nine years ago, and in battle with the necromancer last October.

She sat up away from him and this time he let her go, releasing her hand with a lingering touch.

"I should go home. Noah must be worried."

She turned and slid out of the bed on the other side, but by the time she was upright on her feet, he was in front of her, leaning a shoulder casually against one of the bedposts.

"Run, run, as fast as you can . . ." he said softly, his meaning all too serious and all too clear.

"Gideon, please," she begged quietly, unable to meet his direct gaze as her heart pounded out a frantic rhythm.

"I see what you are running from, Magdelegna. But you will not succeed. The huntress is a part of you. Back before time was time, our people lived in prides just like the lions do. And like lionesses, your ancestral females were born to the hunt, built sleek and beautiful and deadly in the most magnificent ways. It is deeply embedded in your genetic code, in spite of all of our evolution and civilization, and is as much a part of you as your empathy. I am sorry, but this code, *Neliss*, is the one thing you can never escape."

"But it is worse when you are near me. Tell me that is not true."

"It is very true. But instead of thinking of it as worse,

I would hope you would think of it as natural. It is, you know. It is natural that your baser nature appears when your mate does."

"You are not even my mate yet. What happens if . . . if we have sex?" She wrapped her arms tightly around herself to ward off a chill. "Will it become wor—more frequent? Stronger? It overtakes me so easily, Gideon."

"I understand how unnerving that can be, Legna. It haunts me as well whenever I come close to you. Even if I cross a path you have recently trod, your lingering scent stimulates the dominant in me, the part of me that urgently needs to be with you. Near you. Wrapped around you, with you . . . with you wrapped around me."

The phraseology was intensely suggestive, but it was lost on her until he reached out to her, past her shoulder to take hold of her braid, wrapping it around his large fist twice before using it to coax her closer to him. When she was close enough for him to lower his head to her ear, he brushed his mouth over it in an unbelievably erotic caress.

"I crave the time when you are wrapped around me," he told her, the heat of his breath and his words flying through her like an arrow to its mark. Her entire body lit up with the heat of response, a flood of molten liquid rushing madly to awakening places beneath her skin.

"Gideon," she breathed, unable to draw in enough air to sound his name more firmly.

"Mmm, I love when you speak my name, *Neliss*," he said, his tongue touching to the sensitive lobe of her ear just long enough to draw it between his gentle lips. "I will love it just as well when you cry it out. And even more so when you scream it."

"Gideon, please do not do this," she begged, the words falling from her in soft, short bursts of breath. "I am not ready for this."

"I think you are."

To illustrate his argument, Gideon lifted the knuckles

of his left hand to her breast, skimming over the taut thrust of her clearly aroused nipple. Legna practically melted under the touch, her body swaying into his as he turned his hand over and cupped her through the rich satin of her dress.

"Yes. Yes," she relented. "My body is ready. But Gideon . . ."

"Hmm." He brushed his mouth over her jaw until he was nearer to her mouth. "A Demon of the Mind whose mind is not as willing as the rest of her. A remarkable dilemma, Magdelegna." His mouth hovered so close to hers, an awesome temptation to her weakened resistance. She remembered his kiss too well, the flavor, the artistry, and the intensity beyond anything she had ever known. "I will make a bargain with you, *Neliss*," he offered, continuing to caress the shape of her breast, eliciting an unchecked moan from her. "Whenever I take something from this delightful body of yours, I will give you anything you desire that will appease your reluctant mind."

Gideon stepped away from her, releasing her so unexpectedly that she had to stop herself from following him. She looked into the white-hot fire of his eyes, understanding instantly the effort it had taken for him to deny his needs. The taut set of his jaw was only the beginning of the rigidity locking up every muscle in his body.

"This time, I give you your wish to go home. Go. This instant, Legna."

Another command. Albeit a welcome one. One she wanted to follow almost instantly. But she hesitated just the same, her gaze still locked to his, unable to break away.

Gideon's hands curled into fists.

"Legna," he warned.

Legna crossed the distance he had put between them in a heartbeat, throwing herself against him. Gideon caught her to himself even as she locked her mouth to his and thrust her hands into his hair at the back of his head. She held him to her, aggressively seeking his tongue, tasting him with wild savagery as his arms wrapped tightly enough around her to lift her onto the very tips of her toes. She disengaged as sharply as she had begun, panting rapidly for breath before she pulled him back to her hungry lips.

His hands were sliding over her, everywhere at once, his touch matching the ferocity of her kisses. Wildfire scorched her wherever he grasped her, setting her to burn. His body was pure strength against hers, solid and unforgiving, hot and hard and just as aggressive as hers was.

Gideon caught the satin fabric at the back of her dress up into a vicious pair of fists, using the material to pry her away from him. He held up a hand to keep her at bay when she moved forward with a sound of protest.

"If you touch me again, Legna, I will have you," he warned, his voice hoarse with pent-up need and barely leashed impulses. "Do you understand? No turning back, no more time." She drove him to the brink with just a kiss, his control shuddering with weakness. Gideon's whole being was rocked with this outrageous desire for her that she wasn't ready to appease. She thought she was at war with parts of herself, but she couldn't know how much his feral half was raging to be let loose on her. It was all he could do to maintain control of himself.

Gideon's caution humbled Legna, and her eyes widened with her remorse for forcing him to be the one to maintain control in spite of her aggression. She felt the haze of his mind within her own, felt the baton of respect and concern for her he was using to beat back every inborn instinct he had. He wanted her to come to him with clarity of thought, with an honest need that transcended just the physical chemistry that so overwhelmed them. The amazing part was that he wanted it for himself just as much as he wanted it for her.

"So, once again you are the one to show far better control between us," she said quietly, taking a ginger step away from him. Slowly, he released the fabric of her dress, the satin slipping from his fingers after a long, highly charged moment. "I will go home, as you say, because I must put Noah's mind at ease. I know he is worried. I can feel it. But I will not take long, Gideon. The night has just begun and I want to spend it learning exactly who you are and what we will be with one another."

Gideon nodded once, a short movement that radiated the strength of the tether he had upon himself.

"Do me one courtesy, *Neliss*. Remember at all times that I am a part of your mind now. Take great care in what you do and what you think." He exhaled slowly. It galled Gideon to confess his weakening discipline, but he had to make this clear to her. "My self-control is stretched far too thin as it is. For all my age and experience, I cannot fight what is happening to me. Do you understand?"

"I do. I will do my best, but I am similarly afflicted and I may make mistakes."

"I understand that quite well, Legna. But there is a vast canyon between understanding and execution. However, I will maintain a reasonable mind. That is a promise."

"Thank you."

This time she moved forward slowly, her intent quite clear as she watched him with careful eyes. She reached to kiss him gently, briefly, stepping back with a sensation of awe over the tenderness he had used while returning her kiss. She absently touched her mouth for a moment, then raised the same hand into a graceful twist, sending herself home.

* * *

Legna appeared in her bedroom, startled to see Noah was already there waiting for her. Suddenly self-conscious, she touched her hair with one hand and covered her reddened mouth with the other. Noah turned from the window to look at her and she turned away and moved to her wardrobe, making herself busy with her back to him.

"I would have come down to you," she said as neutrally as she could.

"I was worried. After Kane told me what had happened, I went to see Jacob. He told me when he left you with Gideon you were sleeping, but I grew concerned when the entire night and next day passed without word. Jacob told me what you did for him and for Bella. I am amazed, to say the least."

"I know." She reached to absently recrease a fold in one of the dresses hanging before her. "I rather amazed myself."

"Legna, when are you going to tell me what the hell is going on?" he demanded suddenly, his hurt at being left out of the life she had always shared with him coming through in spite of his efforts to maintain an even tone.

"It is senseless for you to try and hide emotions from me in any event, Noah," she chided softly, finally turning around to meet his eyes.

"Legna," he uttered, the shock that washed over him so potent that it made her catch her breath. He crossed over to her in only two steps, reaching to grasp her by the chin and turn her face up to his. "What the hell is this?" he interrogated her roughly. "What happened to your eyes?"

She could not answer him. She was suddenly overwhelmed by Gideon's virulent concern for her.

Legna, what is the matter? I can feel your distress.

Nothing. Please, do not worry.

You are lying to me. Tell me what is going on.

Noah and I are talking. Gideon, trust me. I will be just fine.

Legna felt his reluctance, his urgent desire to protect her no matter what. But to her relief he gained control of the instinct and moved to the back of her thoughts, allowing her the freedom to deal with her brother in her own way.

"Legna, answer me."

"Noah, I cannot give you the explanation you desire if you are going to rail at me."

"I beg your pardon, Legna, but I think a brother has a right to be upset when his sister's eyes have changed from a pretty gray-green similar to his own into this bright silver that looks just like—" Noah went pale as realization dug deep claws of shock into him. "Sweet Destiny, Legna, *are you insane?*"

"Noah, I refuse to get into an argument with you over this," she said, jerking her head out of his grasp. "And it is not as though we have any choice in the matter."

"This . . . is impossible," her brother growled bearishly. "He's more than seven hundred years older than you, Legna! His power is like nothing ever seen before. Do you have any idea what an infusion of power that potent can do to someone as young as you are?"

"So far what it has done is allow me the grateful opportunity to save the life of a greatly beloved friend. A friend who happens to be the wife of a man you care for very much, Noah. As strong as he is, how well do you think Jacob would survive the loss of Isabella? Do you think he would even make it through a year? Did you think Father would have if he had not been Summoned so soon after Mother's death?"

"Legna!" Noah's temper flared, sparked by the suppressed issues beyond what she had dared to speak of. It was one thing to share memories of joy, and quite another to actually discuss the nature of their parents' deaths. "You are trying, as usual, to divert this conversation from its true point, Magdelegna."

"And that is?"

"You! Your well-being! Do I need to point out that you have just spent twenty-four hours sleeping off this exertion you are so proud of? What if it had been worse? What if conducting that kind of power had burned you out completely, something sleep cannot cure?"

"I have thought of this, Noah. Contrary to what you and Hannah seem to perpetually think about me, I am no longer a child. I am aware of the ramifications of my actions and the actions of others. Would it please you to know I am having a significant amount of trouble accepting this and that I am anxious enough without your predictions of doom?" She turned and slammed the doors to the wardrobe shut in a rare show of frustration. "I hardly know him, Noah, and now he is taking over half of who I am. Anything I do know about him has been from stories I heard as a child that, to be frank, could be pretty frightening at times. So trust me when I tell you I am sufficiently terrified to satisfy you!"

She sighed softly then and turned to face him slowly, her arms crisscrossing her waist. "My entire life was turned upside down a little over twenty-four hours ago." Legna leaned back against the wardrobe doors, closing her eyes and releasing uninvited tears down her cheeks in the process. "All I have wanted to do since this started was talk to someone about it. The someone I chose to share this with, I found lying in a pool of her own blood on her living-room floor."

"Legna," Noah said, his eyes as sad as his hoarse voice, his anger instantly evaporating under the shower of her tears. "I did not mean—"

"I know you did not. But you have to understand, I have been fighting to keep my perspective on everything in my life ever since I was dragged out of it and entrapped in that horrific five-pointed prison last October.

I have not been at peace since that day, Noah. The only way I can discuss the incident with you is in an argument, and Hannah is not much better. I do understand it is because of what happened to Father and how it affected you both." Legna pushed away from the closet and crossed over to him, reaching to take up one of his hands between hers. "It was Gideon who figured out why I have been so restless, and it was he who finally helped me rest."

"Legna, that is just his abilities. It does not mean—"

"Noah, please. Can you stop arguing with me and find it in yourself to support me in this? Gideon and I have not made a careless decision based on some kind of whim. We were chosen by Destiny for this. Yes, it was up to me to make the acceptance, but you do not know what the Imprinting feels like, how strong it is. Need I indicate Jacob and Bella as an example? She was a human, completely taboo by our laws at the time, and yet Jacob found himself betraying centuries of morals just to touch her. No matter how much it tore him apart."

"You cannot liken Gideon to Jacob. There are things—" Noah broke off, running a frustrated hand through his hair. "I know you, Legna. You are extremely sensitive to the art of compromise. Gideon will never compromise. He demands and acts and expects that no one will contradict him. If they try to do so, he merely ignores them. I cannot bear to think of you in a relationship like that."

"Noah, I beg you to stop making him out to be some kind of manipulative monster, because you know it is a lie and I will not stand for it. I love you, Noah. I always will. I understand your fear, but you have to look beneath it and understand what you are feeling. I do not believe it is Gideon's age or power or rude manners that truly scare you."

"If you are going to start psychoanalyzing me, Legna, just stop it right now," Noah warned her.

"You have had my undivided love and attention practically since the day I was born, Noah. Has it never occurred to you that you are simply unwilling to share me with anyone else? You joke about it, but there are reasons why you are not interested in finding a companion of your own. Why should you? You have a perfectly kept home, a beautiful hostess to manage your social affairs, and she is pretty much emotionally maintenance free. I give you completely unconditional love, respect, and admiration. I keep you company when there are so many around, but none are really close enough to your heart to safely be a King's confidant. There is only one thing I cannot do for you, and I already know you have your ways of obtaining *that*."

"Legna," he protested, his face flushing. "That is not true."

"Which part?" she countered, raising a single brow.

"I . . ." He hesitated, looking away from her penetrating gaze, realizing that she saw so much more than he had ever given her credit for. "Well, for one, the rafters of my 'perfectly kept home' are full of cobwebs," he said sheepishly.

Legna suddenly, gratefully, found herself laughing. It was a short burst of amusement that instantly defused the painful tension between them.

"As if it would kill you to spare a thought to giving them a two-second toasting and getting rid of them yourself?"

Noah smiled in spite of himself, shaking his head solemnly. He sighed a long breath of unwinding tension. "Listen, I cannot tell you I am happy for you when I am not. I cannot pretend to encourage you to leave me when it is going to break my heart. I guess what I am saying is . . ."

"You need time," she finished for him. "A phrase I have been using a lot myself recently. I understand how you feel, Noah. I would appreciate it if you took the time to understand how I am feeling in return, okay?"

The Demon King nodded silently. He then reached out to his sister, giving her hand a warm squeeze for a minute that reassured her of the things he couldn't say at that moment.

"I will let you get changed," he said, moving to the door of her room, opening it before hesitating a moment. "Are you going . . . out?"

"Yes."

"Do me a favor? Make time to have dinner with me to-morrow?" He jiggled the knob on the door as if inspecting its integrity. "I will be able to tolerate this better if you take the time to reassure me and tell me that you are doing all right."

"Only if you swear to me Hannah and the children will be miles away," she bargained.

"As I see it," he countered, a small smile twitching across his lips, "the way your abilities are developing, you could see to that yourself."

Noah left, shutting the door gently behind him. As soon as he was gone, Legna moved quickly to her bed and let herself fall down onto it with a huge sound of relief.

Well done, Nelissuna. *Very well done.*

Thank you. Gideon?

Mmm?

Please tell me we will not devastate my family because of this.

It will work itself out. Just keep that in mind. I am waiting for you, sweet. And by the way, I know you want to stop to see Isabella. That is strictly against my standing orders as her doctor.

You know, this is going to get on my nerves very quickly. Remember how you said we needed to convince Noah that you will make me happy?

I do.

Well, it would make me very happy if you would vacate my head for a little while.

As you know, that is pretty much impossible.

Try!

As you wish. For now . . .

She felt him fade from the forefront of her thoughts.

Chapter 7

Legna appeared in the third-floor parlor, in the suite of rooms she knew housed her friends, with her newly habitual pop to announce her arrival. She turned as the male sitting behind her put aside his book and rose to his feet.

"Legna, it is good to see you up and around," Jacob greeted her.

"Thank you. It feels good. I wanted to find out how Bella is."

Jacob moved to the bar across the way and retrieved two glasses and a decanter of a creamy, yellowish milk.

"She is sleeping a lot. I suppose that is to be expected." He turned and moments later was handing her a glass full of the rich beverage. "I did not get a chance to thank you. You have my undying gratitude, Legna. If ever you need anything, just ask."

"Thank you," she said again, taking a delicate sniff of the contents of her glass. "Hmm, very nice. Giraffe?"

"Very good," the Enforcer complimented. "Many confuse it with zebra."

"A rather spirited choice first thing in the evening," she remarked. "Are you all right, Jacob?"

"I will be, once this crisis has completely passed." He swirled the milk around in the glass for a long minute. "I have this image burned into my head of Bella lying in her own blood . . . and I cannot . . ."

Jacob broke off, clearing his throat and looking up at the ceiling as he drew a deep, unsteady breath.

"It will pass with time," Legna said soothingly, instantly adopting the calming, centering pitch she used to ease others. "Just remind yourself that she is safe and will be well again soon."

"I know. But I have to admit, I am having a hard time leaving this house even with all of the guards posted outside, even with Noah a shout away. I did not feel that she was in danger until it was almost too late. I just do not understand it. She's here in my head 24/7. How could I not even notice when she was being brutally attacked? When she dropped from consciousness and was suddenly no longer there?"

"Jacob, you are being too hard on yourself."

"I should have known when she said she was not feeling well that it was a premonition of some kind. Even with this pregnancy, Isabella is not a nervous person by nature. She always takes so much in stride, so easily. She has premonitions all the time now, and I should have known that they are commonly the cause of such strong agitation as she was experiencing when I left her. I do not know why I did not think of it. And I do not know why she did not understand it herself."

"Premonition is the most obtuse ability in the world. You know that, Jacob. She has only lived with the ability for five months. She has no idea how to always distinguish them or how to interpret them. And for that matter, what makes you think you should be able to do so any better than she does? You are a tracker and a hunter, not a soothsayer."

Jacob resumed his seat on the couch, sighing deeply and rubbing at the bridge of his nose. He looked exhausted and Legna could feel the knots of emotion he had tied himself into. She took a seat beside him, reaching to lay a comforting hand on his knee.

"You are not responsible for this, Jacob. And if I know Bella, she will be quite colorfully upset if she catches you blaming yourself. How do you expect her to heal and remain calm and peaceful if her mate is in turmoil? She may be sleeping, but she feels you. I know that for a fact."

Jacob looked at his monarch's pretty sister, his keen eyes missing nothing as he scanned her from head to toe. He reached out to touch her gently beneath both of her altered eyes.

"Now I understand," he said suddenly. "You are the reason why I keep feeling Gideon even when he is not around."

Legna drew her bottom lip between her teeth and nodded in affirmation.

"You carry his scent . . . but not yet completely." Jacob tilted his head to study her more closely. "It has been a very long time since I have seen two Demons Imprint on each other. It is a remarkable gift, Legna. You are very lucky."

"You know what," Legna laughed softly, "you are the first person to have anything positive to say about this. And that includes Gideon and myself."

"I take it Noah had the equivalent of a meltdown?"

"Apropos analogy for a Fire Demon, would you not agree?"

"Noah is remarkably even-tempered for a Demon of his ilk. The only one who really gets him hot under the collar regularly is that prolific sister of yours."

"I know," Legna chuckled. "I suppose I ought to count my blessings. I can count on one hand how many times I have truly ticked Noah off."

"That is because you are the baby sister, and for all of your life you could do no wrong in his eyes. I hate to say it, Legna, but you are spoiled rotten."

"Is that so? I should like to see you try being the household diplomat for two Fire Demons for nearly three centuries and then tell me how easy I have had it," she challenged.

"Thanks. I will pass on that honor."

They toasted each other, trading chuckles.

Legna materialized in Gideon's parlor about an hour later. He was sitting in the shadows behind her and she turned to him with curiosity.

"Gideon?"

When he did not respond, she stepped closer to him. That was when she realized that, in essence, he was not truly there. His corporeal form was sitting in a large chair, but his astral self was somewhere unseen. It was the strangest feeling, she noted, that he was physically close, spiritually distant, and also being kept in a quiet corner of her brain at the same time. He was utterly unaware of her intrusion near his body, his focus completely dedicated elsewhere. She took advantage of the moment to look him over once more.

She moved to stand before him and then began to circle the chair, studying him from all profiles. She did not know why she always felt this compulsion to survey him like this, but it did not keep her from doing it. After one revolution, she stopped in front of him again. He was alone, wherever he was. It almost seemed as though he was out on some sort of solitary, spiritual walk. Mind Demons were experts in meditation, so she sensed this with her experience and power as well as her connection with him. She remained quiet in his mind, though, as she knelt between his feet, settling her hands on his thighs. She moved her palms up the corded length of the long muscles and then traversed back again with the edges of her fingernails.

The stimulation made Gideon stir. She was purposely

breaking the concentration he had fixed on his projection, perhaps just to see if she could. He was incredibly focused, and she knew that, so she pulled out all the stops and leaned forward between his knees until she could touch her mouth to his.

The kiss brought him back with a jolt.

Gideon immediately reached for her, his hands gently cradling her head. Legna felt his thighs tense against her sides as he took over the kiss and turned it into a desperate, nearly brutal thing. His mouth punished hers, and she accepted it willingly, payment for her disruptive teasing. His fingers tunneled through her heavy hair, gripping her with a pure hunger for the feel of having her within his grasp. He broke away from her bruised mouth, pressing his forehead to hers as they both tried to catch their breath.

"Mine," he said roughly. He wanted to deny the possessiveness, knowing how ridiculous it was, but he simply could not do it. The need to stake his claim on her was rubbed harshly raw, more and more every time he let her slip away without making her his. "You are mine, Magdelegna, and it is so hard to let you go as you wish me to, even for those short spans of time."

"I know," she whispered, pressing her soft lips to his mouth once more. She kissed him with all of her heart, and he clearly felt the sincerity. It served to soothe him greatly, allowing him to loosen his hold on her enough to bring his hands forward over her ears, his thumbs stroking her flushed cheeks gently. "It is so hard," she complained softly. "How do you remain an individual when you are also part of so powerfully driven a pair?"

"Irrational or justified, it is what it is." Gideon was realizing the logic of that for himself even as he spoke the words. "Perhaps, in time, it will be less acute. I have no desire to rob you of your individuality, nor do I wish to lose my own. It is difficult for me as well . . . I have been so solitary throughout my lifetime, and now, to be suddenly given such riveting company . . . I fear I cannot do you the justice you deserve. And for you it will be worse; with the influx of power you are beginning to experience it will be taxing, to say the least."

"I know." Legna reached up and splayed her palms over the dark silk covering his chest. "I suppose at some point, if I start to go crazy, you are going to have to knock me out or tie me up or something."

"Hmm. The latter has possibilities," he mused with a growing smile that erased the tension in his face.

Legna laughed, giving him a shove.

"Gideon, you are nothing but an ancient pervert," she teased him.

"And this is an issue because . . . ?"

"You are horrible!" She pushed away from him, gaining her feet.

He reached to take her hand, pulling her closer once more and continuing to do so until she had nowhere else to go but his lap. She took the seat, her voluminous skirts spreading over them both.

"I will forgive you, this time," she conceded.

"Thank you," he said with honest graciousness. "Now, my beauty, tell me what you would like to do to get to know me better. I find myself looking forward to your discoveries."

"Well, I did not think of anything specific. I imagined time would fill itself."

"That is dangerously liberal, sweet. If you leave it up to the natural course of things, I can tell you exactly what we will end up doing."

Legna giggled, blushing because she realized he was right. Even just sitting in his lap and talking as she was, she could feel the mutual awareness that sparked between them, constantly simmering and waiting for just a little more heat to bring them up to the boiling point.

"Very well, I am open to suggestions," she invited.

"Again, too liberal," he teased, his eyes twinkling with mischievous starlight.

"You are incorrigible. I never realized you were a sex fiend, Gideon."

"I am now," he amended, drawing a finger down the slope of her nose. "Have I mentioned that it has been quite some time since I have found myself attracted to a female?"

"If it is anything under a thousand years, I do not want to hear about it," she warned.

"Did I mention I was a virgin?" he edited himself innocently.

"That is just wonderful, darling," she cooed with satisfaction, giving him a approving pat on the cheek.

Gideon threw back his head and laughed. She delighted him to no end and he could not remember ever feeling so light-hearted. It seemed sometimes as though he had been born too serious for his own good, and that he had been straitjacketed by it for centuries. It was a balm to his soul to be able to banter with his beautiful intended.

"I never suspected you had a sense of humor," she mused aloud, studying his face as if he were a fascinating puzzle to be figured out. "See? Hardly ten minutes into the night and I am already learning fabulous things about you."

"Imagine what will happen in an hour," he said.

"That sounded suspiciously liberal to me," she rejoined slyly, reaching to wind her arms around his neck. "Did I mention that you look like you just stepped off a pirate ship? This outfit is very . . . roguish."

"Roguish?"

"'Roguish' is a word from the English language," she lectured. "It means . . . to be like a rogue. In your case, to be in the style of a rogue. Roguish."

"I know what it means, *Neliss*. I do not believe I have ever heard myself described in such a way before. I shall have to take your word on that." He reached up to push back some of the heavy fall of her hair. "You always wear dresses like this, and almost never bind your hair. Do not take this as a complaint, but I was wondering why that is."

"I like dresses. I never quite took to the idea of skirts above the ankle. I guess I am an old-fashioned eighteenth-century girl."

"I see. And just when, exactly, should I begin to look for those pigs that will be flying by?"

"You know, you sit there and accuse *me* of having a smart mouth?"

"Well, you were wondering what part of you was going to show up in me," he rejoined.

"Oh. Ha ha. Your stellar wit has charmed me straight to my toes," was her dry reply.

"In any event," he continued, ignoring her sarcasm, "your style suits you quite well. It suits me as well."

Gideon reached out with a single finger to trace the cream silk of her neckline slowly. The dress was a heavy sheath from shoulders to upper thighs, after which it flared out in a skirt and train of enormous folds of glimmering, iridescent material. The neckline, however, was the antithesis of the otherwise demure style of the gown, cut deep enough to allow his light touch to skim over the very tops of her breasts, taking her breath from her in an instantaneous rush.

"I cannot explain to you, Legna, how much you affect me," he said, his voice filled with the fascination reflected in his eyes as they devoured her beautiful flesh, from her neckline to the obvious thrust of dark nipples beneath the light fabric. He leaned forward slightly, bowing his head until his mouth brushed the line of her breastbone. The erotic kiss played havoc with her equilibrium and she clutched his shoulders for an anchor. His lips drew hotly over her silken skin, upward in a line that brought him to her extraordinary throat. She was shuddering with wave after wave of stimulating chills of pleasure as he nuzzled her throat and neck, paying great attention to the smallest touch and the effect it had on her. When he pulled back, she made a petulant sound of protest, making him chuckle softly. "Be careful what you purr for, little sweet. You are too tempting a delicacy for me to resist for very long."

"So I see," she said softly, her warm eyes meeting her mate's, barely a nose length away. "What you do to me seems so simple and harmless, if watched from an outside perspective, but when you are inside . . . it feels like fire and magic."

"Mmm, I promise, *Neliss*, this is only the beginning of the fire and magic you will feel from your . . . inside perspective."

Legna's face felt as though it had suddenly caught on fire as she blushed over his purposeful twist of her words. Hearing him say such things turned her completely inside out, setting her imagination on curious tangents that were remarkably vivid and blatantly lacking in decorum. With him sharing her mind, she was positive he was aware of every last one of them. It made her worry what he might think of her, and she wished she could make those parts of herself less obvious to his exploration through her psyche.

"Legna, your imagination delights me. I would be hard put to try and ignore it," he explained in response to her private rumination. "Never be ashamed of anything about yourself, *Neliss*. Never feel you must apologize for your experiences or curiosities. You lived a full and varied life before me, as I did before you. Neither will I be like Jacob, frantic every time a male enters your sphere. We are for each other. This cannot change, and I have faith in that, as well as trust in you." He soothed her bristling nerves by rising to his feet, setting her on her toes in front of him. He held her close, his hands circling her shoulders like a cloak, cradling her against the incredibly warm length of his body. "In your thoughts I find enough adventure and stimulating inquisitiveness to last us another millennium, and I will relish every experience you wish to explore."

"Even though you have probably done everything twice already?" she countered.

"I have done nothing with you. Nothing but these two days past, in truth." He reached to run smooth knuckles down the length of her throat. "There is no experience in my life comparable to the way your kiss makes me feel. Even this simple touch against the universe's softest skin is new and breathtaking. You know these are not just pretty words, Legna. You can feel it as I feel it. You can enter my perspective and know I speak the truth. Do not shy from my age and wisdom. It is all for naught when it comes to experiencing you."

Truth. The truth was, he never lied. Everyone knew that, and now she knew it as fact as well as faith. The only time he was capable of deception was when he was deceiving himself about the emotions and feelings he guarded so heavily. All of what he was saying now was an absolute truth, though. He had lived the centuries since the wars in seriousness and reservation, never once risking himself to the inevitability of loss, never allowing emotion to cloud his judgment or actions.

Until now. Now he suddenly decided to invest himself without reservation in her. Or was he really? He seemed so accepting, but was he truly accepting even the deepest nature of what the Imprinting would mean to them both? For that matter, was she?

"I think I am ready to choose an activity for us," she told him, once again forced to clear the persistent catch in her voice that appeared whenever his tenderness did.

He did not respond. He was too absorbed in the touch he was running over her skin. It had expanded to her face, shoulders, and, once more, the length of her exposed breastbone. He clearly could not resist these temptations. It was as if he was so lost in the experience that he did not even realize he had escaped into the sensual tangent.

It was safe to say, standing as close to him as she was, that she was very aware of the rise in his aroused sensuality. Even if his hand had not been burning across her skin, the unapologetic hardness of his body pressing with erotic familiarity against hers would have told her how very much lost in his need for her he was. Gideon had to be the most sexual creature she had ever encountered. And yet, only a few short days ago, if she had been asked her opinion on that particular subject, she would have made suppositions that were quite the opposite. Was he telling her the truth when he said it was because of her?

"I never lie, my beauty," he murmured, reminding her of her own understandings about that. His lips against her hair, just beneath the back of her ear, were warm and smiling even as he kissed the thrillingly sensitive spot. "And even if I were just a dirty old man, *Neliss*," he whispered like the warmth of sunshine in her ear, "it would never account for the tenderness you see in me even now." He tightened his hold on her, drawing her so close that he burned hotly against her. "And you would have been in my bed, beneath the press of my body, open and inviting me in by now."

The raw observation and the aggressive heat of his body made her gasp, a mix between shocked sensibilities and excited delight. Legna looked up into his famished eyes, licking her lips with a hunger all her own.

"If we do not find something to do, we will end up in bed together," she reminded him with her heart pounding so obviously against his chest.

"Yes. Perhaps without the intention of rousing until Jacob and Bella's Beltane wedding," he mused, the pleasure of the speculation quite evident in his expression.

It was an attractive thought to Legna as well, especially as his mouth dipped beneath her hair to continue to tease the sensitive skin of her neck. But just the same, she took matters into her own hand, so to speak, and teleported out of his grasp, reappearing all the way on the other side of the room. Finding his arms so abruptly vacated, Gideon gave her an eloquent look. She was going to pay for her little trick one day, and his eyes promised it to her as thoroughly as a worded threat.

At the moment, however, she had to direct their energies elsewhere if she was ever going to have enough time to think straight about this situation. He was far too threatening an allure for them to chance too much flirtation. He was an alpha male, coded by genetics, experience, and a knowledge of the ages that told him how to get his way whenever he wanted it, that he deserved to get his way because of his superiority of health, strength, and intellect. He was to be the male of their particular pack who was deferred to as the most powerful, the most beautiful, and the one whose wishes were paramount to all others.

And she was to be his mate.

The alpha female, the huntress, the mistress and mother, the disciplinarian and the comfort of nurturing and stability. Legna realized that it suited her all too well. Even the huntress. Though only newly introduced to this part of herself, she knew it was well matched within her, that she had taken too much pleasure in her brief appearances to try and deny it now. That did not mean it did not frighten her to learn this about herself. She was a diplomat, the peacemaker and peacekeeper in both her family and in her brother's court. It was so alien to her nature of over two centuries to embrace violence and aggression. But this was what would be, an inevitability. As Gideon had said, she had made her choice. The problem was reconciling herself to it, finding joy in it. Could she ever be happy with such an alteration in herself? Could she be what he needed? Even now she could not give him what he required from her. She knew he restrained himself with pain, knew it fed the canker of loneliness he had lived with for so long, to be kept from the haven she could supply for him.

It was only his concern for her that kept him from taking what in essence was very much his, just as he was very much hers for the taking. But just as he was the gift, she could not yet comprehend how she could be a worthy recipient. There was then the deeply entrenched fear of him that had been instilled in her for so many years of her life. She had been molded to feel this, the respect of his unknown and immeasurable power, the wonder and responsibility of age and wisdom that would come to any who sought for it as Gideon had. How was she ever going to circumvent that fear? How would she even feel herself an equal, as Noah had almost always made her feel, in his house?

"With the help of your chosen mate," Gideon answered from across the room. "Legna, allow me to show you everything you fear as closely as I am able, as close as you are willing to come. Familiarity will help to wash it clean, will allow you to replace it with all you will need to walk beside me for our life. I can introduce you to your growing power, and I can also assure you that beneath all of mine I am no different than Noah or any other male Demon among us. I can also show you the advantages and the enjoyments that come from embracing not only the more instinctual side of yourself, but the same side within me."

"I do not doubt that, Gideon. That is just the problem. I do not know if I want to embrace it."

"It is fear of the unknown that holds you in conflict. You are driven by impulse and by nature in these moments and it frightens you, and I can understand that. You are far more comfortable with the idea that you are an intelligent being of high moral standards and civilization. This is how you have become the genteel and valuable creature that you are in your brother's realm. But in all things there must be balance. You cannot control these impulses when they happen, because you need savagery just as much as you need sensitivity. It is time for you to integrate the huntress with the diplomat, Legna. You do not have faith that your mind will eventually learn to regulate itself, choosing appropriately in the situations of the future. You persist in thinking that to explore the baser side of your nature would mean a total loss of control. This is the heart of your fear.

"You have not changed in essentials, Legna, and I cannot conceive that you ever will. The predator with intellect and morals will choose her battles very carefully. No true hunter hunts in excess of its needs. This is what makes the difference between a sophisticated assassin and a ruthless killer. You will bring your weapons of conscience and tolerance with you. The cold killer leaves them behind. You have perfected the cultivation of your morals and they will not abandon you. Nothing of any import will be lost in the process of nurturing the huntress. You will lose nothing, and gain so much more."

"You sound so certain," she said wearily, turning to look out of the window she stood near. "But lemmings are chock full of animal instinct, and look what happens to them."

"You are forgetting that you are an intellectual being, quite capable of realizing it is a pretty bad idea to run off a cliff," he scolded gently, slowly approaching her from behind.

She was aware of his advance, but then again, he did not hide it in any way.

"If what you say is true, then why do I feel as though I cannot stop this urge to run off a cliff and straight into your bed? It burns and beats at my every last cell, springing into this high-strung awareness every time you come near me as you are doing now. With each step you take, the fire grows, taunting me, urging me to throw morals and caution out the window and just"—she turned to face him, her eyes burning with intensity, her breath coming quickly—"just devour moment after moment with you."

"It feels reckless, Legna, I know. It is not normally in you to want to expose yourself in such ways to a male who, for all intents and purposes, seems a total stranger to you. You forget to take into account, *Nelissuna*, that this is no normal binding between us. The nature of the Imprinting is older than time, meant to drive those who are genetically compatible together in order to perpetuate the species's evolution and continuation. It is what drives the wolves to make hierarchy in the pack where only the alphas are allowed to reproduce. The bucks of a hundred different types of animals are propelled do battle until the strongest and most magnificent of the males is chosen to lead and propagate the herd. Like these long-lived examples, we are also compelled to perform these rituals of joining.

"The difference is that we have a special intelligence that sometimes attempts to countermand nature's plans for us. It is perhaps just one more battle that needs overcoming in order to satisfy Nature herself that we are as compatible as she would have us be. You and I are two of the finest examples of our people, Legna, so it is no surprise that we are biologically compatible. However, it is our vast intellects, our abilities, and our consciences that also dictate whether or not we should carry the privilege of Imprinting between us. This is why it is my belief that we are not so much unacquainted as you may think."

"In what ways?" she asked, moving to the fireplace to warm herself, coming closer to him in the process.

"Well, in Demon ways, for one. I may have come from a more barbaric age than everyone else around me, but who do you think pioneered the strong ethical and moral codes the youth that came after me would follow? The laws that govern you and the respects you hold in your moral code are of my origination and my making.

Your beliefs, and mine, are the same. So in this way we already know one another at the heart."

He paused then, a tangible cloud of troubled emotion skidding over him suddenly. It was powerful enough to make him turn his face away from her, as if he were ashamed of what he was feeling. She could feel him struggling with something very dark and extraordinarily heavy inside of himself, but as usual he held it tightly concealed within himself, even her special access into his mind proving not strong enough to see behind the walls he erected against the world around him.

"I never wanted to see a repeat of the Druidic Wars in my lifetime, Legna. I had to do everything in my power to change what we were. How could any being of conscience, however late in coming that awareness may have been, do any less? The way the Druids were massacred, locked up from their Demon mates by those of us who were unattached . . . it was a cruelty I pray you will never see the like of. We who knew nothing of how it felt to be Imprinted could not even begin to understand what a horrific hell it was to sentence both halves of the mated pair to such an inconceivable torture. The Druids were left to starve to death from the deprivation of the energies of their Imprinted Demon mates, and the Demons were driven completely insane because—" Gideon broke off, this time turning his back to her as if he wanted to look out the window she had just abandoned. But this time, it was futile for him to even bother trying to cover his emotions with actions. The guilt and the shame washing through him were almost suffocating.

"Gideon."

He started when her hands suddenly were on his back, stroking him in a gesture of comfort. The soothing heat she was sending into him like soft pulses of compassion steadied his pounding heart and provided a balm to ease its ache. It was such an overwhelming gift in the face of what he was telling her, and he felt as if he should not accept it. But he had hurt for so long . . .

Then Gideon recalled that it was just that he should hurt. He deserved to live this long with the weight of his sins upon him. He could never allow himself to forget how he had allowed the passions of hatred and prejudice, anger and fear, to cloud his judgment once. For him, it was not stories of people long dead told in detached history lessons in Demon classrooms or a lesson taught to instill moral belief in the young. For him the names and faces involved had been alive and touchable. He had been the fosterling of the Demon King, Jonas, who had been so brutally murdered by the deceptive and demented hand of the Druid monarch, Isere. And in just a single moment of trust extended in an undeserving direction, it had all come to an end. It was a moment that had started a war; an instant that had given birth to a millennium of regret and guilt, and, as of last Samhain, he had come to realize it had caused ages of suffering for all the Demons who had so desperately needed their obliterated Druid mates. What would she think of him, his beauteous mate, if she knew he had been one of the loudest voices screaming for Druid heads? Sensitive and sweet as she was, how could she ever forgive him for that?

"Tell me the rest," Legna requested, unaware of the questions haunting him but, nonetheless, using her voice as a coaxing instrument of absolution. She knew what he needed, even if she didn't understand exactly why.

"You tell me the rest, Legna," he said hoarsely. "The irony of it is astounding. Here I stand, Imprinted on a mate of unparalleled beauty, compassion, and strength, after all these centuries. Would that I could believe I deserved such a treasure, but whether I believe it or not . . ."

"It is what it is?" she said in soft echo of his earlier words.

Legna moved around Gideon until she was standing in front of him, looking up into the face he tried to avert from her. She caught his head between her soft hands, making him look down into her compassionate expression and forgiving eyes.

"The problem is," he said in a rush of soft words, "aside from my trouble reconciling myself to the idea that I actually deserve you, *Nelissuna,* I am quite rusty in matters of affection and romantic emotion. I am afraid I have no idea how to go about earning your trust and your good opinion, never mind being what you need . . . beyond that."

"Well, you can put your mind at ease on one score, Gideon. You already have my good opinion. I know"— she stopped his protest with a raised hand—"I know I was very hostile to you this past decade, but we both know that was wounded pride. Now that I understand your thinking in your behavior toward me, I can look on you much more fairly. For instance, now I can see that it takes a good and honorable man to sacrifice such a genetically empowered urge for the sake of someone else's feelings and needs, as you did for me . . . and, I believe, for Noah. You were protecting his relationship with you in as much as you were protecting me, Gideon.

"You even faced great condemnation and shame because of your efforts to protect me, and I can find many reasons to find you worthy of my good opinion in those actions alone. Add to that the way you give so selflessly to those I love when they are so traumatically injured, saving them from death as no other can, and it is a very firm step on the road of one day becoming my savior. My knight in shining armor . . . roguish garb aside." She smiled, a dimple in her cheek flashing as she did so. "But we shall not tell Noah about that because it would devastate him to think he had been unhorsed from his position as my one true hero in life."

"I swear to you he will not hear of it from me," he

promised her, his eyes shining with bright, starlit hope as he looked down on her, drinking in the curves of her luminous face. He followed the touch of his eyes with the touch of his fingertips. "Legna, I have lived so long, and there is so much you do not know about me. You may find yourself faced with a desire to change your opinion of me once more."

"Before I make such a rash choice as I did nine years ago, I promise we will discuss the matter together before forming a judgment."

The promise comforted him greatly; she could both see and feel it as he relaxed just a little bit more. She was aware that anyone as long-lived as he was had to have made quite a share of errors, but the atrocities of war belonged where they had taken place, far in the past. Gideon was clearly capable of punishing himself much worse than anyone's outside retribution could.

"Now," she continued, reaching for his hand and folding it between hers as she tangled their fingers together, "I think it would be nice to walk in the gardens. Afterward, I might enjoy a game of chess, if you are so inclined."

"Hmm." Gideon smiled as he followed her firm lead. "I have always been curious as to where you got your penchant for gardening," he mused. "I will have to turn the sun patio into an arboretum. It does not get use because of the sheet glass and it will provide a great space to work in."

Legna felt her heart dip and flutter at the insinuation that they would one day be living together. She knew, of course, that it was inevitable and that was why Gideon spoke of it that way, but still it turned her flighty stomach over with immediate anxiety.

"I hear your thoughts, my beauty," he whispered into her ear suddenly, making her stop at the threshold to the back porch in order to meet his eyes. "I cannot console you on this point. You will be mine one day soon, and you will join my household. I know it. You know it.

Fear me if you must, but do not fear the inevitable. You will make a home with me long before you will feel you have come to understand me. Perhaps even before you trust me."

Legna knew he was right, and immediately the logic settled her ruffled nerves. She moistened her lips with the soft slip of her tongue.

"I am sorry. You are right, of course." She fiercely protected the boomerang thought she had, a worry over Noah being left alone, over leaving her childhood home and all that it would mean. It could mean so much happiness for her, and so much pain for others. She regretted that pain already.

"I can oblige you your walk in the gardens," Gideon was saying as he led her into the vast wilderness of his half-tamed gardens. "But chess is such a rudimentary skill for you. In fact, it will be impossible to play fairly with each of us able to read the other's intentions."

"Ah, but therein lies the challenge, Gideon. He or she who learns how to master the blocking of the other's thoughts will soon become the victor." She smiled, but Gideon did not feel the irony she felt behind it. "I say it is an excellent challenge."

"Since you put it like that, I find myself inclined to agree."

Gideon stopped his progress abruptly, the ripple of it moving up their joined arms, tugging her to a halt that reversed her momentum and sent her bumping into his tall frame with a little grunt of surprise. She blinked to clear her disoriented sense of direction, looking up into his determined gaze as his hands came to cradle her face once more. He lowered his mouth to hers, kissing her with timeless tenderness, the usual lust for one another that sprang between them being held firmly at bay.

He wanted to her to know that the only part of his body engaged in this moment was his grateful heart, and this was the only way he could tell her.

Chapter 8

Legna was awakened the next evening by the wild tromping of well-known little feet that echoed through the stone corridors of the castle. Of course, the exasperated female voice scolding after the retreating army of children was also quite familiar.

Legna yawned and stretched between the warmth of her covers. She started in surprise when her hand hit a solid wall of flesh. She sat up in sudden shock, looking straight into Gideon's eyes.

"Are you insane?" she hissed, yanking up her covers to make sure she was well concealed while at the same time flicking worried looks at the two doors leading into her room. "Noah will sense that you are here!"

"Good eve to you, too, *Neliss*," he countered casually, as if he had no cares in the world. When she continued to glare at him, he chuckled and sat up to face her. "I am in astral form, sweet. I felt you beginning to wake and wanted my face to be the first you saw when you opened your eyes." Gideon reached out to brush back her mussed hair, a tender smile crossing his lips.

"That is terribly sweet of you, Gideon," she whispered with continued agitation, "but what makes you think Noah cannot sense your energy even in this form?"

"He will most likely mistake it for that part of you that

has become me. And if he does not, should you desire it, I can leave the moment you feel his approach. Personally, I am not so intimidated by your brother as you seem to be."

"Gideon, this is not about intimidation. This is about respect for my brother's house . . . not to mention his feelings. I want this to cause as little pain to him as possible. I was hoping you would understand that."

"I do understand, *Neliss*. However, your brother is quite mature enough to realize that I will come to visit with you here until you come to live in my home. I suspect he will tolerate it if it means putting off that eventuality."

"I understand your perspective, Gideon, but this is still news to Noah. You must give it some—"

"Time?" he finished for her.

She sighed, understanding what an annoyance that word must be becoming to him. She was equally frustrated that all these troubles stood between them.

"I am willing to take the time to sort them out with you, Legna. Stop fretting. You attribute me with a temper I do not have. A man who has lived as long as I have has learned much more patience than you are giving him credit for. Now kiss me so I may leave and settle your worried mind."

Legna smiled, tossing her hair back over her shoulder as she leaned across to him, her mouth turned up invitingly to his. He reached to hold the back of her head with one large hand, drawing her firmly to his mouth.

Kissing him in this form was a new and entirely different experience. Since he was made up of pure mental energy, solidified only by the power of thought, there was a tinge of feedback that rushed over her damp lips and the warm, wet interior of her mouth as he explored it for a long, stunning minute. The only thing she could liken it to was the sensation received when licking a battery . . . only it was ten times as strong in effect. He laughed against her lips when she began to giggle at both the thought and the ticklish feeling.

He drew back, gently caressing her down the side of her face as his eyes continued to shimmer with bright amusement.

"You will never bore me, sweet," he promised her, kissing her ever so briefly before dissipating beneath her touch.

She sighed, feeling the loss of his presence more keenly every time they parted. She knew it was only a matter of time before they would not be able to part at all. The time when nature would overtake sense. She only hoped that by then she would have already made all of her reconciliations within herself.

She slid out of bed quickly, somehow managing to shower once more with her eyes closed the entire time, in spite of the chuckles echoing over and over through her mind. By the time she was dressed, she was flushed from being torn between scolding Gideon and laughing with him. Unfortunately, the scolding would have been highly ineffective, considering he was already privy to her dilemma between the two options.

So she lifted her nose into the air and decided to completely ignore him.

When she reached the bottom of the steps, Hannah was pacing back and forth across the entire length of the Great Hall. Legna was at once awash with her sister's emotions and could not resist the groan that swung through her thoughts.

Be brave, Neliss, Gideon encouraged her, reading from her thoughts what she was sensing from her other sibling.

Wrath of a Self-Righteous Fire Demon, take two, she thought wryly back to him.

Did you expect otherwise?

No, but a girl can hope.

Complete your task, Nelissuna, then come to me.

I will, but remember I promised to have dinner with Noah later.

I recall. I do not plan on making you miss your appointment with your brother, Legna. Only to have as much time with you between now and then as is possible.

Legna gave him one of her mental nods and turned to face down the simmering temper of her distraught sister, once more preparing to defend the Imprinting, which she had no control over in the first place. Except, this time, it meant quite a bit more to her than that.

When Legna appeared in Gideon's parlor, he was walking across the room, shrugging into a long coat of a rich brown leather, reaching back to pull the long tail of his hair out of the collar just as Legna was cocking a curious brow in his direction.

"Are we going out?"

"No," he responded, his tone as serious as the tension she sensed within him.

"What's wrong?"

Gideon paused in the middle of strapping a knife in its sheath to his thigh. Body Demons rarely, if ever, armed themselves. It only served to perplex Legna further, his thoughts kept as far from her as he could manage for some reason.

"Noah has called a Council meeting. Elijah is expected to give his report on Bella's attack. I was told to . . . come prepared."

"Who told you this? Noah mentioned nothing to me."

It gave him only a moment of pause to hear this, then he shrugged.

"Your brother has formed a habit of leaving you out of the loop since October's incident. You are not on the Council, so he sees no reason to inform you of these things."

"Not on the . . ." Legna's jaw dropped open as her eyes widened in shock and building outrage. "I am one of the most powerfully effective diplomats and mentors in our society, and he chooses not to inform me of critical happenings that require you to come armed to a Council meeting? I am not a child, despite what you or my brother might think, and I know full well that the only reason for you to be armed is if you plan on engaging in battle with a Nightwalker species that is somewhat or completely immune to your abilities."

"I never said that I thought you were too young to be capable of understanding the situation. Legna, do not lump me in with the protective actions of your brother. If you will recall, it is I who is being forthright with you about the nature of what is going on."

He was right, of course. In a way, she truly was acting like a child, throwing a temper tantrum because the big kids were clearly not going to let her play in their games. It made her angry with herself and with Noah all at the same time. Legna folded her arms across her middle tightly, blinking back the childish urge to give in to tears.

"Come, sweet, you are being too hard on yourself," Gideon soothed, crossing over to her and pulling her into the comfort of his arms. "Now that I am a part of you, I am beginning to understand how come you became so angry with me for calling you a child. Despite your age and accomplishments, no one in your family has ever quite stopped treating you like the baby of the family. It is a wonder you have developed the sophistication you have despite their unwitting repressive behaviors. It is even more miraculous that you have maintained your patience with them for all these years."

"I am being sensitive because they have both taken turns at scolding me within the past twenty-four hours," she argued with herself aloud. She sniffled and dashed the dampness from her eyes before she made a complete fool of herself.

"You do not need to feel embarrassed with me, Magdelegna," he told her softly, reaching to pick up one of the long coils she had styled her usually softly curled hair into. He smiled, rubbing the curl against his lips affectionately. "Always feel free to show your honest feelings to me. I am most likely aware of them in any event."

"Gideon," she whispered, her hands reaching to splay over his broad chest, "I am . . . I feel fear for some reason. I am filled with the sickly sensation that if I let you go, I may never see you again."

The confession did amazing things to Gideon, turning his heart completely over in his chest, for starters. She was allowing herself to become more closely attached to him, otherwise why would she dread his loss? He closed his eyes as he was rushed through with pleasure at the realization and a swell of hope so powerful it made him numb. Unable to resist the impulse, he drew her tightly into his embrace, hugging her so securely that he heard her breath escape in a rush from the compression of her rib cage. Her feet waved a couple of inches off the floor, and she laughed in a mixture of delight over his affections and unsure fear as he swung her slightly from side to side, continuing to clutch her for a long chain of minutes. When he finally set her back onto her feet, she clung to him with her comparatively slender, feminine body as if they had been stuck that way by the irrepressible connectivity of static electricity.

Gideon's hands were gloved, she realized for the first time as he brushed her hair back in an attempt at giving himself a clear field of vision while he looked down into her face.

"You look beautiful tonight," he said, stroking the very different mass of tight curls first, and then the shimmering azure silk that spilled off her shoulders in a delicately embroidered and beaded shawl. The dress she wore was as long and trained as all her others, the black silk of it also beaded and fringed with intricate care. "Was this all for me?"

She nodded, too wound up to make any pretense at sarcasm or jokes or evasiveness. The appreciation in his eyes as he took in her efforts made the honesty well worth it.

"Just so you know, I find you to be equally stunning even when you wake up tousled and perturbed with me," he told her, his crooked smile making her smile shyly in return. "It is your desire to please me, above all, which has won my pleasure, not the methods you used to try and do so. However"—he reached to slide blue silk back from a bared shoulder, leaning forward to kiss the exposed spot gently before meeting her gaze once more—"you do wear it well."

"I want to come with you," she blurted out suddenly, the words coming to her lips even before he could find the thought forming in her mind.

"Why? So you can pace the hall while the Council meets? To what end? Only to have to pace it some more after I leave for whatever action it is that Elijah has planned for me? I believe it would be better for your peace of mind to remain here where you can follow me in your thoughts with no one to disturb you." He rubbed the soft, rosy rise of her cheek with a leather-covered thumb. It was a uniquely masculine caress, as well as breathtaking and loving. Legna had to maintain her focus with a little more effort than usual. "Remember, Legna, for the rest of your life you will always come with me."

"No. This is wrong!" She pushed out of his hold, wrapping herself in her shawl and her own arms once more as she paced several steps away before turning quickly back. "Can you not feel what is inside of me? I am ready to scream with this feeling that no one should . . . that I should . . ."

She had to stop and sort through exactly what it was she was feeling. She had denied these instinctual aspects of her being for so long, now she had no experience with which to compare them. She drew a frustrating blank on how to describe or identify the sensation she was feeling.

"What you are feeling, Legna," Gideon rescued her with a soft, soothing pitch to his voice, "is the desire to remain at my back. It is an instinct designed for both your self-defense and the defense of your mate."

"Yes!" she exclaimed, returning to him in order to reach for him, her slim hands clutching the leather that covered his powerful upper arms. "We were meant to be back to back when you face danger. I can feel it. It is a clawing need within me. . . . It . . . reminds me of what it feels like when you are swimming and remain beneath the water too long. It is a need as desperate as the urge to draw breath when starved for air. You must take me with you."

"Not this time, *Nelissuna*." He tried to deny her gently, but her need and determination were sharp. She could take offense easily, no matter how diplomatic he tried to be. Gideon hoped he would be able to appeal to her logic. "You do not have enough experience working with these instinctual emotions. They are new, and, as you know, can be overwhelming. Until you learn to acknowledge them and integrate them into yourself, you are in danger of losing focus and control. I do not have to tell you how dangerous that is in a volatile situation.

"We will take the time to train you, to train myself as well, after I return to you. Understand, I will be unable to feel comfortable having you at my side in battle right this moment. Not because I do not want you to fill your place behind me, but because in this situation I would spend too much time worrying about you. It could cause one or both of us to become injured."

He was correct, of course, but it only served to spike a streak of frustrated anger and self-contempt in Legna. She had been running from this side of herself as if she were a frightened child, shutting her eyes tight and wishing the monsters within herself away rather than facing them down. Now she would begin to pay for that. She had been so arrogant to believe that she had to keep herself above such urges. In that moment she would have given anything to already be reconciled with those exact same urges in order to aid her mate as she was supposed to. If something happened to him because she was not there to be his additional eyes and strength, it would be her fault.

"Stop, Legna, this serves no purpose," he said firmly, the leather of his gloves cool and taut against the skin of her face as he forced her to meet his gaze. "Do not waste your time with self-recriminations when there is nothing to be done about it at this moment. Instead, find a comfortable place here and follow me from within. I still need you, sweet. Your experience, your abilities, and your intuition could serve me just as well as your physical presence could in this matter. I need you to see what I may miss, and to maintain a route of escape should the need arise. And no, I do not expect it to. It is just my nature to be prepared."

Legna absorbed his request for what seemed like a minute too long, but then she broke out of his hold and turned her back to him. Her thoughts were so chaotic that Gideon could not make sense of what she was thinking about specifically. It wasn't until she reached for the second knife and sheath he had left on the table that he began to understand her intentions.

With the grace she had that surpassed even that which should have been natural to her because of her bloodlines, she moved back to him. After touching him lightly across his chest with an affectionate hand, she quietly bent to the task of securing the sheath to his other thigh.

The profundity of her actions left Gideon utterly speechless. All he could do was watch and feel as her deft fingers fixed the higher strap and buckle on the high inside of his thigh. To say the experience was erotic was an understatement of terrible ineptitude. It didn't matter that it had not been the intention of either of them to see the action in such an intimate light. What mattered was that they were both aware of it, that they both were aroused by the intimacy of her actions on far deeper levels than just the fact that her hands were touching him.

She was his one true mate, his second half, the feminine side of himself that flourished on intuition and protective instincts. She was the side that turned calm before the battle so as to see to complete preparation for what was to come. She was center, focus, and everything moral that would guide his actions. She was the strategy and logic that would take him along the best course to victory while exercising caution for his own safety. She was mercy for those who would lie beaten at his feet, satisfying him with victory while sparing him the poisonous joy of killing when it was no longer needed. She was the peace and the light that would keep him from burdening himself with the heavy weight of taking a life, no matter how justified it was.

He was her one true mate, her second half. As she armed him, she felt him slipping deeply into her soul, becoming the masculine side of herself. This was the place within her that thrived on defending what was hers, the part that would mark her territory with the blood of her enemies if they dared cross the lines set before them. He became her sense of authority and righteousness, the part of her that was battle scarred and warrior skilled. He was her physical prowess, her devious cunning, and the part that would endure the pain and wounds of hell rather than see injustice done. He was the darkness and the conflict that kept her from becoming too complacent in the soft nature of peace, leaving herself open to the attack of those who were not so honorable in ideals as she would have them be.

Legna's hair hung down the far side of her head, leaving the nearer side of her lovely face and throat exposed as she concentrated completely on performing her task with an efficiency worthy of trusting his life to. With his special sight, Gideon's eyes focused on the thrum of her strong pulse even as he shared it with her already in his own body and his own spirit. She secured the second strap of his weapon and straightened, her steel-colored eyes reflecting the female warrior within her that saw to his preparation with meticulousness.

She unsnapped the hard piece of leather that kept the knife in its sheath and pulled the weapon free. The sharp metal of the nine-inch blade sang shortly as it slid over the metal rim of its holder. Legna held the blade in the light. She turned it over, inspecting it carefully for a moment before being satisfied enough with its quality and razor readiness to return it to its home, nimbly securing the snap over it once more.

Finished with that task, she inspected her mate from head to toe, carefully judging his readiness. When she finally met his burning eyes, Gideon allowed himself to take a breath.

"I never knew the short dagger was your expertise," she mentioned softly.

"It is one of them. One who lives a life of my length would be foolish to not take the advantage to become an expert at all combat weapons." He watched her expression carefully, searching for her thoughts.

"Yes. I know. I suppose in a sense we can count ourselves lucky that our innate powers outstrip the destructive capabilities even the most advanced technology can produce. We have little need for the weaponry of that ilk, even if we were compatible with such things."

She moved a step closer, her elegant hands reaching for the warmth of his chest beneath the gap in the leather coat, her nails pulling ever so slightly at the cotton fabric of his shirt. He slipped his hands around her slender waist, the possessiveness in the grip hard to mistake as he drew her even nearer. He said nothing, but he reached to kiss her within the span of the next beat of his heart. As their warm lips meshed, so did their intent. The exchange was part tenderness, part desperation, and a large portion of unspoken feelings and desires twisted up too tightly in the worries of the moment to find any clearer expression.

"Will you be here when I return?" he asked, his words warm and more than a little urgent against her mouth.

"Yes," she promised him, sealing it with the fiery longing that came through in the sworn oath of her lips.

Not wanting to distract him any more than she already had, she broke away from their kiss, leaving his grasp with a definitive backward breaking movement that took her a sufficient distance away from him, and him away from her hunger and frightened needs. If not totally, at least from the physical manifestations of them.

He understood her actions completely and was grateful for them. He needed his wits about him, and she had the ability to rob him of them with such ease when she engaged him in the artwork of her mouth and the complexity of her emerging needs and thoughts.

"Hang on," she murmured, taking a deep breath as she closed her eyes and, extending her slender arms out to either side of her body, splayed her hands in a focusing movement.

The last thing Gideon saw was the silk of her shawl snaking off of her smooth skin, pooling on the floor around her feet. In a flash, he found himself reappearing in the hall of the Great Council with a nearly silent pop and no other sign of smoke or mirrors.

Jacob was the first to rise out of his chair after the Great Council had finally convened.

"As you all may or may not know," he began, "our female Enforcer was brutally attacked a couple of nights ago." The announcement elicited several surprised mur-

murs from those who had not been updated through the flow of gossip. "She was finally strong enough this evening to begin to tell us what had happened to her. Once we combine her information with Elijah's"— Jacob gestured to the enormous blond warrior sitting on one of the sides of the triangular table, rocking back on the rear legs of his chair—"and then further combine their information with that of the medic who healed her, I think we will all be updated and informed enough to make secure conclusions and begin to take action. Since Noah, myself, and Elijah have already processed this information between ourselves, we will also provide suggestions for courses of action we feel are appropriate.

"For obvious reasons, I will be the one the retell my mate's story. She is not strong enough yet to venture from her bed, and I believe you all can agree that her safety and the well-being of the child she carries must be attended to above all other courses of action."

Councillor Ruth made a derogatory sound under her breath that was par for the course for the female Mind Demon. However, tonight, Jacob was not in his usual tolerant frame of mind. Normally, he managed Ruth's tart remarks and jockeying for power and position with the forbearance shown a mouthy child, but Ruth's disparagements against Jacob's wife had grown too bold to continue to pass without acknowledgement. It did not help matters that Ruth should pick so unwise a moment to taunt him.

When the Enforcer's fist came down on the table hard enough to send a horrendous crack through the solid wood, Councillors and King alike were startled in their chairs. However, it was nothing compared to the dangerous vocalization that poured out of the Earth Demon's throat as he narrowed cold, bitter eyes on the vindictive Ruth.

"You will refrain from expressing your negative sounds and opinions about my wife to this Council, Ruth," he growled his warning, his tone so low and dangerous that many of the Councillors experienced a deathly chill. "If you do not, you will find yourself answering to me. Do I make myself perfectly clear to you, woman?"

"You dare to threaten me?" she retaliated, gaining her feet as she faced off with the Enforcer in what had to be the most unwise action in Council history since the decision to go to war with the Druids.

"Ruth, sit down," Noah warned with a hiss. "If you do not, you will find yourself removed from this Council for the rest of your days. Do *I* make *myself* clear?"

"You do not have the power to do that!" Ruth declared, her obstinace so complete she simply did not understand the hole she had been blindly digging for herself. Perhaps in those first months of her daughter's loss this could be understood, but she had been spewing ill will and hostility toward the Enforcers continuously. However, the Council understood that the Enforcers were not to blame for the damage to her family, and her tirades and animosity had left her very few friends on the uneasy Council.

"I do," Noah countered with the cool confidence of his omniscient position. "If the Council supports me in majority, you will find yourself excommunicated from this gathering. And I think you need to realize, Councillor Ruth, that the woman you treat with such contempt, who sits by Jacob's side in this Council, will hold in her hands the deciding vote of the majority I need once she is well enough to sit with us once more. Now *sit down.*"

Ruth paled under the clear threat, her entire body shaking with her pent-up outrage and impotent position. But she somehow managed the wisdom to hold her tongue, tossing the blond mass of her hair in a gesture of silent defiance as she finally regained her seat. There was no mistaking the hatred in her eyes as she glared at the Enforcer.

"Continue, Jacob. I apologize for the interruption," Noah urged him gently.

Gideon flicked an aluminum gaze of curiosity at Ruth as Jacob took a minute to compose himself. He understood Ruth's unchecked emotions. Her daughter had lost the most valuable treasure a Demon could earn. She had lost the Druid mate who, without a doubt, would have become Imprinted upon the young Demon female for all time, earning her a place in the emerging history of a new era for all of Demon culture. This was the very type of Destiny that a being who craved power like Ruth did would have exulted in. To be mother of such a daughter, what a wondrous thing that would have been.

But Gideon's compassion was entirely for Ruth's daughter, Mary. The death of her male Druid had deprived the young Demon of ever knowing what it was that he and Legna were just beginning to discover and had already grown a healthy awe and respect for.

Then Gideon abruptly felt the weight of his realization that, had it not been for Isabella and her remarkable abilities, he too would have been cursed to this fate. The thought made his entire body run cold despite his efforts to control the ebb and surge of the thick emotion. To lead a life without Legna, and without ever knowing what he was missing, was unthinkable. When had he begun to feel as if all his long years had been a labor leading him up to this point, so he could draw her to his side? When he thought back over the past nine years, time he had wasted and left her unprotected when, instead, he should have been keeping her close and safe . . .

Gideon tightened both hands into fists, the soft creak of stressed leather lost under the voices of the Council. He glanced around the table at those who could sense his thoughts and feelings, if they dared, including the avaricious Ruth, and he struggled for control.

Easy, dearest. Focus on the moment, and remember how close I am now.

Her comforting voice was nothing compared to the powerful effect her use of an endearment had on him. His fingers moved to silently grip the arms of his chair, almost as though he had to hold himself down lest he soar with the simple pleasure. He couldn't explain the ridiculous effect, but there was no way to deny it.

If I had known it would be so easy to please you, I would have done it sooner, she sent to him, her laughter lightening his heart as it moved through his body and soul.

When have I ever given you the impression that you did not please me, Neliss?

Hush, flatterer. Pay attention to Jacob.

Gideon smiled with a corner of his mouth and turned his attention to do just that.

". . . originally thought it was the attack of a necromancer," the Enforcer was saying. "She had been struck by several charges of what looked like their signature use of electrical abilities. What we could not immediately understand was why she had not been able to dampen that type of power as she has done in the past."

Jacob paused, rubbing his hands together as if they were chilled. It was no wonder, Gideon mused. He would have felt just as cold if it had been him before the Council describing an attack on Legna . . . and being forced to relive the fact that he had failed to protect her, whether it was avoidable or not.

"The reason why Bella could not dampen her attacker's power is because the majority of it came from a handheld, Taser-like weapon. It was technology, not supernatural ability, that initially injured her. She opened the door and had no chance to protect herself. She was fired upon immediately. The only thing she remembers clearly after the original shock was that one of her attackers came up to her as she lay stunned and wounded on the floor and proceeded to—" He broke off, his throat working as his fingers curled to clench into fists. It was as if the inconceivable words had lodged themselves in Jacob's throat, strangling off his very breath in the process.

To Legna's clear relief, which Gideon felt as if it were his own, Elijah stood up and laid a hand on Jacob's shoulder, urging the Enforcer to take a seat. The warrior turned to the Council and picked up the story.

"Bella remembers vividly that one of the assaulters purposely began to traumatize her about the abdominal area. Kicking her . . . even going so far as to use blunt weapons like bats or long sticks. She is not certain which. Her injuries were consistent with a beating, were they not, Gideon?"

Gideon gave the warrior a single nod.

"It was as with hounds on a fox," Gideon informed softly. "She lay in the center of a pack as it attacked her all at once. The primary target was Bella's unborn child. Secondary was Bella herself. It is clear that her assaulters intended her to die. Had that happened, we would have had no first-person account of the incident. Luckily, my—Magdelegna," he corrected himself quickly, feeling the sudden weight of the Demon King's eyes on him and wishing above all else not to disturb Legna any more than she already was, "Magdelegna," he continued, "found Bella within minutes of the end of the assault."

Speaking it out loud made Gideon realize just how close she had come to danger that day. Had she not been under his compulsion to sleep, she might have risen sooner and been with Bella at the time of the attack. Gideon felt something dark pour a stain over his soul like black ink on paper. Again, so close to losing her, and never having truly had her to begin with. The understanding was awful enough, but the feelings writhing beneath it seemed to want to rise up and choke him, just as they had Jacob. He fought for control of it all, but it was Legna who made the most impact.

Shh . . . Ease your heart, my mate, she soothed him. *You are mine now and there will be no harm to either of us that can ever change that.*

"It is clear that outside of Isabella's injuries, everything else in that room was staged," Elijah continued, his straightforward warrior's voice stark in the middle of Gideon's suddenly heartened spirits. "It was made to look like necromancers, but I am not convinced of that. Why destroy the place and leave obvious signs? Clearly there was no battle. Why sign their names to it with such senseless destruction?"

"Not necromancers?" Ruth asked. "But can you be sure?"

"No, actually, we can't," Elijah agreed. "Necromancers are still humans, and they can still use technological weapons. These are the requirements of fact. An enemy with motive," Elijah ticked off his facts on his fingers, "one who can use technology, and one who knows we despise the necromancers, thereby the attempt to frame them. Sans the necromancers themselves, of course, who might still be a possibility. More importantly, they had to know of Jacob, Bella, and the significance of their unborn child."

"Who else would know about the emergence of Druids and their role in our future?" Jacob asked.

Gideon's blank expression might not have aroused the suspicions of anyone at the Council table, but Legna was concentrating so completely on his thoughts that there was no way she could have missed the wash of dread that slipped through him, accompanied by the ghost of guilt that followed.

You know something, she whispered.

Not now, Legna.

Legna understood. There were powerful male Mind Demons in the room who were capable of penetrating even Gideon's formidable defenses should their suspicions be aroused. She silenced herself immediately, filling his mind with images of comfort and cotton-candy thoughts that would cause a significant haze over any curious Demons trying to pull information from her mate.

"This connotes Nightwalker. Rumor spreads quickly in our world, and it would not surprise me if a species has heard about the Druids and felt threatened by their perpetuation among us."

"That leads us to how to eliminate or confirm each species of Nightwalker," Elijah remarked. Other Nightwalker races were his forte, so the Wind Demon was in his element, so to speak. As head of the warriors, Elijah had the duty to see to the resolution of altercations between Demons and other races. "Let's start with the Shadowdwellers."

"The attack took place at sunset," Noah said.

"Exactly," Elijah confirmed. "Shadowdwellers cannot bear even the slightest amount of sunlight. Their sensitivity is worse even than that of the Vampires. As we know, some members of the Vampire race can tolerate some sun the older and the stronger they become. But that is absolutely impossible for Shadowdwellers."

"The Mistrals are notoriously nonaggressive. I cannot imagine them going to this trouble to commit such a violent act," Jacob added.

"But I can easily believe it of the Lycanthropes," Elijah rejoined. "Though we have held a tenuous truce with them these past thirteen years, there are still those who resent the Demons enough to cross the lines of peace."

"To what end? To destroy a pregnant female? It does not make sense," Noah argued. "Lycanthropes are not known for that measure of focus and specificity."

"I tend to agree," Gideon spoke up. "Lycanthropes would turn to their instincts in the heat of such an attack. They would not have been able to resist the urge to mark Isabella, tainting her with their blood in the process. There was no hint of claw wounds or animal bites, not to mention the fact that her blood was free of the taint of Lycanthropy."

"And yet, what better way to hide that the attack was theirs than to resist the impulse? They were in human form, if it was them. Bella was attacked by bipeds."

"Vampires?"

"All criteria make it possible except for motive and technology. Of course, it would be no trick for a Vampire to charm a human into using such a weapon."

"Motive is my concern," Gideon said quickly. "Lack of one, that is. There is no cause for it."

"Yet they cannot be ruled out," Elijah countered. "There could be something we are missing."

"I will rule them out," Gideon said succinctly.

Noah turned his head, cocking a brow.

"You will go to Damien with an accusation like this?" he asked, knowing full well that there had always been something between the two Ancients.

"But I was planning on sending him to Siena," Elijah complained. Gideon felt Legna's reaction sharply, the emotion of shock and fear almost blocking out Elijah's explanation. "You know her best, Gideon. I realize your innate Demon abilities will not be able to affect her much, but you will be able to see enough of her body chemistry and functions to know if she is lying to you or concealing anything. I trust you feel capable of sufficient hand-to-hand combat if it should come to that?"

"Of course," Gideon said with the simplicity of perfect confidence. "And I do not see why I cannot do both tasks. I am the wisest choice in either direction."

"He has a point," Noah agreed.

Gideon felt Legna's instant disconcertment at her brother's eagerness to send him into volatile duty. If she could have controlled his body, she would have made the Ancient slap the Demon King.

"Very well. While you are doing that, I plan to move in the circles of the humans who take delight in stalking Nightwalkers," Elijah said. "The sanctums of those self-proclaimed hunters are easy to penetrate, especially for those with clear physical and battle prowess."

"The remaining issue: necromancers. They will be what is left through process of elimination," Jacob said quietly. "It is very likely that the obvious may end up the right answer. But we cannot rest on that without safely eliminating the rest."

"We will reconvene when Elijah returns from his reconnaissance. I trust that will give you time to complete your tasks, Gideon?"

"Ample time, Noah, I assure you."

"Very well. I will see you all then. Council is adjourned." Noah rose to his feet, pausing in the act of straightening to touch Councillor Ruth's hand, whispering a single-word command to her under his breath.

The Council dispersed with the exception of Gideon and Jacob, both of whom remained in their seats until the room had cleared entirely. When the door had shut, Jacob turned to the medic.

"If you require someone to watch your back, I will be glad to accompany you."

"No, thank you, Jacob. I think this is a task best completed by an individual. If two of the most powerful Demons in our society were to appear on foreign doorsteps, it would put the receptions completely on the defensive, perhaps even provoking an undesirable altercation."

"I see your point. However, if you should encounter trouble, you merely have to instruct Legna to come to me and I will assist you to the best of my ability."

"I do not think it will come to that. Damien has been peaceable for centuries, and Siena is no fool. She knows I would not enter her territory without being monitored."

"Are you going now?"

"Yes. I see no reason to delay the action. I am already prepared."

"I noticed," Jacob remarked. "I have not seen you

armed in some time. I figured Elijah must have given you some forewarning of possible events."

"He merely told me to come prepared for all possibilities of combat."

"He would put it that way," Jacob chuckled. "The man is a warrior through and through, for all his clowning around."

"True. Shall I stop in to check on Bella before I go?"

"Not dressed like that. You would give her palpitations if she knew you were going into danger for her benefit."

"Luckily, I am mostly immune to Bella's powers and could cure such palpitations with a thought," Gideon mused.

Jacob raised a brow, taking the medic's measure. He could not recall the last time he had heard the Ancient crack wise about anything. It was not a wholly unpleasant experience, and it amused the Enforcer.

"I . . . am aware of what is occurring between you and Legna, as you know," Jacob mentioned with casual quiet. "I am only recently Imprinted myself, but should you require—" He broke off, suddenly uncomfortable. "Of course, you probably know far more about Imprinting than I ever will."

He is reaching out to you.

Legna's soft encouragement made Gideon suddenly aware of that fact. It was one of those nuances he would have missed completely, rusty as he was with matters of friendship and how to relate better to others.

"I am glad for the offer of any help you can provide," Gideon said quickly. "In fact, I had wanted to ask you . . . something . . ."

What did I want to ask him? he asked Legna urgently.

I do not know! I did not tell you to engage him, just to graciously accept his offer.

Oh. My apologies. Still, you are clever enough to think of something, are you not?

Legna knew he was baiting her, so she laughed.

Ask him why it is you seem to constantly irritate me.

I will ask him no such thing, Magdelegna.

Well then, you had better come up with an alternative, because that is the only suggestion I have.

"Yes?" Jacob was encouraging neutrally, trying to be patient as the medic seemed to gather his thoughts.

"Do you find that your mate tends to lecture you incessantly?" he asked finally.

Jacob laughed out loud.

"You know something, I can actually advise you about that, Gideon."

"Can you?" The medic actually sounded hopeful.

"Give up. Now. While you still have your sanity. Arguing with her will get you nowhere. And, also, never ever ask questions that refer to the whys and wherefores of women, females, or any other feminine-based criticism. Otherwise you will only earn an argument at a higher decibel level. Oh, and one other thing."

Gideon cocked a brow in question.

"All the rules I just gave you, as well as all the ones she lays down during the course of your relationship, can *and will* change at whim. So, as I see it, you can consider yourself just as lost as every other man on the planet. Good luck with it."

"That is not a very heartening thought," Gideon said wryly, ignoring Legna's giggle in his background thoughts.

Jacob rose from his chair, pushing it in as he stretched out muscles stiffened from sitting too long.

"I will see you soon, Gideon."

The Enforcer twisted into the form of a dust spiral and exited up out of a window.

How are you feeling? Up to teleporting me to a place I send to your mind?

I believe so.

So he did just that.

Chapter 9

Gideon materialized on a vacant street corner beneath a broken street lamp. He looked around carefully, taking a step backward until he was against the brick of the corner of a building and settled deeply in the shadows. He manipulated his eyesight until he could not only see clearly in the darkness, but could see at any distance he wished. He was aware of how impressed Legna was by the new way he was looking at things.

It was actually her first real situation where she would experience the use of his powers from a behind-his-eyes perspective. Gideon found himself hoping that she would not witness too much more than tricks of his eyesight and other simple biochemical alterations.

Stop fretting about me and what I will see. That will be just as bad as you worrying about my physical presence.

You are correct. Thank you.

You are welcome.

Gideon continued to scan his surroundings, using a clever alteration of body chemistry to extend an attractively scented trail as bait for the creatures he was looking for.

It wasn't long before a dark figure appeared in the street some distance down. In a blink of an eye, he had skimmed the half-mile distance and stood even closer to

Gideon's position. The medic spiked his body chemistry with adrenaline. This served two purposes. One, it prepared him with heightened strength and reflexes in the event of an altercation; two, it called to his possible adversary like ambrosia.

The Ancient's target moved faster than even Gideon's improved eyesight could track, but the medic didn't even bother to try. He felt a viselike hand close around his throat, slamming him against the wall until he felt brick digging into his scalp, the leather of his coat the only thing protecting him at other points of contact. Gideon felt Legna's emotions jolt, but to her credit, she poured her faith into the reassuring whisper he sent to her. She remained ready for any consequence, though, and it pleased him.

Gideon watched calmly as the beast reared his head back, his mouth opening with a hiss and a display of long ivory fangs. The Vampire feinted for his neck but suddenly stopped, its dark eyes widening with surprise. Slowly the other Nightwalker eased back, his wide gaze moving slowly downward until they rested on the blade of the knife that had just pricked through his shirt and the skin over his heart. He finally took the time to meet his prey's eyes and, with a sigh and a curse, he suddenly released Gideon.

"Demon! Bah!"

Looking quite put out, the Vampire stepped back until Gideon finally turned the blade away and with a nimble flip, resheathed it as silently as he had drawn it.

"My apologies," he said graciously, "for the trickery. But I needed to attract someone's attention and it was the quickest method I could come up with since I was certain you were all out hunting by now."

The Vampire grunted in reluctant agreement "What do you want, Demon?"

"I want Damien's hunting grounds. Would you be privy to the information?"

"If I were, why would I give it to a Demon?" the other male queried.

"I do not intend to harm him, only speak with him."

"My question has not changed."

"Indeed," Gideon agreed. "But you would know if I were lying, and you will have to be satisfied with that."

The Vampire tilted his head to the side, his darkly handsome features a study in speculation.

"You have a point. Still, I will only tell you to concentrate your search in San Jose. Other than that . . ."

The Vampire gave him a mock, open-armed bow before leaping into a flight that took him into the shadowed recesses of the taller buildings across from Gideon.

Do you need me to take you to San Jose? Legna asked him.

No. Rest. It is close enough. Save your strength for later. Do not worry. Damien and I are acquainted. I am in no danger from him.

But I can feel you aren't as positive about that as you would like to be. Do you suspect him in this attack on Bella?

I will know the answer to that shortly.

Damien's head lifted suddenly as he caught a powerful and familiar scent wafting on the mountain breeze. He turned his head quickly even as he crouched down low, the long braid of his black hair whipping like a flagellum with the abrupt movement.

"Gideon?"

The Demon stepped out into a shaft of moonlight, the exposure bold enough to relax the Prince. Damien regained his height and the elegance of his more human composure, dismissing the wary beast of moments ago with an easy thought.

"Damien," Gideon greeted with a respectful nod.

"Come to hunt me down in my own hunting grounds?" Damien asked.

Legna had never seen a Vampire as old and as potent as

Damien, the Prince of Vampires. Through Gideon's eyes, she was astounded by what she saw. He was as powerful and broad in build as the warrior Elijah, except where Elijah was blond and always seemed to be enjoying a good joke, this creature was dark in dramatic ways.

He had blue eyes so dark that they almost appeared to be black, the pupils nearly indistinguishable from the irises. His hair was raven black, with that blue-black sheen that often tinged the feathers of those cunning birds. Unlike those she had seen of his ilk previously, this Vampire sported a closely barbered beard and mustache. There were lines and grace to his face that made him naturally handsome, but Vampires had a glamour of sensuality that enhanced the effect even further. His features, from cheekbones to generous lips, were highly seductive as they broke into an amused smile.

"Gideon, you old dog, you have taken a mate," the Prince accused with humor sparkling from those fathomless eyes. "And I believe she finds me quite attractive."

Gideon heard Legna gasp in shock and tried to repress a feral smile as he became aware of the burning blush she sprouted.

"I would not cross that particular line even as a joke, Damien," Gideon warned him smoothly.

"My apologies. I could not resist." Damien looked steadily into Gideon's eyes for a moment. "She must be young, not to realize I would be able to read her presence within your mind."

"She is young, but I would not underestimate her if I were you."

Gideon's confidence, which radiated throughout the statement, helped Legna regain her perspective and balance. She blew the image of a gentle kiss to him, making him smile.

"No, indeed," the Vampire agreed. "You have come to ask me if I have betrayed your confidence, have you not?"

"I have. Outside of my people, you are the only one

who knows the significance of the female Druid who is mated with our Enforcer. You know because I told you myself. I want you to tell me you had nothing to do with the brutal attack that was visited upon that same female. An attack that nearly resulted in the deaths of her and her unborn child."

Damien's entire countenance changed. The seductive humor and handsomeness faded just enough to allow fangs and animalistic ferocity to reflect in his blackening eyes.

"Who would commit such an atrocity?"

Legna felt the relief that ricocheted through Gideon. She knew, in that second, exactly what Gideon did. The Vampire had done nothing to harm Isabella.

"I am sorry I had to ask, Damien," Gideon apologized with a heartfelt bow to his acquaintance.

The Vampire blew the apology aside with the wave of an elegant, long-fingered hand.

"Understandable, considering. You will be asking Siena about this, I take it?"

"Of course. Though this is not her style, it could be rebels from amongst her people. What of yours? Anything I should know?"

"Not really," Damien mused, thinking on it a minute longer. "We have our outlaws, those who kill indiscriminately for the perversion of the pleasure death-fear gives them. But I believe they are too busy running from justice, avoiding the sun, and making their kills to be bothered with your politics and propagation."

"I agree. I did not think there were Vampires present at the altercation site, but it does not hurt to be thorough."

"Would you like me to speak with Tristan?"

Gideon shook his head negatively at the mention of the Shadowdwellers' monarch.

"The attack was at sunset. Far too much daylight to have anything to do with them. But thank you for the offer."

"I tell you what I will do, Gideon, as a return favor for your warning about the necromancers. I will get my Vanguard to scour the dens of the human Vampire hunters and see if they hear anything."

"Thank you. That will be a help. Elijah is on a similar task. But I believe your intelligence on these people is much more complex and thorough than ours."

"That is because you do not normally have anything to fear from normal humans who are without dark magic. You are too strong for that. However, while we are strong, we Vampires have that one weakness that humans can exploit far too easily. Being forced to sleep in paralyzed weakness during daylight makes the average human far more of a threat to the average Vampire, requiring us to have a deeper knowledge of their ways. At least you can fight your lethargy, can hear the approach of enemies, and can use your abilities at near full strength in spite of your sleep under the sun. Very few of my people can claim the power to do the same."

"I understand that quite well," Gideon reminded him.

"I was reiterating for your young female," Damien said, showing a fanged smile and mischievous wink.

"You are never happy unless you are flirting with danger. A frightening quality in a leader of an entire species," Gideon returned dryly.

"Nonsense. I am merely pleased with your good fortune. Enjoy her well, my friend. You have earned her."

Gideon thanked the Vampire once more, then each gave a short bow to the other before the Vampire took to the sky with an enormously powerful leap. The Demon felt his mate watch the departure through his eyes with significant awe.

I have led a life far too sheltered, I am realizing, she mused to him.

One would think otherwise, having lived at the hub of our court all of your life. I am surprised you have not met Damien before this.

Well, as you previously noted, Noah has a way of making certain I am not present for volatile situations. I would say the Prince of the Vampires making a sojourn to the court of the King of the Demons would no doubt qualify.

I believe you are correct. Now, my beauty, we are ready for one more stop.

By all means, dearest.

Have I mentioned I love it when you say that?

As a matter of fact, you have.

Jacob moved slowly up the stairs, feeling weighted and tired. It was a struggle for the Enforcer to leave matters so close to his home and heart to others, but he trusted Elijah with every ounce of breath he drew, as well as with the life of his wife. The warrior simply adored Bella. How could he not? Jacob's "little flower" had broken the warrior's nose the very same instant she had met him. To Elijah, that was the ultimate quality in a good woman.

Jacob chuckled with that thought, feeling somehow lighter for it. He also realized he was changing his feelings about Gideon lately as well. The medic had never truly done anything outsiders would see as a great offense, but because he had earned Bella's hostility at the start it had naturally gravitated into Jacob's own heart.

Funnily enough, it was Bella who had begun to act with civility and honest appreciation toward the medic first. It was so like her to be that changeable, that forgiving and tolerant. It would have been impossible for her to trust the Ancient with the care of her health and the health of their baby otherwise. She had genuinely formed a sense of humor about the medic's eccentricity of manners. It simply was not in Bella to hold grudges, especially when she understood the great gift Gideon was bestowing on them by lending his formidable skills to aid her pregnancy.

Jacob had wondered why that particular outlook had

not rubbed off on him as easily as the irritation had. However, if he were to be honest with himself, it probably had a lot to do with the fact that Gideon constantly had his hands all over his mate. It was necessary, of course, but that did not change the instinctual hostility it created. Perhaps it was because Gideon was now Imprinted himself that there was a distinctive easing of his negative perspective toward him. There was comfort in the idea that they were now on equal footing, each understanding what the other was forced to feel, from a firsthand perspective.

Gideon had also performed a miracle saving the lives of his family, and Jacob was keenly aware of it. No one else would have been able to save both mother *and* child. This task alone indebted Jacob to Gideon and ingratiated Gideon to Jacob for the rest of their days.

Jacob entered his borrowed bedroom in Noah's home, not bothering with the lights when he could see with perfect clarity without them. Bella was sleeping lightly, already stirring when she sensed him coming near. With a smile, Jacob began to whip up a surprise for her.

When Bella opened her eyes, it was because she was suddenly overwhelmed with the aroma of roses. She sat up, feeling rose petals cascading off of her torso as she did so. She laughed, scooping up handfuls of the luxuriant petals, rubbing them over her face and throat as she inhaled their potent fragrance.

"Jacob," she murmured with pleasure.

Jacob scooped up more of the silky-soft flower parts, dumping them over her head as he took a seat beside her. She giggled, the first expression of her old humor he had heard since the attack. She had been so sad, so depressed, that it made his heart hurt. The simple parlor trick of the flowers was worth gold if it made her laugh.

"Hello, little flower," he greeted her, leaning forward

to kiss her gently, the scent of roses lifting up from her warm skin and all around them.

"I love you," she whispered, her hands cradling his face as she kissed him once more. "I love that you stay with me even though I know your heart aches to hunt for those who hurt me."

"There will come a time, little love, when I will not be able to stay," he said gently, touching her soft features in the dark with exquisite care.

"I wouldn't expect you to, Jacob. Remember, there is a lioness in my heart as well. She will not be satisfied until she is a part of the destruction of those who tried to murder her young. And the only way I will achieve that now is by residing within your heart and your thoughts as you seek revenge for us both."

Jacob nodded, utterly speechless as emotion choked him into silence. There was so much to feel, he couldn't sort through it all. Love and hate, satisfaction and discontent, joy and rage. It all but destroyed him to hear words like "revenge" and "destruction" coming out of his sweet-natured mate's mouth. She had been born to be a peacekeeper, an Enforcer of great laws, and an impressive warrior in her own right, but that she had reason to hate and to fear . . . Jacob felt even more keenly the sense that he had let her down. Darkness was his to deal with, his to protect her from, and he had failed. It stirred a red haze through his mind when he thought of it, when he felt it. She was there almost instantly, trying to soothe him and ease his frustration, but even her touch in his mind was weak and clearly exhausted. It was as if she was merely a shadow within him, and it simply should not be that way. She should be vibrant and overwhelming him with her energy and love, not this soft-spoken fragility that scraped at the interior of his heart.

"Oh, Jacob," she sobbed softly, her weak body leaning against his as she wrapped slim arms around him.

"Please," she begged him, "please don't let this destroy you. I need you so much. I need you here and at peace."

"I will be here, little love," he murmured into her hair, his voice aching with the tragic pain her tears caused within him. "But I will buy my peace with battle, Bella. For both of us. Once done, I will put it behind me."

"Swear it to me, Jacob, because I know you can't break your word. Especially not to me."

"I swear it, Bella. I will bring us to our enemies, and then leave them on the ground behind us. I will not bring that darkness into our bed, near our child, or anywhere where it will fester. I will come to you with a clear mind, heart, and soul. I swear it to you with all of my love."

"I love you, Jacob," she said softly, hugging him tightly, knowing full well that the only thing that would clear his mind, heart, and soul would be their retribution.

Gideon sat crouched in the shadow of a large boulder, his breath white and hard on the freezing air of the bare start of a Siberian spring. He was not dressed for such weather, but it did not matter. He regulated his body temperature as a secondary thought, a shimmer of warmth visible as it lifted away from the exposed skin around his face and neck. He absently tugged a glove tighter into place on his hand as he watched the activity of the village below him. He easily sensed the pulses of about a hundred creatures, all upright, bipedal and fourlegged varieties. He did not dare to skulk for long because he would be spotted and a point of suspicion if he did. He was able to track the mammalian forms of the Lycanthropes around him well enough, but it became more difficult when they took cold-blooded or avian forms. Any animal around him could Lycanthrope, and he would not sense them all.

A true Lycanthrope could exist in three stages. A single animal of any species imaginable was the first. There was a human form for the second, indistinguishable from any normal mortal who could not see beneath the skin and into their genetic make-up. Most Demons could tell just by their scent that they were not truly human. Gideon suspected this was probably true of other Nightwalkers as well. The third and final form was the Lycanthropic form, a combination of the first and second, the specific animal and the specific human usually as large as a human but sporting the specific attributes of the Lycanthrope's animal form, like the fur and claws if it was a bear, or fangs and wings if it was a bat.

These were the classic forms humans referred to as werewolves. But what most humans did not realize was that Lycanthropes were not just limited to the form of the wolf. In fact, there was hardly an animal that was not represented amongst the Lycanthrope populace.

Gideon could alter his body chemistry to blend in with the scents around him, a glamour that only the most powerful Lycanthropes would be able to see through. He did so as his boots slid down the steep path leading into the narrow valley that housed the village. It was deceptively quaint. Gideon could see that there was method to its placement and its sturdy construction. It was made to withstand the inhospitable weather of a Russian winter, but it also would withstand any form of attack if necessary.

As a rule, Lycanthropes were never far from a variety of armory. Lycanthropes were not chemically adverse to technology, as Demons were. Demons were also not the focus of self-appointed human werewolf hunters. If there was a Nightwalker more well-known to human mythology than Vampires, it was the Lycanthropes. As a result, both races were plagued by those who were overzealous in their attempts to prove the myth was real and to kill the mythical monsters as if it would make them heroes of equally mythic proportions.

Though Lycanthrope natural attacks were formidable on their own, when dealing with overzealous hunters and the like, it was always wise to fight firearm with firearm, so to speak. The Lycanthropes were wise enough not to bring a pair of claws to face an enemy with a gun. They would not have survived long as a species in this era of high technological weaponry had they not understood that basic fact.

Gideon walked around the edges of Siena's village until he was approaching her residence, which consisted of a remarkably camouflaged cave. As he passed the guards, he greeted them coolly. As far as they realized, he carried the scent of Lycanthropy and therefore belonged there.

Siena's residence was a cavern more than it was a cave. More so, it wasn't even simple enough to be called an ordinary cavern. It had been carved out of the center of a mountain and shaped into a breathtaking edifice made completely over into the grandeur of a castle, allowing for an enormity and artistry that included multiple levels and conveniences like light and plumbing. It was all carved out of a reddish brown stone, a massive task that must have taken decades to complete. It was a flawless design, just as Gideon remembered it. The only obvious access to the Queen's castle was by way of that one demure entrance. It could be blocked and guarded off in a heartbeat, protecting the entire village and the Queen's household if necessary. There were outer houses around the castle bailey, just as if it were under a sky instead of a mountain, like any other castle from history. It only lacked the unnecessary moat and portcullis to protect it. It was enough of a fortress and did not need those things to help it.

Gideon walked on, entering the castle common room with confidence and a familiarity that came rushing back to him as he remembered the mapping of rooms and the graceful carvings so painstakingly ground into the stone walls around him. Even the common room was decorated lushly, reflecting Siena's wealth and penchant for the finer things in life. It was a great improvement from the last time he had attended this court. Tapestries, artwork, rich carpeting, and elegant touches of the like that had not been there thirteen years before . . . before Siena had ascended to the throne. The reception area was twice as large as Noah's Great Hall, but it no longer echoed so easily against its own walls as people moved through it as he was doing.

It had been easy to gain entry to the immediate common room, but it would be a different matter completely to get closer to Siena, Gideon understood. The Lycanthrope Queen was no fool. She would not have the access points that led closer to her guarded by anyone less than older, highly skilled Lycanthropes capable of seeing through simple Demon glamours with the mere sniff of a keen nose. Luckily, he was no simple Demon. This, of course, was what Elijah had realized, and had been counting on, when he had chosen Gideon for this dangerous task. No one else would be able to do what he was about to accomplish.

What will you do now?

Just watch. And be very quiet. Lycanthropes have a great variety of abilities, some of which would surprise you. The less you give away, the better.

After what happened with Damien, I believe you, she whispered before falling silent.

He was aware that she did not back away in any other manner, though. She was tense, ready for any possibility, determined to protect him however she could if it came to that. It turned his spirit into a tight spiral of pleasure to feel it, to feel her powerful instinct to protect him. It meant that she was coming to care for him, whether she was ready to admit to that or not. The idea delighted him, far more than he had expected it to.

Gideon tucked it all aside for later examination, though. He needed to stay completely focused on what he was doing. Lycanthrope territory was still, for many intents and purposes, a hostile territory. The war had ended only thirteen years hence, after three hundred years of squabbling and outright attacks led by Siena's father. The previous King had been a warlord, satisfied only when he was battling for property, wealth, or position. But his type was never satisfied. When Demons had proved unbeatable after he had spent years antagonizing them, he had satisfied himself with being a constant burr in Noah's side. Kidnappings, marauding, all forms of torture and hassle, until Noah realized that centuries had gone by and there was not a Lycanthrope alive who had not been tainted by the propaganda against Demons. There would never be peace, not even after the warlord died, if there was no intervention.

And so he had sent Gideon into the King's prisons.

As for tonight, it was clearly a night of justice for the Lycanthrope Queen. By the volume of people coursing in and out of the frontmost throne room, and the line of patient subjects leading into it, it was clear she was very busy dispensing whatever form of law it was that tended to the disputes of her people. Noah held similar days of access once a month. It was required that all members of the Council take part in these days of dispensing law. Each Councillor had their own area of expertise. It was what made the Council so well balanced, as a rule, the troublesome temper of Councillor Ruth notwithstanding. But even she held a useful position. Her constant challenges of their ideas and choices always kept them on their toes. If anyone laid anything before the Council without the proper preparation required to argue their point for the obstinate Ruth, they would most likely fail under her scrutiny. As a result, the laws and actions the Great Council created would perhaps not be so very well thought out as they were.

Gideon was finished observing the movements of those in the nearby rooms. He watched as one group of spectators left the throne room and another began to form. As the guards allowed the group to gain entry, Gideon joined them. He was aware of the guards lifting their heads, reaching out to scent something that was not quite right, but before they could fixate on a target, Gideon was well into the room and mingling with the crowd. That did not mean he could not be spotted at any moment, so rather than wait for someone to grow wise to him, he rapidly strode onto the rich purple carpet that led up to the throne where Siena sat listening to one side of an argument, the other party to the complaint under debate waiting with some impatience to her left.

Siena noted his approach almost instantly, her head coming up suddenly as she fixed her golden eyes on him.

The Queen was in her human form, that of a magnificently beautiful woman with golden hair so pure in color it resembled the color of virgin gold filament. Her hair was almost as long as Legna's, but unlike Legna's silky, wavy fall, Siena's was naturally curled, the large coils about fist thick in circumference as they twisted around and around down the length of her back and torso. She had the features of a cat, full of sly points and curves that made her exotic and lovely. This included ears that came up to delicate, elfin points, the only part of her that did not look quite human, but these could be easily overlooked by anyone not searching for the distinction.

Siena stood up when recognition set in, a soft sound from her alerting her guards, who, without delay, stood between the Queen and the intruder, imposing halberds clutched in their hands. The guards were Minotaurs, enormous and powerful creatures with the look and strength of ten bulls, a height that towered over Gideon's own significant stature, and a warrior prowess that would challenge even Elijah's skills.

Gideon halted his approach, one foot on the first step leading to the throne.

He folded his hands across the top of his thigh and

bowed to Siena with respect, remaining with his head lowered until she decided how to proceed with him. His seeming subservience appeared to put her at ease. She relaxed, sitting down slowly before turning her attention to a nearby servant.

"Jinaeri, clear the court," she instructed to one of her female aides. To the petitioners in midhearing, she smiled comfortingly. "Gentlemen, you will be my guests for the next twenty-four hours, during which we will continue this discussion."

It was clear the solution was more than generous enough to keep them content. They both bowed, all smiles and excited pulses. Siena was famous for her lavish court. It was an honor for commoners to be allowed access to it.

Gideon continued to wait, his head remaining bent as the room was cleared. Though he looked vulnerable, both he and Legna were quite aware of their surroundings. Gideon did become aware of the fact that a great deal of Legna's suspicion and tension was directed toward the lovely Queen seated a mere ten feet away from him.

The sound of the throne room doors closing with a clang was the final indication that they were relatively in private. That was, excluding the two dozen guards standing stiffly at all exits and around the throne itself. Gideon raised his head and met the Queen's speculative gaze, letting the curious gold eyes pick him apart slowly, as if trying to discover his intentions by sheer force of will.

"Disarm him," the Queen commanded sharply.

Instantly, the two throne guards flew at Gideon.

The medic, however, was no longer where he had been. He was, instead, rolling across the floor and out of range of the wicked reach of the Minotaur weaponry.

Gaining his feet with sleek agility, Gideon feinted a lunge at the guard to his left, forcing the Minotaur to anticipate and swing his weapon. The halberd had an impressive momentum to it due to its top-heavy weight. Once the Minotaur committed to the swing, he was virtually defenseless until it was completed and recovered. It was plenty of time for Gideon's enhanced reflexes to give him the advantage.

The next thing the guard knew, he had a Demon flying at him, using his own halberd as a sort of step to propel himself into the air and above the guard's horns. It was a daring maneuver—the horns themselves a dangerous weapon, capable of goring a victim with a single thrust and a twist of the Minotaur's powerful neck muscles. But Gideon was well out of reach, even if the guard hadn't been so startled by the unconventional maneuver. By the time the Minotaur had gathered his thoughts, he was bowled over by a powerful kick to the center of his back. Of course, "bowled over" for a creature of that size meant being driven down onto his knee. Still, it was an impressive feat, even for a Demon.

Gideon turned to face his other opponent, catching the shaft of the other halberd hard in the ribs. The blow literally lifted the Ancient off his feet, and Legna was not the only one to hear his ribs snap in response. However, the injury was nothing to a healer of his remarkable power and skill. The ribs were halfway healed by the time the medic finished rolling with the momentum of the strike.

Gideon was back on his feet, facing off with one guard, eyeing the second, and cocking his head to listen to the soft whisper of his mate as it slid through his thoughts. The Ancient Demon smiled, a rare but impressive show of fangs flickering in the light of the throne room's gas lanterns. It was Legna's strategy he followed as he grabbed one of his thigh blades with incredible speed, sending it flying as he sleekly dodged a halberd swing. He drew the second knife and froze himself into a throwing posture.

"Halt!"

The guards hesitated as the Demon and the Queen shouted the command in tandem. The startled Minotaurs turned perplexed looks to their Queen, each snorting with shock at the sight that greeted them.

The Lycanthrope Queen was sitting back in her throne, her chest rising and falling with her own shock and outright panic as she turned wide eyes onto the haft of the blade that almost touched her temple as it held her pinned by her hair to the back of her throne.

Gideon smiled wider, taunting his opponents with a flip of the blade in his hand.

"And I meant to miss," he said darkly, his eyes gleaming with silver warning.

The throne room was utterly silent except for Siena's breath sounds. Suddenly, she laughed, a short, sultry sound that drew everyone's attention.

"Gideon, you bastard, there's silver in that blade!"

"In both," the Demon corrected, relaxing his stance and returning the second blade to its sheath with a flip his mate was realizing was as characteristic as it was a skilled one-motion maneuver.

The Demon moved to the steps leading to the throne, approaching the Queen in order to do the one thing no one else in the entire castle or village could do. He grasped the handle of the knife and, with a powerful pull, withdrew it from its deep embedding in the wood of her throne. The knife was snugly put away in the following second while Gideon made a respectful retreat back down the stairs. He spared a glance to the guards behind him, watching carefully with senses other than his eyes as one Minotaur extended a hand to help the other back to its feet.

"It has been some time, Gideon, since you have graced Our court," Siena noted, her strong voice ringing echoes throughout the cavernous room as she regained her composure with a sly grin and a shake of her hair. Gideon's keen eyes carefully measured the amount of blood that fell in droplets from the tips of the strands of hair his blade had severed. The injury to the tensile, living hair was incidental because Gideon had never meant her any harm. The small wounds, no more or less painful than about a half dozen paper cuts for the Queen, would heal quickly. Had he meant to harm her, severing a large chunk of the gold filament strands could have easily been the equivalent of cutting off her arm when measured in trauma.

"As I recall, I was your prisoner at the time," he reminded the Lycanthrope Queen. Gideon mentally hushed Legna when she snickered over the idea of the feminine Queen getting the better of him.

"Ah, yes, you are correct. I had almost forgotten. But we did not part on bad terms those many decades back, so I trust you are not intent on exacting some sort of vengeance."

"No, Highness. You treated me quite well for a person of such dubious status. I am, in fact, ever grateful for the generous hospitality you showed me."

The statement managed to hush Legna's laughter more effectively than any of Gideon's warnings had. He was suddenly very aware of her renewed and highly hostile focus on the Lycanthrope female.

"So tell me, Gideon, is it my hospitality you seek tonight?"

There was no mistaking the suggestion in her voice and the sly lift of both a golden brow and one corner of her full lips. The Queen stood up once more, slower this time, allowing her tall body to expose its remarkable charms gradually. She was garbed in a simple golden bra, the brief article of clothing accenting an exquisite and full pair of breasts. She wore a thick golden chain that linked around her slim hips, holding a couple of thick veils over the front and back of her long legs. A thinner chain circumscribed her trim waist, the glittering gold drawing attention to the muscular fitness of defined abdominal muscles and the deep inward curves of her sides. The only other thing she wore was the collar of her office, the gold and moonstone choker a one-of-a-kind creation that marked her for who she was to any Nightwalker who saw it, Lycanthrope or otherwise.

She moved to the top step leading from the throne itself, looking down to Gideon as she slowly began to descend. Every motion of her body was a purposeful dance in sensuality. Gold shifted and twinkled flirtatiously, gossamer veiling fluttering with the breeze of her movement. Lycanthropes tended to be highly sexual beings, even more so than Demons, and it radiated from every living cell of the Queen's advancing body. These Nightwalkers were not merely genetic carriers of animal instincts from long ago; they were pure animalism, living a third of their lifetime as little more than an intelligent beast. That fact eddied from the beautiful Queen like raw pulsations of nature.

Gideon was aware of a soft, antagonistic hostility nibbling at the edges of his thoughts and realized the source was Legna, who, for all her control and detachment, was apparently just as susceptible to simple jealousy as anyone else. The Queen halted her approach about three steps away from him, her posture held with proud perfection as she once more took his measure.

Sweet Destiny, you would think a Queen could afford the entire dress, Legna remarked dryly.

Gideon realized he was trapped between potentially unpleasant circumstances. It would be difficult to tender goodwill to the Queen while maintaining peace with this different emotion for Legna. His goal, in the end, was not to upset either of them, and at the moment it seemed very unlikely that he could manage that. It was enough to ruffle even his practiced calm as a soft sheen of moisture appeared on his forehead.

"You come armed to my home. Why is that?"

"Would you do any less when walking into the den of

those who have held you in threat in the past?" Gideon countered. "If invited to Noah's court, would you relinquish the weapons you have, even now, concealed in your hair?"

"You were always the shrewd one." She laughed, her smiles and humor lessening the tension in the room considerably. She came closer to the Demon, her motions more businesslike as she did so. She walked on, and he fell into step beside her. She led him farther back into the cavern, a slow, strolling tour of rooms he had lived amongst once, quite some time ago.

So long as her bedroom was not one of those rooms, Legna warned, her jealousy a fiercely tangible thing.

No, Neliss. *I can assure you it was not.*

And I am to take your word on that?

I would prefer if you did. However . . .

"I see you have not yet settled on a mate," Gideon said to Siena.

"And I see that you have, despite all your proclamations that you never would. I can smell her all over you. She must be . . . delicious." Siena's phraseology was provocative, making Gideon smile inwardly with the imagery it churned up.

I shall have to fully test that theory, he mused.

There was no response, but he knew Legna was too flustered by her mixed emotions of the moment to formulate one.

"I recommend it," he offered amiably. "Especially in your situation. It is far more satisfying than maintaining the status of a virgin Queen, Siena."

Virgin? Her?!

"Yes," Siena said, a crooked smile spreading over her lush mouth. "As delightful as that sounds, I can easily forgo the cravings of the body if it keeps me from being forced to mate with some male I will end up chained to for the rest of my life." It was clear by the contempt in her voice that, for all her natural sexuality, she'd rather roast on a hunter's spit. "It is quite unfair," she remarked, "that I should be plagued by this outdated, obnoxious genetic predisposition to chose one and only one mate for the entire span of my existence." She sighed with lascivious drama. "Imagine the fun I could be having." She became serious instantly, speaking to Gideon as the confidant he had been for her so many years ago. "I have no need for a King, and therefore, no desire to take a lover who would become one. So, a virgin I will remain, very likely to the end of my days."

"Those words almost have a familiar ring to them," he mused.

"Yes, I know. And now you have a mate." She cocked her head, taking a deep breath as she drew in his scent with obvious curiosity. "You are lucky, Gideon," she said with honest surprise and pleasure for him. "You have Imprinted on your mate and she on you. A rare phenomenon for your people, as I understand it. I wish you joy of it."

"Thank you," he responded graciously.

"But perhaps if you bedded the wench, she wouldn't be so jealous of me."

Gideon could not help the release of a groan as he was caught between Siena's wink of mischief and Legna's outraged exclamation in his head.

"Siena, I did not come here to get myself a dubiously cozy bed in the proverbial doghouse. So, if you would please have mercy?"

"As you wish. Tell me why you have come," she said as they entered a room filled with enormous fountains of gold.

Surrounding these fountains was a bath occupied with Lycanthropes of all shapes, breeds, and sexes. All these creatures were in various states of furring, feathering, and undress as they bathed in water that spread the length and width of a football field before the two of them. Gideon wisely kept his eyes averted, not wishing to inadvertently condemn an innocently bathing female to the wrath of a jealous Demon, should he set eyes on her nude body by accident.

"Have you any reason to suspect there may be a faction of your people who have taken it into their heads to resurrect the war by attacking my people?" he asked the Queen.

Siena turned to look at him, the coined gold of her eyes brightening as she speculated a moment.

"I am glad you do not think I had anything to do with this."

"No, Siena. Though there are still many on the Council who fear your intentions, the years I spent with you during my incarceration have had an effect on both of our perspectives about each other's species." Gideon smiled because he recalled that that had been Noah's intention all along. Gideon had endeared himself with his grace and his deep wisdom to a young girl who would one day become Queen. "With the exception of testing my prowess with throne-room pranks, you are above picking petty fights. I know we have done nothing to provoke you to do anything as strong as what has happened."

"Well, if there are rebels among my people, I usually find them quick enough. Explain what happened."

Gideon did with efficiency and a minimum of detail. The Lycanthrope Queen listened intently.

"No. Gideon, my people may pick fights with yours, but to organize an act of such specificity and cruelty? The survival of our young is the highest priority in our moral code, and because it is high in our esteem, we consider it monstrous to do anything that resembles an attack on the young of even our worst enemies."

"I sensed you would say as much, but you understand it was important that I make absolutely certain. For all we were aware, you may have had a social criminal on the loose that we simply had not heard about."

"You are correct, of course. It is strategically unwise to leave avenues of possibility unexplored. If I have learned one thing about you and, I believe, your people, it's that you are not foolish in matters of strategy." She paused for a slow beat. "Gideon, I believe it is time for Noah and me to sit down together. At the very least, we should arrange the parameters for an exchange in ambassadors. With such positions set up and exchanged, there will be less opportunity for these gaps in information. The only thing that will come from not communicating with one another is mistrust and mistake. Before you know it, we will be returning to war for reasons we won't even be clear on."

"Do you think your people are ready to accept a Demon in your court?"

"I believe enough time has passed. I would request you for the position, except I know your Council duties and your new mate will be keeping you quite occupied. Perhaps you can suggest someone in your stead?"

"I am certain I can. As for your half of the exchange, be certain to choose someone very smart, very eager, and very unprejudiced toward our society as your ambassador. It will take an open mind to open the closed ones in the Demon court. Meanwhile, I will courier your request for a meeting to Noah. I will send you word of his response myself."

"I will be awaiting you. In the meantime, I can search through my intelligences to see if there is something that I may have overlooked."

Siena turned to face him, slipping a ring off her finger and handing it to him. She knowingly managed the exchange without touching him.

"This will allow you to come and go in my court in your honest form without fear of being accosted. That is, until we designate the ambassador who will wear it after you. There is no further need for tricks of camouflage. I prefer to know the true nature of that which approaches me. You might remember that for the future."

"I never doubted your abilities to find me out, Siena.

That is why I shed the glamour as soon as possible. I thank you for your information, and for this." He closed the ring in a secure fist. He bowed to her with an elegant flair that made the Lycanthrope Queen smile.

A moment later, he was yanked away, disappearing with a definitive pop, as if being rescued from the jaws of death. The jealous motivation behind Gideon's removal sent the Queen into gales of laughter, forcing her to take a seat when she developed a stitch in her side. The possessive actions of Gideon's mate tickled her with their obvious lack of reasonable logic. If the unseen woman had only thought about it a moment, she would have known it was an utter impossibility and she need not have been so insecure. After all, there was no way Siena would ever allow herself to be attracted to a male, least of all a Demon male.

Chapter 10

Gideon turned to look for Legna the moment he materialized inside the manse. She was not in the immediate area of the parlor, and he moved into the hallway to search for her. Instinct told him to head up the marble staircase, and he did so, taking three steps at a time. He headed straight for his bedroom, moving into the open doorway and spotting her at last.

She had chosen the comfort and quiet of the window seat beneath the largest of all the stained glass windows. She sat with her legs curled beneath her and her shawl draping carelessly off one shoulder. The moonlit colors of the window flashed over her bared skin. A large tree just outside the glass swayed wildly in the wind. The moving branches played tricks with the moonlight outside, sending the color into an illusion of movement that looked like little tinted fairies dancing over her skin.

Legna turned her head to look at him and directly moved to her feet. Her shawl dropped away completely, clearly the last thing she felt needed her attention. She hurried over to him, plainly lighting up with the satisfaction that she would have her arms around him in barely a moment. The sound of silk and beads disrupted the momentary silence of the room, the creak and rush of the tempestuous wind outside almost drowning the simple sounds of her approach.

She was eager elegance as she threw her arms around his neck and allowed herself to be dragged up into his embrace. For an endless minute, her body clung to his at any and every contact point they could collaboratively manage. Gideon buried his face into the sweet curve of her neck, breathing deeply of her warm, living scent as he tried not to hug the breath out of her.

To his consternation, she only allowed him to hold her for a moment before she pushed back and squirmed out of his grasp. She reached for his left hand, using both of her hands to pry his fingers open even though he put up no resistance. The gold and moonstone ring resting in his palm was plucked from its place and tossed carelessly across the highly polished wooden floor, the sound of the bauble skidding far into the darkness seeming to satisfy her.

"You will wear nothing of hers," Legna told him, her tone brooking no argument.

The dictate amused him. He had no intention of wearing the ring. It was for whomever Noah chose as an ambassador for Siena's court, and that most certainly was not going to be him.

"Jealous, *Neliss?*" he teased her as he ringed a hand around her neck and pulled her closer once more. "It is not like you to indulge in such petty emotions."

Legna frowned at him, tensing against his efforts to draw her nearer to him.

"You think my feelings to be petty?" she demanded of him. "Is it just my jealousy you see that way, or all my feelings?"

The temperamental heat in the question gave the Ancient pause. He had not returned home looking for another fight, even if this, too, ended up just being an exercise of his wits. He had not thought he'd have to face such silly possessiveness from Legna. She was usually so well balanced with logic. It was her intellect above all else that made her so compatible with him.

"Oh, I see," she hissed suddenly and softly, her entire body going stiff and resistant against his. "And I suppose all of this seems childish and irrational to you?"

"Of course it does," he said with impatience. "If it were me acting this way, would you not think me foolish and irrational?"

"Foolish! Now I am foolish to you?" Magdelegna wrenched free of him, twisting out of his reach. "I understand," she breathed hotly. "Even after all of this, after everything we have said to one another, you *still* think me a child! To you, this is all just some temperamental little tantrum!" Her quicksilver eyes were burning and furious as she ran her gaze down his length with unconcealed contempt. "Well, at least I *have* emotions! At least I am normal and real and have a live and beating heart that feels its way through life!"

"You mean you let yourself behave recklessly because of the whims of your feelings," he countered sharply. "A moment ago you could not wait to hold me, now you reject me . . . all because of emotional caprice. Tell me, Legna, what benefit you find in that. Can you not see that this, what you are doing now, is how wars start? A simple surge in temper, and before you even realize it, everything snowballs out of control. Wallow in it for yourself if you must, but do not wish it on me!"

"You pompous, self-righteous ass!" she uttered, her face flushing with a beautiful fury that almost distracted Gideon from the point he wanted to drive into her. He understood that she could not help her emotionalism to a degree. After all, she was an empath and emotions were what empaths primarily dealt with, but she needed to learn control of herself or this would never work smoothly between them. "Of course," she said with drowning sarcasm in response to his thoughts, "the fault must be mine. I am the child and you are the Ancient. You could not possibly be wrong about this."

"Legna," he warned tightly.

"Let us test the theory empirically, shall we?" she countered in a rush of breath and furiously intent eyes. "Show me. Show me the great benefits of this almighty control of yours, Gideon. The ability to share my heart has given me close family, dear friends, and the spirit to help others in desperate need of me. Have your cold, unfeeling ways given you these things? Where is your family? Where are your friends? Oh, you help others and wield a mighty power, Ancient, but do you care if you succeed or fail? Do you care if your patients live or die?"

"Of course I do!" he growled at her, his body surging up instinctively to intimidate hers as she hammered away at the tender spots in his psyche. "Do not dare accuse me of insensitivity when it comes to my patients, Magdelegna. You know nothing of what I—" Gideon broke off before he could finish the temper-driven sentence, his fingers curling into his palms as he tried to take a deep breath to steady himself.

"Feel?" she finished for him regardless of his checking himself. "You are damn right I know nothing of what you feel! You will not let me know it! You will not even allow yourself to know it! Tell me, Gideon, what do you see as the benefit of all this steadiness and flat affectation?"

"Things it is best you never come to understand," he returned stiffly.

"Sweet Destiny, do you even hear the condescension you are spewing?"

"It is not condescension!"

Gideon wanted to turn his back to her, to walk away and put distance between them, but he could not force his body to comply. Even as they fought, the pull of her allure remained steadfast and powerful inside of him. As strong as his desire was to push her away, the need for her was even stronger. If that weren't enough, she was taunting him with sins he had left long in the past. Oh, she was certainly ignorant of the fire she toyed with, and if he had any say in the matter, he was going to keep her ignorant. Those sins would be kept deep in the past and had no place in the life of the man he had become as a result.

"Gideon." Her entire tone suddenly altered, from one of fury to something more coaxing and much more dangerous to his peace of mind. When Legna wanted to, she could use the power of her voice to lure others. It lured him even when she wasn't trying, so now he was doubly tempted to give in to her sway over him. "I see the gentleness in you and your tenderness when you heal. This tells me how very much you do care, even though you keep yourself so very still both outside and in. But why is it you feel this is so necessary?"

Legna moved closer to him, banishing her anger of moments ago and driving herself to get answers from him by any means she could possibly manage. She reached out to touch his chest where his leather coat hung open, her fingertips moving softly against the cotton of his shirt. She closed her eyes and openly tuned her empathic senses to him, seeking even the smallest reflection of how he felt when she came this near to him. She needed to know he felt something. Anything. Else, how could she possibly spend all the rest of her days with a man who refused to feel anything for her? For anyone?

But despite his cold, emotionless armor at present, she had felt those distinct cracks breaking through him and ebbing into her today. Emotions. Small shows of emotional surges that he always quickly managed or suppressed, but he had them just the same, despite his quick cover-ups. She had even thought he was enjoying them . . . enjoying her and her effect on his calloused demeanor. She had been a shadow in his mind for all of it. She couldn't be wrong about this!

With her hands slowly sliding up his chest, she purposely allowed him to fall victim to the spell that always overcame them whenever they touched. She used it to her advantage, working it as an avenue into the vault concealing everything he was capable of feeling, if only he would permit himself. She hooked her fingers over his broad shoulders and pushed, until she was urging them to shrug back. The leather coat dropped off his arms a moment later, but she caught it and stepped away slightly to fold it over the back of a nearby chair. She didn't remove her touch completely, however, letting her lingering fingers keep him connected to her whether he was aware of it or not.

Gideon did not understand what she was up to, but it was hard for him to remain tense or on his guard when the warmth of her touch was soaking into him. Still, he would not let her think she was going to overpower his arguments this way.

"You will never change my mind on this matter, Magdelegna," he said with soft heat as she moved closer to him once more. "You have to accept that this is the kind of man I am. I have been thus for twice your lifetime or better. To think of changing me, Legna, is an exercise in folly."

Legna seemed to ignore him for the present, moving her fairylike touch to his gloved hands, slowly working the material free as if time no longer mattered to her. She was completely immersed in every movement, every sensation, and every reaction her activities elicited. It seemed strange that such a simple task would feel so erotic, but it was exactly that.

"Just because you have been unchanged and unmoved for so long," she said quietly, "does not mean it is the way you should stay."

After dropping his gloves onto the chair where she had placed the coat, Legna came around to face him head-on, her eyes stubborn and challenging him in such a way that he found her wickedly seductive. A deep, instinctual part of him bucked and reared at the way she boldly confronted him, demanding he prove his worth to her. Gideon shook his head, trying to regulate his focus and the reflexive rushing of his breath and blood as she tempted him in soft, minute movements and ideals that he knew from experience were flawed. Gideon held himself as still as he could as she moved slowly around him, her hot, thorough eyes scanning every inch of his body before her fingertips slid around the lower strap of his left thigh sheath. The way she freed the joined buckle was nothing unusual, but when she finished and curled her fingers so that her nails glided up the inside of his thigh as they traveled to the upper strap, Gideon's entire body and soul flexed with instantaneous arousal.

Legna heard him utter an oath beneath a guttural sound of stimulation. A sly, knowing smile touched her lips. She dropped the freed sheath on top of the rest of his discarded objects. Then, purposely allowing her hand to trail over his lower back from one hip to the other, she passed behind him to come to the thigh on the opposite side. She did the same thing she had with the first, but it still sent an unimaginable shock of stimulation through him, as if he had not been expecting it.

As she discarded the last weapon with one hand, the other remained on the tightly flexed muscle of his upper leg. He stood so still, flexed so hard with awareness, his attention riveted on every movement and every touch she made, and she knew on a deep, primitive level that she had his desires and attentions literally at her fingertips.

"Think for a moment, Gideon, about the positive and rushing delight the best of feelings can bring to you. You cannot see those that are negative and denounce the whole lot of your emotions because of the harm they can do. Think of what you are feeling now, in this moment. Would you throw this away so easily?"

"This is lust, a-a physiological state of arousal caused by our compatible chemistries . . ."

"Oh, is that all?" she asked him provocatively as she drew her lush and warm body up close to him, ignoring his stiff resistance and cuddling up to him warmly so she could rub her face against a pectoral muscle with kittenish pleasure. "Then why do you not control your body, Gideon? A Body Demon of your age and skill surely has the power to stop reacting to any of this . . . physiological state of arousal . . . even in spite of the Imprinting. Why do you not stop the racing of your heart, the burning of your skin . . ." Legna let her fingertips ghost down over his belly and then dipped below his belt to caress the hard and heavy erection that strained behind the soft fabric of his trousers. "Why not ease away these tattletale signs that tell me you are far more engaged than you wish to admit to me?"

Gideon snapped. There was nothing else he could call it. One minute he was struggling to breathe and staring down the knowingly seductive squint of her eyes, and the next he had his hand around her throat and was heaving all of his weight against her. He forced her to step back in rapid retreat from the power of the raw strength and the fury of emotion surging out of him. Legna had no chance to react or even catch her breath until he had driven her down onto his bed and was nose to nose with her while his quicksilver eyes burned with his rage.

"Do not play with me, little girl!" he hissed into her face as he threw a leg over her and boxed her in beneath his weight. "Your beauty and your seductions of my body and my mind will fail! You should crave that they fail, because I promise you that you do not wish to meet my unfettered temper, Magdelegna! The last time it saw the light of day I screamed for the heads of an entire race! Stop trespassing in this territory, I warn you!"

"This is my territory," she countered with a heated rasp as she grasped hold of his wrist where it was secured against her throat. "As an empath and as your mate, this is my territory! *You* are my territory! Mine! Ugly or beautiful, raging or passionate, you are mine for the rest of our existence, Gideon, just as you claim I am yours, and I will not let you feed yourself to me in select little bites and bits! I will have all of you or I will turn my back on you and take *nothing at all!*"

"Do not threaten me, you insolent girl!" he roared into her face. But Legna felt the clench of terror that gripped him inside and out. It was the reflexive emotion she had been seeking . . . needing. She needed to know that he couldn't easily go on without her. She needed him to know it, too. He had to realize that his world had to change to accept her. He could not keep on as he always had, with her as a lonely little satellite that served his purposes only when he thought to make use of her.

"Are you of so little faith in yourself, Gideon, that you do not think you have learned from those terrible mistakes you once made?" she asked him, her voice so suddenly soft in the echoes of their shouting that it fell harder against him for it. "Because I have always seen in you a man of unparalleled confidence in himself. I never thought you were the sort who would let his past mistakes paralyze him in such a way."

"I am not paralyzed," he rasped out on rapid-fire breaths. "I am in control, Magdelegna. I need to be in control of myself! You do not understand what I have the power to do. You do not conceive of the responsibility my position in this society calls for."

"Yes, I do," she countered gently. "Do you forget so easily how I was raised at the knee of our King? All of my life I have seen him struggle between his natural-born temperament, the one his fiery element sets so deeply within him, and the responsibility he has to all of our people. I have known for a great many years that it was your lessons most of all that taught him to control what he felt so he would never harm anyone in his anger. But, Gideon, it was *my* lessons that taught him to indulge his passions safely and with pleasure. I taught him how to love deeply, despite the losses he has suffered. I guided him to the ways of indulging his fiercest emotions without any harm coming to him or anyone else. Do you not trust me to do the very same for you?"

"You are asking me to destroy a dam centuries in the making, Legna," he said hoarsely, a fine tremor rolling through him that she felt like a vibration. "One created to protect lives and our culture."

"Lashing down what you feel never protected any of us," she said as she reached to caress his face with tender touches. "It was learning right from wrong, coming to the understanding that you had made grievous mistakes, and the actions you took to guide this society into a moral rightness that saved our people from themselves. Now I am sent to you by Destiny to guide you back to those feelings you have denied yourself for too long. Did you think you could have this Imprinting and not give your heart to it? To me?"

"I . . ." Gideon swallowed as he realized she was right. He had, at most, feared she would not come to love him, that someone as sensitive as she was would shun him for all his mistakes. Never once had he considered his return emotions and her need for them.

Never once had he thought she would make him feel . . . so much.

Gideon stared down at her, the hand held around her neck long since eased into absent tracings of her jaw and ear. He realized he was memorizing her, by shape and by the feel of her, mapping her point by point so he would always know every special nuance she bore. He became aware then that he'd left the marks of his fingers in the soft skin of her throat. Instantly his heartbeat stuttered and he was awash with renewed dread for the havoc his uncontrolled temper could wreak.

"Only if you constantly cork it up, stuff it away inside you, and turn away from it. Pretending your anger does not exist is a flawed plan," Legna counseled him as her fingers sank fiercely into his hair. "Not to mention every other volatile emotion you try to ignore. You need to find a safe release for all your passions, Gideon."

Legna watched him carefully, so she easily saw the sly change that swept through his expression and then felt the bent of his mind as he focused suddenly and sharply on her features: the shape of her lips, the curve of her jaw near her ear, and the length of her throat. He smiled just a little, his fingers gliding up over her lips so he could gently toy with her mouth.

"Will you be my release, *Neliss?*" he speculated aloud. "Will it be this mouth that devours my hottest desires? Can such delicate ears tolerate the fury of my cries? Will your pulse beat in sympathy with mine whenever I am in need?"

"Yes," she whispered readily, her heart already pounding out a hard rhythm. "I will be whatever you need. All that you need. Just so long as you feel your need, Gideon."

Gideon knew then the full scope of his need for Legna. For the first time he truly allowed himself to feel what had been growing inside of himself from the moment he had first grabbed hold of her in her brother's gardens those years ago. The whiplash effect of the desire and longing rushing through him was overpowering. He balked at it, but she grabbed at him tightly and drew him down until their lips touched.

"I do not want to hurt you," he breathed into her mouth, his blood rushing in his ears and burning hot in his veins. "We were overwhelming together even when I was keeping myself in check. What if . . . ?"

"Do not ask questions, Gideon. Simply feel your way to the answers. And I know, in my deepest heart, that you could never truly hurt me. Not unless you denied me."

"I cannot. Not anymore."

Legna felt the raw truth of that. Protective restraints and exercises in discipline crumbled and fell to the wayside inside of him as he slowly began to invite the possibilities. Then he let it all soak into him, like a rapidly filling sponge. She became dizzy with the sudden and powerful rush of it, his emotions so untried yet so pure and potent. There were so many waiting to be exercised, but there was no denying what came raging to the front of it all, demanding first attention.

"Yes," she moaned softly against his damply stroking lips. "I feel how you need me now."

"Need? How paltry a word for what I am feeling," he said a bit dangerously. His broad, strong hand ran in a sharp and sudden line down over the center of her body. It sought the hem of her skirt and found access to her bare skin beneath it. Legna gasped raggedly as his fingers burned a path up the inside of her leg, skimming up the flesh of her inner thigh. "I am going to devour you, Magdelegna," he promised her, the darkness of his cravings coming to bear on her fully at last. "You wanted to know my passions? Allow me to introduce them to you."

Legna was so focused on the approach of his stroking hand between her legs that she barely heard him. But when she felt the sudden nip of his teeth against her lip she looked up into his smelted, liquid mercury eyes.

"My first desire, *Nelissuna*, is to see you natural and nude. Then I will *feel* you natural and nude . . . beneath my hands, my body, and, most especially, my mouth."

He sealed the invitation with a crushing kiss, a cross between wild heat and a desperation that transcended the demands of his body. What he described was wholly physical; however, what he wanted to derive from it was purely emotional satisfaction. He wanted to make her his. His primitive side demanded he mark her in every way imaginable, but more than that he would heavily stamp her with the feelings she had demanded from him.

Legna's head was spinning from stimulus and psychometric devastation. Some sort of defense mechanism made her grab hold of him, and she sharply rolled her weight until their positions were reversed and she was above him as he lay on his back. The assertive move made her heart leap with eager and anxious anticipation, her blood hurrying hotly through her as that dominant woman inside of her surged forward to take control once more. She nipped at his lips again and again, then devoured him in one wet, burning kiss after another.

Now both of his hands had found their way beneath her skirts and he gripped her strong thighs as she sat astride his hips. Gideon tried to lie very still, with the exception of a fine tremor that vibrated through his entire body, because if he moved he was going to start ripping away her clothing and he didn't want to delve into that raw place just yet. He wanted to save it and savor it for when he was claiming her with his longing and desperate body. He withstood the feel of her fingers as she unbuttoned the collar of his shirt and then rapidly worked her way down to the waistband of his breeches. She parted his shirt, her hands moving the cloth aside with bold strokes, her torso rising so she could fix her gaze with great longing on the expanse of his chest. Her eyes slid closed as she braced herself against his warm flesh and bent to taste his skin with a lengthy flick of her tongue.

It was a wonder Gideon didn't explode apart on the spot. He had never felt such an overwhelming sensation of pleasure from so slight an action in all of his vast life. He groaned deeply, savagely, as her moist tongue slipped over one flat nipple and then the other.

Gideon sat up suddenly, sending her sinking into his lap as he hastily shed his shirt for her. That was when she first saw the remaining lividity of the bruises across his ribs. She reached to touch him over the injured place, her fingertips gliding with gentleness over him.

"Why do you not heal yourself completely?" she asked him.

"Because it is not necessary. My natural processes will

remove it by dawn. What is natural to your body is sometimes what is best for it."

"Oh. I see," she said with a softly cunning smile.

Her curious touch was killing him. Not because he was in any pain, aside from the agony of her seductive and thorough exploration, but because he had never needed anyone or anything so much in all of his life the way he needed her. And it was the tenderness and concern of her probing fingers that affected him most deeply. He was completely unused to having someone care for him. Someone who showed concern over his well-being instead of assuming that since he was an Ancient and powerful healer, he had no need of concern or compassion. Legna's eyes lifted to his as she felt the loneliness and sadness of the thought that was drifting through him, understanding that it was her actions that had stirred them and her actions that would dismiss them.

Her mate was beginning to understand an emotion she had always taken somewhat for granted, the one she had grown up with and maintained all her life. He was coming to realize the soothing balm that having someone to come home to could have on a soul. His psyche was warming, slowly but surely, and all because of her Imprinting on him. *She* was teaching the Ancient, the one Demon whom she had always thought of as knowing more than even history itself did, in her one true area of expertise. She was guiding him into the realm of his abandoned emotions. Just as he was trying to teach her the advantages in the balance between predatory instinct and civilization, she was showing him how to temper his feelings when he had to and how to abandon himself to them in order to have an existence of color and light and life.

"My light. My life," he insisted aloud, his hand slipping beneath her hair and around her neck, coaxing her forward until she was once more cuddled up against him, her mouth turned up in order to easily accept the kiss he was bringing to her.

The intensity of the kiss, and the emotions pouring from him and into her, brought tears to her eyes. She surged up into the touch of his mouth, bringing him deeper and closer with her lips, tongue, and soaring feelings. She filled him with her compassion and her understanding, her trust and her absolution, and, most of all, she poured her heart into his, the part of her that was starting to love him, no matter what his sins and flaws might be.

The deluge of her emotions flooding into him packed a punch more powerful than halberds and Minotaurs ever could have. Gideon felt a sound of raw emotion vibrating within the joined haven of their mouths and realized he was the one to utter it. The depth of it brought tears to Legna's eyes, and he felt as though his heart was about to tear itself into shreds because it had no idea how to handle what she was pouring into it. *She was so wrong*, he thought to himself. She had claimed that one day he would possibly become her hero, her savior.

But it was she who was saving him.

Legna was the one to finally break the soulful kiss, gently touching her bruised lips over his jaw, his cheekbones, and even the dark brush of his lashes.

"*Nelissuna*," he said, his voice throaty and soft.

"I am here. I will always be here," she soothed him sweetly, meeting his gaze when he brushed a finger under her chin to tilt her head back.

"Promise me, *Neliss*," he said hoarsely. "I have heard those who speculate that I am indestructible, but I swear on my soul that it will kill me to ever lose you."

"I will always be here," she reiterated as strongly as her heart could manage.

He reached to caress her face with warm, tender knuckles.

"Do not leave me, *Neliss*." He was pleading with her,

unashamed of the need and emotion his voice reflected. "Sleep beside me today and all the days to come."

She nodded silently, feeling the relief that sang through him so keenly that it made her throat ache with compassion. He was a creature of such enormous power and indomitable will, but her words now had the power to save or destroy him. It was an awesome realization and a profound responsibility, but she accepted it without reservation.

It was the last consideration she would give to responsibility.

Her entire focus, as well as her body, was flung down beneath Gideon's once more. He loomed over her, his bare, tanned skin hot to her touch as she clung to his shoulders. Before she even realized where his hands had gone, he'd unzipped her gown, loosening the bodice dramatically. He peeled silk and beading away from her skin, exposing her to air much colder than the temperature of their excited bodies. Her nipples tightened under the stimulus as well as beneath the avaricious stare of her lover.

"Ah . . . see, I knew you would be this way," he confessed in a barely audible whisper. "Not just that you are so easily responsive to me, but this color . . ." He reached out to gently stroke the darkly tanned tips of her breasts, first with his fingertips, then with breathy touches of his lips. "Do you feel how this excites me, *Neliss?*"

Legna understood that he wasn't referring to his physical response, although there was plenty of that. He meant the raw surge of possessive craving for her and her alone. She connected with him as no one else had since he had been an unrefined fledgling. Oh, he'd been forced to relent to instances of physical lust before, the Hallowed moons demanding it of him as they did everyone else, but every touch he shared with her made his heart and soul ache with emotion. The unexercised feelings tumbled and jumbled against her, but then his mouth or hands would close around her and they would find focus and set themselves in clarity.

He loved her, everything about her, and he had done so for more years than he might ever admit to aloud. As Gideon stripped away her delicate dress, he worshipped every inch of her revealed skin with kisses and caresses made partially of fiery craving and mostly of devotion. Legna stretched out beneath him, blinking back the rush of tears wetting her eyes as she finally began to learn exactly who he was . . . and how he felt. Who ever would have thought a male so potent and so confident would deem himself unworthy of a girl like her? This understanding made her realize that despite the hundreds of referrals to her youth, she had long ago impressed herself on him as a lady of quality who deserved only the best their race had to offer. So he had never dared come close to her, despite the fact that he was considered the most esteemed of their breed. Deep within himself he had thought that if they'd only known the truth, the Demon people who so highly respected him would shun him as he had expected her to do. He thought a thousand-year-old crime was just as unforgivable now as ever.

Not one of us has the right to judge you, Gideon.

You have every right to judge me, love.

He raised his head to meet her gaze, turning slightly to nuzzle against the hand she held against his cheek.

"You are my one and truest mate, *Neliss*. If I am going to be the same to you, I must earn my place beside you."

"But—" Legna broke off with a gasp when she felt him surge forward against her, driving his hips between her thighs until he had situated himself tightly against her, his broad torso hovering over her so she felt cast beneath his shadow. Unlike her, he was still clothed from the waist down, but there was tremendous suggestion and blatant need in the hardness of the body nestling against hers.

"Shall I do it this way? Through your body? Shall I gain

every inch of progress with every cry of pleasure I elicit from you? I know it in my soul now that only through your love will I find my absolution. Perhaps I have known it all along and that was why I was forbidding myself to reach for it. But I have waited so long, Magdelegna. So very long."

She did not need to be an empath to hear the pain breaking in his voice.

"Is it my body that will give you succor? It is yours to take, then, Gideon," she whispered to him, pulling his head down until her lips brushed gently against his ear. "You are already in my heart."

She felt the start that jolted through him and readily met his doubting look when he sought her expression for confirmation. He must have seen what he was searching for, because she felt a fine shudder run through him. She felt his hands clenching into the bedclothes at her shoulders as his eyes slid closed. Unsure if he was arguing for or against what she was trying to give to him, she reached to stroke confident hands over his shoulders and down his back. Her fingertips then glided over the tight cut of his backside and clung hard to him, drawing him deeper into the embrace of her legs as she wound them around his.

"Legna."

Gideon was amazed he'd managed to get the word past his lips. Everything inside of him felt as if it had become petrified, seized with the solid rigidity of an arousal beyond anything that should be possible. She was past beautiful. She was an inconceivable perfection. There were no words in any of the languages he knew to voice what he was thinking and feeling as he watched her turn a knowing little smile on him, as if she were flaunting her total power to captivate him with just her existence.

"I am waiting for you," she said, her voice low and

sultry and as tempting as the beckoning curves of her body.

Gidon recovered her hands, catching them in his and pinning them to the bed, his body lurching roughly against her as he seized her lush mouth in a kiss. She was caught between the bed at her back and the unforgiving steel of his hard male body. His unchecked aggression delighted her and she made a noise of appreciation low in her breast. She laced her fingers between his, holding his hands tightly in the implausible event that he might try to withdraw them.

He was bruising their mouths with the ferocious need that burned through him, but she gave as much as he did to the erotic twist of lips and tongues. Her teeth scored his lip again, making him pull back and look into her face with an animalistic intensity. In an instant he crossed her arms high above her head, pressing her hands back against the bed and leaving her bare body vulnerable to him.

He switched his hold on her hands so they were both trapped beneath only one of his. Legna was breathing so hard with the anticipation of his next decision that she became a little light-headed. Then his freed hand was slipping over her belly, a bold, masculine caress that scorched her soft skin. He rested his mouth on the curve of her neck that blended into the crest of her shoulder. She felt his hand coast up her rib cage to embrace the full weight of her breast.

She cried out from the stimulation, her body jolting in response. Legna felt wild, liquid heat pour down her body, the rush of it dampening her thoroughly between her legs. He made another territorial vocalization, making her shudder when he released the hold of his mouth in order to push past her hair and whisper into her ear.

"*Neliss*," he murmured, his hand sliding away from her breast, down her ribs and belly. "I can smell your scent," he told her, his breath as hot as the meaning of his words and the path of his hand.

Legna dropped her head back, feeling his hand pressing her back into the bed as it traveled to the southern regions of her trembling torso. His palm was pressed flat against her as he reached the center of the span between her hips.

"Gideon!" she gasped as his touch feathered half an inch closer to her heat and the moist scent that had lured him there.

"Darling," he corrected her, making very sure she felt him withdraw slightly.

She squeezed her eyes tightly shut, trembling so hard she couldn't understand how she was still breathing. She understood him perfectly, but instead of complying, she pushed up and into his body. The slow movement rubbed her suggestively over the unmistakable bulge still trapped within the confines of his clothing. Instinctively his hand moved around to the lower curve of her spine, using the counterpressure to keep her against the uncontrollable surge of his hips.

He swore through gritted teeth, giving her a much better idea of what the word meant now that she was hearing it in context for the second time. She laughed, a low, breathy chuckle that reflected her recognition of her power over the desires of his flesh.

Gideon released her hands, his bold touch caressing her breasts, rubbing and pulling gently on the thrusting tips until she moaned and shuddered with the spears of arousal that lanced through her entire body. She reached to slide her fingers into his hair, holding his mouth and tongue to her neck, which he was feasting on in slow and purposely erotic ways.

Approaching the vee of her hips once more, Gideon could feel the edges of the pool of liquid heat that lay just beyond his fingertips, and he craved the feel of the exotic fluid as well as the sensitive, soft flesh it bathed.

He was locked into the excruciating hold of his urgent body, feeling like he had never known such a wholly riveting need. He felt her in his thoughts, felt her analyzing everything he was feeling to adjust the way she rubbed against him, until it was driving him insane.

Suddenly she caught his ravenous mouth with her own, then she moved from his mouth to his neck and throat, learning with delight that the feel of her wet lips in those areas was an incredible stimulant. She felt the swell and pulsing urgency of his erection, so close to her own heat. It sharpened her own hunger, the need to have him deep within her body gripping roughly through her.

Gideon felt her release him from the touch of one hand and was even aware of the slight jerk of her arm. But he was still unprepared for the strange jolt that accompanied that skillful twist of her wrist. They materialized a half a second later in the center of the bed, her body and his still connected as they had been before the teleport, only this time he was as nude as she was.

That brought him to be unexpectedly sliding through the liquid heat of her aroused sex, making her gasp as he rubbed over sensitive flesh and heightened the cravings of her body for his joining thrust. He uttered a sound of pure primal desire, his hands moving to grip the fabric of the coverlet as he threw back his head and curved back into a full arching of his tormented body.

But he did not give her what she wanted, in spite of it taking every last ounce of control he had left. He moved away from that unbelievable haven she had tempted him with, rising up on his knees in order to do so, pushing her thighs farther apart as a result.

He was wracked with the pulse of his need as he looked down on his irresistible mate. He shook his head in wordless disbelief at her cunning tricks to overpower him. And they had worked, every one of them. Not to her satisfaction, perhaps, but it completely convinced him that he had been wrong when he had assumed sex was too commonplace an act to hold the attention of a creature with a centuries-long life.

And he was feeling the error of his thoughts keenly. Still, he would not deny her equal time. She meant too much to him. It was in her nature to give so wholly to the needs of others before indulging needs of her own. But he was not like others, and he would not be satisfied in that way.

He leaned a little forward, looking straight down into her curious and questioning gaze.

"I want you to say my name," he commanded her, his voice guttural and powerful. "And if you do, I will give you a gift very similar to . . . *this.*"

He was suddenly diving past her eyes and into her body. The feedback of the sudden rush of his power entering her, combining with her very own aura, made her struggle for breath. The sensation fired wild chills down her breasts and belly and thighs. He insinuated himself into the rush of her blood with astounding speed, enhancing and altering the chemistry of her physiology until she was bursting with an intense rush of adrenaline. Then there was the awareness of her most sensitive erogenous zones being filled with the hot pulse of fresh blood and stimulating nerve impulses.

He sent increasing heat through and through her, finishing and beginning again, all the while watching her wide eyes as she rasped for breath. She couldn't focus on him any longer, her vision blurring as she felt herself falling over backward into a black hole of his artful creation.

Legna exploded, the crystal finally shattering as he hit the perfect pitch within her. She screamed out, her body seizing with her pleasure, her entire being wrenching with indescribable pulsations beneath him.

And he had not even touched her.

She was drawing wildly for breath as she finally dropped from the outrageous crest he had pushed her to. She was finally able to focus on the hotly satisfied look in his eyes.

"Come now, sweet, and say my name," he continued to urge her in that superior and coaxing tone. "You are strong enough now to keep it as well as I do." He lowered his mouth to her breasts, laving each nipple with torturous patience and then scoring her across the right one, exactly as she had marked herself on him.

It was like putting a high-voltage current through her, forcing her to arch up off the bed. He took advantage, dragging his mouth over her raised belly, dipping his tongue into her navel as if pushing a magic button inside of her that released a spill of hot liquid over already soaked flesh.

"Say my name, *Nelissuna*, and I will give you so much more," he murmured against her skin as his lips moved lower and lower.

Legna wondered how he expected her to say even *her* name when what he was doing had her throat locked into a perpetual sound of pleasure. The push of his thighs against the backs of hers left her completely exposed as he rose up and replaced his mouth with the touch of his hand.

This time there was no teasing. His fingers slipped into the wet silk at the juncture of her thighs, touching, exploring, and finding in a heartbeat the way to stroke her into new awareness and heightened response. She bucked, crying out as her hips rose and twisted. She felt him slip his touch inside of her, a skilled intrusion that showed her everything a man was capable of learning about a woman when he had a millennium to do it in.

He already knew her from the inside out, and he made good use of it. As he railroaded her with increasing ecstasy, he continued to ask her for his name. He promised her more, but she could not have even tried to imagine more. When he slid down her sweat-drenched body to taunt her

with his mouth, he used the link of their minds to continue
the request and the promises of reward.

Legna felt herself wrench into an explosion of forcibly
parting molecules, a feeling parallel to how she had felt
the first time she had ever teleported. The rush was magnificent and heartbreaking all at once. Wonderful to
feel, tragic to leave behind. Tears coursed down her face
and into her hair, a sob tearing out of her throat as he
pushed on relentlessly.

If she thought him merciless, she was wrong. He was
wholly selfish, her untamed pleasure arousing him to
phenomenal heights. She was the cruel one, refusing his
one request even as he pleaded sweetly with her, using
her delicious body as his begging bowl. He covered her
from head to toe with the attentions of his hands and
mouth, feeling her squirm beneath him in such wholly
erotic movements that it took all of his willpower not to
thrust himself deep inside of her and damn everything
else to hell.

Demon couples did not share their power names, as a
rule, mostly to protect one another from being used by
outside sources to betray that precious secret that protected their beloved mates. But he already knew hers,
having learned it five months ago when he had heard
her former mentor spouting it left and right for all to
hear.

So now, she would have his. It was the most profound
gift he would ever be able to give her, symbolizing a trust
that had to stretch beyond the reasonable. But he would
have nothing that she gave him unless he returned it in
equal measure.

He rolled over, dragging her with him until she lay
heavily over him, her thighs straddling his hips. He
reached out to enclose her hips between his solid hands,
and, with purposeful movement, slid her intimately up
the length of his lethal arousal.

Legna reared up onto her heels, her head thrown

back as she cried hoarsely to the heavens. He gritted his teeth as the burning center of her body called to him, promising a haven like nothing he had ever known.

"Say it, Legna," he begged her, moving her hips again until he was poised so close to the entrance to her body that it would take only one movement to join them.

Suddenly her head came forward, her eyes flashing with fire and intent and the determination of all the decades of her life. Her hands shot to his shoulders, pinning him back onto the bed as she released a savage sound of intent. She locked herself right where she was, refusing to allow him to move her in any way. He felt her tilting her hips so slowly, using all of her strength to fight his staying grip.

"Legna!" he gasped, feeling himself pushing into her, losing his control and his reason as she forced dominance out of his hands. She leaned over, eye to eye with him as droplets of perspiration fell from her body to his. He felt himself being surrounded further and further, the pace excruciating, the hot silver fire in her eyes taking everything away from him.

And then with one last undulation of her body, she gave it all back. She took him into her silken sheath completely, gasping out a triumphant sound of pleasure as he filled her to her borders. She stretched to accommodate him, and it had to be the most incredible sensation of their mutual lives.

And then she closed her eyes, a tremor shivering up her curving spine as she touched her mouth to his, and finally said his name.

"Pentangelo."

It was a powerful name, a name of protection and high expectations. Just as hers was. Indirianna meant "Companion of the Heavens," and Pentangelo meant "Angel of Endless Time." The power of the names was clear enough, if at the very least in how their meanings so perfectly suited the creatures they had become.

And as they made love for the first time with all the power and intensity of the proud species they came from, they became completely lost in each other. They tumbled across the bed again and again, first Gideon driving deeply into Legna, and then Legna coaxing her hot body against Gideon with breathless, sinuous friction. They became tangled in her hair, the tendrils trapping them together into one endless being just as their thoughts melded in the same way. Gideon was capable of manipulating Legna's body into an aria of immeasurable pleasure, but Legna was capable of thrusting the sensations right back into him in the form of raw emotions.

"Legna!" he cried hoarsely, everything about him screaming into her that he was too lost to do anything but feel the amazing summit they had formed together.

Legna's breath came in short, quick moans that began to rapidly turn into higher-pitched exclamations. She was beneath her mate, feeling him as he thrust into her to depths that transcended the physical.

When Gideon climaxed, it was with a primal roar of ultimate masculine ecstasy. The final thrust of his body and the burning rush of his seed pouring into her sent Legna into a volcanic release. It rode out of her on the back of an exultant shout. She tightened around Gideon like a passionate vise, milking him with dynamic thoroughness, leaving the most powerful Demon in all of history without a single ounce of strength.

Gideon dropped onto his mate's damp body with a final sound of contentment. He listened as they both gasped for breath, loving the sound of it for reasons he couldn't even think of.

In fact, thought was beyond them both. Gideon gave a moment of concern to the weight of his body on hers, solving it by simply rolling them over so she was sprawled across him. After that, there was nothing but bliss and the mated pair that basked within it.

Love?

Yes.

Gideon chuckled.

Why did you say yes like that?

Oh, I thought you were asking me a question.

I see.

Then he truly did see what she meant, and his heart flipped over in his chest.

Darling?

Gideon smiled at the warmth the endearment flooded him with.

Yes, Neliss?

Oh, nothing. Just fulfilling my end of the deal.

The deal?

Yes. You made me a deal.

You lost me, he sighed.

Legna lifted her head, propped an elbow up against the pillow of his chest, and settled her chin in her palm so she could look down at him.

"You said that I would get something very special if I called you that."

"Did I?" he asked, his eyes brightening with speculation as he thought back on it. "Actually, I think you have that confused with the deal about saying my name."

"I like your name," she said with a smile. "I always thought mine was awful snobbish. But yours has me beat hands down."

"My name is one of the finest and oldest names in all of our history."

"That's only because you have lived to be such an old tosser."

"Tosser?"

"British vernacular, luv."

"What are you, my dialect coach all of a sudden? Is this your idea of postcoital pillow talk?"

Legna giggled, apologizing with a clinging kiss on his lips. It clearly calmed him, making him smile in a very cat-versus-canary way.

"Is there something you would prefer I say?" she asked compliantly.

"That yes a few sentences back was great. Short, sweet, to the point."

"Yes," she agreed.

"Yes?" he asked, arching a brow.

"Oh, yes," she assured him, her own brows doing a little lecherous dance.

"Mmm, yes," he murmured as her mouth lowered to his.

Yes. Yes. Yes.

Legna?

Yes?

Do not talk with your mouth full.

No?

No.

Chapter 11

Isabella stirred in her sleep, her cheek and nose rubbing against the smooth, warm skin of her soon-to-be-husband's neck where she had slept with her face pressed against it the entire day.

The rub of her lips sent stimulation winging down her mate's spine, stirring him out of his rest as well. She lay at his back, the entire length of her petite body plastered to the back of his, including the leg insinuated between his thighs and the swell of her belly that was nestled into the lower curve of his spine.

Jacob reached for the hand that dangled against his chest, attached to the end of the arm that draped over his. He drew her fingertips to his lips, letting her feel his kiss and his smile.

She smiled against the warmth of his neck in response.

Feeling better? he asked, using their mental connection first because he had missed the feel of her in his mind. All he had been able to do was content himself with her dreams as she had slept and healed.

Much better. I missed you.

I missed you, too.

She pulled her hand free so she could touch him, her fingers drifting softly across his skin, drinking in the missed feel of him.

"Next week is Beltane," she reminded him. "Do you suppose we will make it through the wedding this time?"

"Not if Gideon says you cannot get out of this bed," he countered sternly.

"Absolutely not!" she burst out, making him wince and cover the ear she'd been too close to. She immediately regretted her thoughtlessness, making a sad sound before reaching to kiss the ear she had offended with quiet gentleness.

Jacob extricated himself from her hold enough to allow himself to turn and face her.

"Okay, explain what you meant," he said gently.

"I refuse to wait another six months. We are getting married on Beltane, come hell or . . . necromancers . . . or . . . the creature from the Black Lagoon. There is no way Corrine is going to be allowed to get married without me getting married, too. I refuse to listen to her calling me the family hussy for the rest of the year."

"What does it matter what she says?" Jacob sighed as he reached to touch the soft contours of her face. "You and I are bonded in a way that transcends marriage already. Is that not what is important?"

"No. What's important is the fact that I am going to murder the sister I love if she doesn't quit. And she will not quit until I shut her up either with a marriage or a murder weapon. Understand?"

Clearly, by his expression, Jacob did not understand.

"Thank Destiny all I have is a brother," he said dryly. "I have been inundated with people tied into knots over one sister or another for the past weeks."

"You mean Legna. Listen, it's not her fault if everyone has their shorts in a twist because of who her Imprinted mate is! Frankly, I think she and Gideon make a fabulous couple. Granted, a little too gorgeously 'King and Queen of the Prom' perfect for human eyes to bear looking at for long, but fabulous just the same."

Jacob blinked in confusion as he tried to decipher his

fiancée's statements. Even after all these months, she still came out with unique phraseologies that totally escaped his more classic comprehension of the English language. But he had gotten used to just shrugging his confusion off, blaming it on the fact that English wasn't his first, second, or third language, so it was to be expected.

"Anyway," she went on, "Noah and Hannah need to chill. You saw Legna when she came to visit yesterday. If a woman could glow, she was as good as radioactive." She smiled sweetly at him. "That means," she explained, "that she looks as brilliantly happy as you make me feel."

"I see," he chuckled. "Thank you for the translation."

He reached his arms around her, drawing her body up to his as close as he could considering the small matter of a fetal obstacle. He kissed her inviting mouth until she was breathless and glowing herself.

"I thought I would be kind to you," she explained with a laugh against his mouth.

"You, my love, are all heart."

"And you are all pervert. Jacob!" She laughed as she swatted one of his hands away from intimate places, only to be shanghaied by another. "What would Gideon say?"

"He better not say anything, because if he did that would mean he was in here while you are naked. And that, little flower, would probably cost him his vocal chords in any event."

"Oh. Well . . . when you put it that way . . ."

Isabella stopped speaking so suddenly that it got Jacob's instant attention. She blinked once, her gaze going suddenly blank and her body going rubbery in all-too-familiar ways. Jacob instantly dismissed his playful mood, rising up on his knees as he waited for Bella to come back around.

It didn't last long, and she sat up with a hand on her belly the very instant her vision cleared.

"Get dressed," she told him, moving to get out of bed herself.

"What is it?" He reached out, circling her arm with a strong hand and forcing her to remain in bed where she belonged. He moved around to sit beside her and see into her eyes. "What did you see?"

As much as he was privy to all of her thoughts, the only thing he could not touch were her premonitions. That place in her mind was blank to him, at the most giving off residual sensation of emotion. Right now, he could feel her confusion, and an underlying sensation of anxiety that accompanied it.

"I don't know. I . . ." She shook her head numbly. She was nowhere near mastering this power. She could barely handle the energy drain that had begun to come with it. Interpretation was completely ambiguous, and at other moments like this, absolutely cryptic. "I saw red. Nothing but this color of red. It seemed magnified, you know, like those pictures people take of ordinary objects and you have to try and guess what they are, but it's hard to because they are so distorted?"

"I think I understand. So why do you feel you have to get up?"

"I . . . don't know. Jacob, I just do. Please, I won't understand this if you don't let me follow my instincts."

"No, little flower. Gideon said you are not to move from this bed, and you are not going to disobey."

"Jacob," she snapped, losing her temper. "I have a bad feeling about this. I won't sit here and be coddled while something terribly important . . . or terribly dangerous might occur. What if this is a warning? I have a responsibility—"

"To what?" Jacob asked sharply. "To run around blindly like a chicken with its head cut off trying to find something *red*? Can you not see how ridiculous that is? As well as dangerous for you and our child?"

Bella wrapped angry arms across her chest, her fingers grasping hard at her upper arms in frustration.

"I hate this! Six months ago I was the strongest I have

ever been in my entire life. Stronger even than the most powerful Transformed Demon. Now I can't even get out of this bed when I need to! All in a matter of a few days!"

"Stop this. You were attacked. You are not responsible for that."

"No? And I suppose you were? If you can give yourself the guilts, Jacob, then I sure as hell have just as much of a right—"

She ended the argumentative statement with a gasp. Her head was thrown back violently, her body locking and seizing with brutality. Jacob barely managed to catch her up against himself before she slid from the bed and struck the floor. Instead, he was able to lower her with a modicum of gentleness to the carpeting.

"Bella?!"

He shouted at her as the glassy expression overtook her once more, but this was like nothing they had experienced together before. She was wracked in violent spasms of her body that could only be called a seizure.

Jacob grabbed for pillows, protecting her as best he could, thinking at a frantic speed about how to get help. He closed his eyes and reached out into the night, soaring out into nature and the things within it that he could manipulate. He touched the mind of a wolf. The Earth Demon charmed the animal, coaxing it to go against its natural instinct to stay away from man-made habitation.

Before long, the wolf was loping over the manicured lawns of Noah's home.

Noah looked up from his studies when the sound of scratching came from the door. He reached out, sensing the energy of the animal outside, his brow furrowing in confusion. He got up and moved to the door, opening it to the wolf, who sat on the doorstep looking at him expectantly. There was intelligence behind those sharp blue eyes, an intelligence beyond what the animal itself had. Noah immediately sensed the residual energy of an Earth Demon in the animal's aura.

"Damn it!" he swore as he realized he had been so absorbed in his work that he had not even felt the spike of fearful, tormented energy taking place in his own home. The Fire Demon twisted into a column of smoke and flew like a tornado up the main stairwell.

"Kane?"

Corrine moved into the next room, searching for her mate with growing consternation.

"Kane, if you are trying to exercise our telepathic connection again, I will murder you once I find you," she complained. "This is not fair."

Corrine had woken up to an empty bed, feeling heavy and disappointed at heart because of it. She enjoyed that feeling of waking up, snuggled against her lover, feeling the weight of his embrace even as he slept. They had come so close to losing each other without even knowing what they would have missed. And as she had healed, she had learned what it meant to love and be loved with a depth that no one who was not a part of an Imprinting would ever truly understand.

It helped that her mate was a little dangerous, a lot irreverent, and playfully unpredictable at the moment. Hopefully their mental connection would continue to improve as she recovered from the damage she had initially suffered. If it didn't, she was going to be the butt of these impromptu hide-and-seek sessions for the rest of her life, a life that was considerably extended now that her Druid genetics had been awakened.

Corrine was walking through the kitchen when she felt that terribly distinctive pop that accompanied the arrival of a teleporting Demon. She grinned, rounding the corner quickly.

"No fair teleporting!" she sang out to her cheating mate. She was laughing as she ran into the living room. She stopped short when he wasn't there, frowning and putting her hands on her waist in vexation.

She sniffed the air, looking for the sulfur-and-smoke scent that her fledgling mate always left behind in great quantity, looking for a clue as to how far away he might be in the house.

That was when she was struck violently from behind and shoved face first into her own floor. She landed with a grunt as the carpeting burned across her chin and elbows. The force of the strike bruised her nose forcefully, and as her breath left her in shocked release she sprayed blood over the sky blue fibers.

She knew with sudden dread that it was not her lover who did this to her. He would have killed himself before harming her even accidentally. No, this was an attack, one of vicious malice.

"So, little Druid," a soft, feminine voice of deceptive beauty purred into her ear, loud and clear as her accoster's weight came down hard into the center of her back, forcing what little was left of her breath out of her. "Where is that spawning little whore of a sister of yours now that you need her?"

Remembering what had happened to Bella, the one who had been blessed with remarkable fighting instincts and skills after her Druidic awakening, Corrine suddenly felt the most intense terror of her life. Whatever skills it was she would develop, none would be as powerful as her sister's. If these were those who had attacked Isabella when she'd had all those defenses at her disposal, what chance of survival would someone weakened by a retarded access to her powers have of defeating such an enemy?

"Oh yes, you should be afraid," that singsong voice of threat cooed to her.

The last thing Corrine remembered was being dragged off by fistfuls of her long, red hair.

Legna awoke with a start and a deep, indrawn gasping breath as she propelled herself into an upright position. Gideon, who had been sleeping with both an arm and a leg securely across her, was awake and alert only a second later.

"*Neliss?* What is it, sweet?" he asked, his worry and concern pouring over her highly sensitized emotions.

His attentive feelings helped soothe her, bringing her respirations down to a more manageable level. Legna reached up and pushed back the heavy fall of her hair as she blinked and oriented herself to where she was. She was still not used to waking up in Gideon's home. But what did she expect, after waking in her own bed without fail for almost all of the nearly three centuries she had lived?

She was, however, definitely getting used to all the sweetly achy places she woke up with. Gideon always offered to soothe any of her sore places, and although she knew he was privy to her thoughts and feelings, she always responded with "What sore places?" making him laugh and grin with a purely male smile of satisfaction.

However, those loving feelings they had engaged in for the past days were close to dormant in that moment. Instead, her heart was gripped with an inexplicable sensation of fear. He moved to face her, close enough that they pressed thigh to thigh as they sat facing each other on the bed. He cradled her head and face in the width of his gentle hands, making her look up into his concerned eyes.

"Tell me," he urged softly.

"I . . . cannot. I do not understand. Maybe . . . just a bad dream."

"And does this happen often with you? Just like this?"

She mutely shook her head, tears welling in her eyes as the alien fear continued to claw at her.

"Listen, love, things are not the same for you anymore. You will never be like an average female Mind Demon again. My power inside of you changes everything. I do not know how exactly. That will show itself in time. But remember that it will tend to frighten you as you first begin to figure it out." He paused to kiss her trembling lips, the connection warm and soothing in ways his words could never be. "You have to think calmly. It is just like when your natural abilities first revealed themselves. You have to examine what is happening, accept it, and try not to be afraid of it."

"How do you know that's what it is? New power and ability?"

"I can feel it, *Nelissuna*. I have been feeling it for days now. So have you, but you do not want to acknowledge it."

Legna exhaled heavily, scattering stray strands of hair.

"Thank you for the timely warning," she said dryly, giving him a dirty look far too much like the ones she used to give him. But this time it made him chuckle softly.

"If you like, I can leave and let you figure this—"

Legna grabbed his arm at the bicep when he made a strong movement to get up off the bed, jerking him back down definitively.

"Absolutely not! You did this to me; therefore, you get to enjoy the fallout."

"You make it sound like a punishment," he remarked, his eyes dancing with silver humor. "There is nowhere I would rather be than in my bed with my beautiful mate."

He leaned forward to engage her mouth in a tender kiss, their lips clinging together as if reluctant to release. Finally, he sat back, leaving her warm and happily flushed.

"Charmer," she accused him without malice.

"Siren," he countered, pulling them back together

and into a deep kiss that left them both longing for breath.

"Mmm, what about the nightmare?" she asked absently, her lips brushing back and forth over his, her tongue flicking out to lick against them temptingly.

Gideon pulled back a half inch, arching an inquisitive brow.

"From just a 'bad dream' to a nightmare? What do you remember?"

"I think . . ." She stopped, swallowing hard. "I had this terrible feeling like I was losing Noah, that he was fading away from me."

"Like a Summoning?"

"A little, but it was not a Summoning. Somehow, I knew he wasn't in that kind of danger, but I could not escape the feeling that I would never see him again. Gideon, it broke my heart."

The tears spilling down her cheeks confirmed that emotion, and he leaned forward to kiss them away.

"So, just an average nightmare after all," he mused.

"How do you know that?" she sniffed.

"Because, love, Noah *is* going away from you, just as you are going away from him. It is very likely an anxiety dream, brought on by your move out of your childhood home and the comfort of the reach of your family's love and protection." Gideon reached to stroke her hair soothingly. "I am only surprised it has not happened sooner."

"Are you sure?" Her nervousness was clear, but she was truly relaxing already.

"Yes. And so are you. You know everything there is to know about psychology, you tell me what you think."

"But you thought it was this . . . new level of ability."

"And for the first time in a millennium my diagnosis is wrong. I do despise it when such bothersome things occur. Now I shall have to start the 'No Mistakes' clock all over again."

Legna giggled at him, which was of course his intention. She swung her arms around his neck, hugging him warmly.

"You smell so good," he murmured against her ear a long minute later.

"I smell like sex," she argued.

He nodded, making a loud noise of appreciation as he sniffed and nibbled her neck.

"You smell of very good sex," he amended with a voracious growl and an eager mouth moving over her bare skin with bold appetite.

"Gideon!" She squealed as he went straight for her waist, knowing she was ticklish there. The playful flicker of his tongue and the scrape of his teeth drove her mad, and she twisted as she screamed for him to stop.

When he tickled her she absolutely could not use her classic escape method. She could barely catch her breath, never mind her concentration. He replaced his mouth with his fingers, making her yelp as he reached to draw one pert nipple into his sucking lips, his hands perpetuating the torture that made her squeal with laughter.

She tried using her legs to push him away, but only succeeded in giving him the opportunity to grab her thigh in his free hand and push her open to the approach of his body. He stopped tickling her the moment he thrust deep into her.

Legna's head pushed back, a silent cry locked in her arching throat as her back came up off the bed. Gideon was done with tricks and ploys, and, drawing his lip between his teeth in purposeful concentration, he proceeded to play the interior of her body like the fascinating instrument it was. Nothing would ever equal her abandoned sounds and expression as she met thrust after thrust, her reaction so profound each time it was as if he achieved perfection just by moving. She made him feel like he was a flawless lover, but he knew it was Legna who was the perfect one.

She was meant for passion, for touch and kiss, and for each and every movement that brought them tighter and closer together. Gideon felt her around him, a cocoon of conditions meant to tend to him, created just for encouraging growth and sensation and the remarkable release of rebirth.

She pulled him down to her mouth, knowing that it drove him mad to feel her cries of pleasure vibrating over his lips and tongue and face. It always spurred him on, even when no encouragement was necessary. She met his rhythm with both her reaching hips and her vocalizations. He plunged into her mentally as well as physically, doing all those things to her chemistry that made her go ballistic with mindless bliss.

It was when they both saw starbursts of silver and gold behind their eyes that they broke, a throbbing explosion that made them shout release against each other's lips. He felt her shudder hard around him again and again, the pulsation of her muscles a sweet, sweet torture.

Gideon refused to relinquish his mate's mouth or her body. He needed to cling to her just as he was, soaking in the heat and aftermath of her release. She smiled against his mouth, kissing him again and again with all the emotion in her tender heart, allowing him to stay where he was until he was ready to leave.

"Who said I was ever leaving?" he murmured against those soft, sweet lips he would never stop craving.

"Well, not to sound like Jacob, but . . . Mother Nature?"

He laughed, rolling over until she was once more lying limply over his body. He liked to feel her weight like that. No matter what position they began in, afterward he rolled her onto him as if she were a living blanket. Actually, considering the mass and fall of her hair, it wasn't such a far-off thought.

"I will be right back."

She disappeared instantly, leaving him feeling terribly chilled. It was a mental perception, of course, because he could regulate his body temperature perfectly. But he was happy to prefer the imperfection of a chill so long as it encouraged Legna to blanket his body.

Gideon was smiling with the thought when a surge of energy skimmed over his senses. He sat up just as Legna rematerialized beside the bed, clad in a burgundy dress that had formerly been in the closet.

"Noah is coming."

"I thought so," Gideon said dryly. "It felt like him."

"Get dressed," she urged, rubbing her hands together nervously.

"Legna, do you not think he knows what goes on in this house?"

"Gideon, do you not think you better not make me lose my temper?" she threatened. "Please. Please, will you get dressed?"

She popped out of the bedroom instantly.

Destiny forbid her brother should see her coming from his bed, Gideon thought with a sigh. It was so . . . non-Demon, the way she thought about these things. Legna herself had run across Noah with a partner more than a few times over the centuries, but it meant nothing to her and she accepted it. Now here she was with her future husband, her Imprinted mate, and she was afraid of her brother realizing they had just been having sex?

Stop criticizing my motives and please come down here.

Love, do you not think your brother felt the energy of our lovemaking from miles away?

I hate you.

Perhaps, but only for the moment, he chuckled.

The beautiful catamount circled the house slowly, her muzzle to the ground every now and then as she tried to make sense of the scents she was picking up. The door was wide open and, with slow steps, the mountain lion progressed into the dwelling. She picked up blood scent immediately and made a beeline to it. There was a stain on the carpeting, still wet with freshness.

The wild cat licked at the spot slowly, unable to resist the lure of the aroma, never mind the taste. She had never tasted anything like it before, its composition so alien it left her confused. There was a touch of power in it. Nothing strong, but enough to indicate it did not belong to just a human.

The room was full of the scent of Demons, and the cat flicked wary golden eyes around herself. She smelled the odor of residual fear, the scent of hostility. Something violent, predator versus prey, had taken place in this dwelling, and suddenly the cat understood that she should not tarry there in case others arrived and mistook her intentions.

She turned to lope out of the door, but was frozen in place when a sudden flash of sulfur and smoke blew into the room with uncontrolled violence. The Demon that rushed out of the cloud stopped short once he saw the catamount dropping into a sudden, defensive crouch upon seeing his approach.

Kane had felt his mate's distress for all of a second, and when the minuscule whisper that was her presence suddenly vacated its home in his mind, he became instantly fearful. It had taken him some time to calm down enough to concentrate on his teleport home, his fledgling status making him raw with the knowledge that had he been just a little older, a little stronger, he would not have been so unschooled as to allow his feelings to interfere with his ability.

But now, as Kane looked from the mountain lion to the spot of red sprayed over the carpeting, he was blinded by rage and pain. The scent of the blood was that of his mate, and he knew with every fiber of his being that she was injured and in severe danger. His hands curled into fists, his dark eyes, so much like his elder brother's, flashing with intent and emotion as he advanced on the cat.

She backed up, the hackles on her back rising as she looked for escape. She made her decision quickly, understanding that she could never outrun a teleporting Demon. The cat began to shake, the jingle of the collar around her neck giving the Demon pause. It was incongruous that a wild cat would be wearing a collar. It bought the cat time as she continued to shake, her fur beginning to peel away in long, fist-thick coils of gold.

Moments later, Kane found himself looking into the golden eyes of a woman. Nude but for her collar, she rose to her natural height, which was quite significant. The drift of her hair hid most of her nudity, but the Lycanthrope female was uncaring of that. Her entire focus was on the startled Demon before her.

"I am Siena, Queen of the Lycanthropes," she introduced herself softly, keeping her rich voice warm and compelling as she spoke. He was a Mind Demon, resistant to her suggestive abilities, but it wouldn't hurt to soothe him just the same. "I will let you into my mind and you will see, Demon, that I am not the one responsible for this."

The Lycanthrope Queen? In his house? Kane almost laughed aloud at the absurdity of such a claim. But he knew that collar well enough. Imitation it might be, but he had heard of the complexity of it, seen drawings of it. It was supposed to be so unique that it could not be counterfeited. But how was he to know the difference between even a bad counterfeit and the true necklace?

She had, however, given him the perfect solution. Despite his ingrained distrust of the Lycanthropic species, he narrowed his eyes and ventured into her mind. She put up no barriers, allowing him freedom that could be very threatening to a woman who ruled an entire species. Had he wanted to, he could have had access to any number of secrets. But he respected her offer to him and stayed on the path of her short-term memory.

Siena had found this scene just as he had. Being a male Mind Demon, he could have known instantly if it was a fabrication, but it was not. She was telling the truth, the evidence in her thoughts.

"What brings you to my home, Highness?" he asked with automatic politeness, an impressive courtesy, considering his emotional upset. "What do you know of what has happened here?"

The golden-haired Queen reached to pull an afghan off the chair closest to her, wrapping it around herself as she moved to sit down in a nonaggressive pose.

"I was tracking a group of necromancers. I had no idea this was a Demon dwelling until I entered it, apparently too late, and for that I apologize. Had I known they were going to attack a member of your household, I would not have remained in the tree line." Siena crossed her legs, sitting as if she were clad in a gown of gold and a crown instead of a well-worn afghan Kane's mother had made long ago. "As it was, I saw about four of them, all women, gathering around outside. None of them entered, but they waited for several minutes. I see now they were keeping guard while someone else entered the dwelling. How they did so without my knowledge can have a multitude of explanations. What I do know is that no one with black magic entered this dwelling."

"Then how . . . ?" Kane ran a troubled hand through his hair. "Hunters? They don't use magic, and Corrine is not strong for a Druid, so it would have been easy to overcome her."

"Ah! A Druid! This makes more sense now. I could not recognize her scent. I have never known the scent of a Druid. I do detect the strong thread of human scent; however, it is clearly mutated. I suppose this means your Druid is half human, is she not?"

"Yes. And you weren't able to recognize what she is?"

"My apologies. The combination is too new to me. However, I would venture a guess that your intruders are not in the dark about who and what she is."

"I have to go. I have to find my brother," Kane said anxiously, moving back a step as he tried to shed his overwhelming fear and concern for his adored mate. Siena felt his distress keenly, her empathy with animals allowing her a peek into the animal instincts that Demons blended with their veneer of civilization.

"I will remain here and see what more I can discover," she assured him, the soothing spell of her voice helping him center himself. "No one else will pass this way without answering to me."

Her reassurance helped him. Settled with determination, Kane teleported to Noah's home.

Chapter 12

Noah and Gideon appeared moments before Kane reappeared in his living room. They had just enough time to focus on the room's only occupant before Legna and Elijah also appeared. Gideon quickly moved to his mate, supporting her weakened frame by holding her snugly to the length of his body, his fingertips gently worrying against her face. She had teleported him and Noah, had gone and fetched Elijah, and then had teleported them both to Kane's as well. Even with her growing power, it was still much for her to do in such a rapid-fire manner. Gideon helped her to be seated, picking up one of her hands as it trembled with fatigue and folding it between his own as they all looked at the Lycanthrope Queen.

She was in her third form. The Wereform. In this form she was the figure of her womanly self, coated in the silky, golden fur of the cat, with whiskers, pointed ears high on her golden head, oval pupils, claws, and twitching tail. She sat in her chair with her legs crossed, the afghan that was no longer needed folded back where it had been, her tail curled silkily around her calf.

She stood up when she saw Noah, however, giving him a respectful inclination of her head. Her golden eyes flicked to the others. She first studied Gideon's mate for a long, interested moment. She then moved on to the massive form of the blond giant standing very close to the King. She knew this one, she realized. She had never met him face-to-face, but he was legendary among her people. Elijah, the Demon King's Warrior Captain. To her people, Elijah the Butcher.

There was no mistaking the description. Tall, muscular, and blond, as if he were an incarnation of Apollo, the Greek god of the sun. There was also no mistaking the shrewd green eyes of a well-seasoned fighter. But it was the palpable mistrust he sent lancing in her direction that confirmed his identity to her. It was the exact feeling she would expect from a man who had spent centuries killing her kind in order to protect his own.

However, Siena's focus belonged on Noah, and she turned it there quickly.

"Noah, it is an honor to finally meet you."

"Siena." Noah bowed slightly, his eyes roaming her figure with minute note of every detail. He was clearly sizing up the woman who had single-handedly ended the war between their peoples. "I have long desired meeting you as well."

"Then we have been remiss, each waiting for the other to make the first invitation. I regret that this meeting comes under such tragic circumstances."

Noah nodded in appreciation for her sympathies. Elijah, meanwhile, had moved to the area where the attack had taken place. The warrior touched the drying stain of blood, scenting it to affirm to himself that it belonged to Corrine.

"We can't tell Bella. This could kill her," he remarked tightly. "Not until we know for sure in either direction what has become of Corrine."

"I have a feeling Bella is going to find out on her own soon enough," Noah remarked, his concern etched deeply across his brow. "These visions of hers . . ."

"I will return when we are finished here and induce

sleep," Gideon said. "She will not be aware of anything in that state. Also, it will allow her to heal so that if we must deliver bad news to her, she will be stronger."

"We are not delivering bad news to anyone," Kane barked suddenly, his hands curled into vicious fists. "Corrine will be found and brought back to me if I have to search every corner of this planet myself. And Destiny had better help those who took her from me."

"In time," Noah agreed soothingly, a hand on the younger man's shoulder. "We all will see to that. But we must start with the basics. I should like to begin with an explanation for your presence here, Siena."

"Of course." Siena stood up, moving with pantherish grace to circle the scene of the crime. "If you would introduce me to your people, Noah, I would be happy to share my knowledge with them all."

"My apologies, Siena," Noah said. "You have met Kane, I imagine. This is my Warrior Captain, Elijah. You are already acquainted with Gideon, our medic, and his mate, my sister, Magdelegna."

"A Princess for your mate, then, Gideon? You did not mention that," the Queen noted, looking amused by the thought.

"No, Siena. Our royal house does not work in the same fashion as yours. Council chooses our royal leaders and only their offspring become Princes," Gideon explained. "But it is a title of respect only. There is no birthright to our throne."

"I see. A wise custom. I know many a fool sitting on a throne because of their inbred rights to it." Siena linked her hands behind her back, removing her gaze from the openly disturbed stare the warrior was giving her. "I will start at the beginning."

Siena spent a moment looking over the menacing presence of the blond behemoth to her left, then moved closer to the more receptive Demons gathered around. Her fearlessness unwittingly impressed itself on the warrior. He knew she was very aware of his hostility, and yet she made no outside sign of it affecting her in the least.

"After Gideon visited me," Siena began, "I personally arranged for my Elite personnel to assist in the investigation into this unpardonable crime against your Enforcer female. Several reported running into your very adept and thorough warrior." She extended an elegant hand in Elijah's direction. "However, as I explained to Gideon, we who are more frequently the prey of a human hunt have a more advanced intelligence of this self-serving network of mortals."

"Your assistance is generous," Noah remarked, "considering we sent Gideon to you with only our suspicions in tow."

"No matter," the Queen said, waving it off. "I would have made a similar choice, considering our history." The Queen's gold eyes flicked back to Elijah for a moment before returning to Noah's expectant expression. "My Elite returned a few days ago with reports so intriguing that I felt I needed to seek the truth of the matter with my own eyes. What I encountered was a militant group of unique collaboration. It consisted of both powerless and empowered humans."

"Wait a minute . . . you mean necromancers and hunters working together?" The idea was shocking to them all. How would two such diverse groups even find each other? What did it take to get two such prejudiced and vindictive factions to collaborate?

"To be more specific," Siena continued, "sorceresses and female hunters."

"*Women?*" Elijah demanded.

"Women," she confirmed. "Exclusively women."

"Exclusively . . ." Noah shook his head in confusion. "I do not understand that. I did not think gender would matter."

"Yet somehow it does," the Queen countered. "When my Elite General began to hear rumors about this group, she infiltrated it as quickly as she could. She has since come to realize it is a highly powerful and more complexly organized party than one would expect for such a recent insurgence of empowered magic-users. My own investigation has convinced me that they have been gathering since long before you first became aware of the return of magic-users. But I believe the specificity and coalescence of this female group only began recently. There still seemed to be a sense of newness to it. Not too new, but just young enough to keep expectations very high. Something occurred to bring these women together, something very specific.

"The magic of the necromancers is powerful. Let me assure you of that straight away. These are no amateurs. Though I always have to question just how expert any of them can be, considering their mortality. Still, my Elite related stories of power and spells the likes of which I had never before heard of. I believe it is only because my Elite General chose half-breed spies that they were lucky enough to go undetected amongst them."

"Half-breed?" Kane asked. As the youngest of them he was the least experienced in these details.

"Half pure Lycanthrope, half human," Elijah explained with quiet solemnity.

"I'm not sure I understand the difference."

"A half-bred Lycanthrope cannot change into Lycanthropic or animal form. Instead, they exist in the constant form of a human. They look human, smell human, and have an ease living between the human and Lycanthrope worlds that we full-blooded Lycanthropes are not easily capable of. The distinction is that a half-breed acquires all the senses and abilities of the animal form they would have been able to take had they been fully bred. For instance, a feline's ability to see in dim light, its sense of smell, retractable claws, and so on," Siena explained.

"This ride on the fence between races allows them to go easily undetected. Even to magic," Elijah said.

The Queen's eyes went back to the warrior with interest. "You know much about us." The Queen studied Elijah for a long minute more, the roam of her eyes slow and meticulous as they both understood what his detailed knowledge had once been used for. "The female half-breeds," she continued at last, "infiltrated the group under the guise of hunters. I promise you, this was no small feat, considering the overpowering stench such a throng of magic-users produces. But my General, Anya, quickly began to hear reports of an attack perpetrated against a female human who had lain with a Demon, although these women referred to them as a 'male succubus and his human whore.' They were clearly aware that the human woman was impregnated with its 'spawn.'

"It was easy to assume this was your Enforcer's mate they discussed. I risked possible detection and accompanied Anya to the next meeting. All I can say is that they are eerily well informed. They knew specifics about your people that even my father's spies and assassins were never able to discover over all our centuries of war. I assure you, the Elite spies are quite adept in their fields, but never have they known such intimate details as I heard from these women."

"I'm sure you undercredit them," Elijah remarked darkly, his sarcasm blunt.

Clearly the Demon warrior was not pleased by the fact that the Queen's resources had proven to be better than his own. He prided himself and his warriors on being the best at what they did. It sat ill on him to have been bested by, of all people, the Lycanthropes.

"So how does this investigation bring you to Kane's doorstep?" Noah asked.

"I was present when orders were given for a group to 'begin their assignment.' Without knowing the nature of the assignment, I felt it would be wise to follow them. I did, and the rest is as I explained to Kane."

"But there is something missing," Legna spoke up

suddenly. "You have seen something and have not realized its significance."

"That is possible," the Queen agreed, arching a brow of curiosity as she looked at Legna. This female Demon was a powerful woman. Siena could sense it quite strongly in spite of the fact that, out of the array of Demons before her, Legna appeared to be the least prone to animal instincts. "What is it you suspect?"

"Emotion. Strong emotion. This is not a random attack."

"No. It wouldn't be, would it?" Elijah said with sudden clarity. "Out of all of us, what is the one connection that Corrine has that no one else does?"

"Isabella. Damn," Noah hissed. "She is our Enforcer's sister."

"And accessibility," Elijah added. "If they know so much about us, it seems logical to assume they knew Corrine is in delay of gaining her Druidic powers. She is vulnerable, weak . . . and they knew she would be easy prey."

"Hmm," the Queen mused. "Perhaps this will make better sense to you, then. An agent reported to me that one of the group leaders had become incensed over the failure of the original attack. Though I did not see this myself, my Elite told me that to describe her as livid would have been too mild a terminology. She kept screaming about how they had failed to destroy the 'Demon bastard' and his 'whore vessel.'"

"Obviously she meant Bella and the baby," Noah remarked.

"I do not agree," Legna murmured. She got the attention of the room with the statement. She got to her feet, moving past Gideon's staying hand of protest, pacing as she forced herself to think. "The rage does not make sense. Understand, I am fully aware of the temperament fanatics such as these can reach, but psychologically speaking, rage of this manner indicates a very intimate connection."

Legna raised a hand to her temple, rubbing it as she tried to think. Gideon was watching her closely but remained silent. He could sense she was close to something and did not want to disturb her, even out of his concern for her weary state.

"Okay, let us look at this entire picture," she said aloud, even though it seemed she would not have even noticed if they had left the room. "The attack on Bella did not take on the nature of a random act of violence, or even an efficiently motivated one. If anyone had wanted Bella destroyed, they could have done it with a single shot from a distant hillside with a high-powered rifle. After all, humans have no trouble at all using such weaponry. Consider: What was the purpose in taking the risk of getting so close to her? Why add the variables of a stun gun that might malfunction or miss its target? If they wanted her dead, why not cut her throat and be done with it? Why the multiple wounds that would not be fatal unless untended over time? And then the brutal attack on the baby. Kicking? Punching? When, again, a single act of well-aimed violence would have sufficed?"

"Suffering," Gideon injected suddenly.

"Exactly. Someone wanted Bella to suffer before she died," Legna agreed. "And by doing that, they would have made Jacob suffer. They risked capture, injury, and death to do this thing. Fanatics or not, why would humans risk such personal threat? The only reason I can see is the vindictive motive of . . . of Jacob being the one to find Bella dead. And he would have, had I not come to visit her. I think the referral to 'Demon bastard' was not a referral to the baby, but a referral to Jacob. Frankly, it sounds a lot like personally motivated revenge to me. And no revenge against Jacob would have been sweeter than murdering his beloved mate and their unborn child in such a way as to make it very clear to him that they had suffered torturously the entire time. It would have destroyed him."

"Revenge . . ." Noah's eyes lit up with disturbed awareness. "Ruth," he hissed.

"Yes," Gideon agreed. "It would explain so much. Including how it is that they suddenly know so much about us."

"Ruth . . ." Noah shook his head at the painful prospect of his realization. "She's unbearable, but a traitor?" he argued with himself.

"She blames Jacob for the pain her daughter now suffers due to the accidental loss of her Druid mate," Gideon added. "My guess is that it was Ruth herself who entered the house after Bella was unconscious. She knew full well that pain would nullify Bella's power absorption abilities. She attended the attack personally in order to . . ."

"To batter the unborn child," Elijah finished, "completing her revenge firsthand."

"Ruth, as a Mind Demon, must have figured out a way to mask the link between Jacob's and Bella's thoughts," Gideon put in. "I remember him saying he did not feel the trouble she was in until Legna arrived on the scene. Being familiar with that connection now, I find it is almost impossible to break, even when you want to. But Ruth could have that power."

"Isn't this too obvious?" Elijah complained. "Ruth is not stupid. She knows we would get to the bottom of this and begin to suspect anyone with an attitude against Bella and Jacob."

"Exactly. She is probably hoping we will discount her for her obvious hostility, providing her an excellent defense," Noah said. "But there is impetus for this most recent attack that would make Ruth as primary suspect make even more sense," Noah added gravely. "She was recently voted out of the ranks of Council."

"What? When did that happen?" Kane asked.

"The Council, sans Jacob and Isabella, voted three

days ago. The vote was unanimous. We did not publicize it to spare Ruth as much embarrassment as we could. But I see now she would have even more motivation for rage and revenge against the Enforcers, if indeed it was she who orchestrated the attack."

Siena moved to stand before Noah, aware of the fact that Elijah was bristling with distrust as she did so. It was clear he didn't like her being so close to his monarch. The Queen ignored the brute's continuing hostility.

"I must warn you that this most recent abduction was not the only plan about to be executed by these women," Siena announced. "The human women are planning another course of retribution on what we must assume is your Enforcers. And this, Kane, is what leads me to believe your mate is not dead." She glanced at the young Demon with heartening encouragement. "If they had wanted to make a statement by killing her, they would have done so right here. This blood is really incidental. I think that they have kidnapped her. With Corrine in their custody, they have an intolerable leverage over you all. I do not know what use they expect to get out of it, but it cannot be anything good."

Siena took her turn at pacing thoughtfully before the gathering. "If we are to remove their leverage, we must rescue Corrine as soon as possible," she mused. "There is only one course of action to be taken, as I see it. If you will allow my assistance."

"By all means," Noah encouraged, holding up a silencing hand to Elijah, who made a sound of protest.

"We must search the premises of these female forces and try to locate Corrine. However, the only ones who have a hope of getting past their notice are half-breed females like Anya, myself, and . . . Magdelegna." She pointed to the mildly startled Mind Demon.

"Me?" Legna asked dumbly, surprised to even be considered for something that would definitely take her out of her comfort zone.

"You are a Mind Demon, yes? You can trick minds, alter perception, and toy with their heads in ways that will give us most excellent access." Siena couldn't help the impish urge to fling a sly look at the grumpy blond warrior, and with a wriggle of whiskers she said, "See? I know you, too."

"In that case, why can I not just teleport into the compound and find her myself?" Legna asked. "I can take images from your mind—"

"No. The compound is a honeycomb of underground caverns. I have no idea where she might be, and we could end up teleporting into the middle of a necromancer's tea party. I think the only way you would be able to find her is to get close enough to sense her thoughts and emotions. The only way this will happen will be through the so-called front door."

"I would sense her thoughts and emotions," Kane argued, looking every bit the frustrated husband.

"And you would be very obvious as the only man in the compound," Siena said dryly. "Since Anya and I are known there, we will not be suspect as we help Magdelegna to locate your mate. Once we find her, Magdelegna can teleport us all to safety."

"And I can mask our presence and our escape," Legna added.

"From Ruth?" Noah was shaking his head. "Legna, she practically invented what it means to be a female Mind Demon. She was the first, and she is the strongest."

"But Legna is no longer a typical female Mind Demon," Gideon spoke up. "She is developing uncommon power and abilities. You have seen this for yourself."

"Developing being the key word," Noah argued, his worry for Legna paramount in his mind. "If any of them are detected, we will not only lose any advantage we have, but we may potentially lose these other women as well."

"I doubt that," Gideon remarked. "True, these are powerful enemies, and not to be underestimated, but I have never known a necromancer able to prevent a tele-port when the Demon was not controlled by a penta-gram. Even Ruth is not capable of that."

"Then it is settled," Legna said. "We will seek Corrine in their stronghold. Once she is rescued, we can worry about the next attack they are planning."

"And if she is not being kept in that place?" Kane asked tensely.

"Why wouldn't she be?" Siena countered. "They have no reason to suspect we are on to them and their locale. And should that be the case, where better to find the information?"

"Then it is settled," Gideon agreed firmly. He was not pleased by the idea of Legna going into danger, but he was going to make sure he and several others were going to be close by should any of them need assistance. And he would be in her mind the entire time.

"Hardly. Legna is not exactly a low-profile member of our society," Noah pointed out. "Ruth would recognize her in a heartbeat, mental blocks or no. Every Councillor knows the face and form of the King's sister."

"I will alter her appearance sufficiently," Gideon said. "It is within my power."

"Excellent. How much time do you need to prepare?" Siena asked Gideon.

"Very little."

"But I need time to rest," Legna pointed out. "I have taxed myself."

"We can't afford that kind of time," Kane argued anx-iously. He felt Corrine's absence keenly. His mind felt so hollow, but it was nothing compared to the fear of the unknown. What, he wondered, was happening to her? He couldn't bear the thoughts that began to race into his head and claw through his hollowed-out heart.

"He is right," Legna agreed. "Give me two hours. Some energy supply from Noah, a little healing from

Gideon, and some meditation should refocus me sufficiently."

"Very well. I will be prepared as well." The Queen turned to Noah. "When you are finished aiding your sister, I should like a moment with you."

"By all means," Noah agreed, much to the displeasure of his Warrior Captain.

"I offer my help in this venture not only as a gesture of goodwill, but because I feel this feminine force is dangerous enough to warrant my personal scrutiny," Siena was explaining to Noah half an hour later. "What you do with the information about the Demon traitor is at your discretion, Noah. I know you have your own justice system. But I will warn you now that if in the future you plan to send further spies into this stronghold for yourself, we must keep each other well notified of our actions.

"I will have my Lycanthropes picking this group apart with brutal efficiency the moment we are able, and I would hate to see any Demon warrior accidentally injured because they were gathering intelligence for you and a miscommunication left us unaware of their innocent presence. There is a great need for us to exchange ambassadors. My court will welcome any Demon of your choosing."

Noah leaned back in his seat, absently turning the signet ring on his middle finger as he considered the offer for a long moment. It was not usual for Noah to show signs of perturbation, but it was clear he was more than a little worn out by all the attacks against those he loved.

"I have only one Demon I could entrust with such a task, but you will have to give Magdelegna time to decide before I can make that a definite promise to you," the King said quietly.

"An excellent choice," the Queen said after a long

minute. "I do not know why I did not consider it myself. Especially since her mate is already quite a familiar face to my court. As for my part, I have a very special female in mind. She is named Myriad. She would be an excellent ambassador for your court not only because she is remarkably open-minded, fearless, and strong, but because she is not the sort who would come crying to me with easily bruised feelings. She, too, is a half-breed, which may help others become comfortable with her more quickly than perhaps a purebred could achieve."

"When this disturbance is resolved," Noah said, "send her to me. Legna will give you her own decision about becoming your ambassador after I request it of her." Noah rose to his feet. "I think I also should tell you that a part of our justice system, which you spoke of earlier, consists of an absolution for true acts of self-defense when they are called for." Noah crossed to a near window and pressed his fist to the glass. "I tell you this because there may come a call for you to take part in destroying this corrupted Demon female should she pose a threat to you or Legna, and I must have you understand that we will not seek atonement from you if you are forced to destroy her.

"I would be responsible if you hesitated because of my failure to tell you these things, Siena, and were injured or killed as a result. It was your ascension that stopped the war between our peoples, and I will not forget that this peace means as much to you as it does to me. I know that were I faced with a hostile Lycanthrope right now, I might hesitate to defend myself for fear of it rending our tenuous hold on this time of tolerance."

"I understand," Siena said softly, making no secret of her remarkable respect for his thorough forethought. "The information is happily received. However, I don't see attacks or battles as a part of this mission. This is an extremely large group. We would be outnumbered in a battle."

"We will not be far," Noah said. "Gideon, Elijah, and I will be monitoring you. We will back you up immediately if needed."

"And we will make all efforts not to cause trouble," Siena agreed. "There will be a time for battle. Unfortunately, it seems to be a recurring theme in history." Siena paused a long moment. "May I speak freely, Noah?"

Noah turned at the question, looking at the woman who was sliding a thoughtful hand over the spines of the books on one of the shelves of his personal library.

"By all means," he invited her.

Siena gave him a tiny smile and continued to meander the room as she spoke. Her movements, matched with her mellow speech patterns, were soothing in an enigmatic way. It seemed as though the only sound she made as she traveled was the soft brush of fur on fur. The lazy swing of her tail was practically hypnotic. Even in this hybrid form, she was an incredibly lovely creature.

"One does not need to be a telepath or an empath to know you are preoccupied with your sister's relationship with Gideon."

Siena stopped to pick up a glass globe that had been etched with maps of the world. The piece was clearly an antique of tremendous age and value. The borders of the countries were misrepresented, and other areas were missing completely.

"Yes. It is a complicated event."

"I see. I had thought Gideon was highly respected amongst your people."

"He is. Of course he is."

"Yes, he is quite old and quite empowered."

Siena rested the globe back into its display holder, turning it until the Russian territory was facing forward. Strangely, it amused the King. Lycanthrope history was deeply rooted in that land, the accent of which could be heard in the Queen's warm speech. Her action was almost like a subliminal need to leave a declaration of her presence behind. He supposed that living half of her existence as an animal was bound to leave her with unavoidable instincts, such as marking territory. His own people were affected with similar needs.

But Noah was actually more curious about her current line of questioning. He had never doubted Siena's intelligence or perceptive abilities, not to mention the strength it had taken to hand down a decree to her people only three days after her ascension to the throne that the war with the Demons was to end immediately.

Also, she had paid careful and quiet attention to Elijah during the meeting. Though she had said nothing, done nothing to indicate it, Noah had a feeling she knew that it had been Elijah who had led the team of warriors who had finally defeated her father thirteen years ago. The battle had been the last of the war, her father's resulting death giving Siena the key to her throne. Noah was forced to wonder what effect it would have on a woman like Siena to come face-to-face with her father's executioner.

"I was always curious," the Queen continued after a distinct silence, "as to how a Demon of such ability had managed to be captured by my father. I realize now, as I come to know your people, that you sent him to make that sacrifice."

"I sent him, but the idea was all Gideon's," Noah credited quietly.

Siena's gold eyes flicked up to meet his. Her eyes were incomprehensibly beautiful, but it was not nearly as startling a feature as her keen intellect. Noah was quite impressed but simply returned her gaze as he locked his hands behind his back.

"Gideon was the only Demon by both type and wisdom who could have done such a thing," Noah continued. "As a Demon of the Body, he has no natural abilities for escape, such as teleporting, so he gambled on the idea that your father would be pacified enough to let him remain imprisoned. Knowing this, your sire had no fear of Gideon slipping away with intelligences that might benefit us. It stood to reason he would thrive on the idea of the advantage holding Gideon over our heads might give him."

"My father was a bit of a fool," Siena remarked without humor. "He never bothered to find out that Gideon could astral project. It was when I discovered this that I realized you all could have had all the information you needed to destroy us in a genocidal fashion, but you were not acting on it. It was the beginning of the change in my perspective about your people."

"Gideon is a veteran of war and its ramifications. It has always been his highest priority to find wise and logical ways out of conflict. He put a great deal of faith in the reports of your remarkable intelligence and your outspoken displeasure with the warring ways of your father. Without these important factors, Gideon would never have suggested the assignment, not to mention embark on it himself."

"It was still a very dangerous chance to take."

"With your father away at battle, leaving you in charge of the court, we expected you might speak to your captive once or twice. It was our hope that with those slight opportunities, Gideon could find a common enough ground to begin the processes of understanding and tolerance between you. A mandatory factor when trying to achieve peace."

"Yes. I know. It was for the best. The five years Gideon spent at Our court made an impact, I believe, on both sides." Siena moved to run fingers over a nearby desk. "But I am forced to wonder something, Noah. It is clear from this information that you trust Gideon. Enough to trust him with the future of both our races. That you hold him in high regard and enormous esteem even on a personal level is also apparent." She turned that pinning gaze back on him. "Why would you be against having such a man as mate to your sister and a member of your family?"

"It is not so much that I do not trust him or do not want him—" Noah broke off and looked back out the window he had been gazing out of before the conversation had begun. "It is a complicated situation. There are things involved in this type of union that could be painful for my sister." Noah looked back to the Lycanthrope woman. "What brother of any substance would greet the idea of his sister's potential hurt with open arms?"

"One who did not love his sister as much as you clearly do," she agreed graciously. "It is almost . . . almost uncanny how alike we are after all. I was raised on stories of Demon savagery, told how uncouth and barbaric you were. Stories that included the Druidic Wars and a long list of other opinions from other races holding other grudges." Siena paused to shake her head, the motion of expressed regret accented by a twitch of her ears. "When I got to know Gideon and began to see the depth of your morals and the culture that surrounded them, I realized how untrue it was. It was wise of you to trust him with the task. You should not lose your wisdom now, Noah."

Noah drew in a deep breath, and then released it in a long sigh.

"You are correct, Siena. And I have said the same thing to myself many times. Perhaps, soon, I will actually begin to listen to myself." Noah gave her a charming smile and with it changed the focus of the conversation. "For the moment, I should like for us to complete the details of the ambassadorial exchange."

"I have been considering something else first," she announced. "I believe we should have a social gathering before the exchange of our diplomats. Perhaps it will relax everyone to begin the integration in the same casual style we began ours."

"An excellent idea. I propose Beltane. There will be weddings, a festival, and we will have sporting competitions."

"That sounds like an excellent idea. Perhaps I can suggest some of the things we do on Beltane to make it a truly blended occasion?"

"Of course. Please," Noah indicated two plush chairs that faced each other next to one of the shelves. "Let us discuss it."

Chapter 13

Gideon approached Legna quietly, not wanting to make any distracting sounds as she sat deeply entrenched in her meditation. He sensed clearly the order she was putting her mind into, the thoroughness she used to catalog the new infusion of his power she had been adjusting to ever since they had become fully Imprinted.

By meditating as she was, she was helping to keep at bay anything other than the focus on her approaching foray into enemy territory. A visitor in her mind so regularly, Gideon had a renewed respect for the strength and mental discipline it took to manage her empathy. Without that impressive will, she would have been driven insane by the sheer amount of random emotion people were constantly projecting every minute of every day. Her control was perfect and kept everything about her neatly restrained.

Everything, perhaps, except how beautiful she looked to him. Better yet, she was being beautiful in his home, the place where he had spent so many solitary centuries never truly realizing what he had been missing. She sat centered on an antique Persian rug, the design unfolding all around her as she maintained her cross-legged position. Gideon realized then how much his passion for her seemed to be growing with every day and every minute they spent together. Even this separate togetherness, when she was deep into her own tasks and he was in his, was a prime example. Of course, his task at the moment consisted mainly of looking at her and admiring all the details of her beauty, both inner and outer. She had the most perfect skin in the world, luminous even though she was clearly a little tired. Her coffee-colored hair snaked all around her body, just a happenstance of how it had settled around her, and he could not help following the winding path as it traveled her breathtaking figure. It was like a spark to tinder, and the heat for her that was always only banked within him flared to new life.

"You are distracting me," she whispered, opening one eye to look at him.

"I am sorry," he said, grinning in a way that belied his apology. "I will attempt to refrain."

"You do that," she giggled, closing her eyes again.

He didn't leave, but he did try to keep from thinking in less than seemly ways. It was not an easy task. His gaze kept wandering over to her, drinking her in. He noticed she had a beauty mark on the bottom of her left foot and it made him smile. He had somehow missed that one in his methodical task of learning every inch of her body.

"Gideon!" she hissed softly.

He laughed, covering his irrepressible smile with a hand movement. Her thoughts might have been kept distant from him, but it was clear she was very aware of his. He began to contemplate having a little fun.

As he mused over the possibilities, Gideon felt an eerie change in the room. He went still, trying to name the source of the strange sensation he was feeling. It was cold, paralyzed, and bearing a level of emotion that was far too deep to belong to him.

That left Legna as the most likely source. Her eyes suddenly opened and she looked up at him, but she did not seem to focus on him. Gideon's brow furrowed as he tried to see what she was thinking, but barriers had flown up around her mind that, combined with the distancing of meditation, kept him in the dark.

"Legna?" he asked softly, crouching down to come eye to eye with her.

He became aware of the fine vibration that was humming through her. He reached to analyze her body chemistry and physiological reactions for a definition of what she was feeling.

It was fear.

Not just any fear, he realized as he reached deeper, but a solidifying terror unlike anything either of them could have conceived. Adrenaline was racing through her, causing chaos in her biorhythms to the point that Gideon hardly knew where to start to help calm her. Whatever this was, it was probably the worst thing that could happen so close to her undercover assignment.

"Legna, what is it?" He used a firmer voice, demanding an answer from her.

"Mama."

The single word completely obliterated the Ancient Demon.

Stunned, he fell back onto the floor, wiping an unsteady hand down over his shocked expression. He tried to think, but he couldn't. Now it was his fear that was rising. Gideon had no idea how she was recalling that day. He had no access to her mind the one time he needed it the most. All he could do was feel the painful wrenching of his own terrified heart as he watched her eyes grow wider and wider.

He didn't need new power and new skill levels to remember that day. It was clear as crystal for him. That day. That terrible day when Gideon had looked up from his position over Legna's mother to see the equally wide eyes of a four-year-old girl who was seeing something no child should ever see.

She was seeing her mother's mutilated body, and a male Demon who was drenched in her blood from silver hair to booted feet, clutching the dead woman to his chest as he leaned over her.

Nothing compares to the scream a babe makes in a moment like that. There was no way to explain to her that there was only so much a healer could accomplish. No way to explain how a beautiful and beloved mother could end up looking like she had looked in that instant. He had been over seven hundred years old at the time, and there was no explaining it to him either. And knowing that had been the first time the child that was Legna had ever laid eyes on him had haunted him for the next two hundred and fifty years. It was that moment alone that had kept him at a distance from her when they had actually belonged together all this time. That child was the child he had seen for so many decades every time he had looked at her. Looked at her looking at him as she was subconsciously trying to remember what it was they had decided to take away from her in order to preserve her precious mind.

Gideon turned his face to the heavens, tears of pure agony burning in his eyes as he prayed for a miracle he couldn't even begin to guess at the nature of. All he knew was that he would be destroyed the moment she stopped loving him, the moment she rightfully began to blame him for his inadequacies, for his failure to save that life, for his failure to protect her young eyes by having the forethought to seal off the room. The thought alone was enough to stop his heart from beating. He heard her begin to weep, but he could not bring himself to look at her. He felt his soul shredding, flayed away from him bit by bit, seemingly with every tear she shed. When she was suddenly on him, wrapping herself around his throat, he was pretty much expecting it. He didn't fight her. He had no right to.

It took him a long minute to realize she was hugging

him, not throttling him. Numb with incomprehensible shock, he dared to allow himself enough hope to lay a hand on her back. It was at that moment he realized he had expected never to touch her again, making the contact feel like a miracle cure.

"Legna," he whispered hoarsely. "I am so sorry."

She said nothing, instead sobbing as if her heart were breaking. He let her go on, thinking to himself that she could cry until next Samhain if she wanted to and he would be the last to gainsay her. This moment was almost three centuries in coming, and she deserved to mourn.

Noah had lived not only with the weight of his mother's murder and the responsibility of raising his sister after his father's Summoning, but he had lived with the knowledge that he had made a decision for his sister that he'd never found the courage to reverse. He had always dreaded this moment, just as Gideon had.

Gideon wanted to ask her a hundred questions, but this was not about him, so he did not. He enclosed her in his embrace, soothing her as best he could with his presence and his warm touch. He brushed her hair from her damp, flushed face, gently tucking it behind her ear over and over again, a rhythmic stroking that carried with it silent words of love and understanding. Her cheek was nestled into his shoulder, her tears soaking through his shirt, her sobs held deeply in her chest so that they sounded like the painful cries of a small animal.

It was almost an hour before she spent herself completely, an occasional shudder wracking her as she drifted into an exhausted sleep. Gideon still did not move in any way. He let her rest, ignoring his own comfort completely. Nothing could make him more comfortable than the feel of her arms around him, even limp with sleep as they were.

She made a sound, jerking slightly as she woke some time later. She lifted her head, searching for his eyes. He obliged her, not even trying to hide the uncertainty within himself. She reached to touch his face, drawing her lip between her teeth as she moved her fingers over him in a strange pattern.

"You were crying," she said at last, her voice hoarse from emotion.

He instantly understood that she was not talking about the here and now, but about that tragic day so far in the past.

"Yes, love," he said simply.

"Why would you cry for my mother?"

"Because no one should have to die like that," he said. "Because for all my ability, I could do nothing for her. As I was for your brother, I had been her *Siddah*, and it destroyed me to think I had done so poorly by her that she had not known how to properly defend herself."

"That is not true. It is because you were *Siddah* to my brother that he was able to become both the man and King that he is. No one could do better than that, and I know you did just as much for Mama."

"I was older when I fostered Noah. It was different."

"Mama was a Body Demon. Female Body Demons are the least powerful of our society."

"I know. And that was why she was chosen by her murderer. He knew she had no hope of . . . but if I had taught her . . . something. Anything."

"You were the one who found her?"

"Just before you did, sweet. I thought I would turn to stone when I looked up and saw you there, looking at me as if I were something straight out of hell."

"And you and Noah had my memory altered."

"Yes."

"Why did you not tell me sooner?" she asked at last, the one question he had been truly dreading.

"I made a promise. A promise I have kept your entire lifetime, *Neliss*."

"A promise to Noah."

"Yes. But you cannot blame him for that."

"No. I would not. Noah has protected me all of his life. This is no different. I would not be the soul I am if not for his choices in this. I understand now why he was so upset to find out we were Imprinted. Both he and Hannah must have suspected this would happen. You must have as well."

"Yes." He swallowed past the lump in his throat. "I did not know what to hope for . . . that you would find out before we made love . . . or after. I was terrified you would feel abused in some fashion. Or worse, would turn away from me before even learning who I am."

"I see." Legna reached to push back his hair, pressing her forehead to his, putting them eye to eye and nose to nose. "I know you," she said in a whisper. "Just as I know myself. How could you ever be afraid that I would think you capable of such a monstrous act?"

"Because I am afraid of anything that might mean I will lose you," he confessed.

"I told you, my love, I am not going anywhere. I am here, right where I belong. My heart lives with your heart, my soul with your soul. I love you, Gideon. You have to start believing that, and believing that you deserve it."

"I will never deserve it," he said roughly. "But I will endeavor to do so for the rest of my days. I love you, *Neliss*, as I have never loved in the whole of my life. You are my heart, my breath, my every thought and every aspiration. You are the true source of my power, because without you I am utterly powerless."

"Love," she whispered softly, setting his heart to flight as she pressed her mouth to his tenderly. "I need to know only one thing, and then we will never need to discuss this again."

"I know," he agreed hoarsely. It took him some time before he began to tell her what she wanted to know. "He was the only Demon besides you to ever be retrieved from a Summoning pentagram. We thought we had saved him in time. By the time we realized how wrong we were, four females, including Sarah, your mother, were dead. Jacob executed him eventually, but it was a poor compensation. There was a time I thought Noah might never recover. He could not do for himself what he and your father had done for you."

"No wonder he has been almost maniacal in his protection these past months. The Summoning must have brought up so much in his mind. I think I finally understand why he could never discuss it with me. I think he was afraid that if he did it would give him away, that it would dredge up enough emotional memory to trigger what everyone had repressed within me." Legna reached up and stroked her fingers along the line of his jaw. "And then he was forced to let me go to you, knowing so much that I did not. He even tried to warn me. It makes sense now, when before it seemed so irrational. And Hannah. She knew also and was so afraid for me."

"They love you, sweet. So many of us love you. Even that acerbic little Druid you insist on being friends with." He winked, softening the remark enough to make her laugh. She reached to hug him with all of her strength, and he basked in it gratefully.

"Well, I am going to protect that little Druid because she is my friend, and she once did the same for me."

"Which definitely elevates her in my esteem," he said, kissing the top of her head through the depths of her hair. He reached up and touched the silky mass with both affection and purpose, closing his eyes and concentrating as he stroked it. Then he lifted the entire mass of it into his hand.

Legna felt a twinge of feedback along her scalp and pulled back from him to look at her hair in his hand. She gasped when she saw the black tresses, a full three feet shorter than they normally were, and the cropped coffee-colored remains fluttering down over their close bodies like dozens of feathers.

"Tell me you can fix that later," she said nervously.

"Love, I once regrew your hair from scratch after it had been burned off. I can do anything."

"Show-off," she said dryly, touching the alien locks. "How did you change the color?"

"Just a rudimentary tweak of pigmentation chemistry. Straightening it was even easier. But this is not the end of my tricks. If you are up to it, we can find a mirror so I can show you."

"I am fine. Puffy eyes aside, as long as I have you, I am fine."

"You have me," he assured her, helping her to her feet. "And as for puffy eyes, you will not have them by the time I am done."

"Remind me to stop if you catch me touching my face," Legna whispered to the Lycanthrope Queen.

"I don't blame you if you do. I never suspected Gideon was capable of such an alteration. It is remarkable."

"He said it was easy. He always says that. He explained that it was simply a matter of changing musculature structure and bone malleability. So now, I have a whole new face."

"I think choosing an Asian appearance was a brilliant touch," Siena whispered, glancing up at a woman who passed their table. "That's the second time she passed us."

"I noticed. She is feeling a little nervous, but it does not seem to be directed at us."

"Well, so long as she doesn't jump us the minute we leave the restaurant."

"No. No hostility or negative intent," Legna remarked.

"Ah, there's Anya," Siena said suddenly, reaching to wave to an exotic-looking young woman with hair that, if just a few shades lighter, would be as fiery red as Corrine's.

It was wrapped into an intricate chignon, but it was clearly held in place by only a single long hairpin made of heavy silver, or what looked like silver.

Legna noted that the Queen had also bound up her hair, and by the way she repeatedly gave it a covert touch, it was clear she wasn't used to it. That was when Legna realized Lycanthropes were actually uncomfortable with their hair up. Their enemies might potentially know this, and so the Lycanthrope women had indulged in the extreme to further throw off suspicion. The sense she was feeling from them told her it was akin to a near strangulation for them. She had lived so far removed from the war, again by Noah's design, that she had not learned this interesting detail.

The Queen cast Legna a look, seemingly knowing what she was thinking, because she leaned over and enlightened her a little.

"When you see one of us change form, you will understand better. You will also understand that, when bound, our hair represents peaceful intentions."

It was an enigmatic statement, but it was enough for the moment.

The half-breed female moved directly to them, greeting them as if they were old friends, their manner warm and as boisterous as that of any girlfriends meeting for a night out.

"Anya, this is Maggie. Maggie, Anya," Siena said, using Legna's altered nickname to keep them in character.

"Hi. Ready to go?"

"Right now?"

"No time like the present," Anya said, rising to her feet right away.

Legna took a deep breath and followed the two Lycanthropes, letting their powerful confidence soothe the last of her nerves.

In less than half an hour, they were entering a dance club. They blended in perfectly with the mostly female clientele. Anya led the other two women directly to the back of the club, taking them through a door that, when closed behind them, dimmed the pulse of the music they'd left behind. She turned and gave a slight hand signal, alerting them that they were about to cross the magical ward set up to filter those who came that far. If anything was going to go wrong, it would be right then.

Siena and Anya had both passed the ward before with success. They could sense its energy and its sickly resource of evil magic, but they only knew that it was an alarm . . . not what the alarm was geared toward filtering out. Siena suspected males were obviously key on the list, and Legna dreaded the logic that Demons were, too. Especially with the high likelihood that Corrine was imprisoned within the magic-users' secret sanctuary.

But Legna felt Gideon's mind strongly in hers, reassuring her that he was in complete control of his protective alterations of her bio-signs. He was very close, probably just outside the club itself by then. Legna could even sense that Kane and Elijah were nearby. Her brother was the only one still out of her range.

All it would take was her faith in Gideon's power.

With deep breaths, all three women advanced. When Anya exhaled with relief at the end of the corridor, they all did.

Legna paused to listen to the voice murmuring praise and reassurance in her mind as they hurried down a flight of stairs that suddenly spat the three women out into an overlit underground chamber, apparently directly beneath the club they had first entered. Legna reached for the males lying in reserve once more, finding them all to be close. She focused, making sure she was ready to teleport them all to safety in a moment's notice. It would probably wipe her out to do so, but she no longer doubted she could do it.

Outside of the garish lighting, the room was actually warm and cozy, decorated in Persian rugs and antiquated furniture. The stone walls and floor were a reddish color, and they were the only thing that made the room seem as if it was underground. Otherwise, it was decorated with comfort and conveniences in mind, rather like an old gentlemen's club or an exclusive cigar club. Except in this instance, it was full of women, and gentlemen weren't invited.

"It almost looks like a Lycanthrope dwelling," Siena whispered. "We mostly live in caverns like this, decked out in rich appointments very nearly identical to these."

"It would not surprise me if this was exactly that," Anya remarked, her eyes clearly those of a soldier as she assessed the room, its exits, and the entire situation they were walking into. "An abandoned dwelling that was left behind as the city above us was built. It is not Russian territory, but it is not unheard of."

Suddenly, a wall of putrid stench seemed to strike them all at once. It took everything in the trio's willpower not to react violently to the awful reek of the necromancers who were suddenly all around them. There were so many of them they could barely breathe. Legna turned to the Queen with wide eyes. Reports or no, they had never suspected there would be so many of them. This human cross-section of magic must have been gathering for years. Everything they were looking at, the specificity of the banners and symbolism decorating the walls of the gathering hall, as well as the numbers that gathered there, spoke of the time it must have taken to corral and woo so many of these women to the same cause. New or no, this had been quite some time in the making.

"My impressions are that the gatherings began long ago, but the organization itself has only solidified over the past few months. Apparently," Anya remarked, "they have grown considerably in strength and numbers since then."

"Apparently," Siena agreed grimly, looking around with barely masked disgust and anger. Legna reached out, settling her hand on the Queen's arm, sending out a blanket of soothing emotions and easing thoughts. She pitched her voice with low, gentle charm.

"We are here now. It will go no further than this," she reminded her.

The Queen's rage seemed to ease. Siena sighed with a guttural sound of frustration. "Women. Men I expect, but why women?"

"I guess female empowerment goes both ways, Siena, good and evil."

"Such a waste," Siena mourned.

"I know," Legna soothed.

They began to move into the thick of the crowd, fighting their revulsion at the smell. Gideon flowed through Legna's thoughts, calming her as she was overcome with the urge to bolt. The desire was all the more strong because the women on either side of her were feeling the exact same thing. It was understandable. To these human predators, *they* were the prey, a role they were not used to and definitely not comfortable with. The instinctive sensation was no different than what a fox thrown into a den of hunting hounds might feel. Even Gideon, strong and powerful Gideon, could not entirely hide his concern for her well-being. Had he been in her stead, he wasn't certain he would have been able to remain either. Or so he tried to tell her as he steadily calmed her fear. But she couldn't imagine her powerful and Ancient mate being afraid of anything.

Legna was aware of him notifying the other three males of the situation, and keenly felt Noah's reaction to the news. But he put his feelings aside, no doubt because he was aware she would be sensitive to them. She sent him a silent impression of gratitude that helped calm her brother.

The trio advanced, Anya introducing them to others as they entered the den. The women all talked and behaved as if they were at a high-society social—except in this society, discussions were often about the recent deaths, or "victories," over certain Nightwalkers they had encountered. Legna could not remember ever coming across such a gathering of bloodthirsty females in all of her lifetime.

It was a reflection of how the black magic permeating the room was poisoning the very souls of these women. Having learned about instinct and nature these past days, Legna understood that a huntress only hunted for what she needed, and only killed for survival and self-defense. She never sought out trouble, and she left the challenges for power to the males of the species.

These corrupted women killed in a warped view of self-defense and sought trouble with all their energy and focus. It was this unnatural, mutative behavior that made their scent so abhorrent to creatures as in tune with nature as Demons and Lycanthropes were.

It was becoming more and more unbearable as time passed, but they gritted their teeth and bore with it. The crowd was beginning to take seats in an area of chairs that had been lined up row after row. Legna warned Gideon to this, putting him on a heightened alert. It would make the gathering suspicious if they did not follow suit, so the spying trio took seats in the back row so no one was behind them, and to give themselves a small amount of relief from the stench.

They were facing a stage, one that rose in inclination the farther back it went, like a classical theater stage. It was constructed from white marble, including columns. The color bore significance. It represented their idea of good, of the female virgin who was pure and just. The psychology of it was clear.

The good guys always wore white.

So Legna was not surprised when a female trinity appeared in hooded robes of pristine white silk. Each woman took a position on the stage. There was right, left, and middle. Legna immediately recognized the traditional Triad, the one representing the Maiden, the

Mother, and the Crone. Future, present, past, respectively. No doubt Siena, coming from a species that had a deeply rooted faith in the Goddess these figures represented, was appalled and horrified by the abomination. Legna felt it emanating from the half-breed female as well.

The middle position was the traditional position of the Mother. If Ruth was one of the leaders there, it would be as the center figure. It would suit her sense of vengeance for her betrayed daughter.

Legna tried to get impressions from the three on stage, but she dared not do so with any strength. There was no doubt in her mind that these were impressively powerful women. There was a necromancer somewhere onstage who was over twenty times more powerful than the necromancer Legna had destroyed in October. And though that one had been a relatively easy kill, it was only because they had been able to take those magic-users by surprise.

But Legna was positive one of them was a Demon. They had been right about that much. And as they reached to pull back their hoods and began to speak to their audience, Legna was riveted on the central figure.

It took her a moment to realize that the Mother figure was not Ruth. Quickly she glanced to the other two positions.

It was the Maiden who was the Demon betrayer.

"Mary!" Legna hissed.

Not the mother, but the daughter herself. The mother was surely not far behind, since the fledgling Earth Demon simply did not have the power or the wisdom to plan such crafty attacks. Ruth was hiding behind the visibility of her daughter, Legna knew it as sure as she knew her power name. Mary did not have the knowledge Ruth had, no matter what she had seen all the years in her mother's house. And there had been many years. The foolish girl was still a fledgling, one who knew little more than what her mother told her. And apparently, her mother had told her enough to engender a hatred and a need for revenge that centered on Jacob.

Legna recalled that the girl had never been fostered by *Siddah*, her mother refusing to choose them at the infant's birth. Now she stood there as a poster child for why the Fostering was so necessary. Ruth certainly had never taught the girl anything about respect and temperament, never mind the moral limitations of a Demon's powers.

The Maiden Demon was a female Earth Demon, the most powerful element a female Demon could be born to next to the element of Fire. And to see it wasted sickened Legna. Worse, Mary had thrown her lot in with these human deviants. For all the times Noah had joked about treason, this act was the ultimate betrayal. Not even he could have come up with this concept. Not even as a joke.

Job, Mary's father, must be spinning on his pyre. Thankfully, he had not lived to see this blasphemy. The honor of Ruth's entire family would be scarred in a way from which it would not soon recover. Ruth as well as Mary would have to answer for these actions. Even if she was not taking part in this, although Legna suspected she was. Until a Demon child became an adult, its parents and *Siddah* were as responsible for its behavior as the fledgling itself. And no one could be more responsible for this than Ruth. She might as well have been in the Mother position after all.

The Crone was the necromancer, Legna noted, sending this intelligence to the men along with her other realizations. She was the eldest of them, but far from old and decrepit. The Mother was the leader of the weaker hunters, insignificant in the dark of night, deadly as venom in the wash of the daylight sun. This woman was physically fit and well trained, and it radiated off her. Her confidence alone was formidable.

"The Demon will be returning to his territory soon," Mary said with confidence.

The statement surprised her, and it also did not. Jacob would never return to the site of such an affront to his safety. The location had been exposed, and it was to be shed from his life as a snake sheds its skin.

This was devised information. Noah had planted it with Ruth somehow. Now the intelligence was clearly filtering down into the plan for a repeat attack on Jacob's household that was being laid before the masses. This time the enemy planned on taking a small army, and they were not going to play psychological games. They planned to take the Enforcer himself, as well as his mate and unborn.

Legna actually felt pity for them. Mary had told them nothing of what they were truly facing.

Trying to capture a being like the Enforcer was rather akin to trying to catch a porcupine barehanded. The task was not impossible, but boy would you pay for it in the ensuing struggle. To these befouled women, Jacob was just a spawn of the devil, his mate his enslaved whore, and the child she carried some sort of Antichrist. Mary only fed their prejudices, stirring them up with the fire of their own fear and hatred, and leaving the humans woefully unprepared.

Do not underestimate them, Nelissuna. *They represent a formidable power. We will be hard-pressed to be rid of them all.*

I know. But it is such a waste.

I agree. Mary the most tragic of all.

Ruth will answer for her part in this, Gideon.

Another waste. But Ruth is no child. She knew what she was doing. She cannot claim ignorance at her age, Neliss.

I know, she thought sadly. *We can be grateful for one thing, though. Mary is too young to have ever been* Siddah *to anyone and therefore will know no power names to give to the necromancers.*

I hope you are right about that. Ruth has been Siddah *to many. Mary may have heard a few things over the years. And I suspect Ruth herself is no longer above such a heinous act.*

Let us pray that she has not already done so.

The three interlopers had to wait some time before the meeting broke up and they were able to rise and move toward other sections of the caverns. Legna used the cover of the milling crowd to hide her outreaching senses. The necromancers might pick up on them, but they would have a hell of a time singling her out so long as she and her companions kept moving. Still, she masked her efforts with surprising skill.

Legna could not immediately feel anything resembling Corrine's distinctive presence. She supposed Corrine's emotions were depressed by unconsciousness. That was when she felt Gideon powering through her. He was doing what she could not, where he could not do it. He sought through her for an injured presence, the blood left behind assuring him that Corrine was definitely injured. She would not have had enough time to heal naturally, so for Gideon this became a beacon for him to follow. With their powers combined, Legna drew a bead on the Druid's location. She looked at Siena, who was also alert. Legna did not know their exact nature, but the Queen clearly had perceptive abilities of her own.

The Queen whispered to Anya, who walked to the entrance of the cavern section the other two were headed into, striking a casual pose as she guarded their backs for the time they needed to locate Corrine's exact position. It took Siena's warning touch to keep Legna from beelining to her objective. Legna was no warrior or spy. The Lycanthrope knew more about such things.

Gideon was aware of his mate approaching several guards in Corrine's vicinity. He pushed any anxiety he might have felt far away from himself and concentrated on feeding her his power. He trusted Siena's prowess as a fighter as well. He had seen her practice, day after day, all of the five years he had spent at her side. She was a formidable opponent.

"I have an idea," Siena whispered, moving them back until they were flattened up against a wall just a curve away from the guards.

She reached up to loosen her hair, shaking the huge coils free, unable to suppress her sigh of relief as she did so. Legna watched with fascination as the curls moved into perfect position, springing up where they should not have been able to. It was then that she realized the changelings' hair behaved almost as if it were a living appendage. This was another thing she had not known about the Lycanthrope species.

"I know how to throw suspicion off the Demons, at least," she murmured.

The Queen then shrugged out of her shirt and stepped out of her skirt, standing nude as she handed the clothing to Legna. Then, as she continued to shake her head, the length of her golden hair crept over her skin, coating every inch of it in the soft filigree. The hair began to transform into fur as the Queen dropped to all fours.

With a final shudder, the woman turned into the wild beast. The mountain lion looked up at the female Demon staring at it with undisguised awe. But Legna quickly shook herself out of the daze when the cat crouched down and crept closer to the guards. Suddenly she sprang, loping into the distant cave quickly, releasing a scream that sent chills down Legna's spine.

Careful, love, Gideon soothed. *It is an enchantment. The scream of the mountain lion has terrifying effects naturally, but she has an added power of compulsion.*

Legna could believe it. She had to concentrate very hard not to give in to the fear the guards were giving in to. The women cried out and bolted from their positions. They tore past Legna as if the hounds of hell were after them. Legna resisted the urge to giggle and hurried into Siena's wake. The Queen was laughing herself as she shook out her hair one final time. Oblivious to her nudity or anything else, she led Legna into the small cave that had lain behind the guards. On a pallet of straw, chained cruelly to the wall in a way that left her suspended by her bleeding wrists, Corrine hung limply, her face buried under the curtain of her hair.

Legna hurried to encircle her with strong arms, holding her weight up as she pushed back her hair. If she was too badly injured, it would be dangerous to teleport her. She had been abused, her face covered in bruises and blood, but Legna felt Gideon assuring her quickly that she was able to be transported.

Legna motioned to the Queen to join her.

"No. I must continue this little charade. I have to exit via natural means, be it the front door or one of the hidden ones I guarantee you are located in these caves. That way, they will not suspect me as anything but the lion."

Anya hurried into the cave, breathless with her excitement.

"They're coming!"

"They'll kill you," Legna argued. "This is suicide!"

"They have to catch me first." The Queen laughed, shaking her hair until it once more spread over her.

Legna didn't waste time watching the transformation. She grabbed Anya's wrist and closed her eyes. They teleported with a hearty pop, rematerializing moments later in the alley next to the club they had entered from.

Gideon and Kane were already hurrying around the corner.

"We have to get out of here. Siena's game is dangerous."

It was clear by the flame in her mate's eyes that Gideon was not pleased with the Queen's reckless behavior. But Legna believed there was sound method to the madness. The human women would suspect Corrine had escaped while they were busy chasing a mountain lion that had inexplicably entered their caves, no doubt by one of the rear escape exits Siena had mentioned.

Chapter 14

"You have been very quiet tonight," Noah said to his sister. "I guess you are pretty shocked about this whole business."

Legna didn't respond, she just watched her brother as he walked around the triangular Council table they had used for their recently ended meeting. The newly discovered liberty of wearing jeans allowed her to prop her feet up on the wooden table with casually crossed ankles. She seemed to be enjoying the somewhat unladylike position.

Jacob and the others had gone home not too long ago. Gideon had removed himself with Kane and an excuse about checking on Isabella's and Corrine's health, but he knew Legna had wanted to be alone with Noah for a little while. Legna understood Noah was pleased she had stayed behind, and she hated to shatter his contentment, but the sooner they discussed this, the better.

"Noah?"

"Yes?"

Noah looked at her, hesitating in his task as he did so.

"I remembered."

Noah's brows drew down in a moment of noncomprehension. But as he read his sister's serious expression and the grave stillness in her eyes, it dawned on him sharply what she was talking about. He almost laughed aloud in his sudden tension. He had imagined this day for two and a half centuries, even down to the words "I remembered," and still it had taken him by surprise.

Noah moved to sit in the nearest chair, sinking into it as if gravity had suddenly increased for him. Legna watched and waited while he gathered himself, trying to erect a mental armor but having very little success with his emotions already in turmoil. It didn't surprise her. Noah's entire element was based on volatility. It was a credit to his power that it didn't take over like this more often.

"You do not have to explain the details of what happened. Gideon has spared you from that. But I thought you should know," she said.

"I had a feeling this would happen." Noah reached to rub at an invisible spot on the table. "I suppose you are thinking that I should have told you sooner, yes?"

"Yes," she agreed. "But I also understand why you did not."

"I am sorry, Legna. I had hoped you would never have to remember that day. I . . . I was terrified when I realized what was happening between you and Gideon. I knew a power rush like that would open all kinds of doors."

"I know. When it was finally unlocked, I also realized why you and Hannah have been twisting into knots over this. I must say, I am glad it is not Gideon you truly object to."

"No," Noah agreed. "It was not Gideon himself. Just the possibilities of his influence resurrecting these memories. I hope he was there when it happened."

"Luckily, yes." Legna paused for a long minute, meeting his troubled eyes. "You must promise me that you will stop trying so hard to protect me. It cannot succeed flawlessly, and you are just wearing yourself out. And if I go to the Lycanthrope Queen as your ambassador, you must keep me apprised of all things. To leave me in the dark would be foolish."

"Then you are considering the offer?"

"Yes. But I must discuss it with Gideon first. Tell me, Noah, why you thought of me for this task."

"As I said, because I trust you. Your loyalty and your open mind are exactly what I require. You know you are my best diplomat. I can send no less."

"You must trust me in this as well, Noah. It is not your job to protect me anymore."

"I'm afraid that will be a nearly impossible habit to break," he told her. "However, I shall endeavor to do so." He gave her a wan smile. "I hope that some day you will be able to remember beyond Mama's death to when she was alive and loved us both. They are excellent memories."

"They will be worth living through this last one if they are as good as I hope for." Legna dropped her feet to the floor and approached him. "Now, there is something I need you to do for me."

"Anything, little sister."

"I need you to talk to Gideon. Yes, he is behind my eyes, and yes, he is somewhat immune to emotional ramblings of distraught brothers and sisters." She smiled as she stood behind him and leaned forward to wrap her arms around his shoulders and hug him tightly. "But he deserves better than what he has been getting from you and Hannah this past week. Despite what everyone seems to think, I believe it is important to him that he earn a family, and I want to give him mine. I do not know a better one." Her voice lowered as she rested her chin on his shoulder. "And I love him, Noah. With all of my heart and soul. He has a conscience of such depth, and a capacity for needing me I never thought possible. How can I help but feel deeply for him?"

"I know," he said just as quietly, rubbing her hand warmly. "I have been feeling that keenly all night. I am happy for you. I truly am. I have been very selfish lately. For all my announcements that I was afraid of your pain, it was my dread of you facing me with the truth that was my motivator. I am sorry for that."

He turned his head to look at her as she released him from her hug and moved to slide her bottom onto the table near him. She crossed her ankles and began to swing her linked feet back and forth.

"Today," Noah continued, "someone reminded me of Gideon's value to our people, and I realized that I had been forgetting to acknowledge that. It is a sad repayment for all he has done at my request over the centuries." He smiled, reaching to tug on the alien black hair that Gideon had yet to return to its natural state. "It is not the same without its true length," he teased.

"Oh, stop," she scolded, laughing as she freed her hair from his fingers with a tug.

"Should you not be getting home to your betrothed?"

"Mmm, I suppose I should. I want to make certain the guest rooms are prepared for Bella and Corrine's stay with us. I am glad they will stay out of the way, protected by the fact Ruth is not likely to think to look for them in Gideon's infamously off-limits household. As advantageous as their abilities are, they and Bella's baby have been through enough."

"Agreed." Noah watched her hop off the table. "Legna?"

"Yes?"

Noah reached for her hand, pulling the back of it to his brief, affectionate kiss. "Tell my brother-in-law that I hope he appreciates the precious gift I am giving him this Beltane."

Legna smiled at him, but her mouth trembled as tears brightened in her eyes. She leaned in to kiss his forehead and then turned away, hiding her emotional expression as she disappeared without a sound.

* * *

Gideon's silvery eyes flashed in the moonlight as he scanned the area before him. He was perched on the roof of Jacob's home, blending into the darkness of the shadows around the chimney, leaning his weight gently against the back that supported his, just as he supported hers. He felt her power blanketing the area. She was in search of the heightened emotions of those who would be descending on them that night with ill intent in their hearts.

Gideon was aware of the hidden pulses and body warmth of the others, easily discerning their location as he turned his eyes from one place to the next. Jacob's heart was the slowest in beat, weighed down, no doubt, by the stillness that often preceded acts of terrible retribution. Elijah was another story. The warrior was notoriously serene on a hunt, but Gideon could sense the speed of his breath and blood was not normal. He suspected that the Lycanthrope female who was near him might have something to do with that. Elijah seemed to be very uncomfortable around her. The warrior knew what it was like to fight her kind, so it was understandable. Working with one's former and recent enemy had to be unnerving.

The Queen herself had enjoyed the invitation to join this little ambush. Her body chemistry, pulses, and senses were just different enough to be alien, but he knew enough about her physiology after his five years of "captivity" to know she was anticipating the hunt, the battle, with every ounce of the instincts that ruled her kind.

There was Noah as well, of course, plus the Lycanthrope half-breed, and, to even Gideon's amazement, the Vampire Prince. He had not been tendered an invitation but had somehow learned of the action taking place here this night. Damien was an ally who transcended all others. To begin with, the attackers would not be expecting anything other than Demons to be involved in this. At most they would be prepared for the Enforcers to still be as heavily guarded as was last reported. They would surely not be prepared to do battle with Lycanthropes and Vampires. Such a collaboration of Nightwalkers was unheard of in all the centuries they had existed in the same universe.

Gideon felt Legna go very still, the heightened sensation of her scans returning his attention to the roof they were perched on. He raised his head and reached for what she had sensed.

Heartbeats. Dozens of them. And power. A great deal of power.

Gideon closed his eyes and reached to astral project to the rear guard of warriors that were hidden farther back from his recon position. Once he warned them it was time to make ready, he returned to his body and moved to lie on his belly beside Legna, who had already done so. They watched the cliffside horizon, feeling keenly that they were coming by the beachside.

Jacob's hunting senses roared to life along with those of all the others. He was at point for a reason. He was the first line of defense, Elijah the next. The attacking force would find it difficult to circumvent these initial defenses. And even if they did manage to get past these formidable fighters, they would have Noah to contend with next. If Jacob had not been so full of high adrenaline and the need to purge himself of his building anger, he might have spared his coming enemy a thought of pity.

Then again, probably not. These animals had come to his home, orchestrated an attempt to assassinate the one thing that meant more to him than his own life. Though they had failed, they would answer for her pain and injuries. They would hear his rage over every shudder and shiver of fear they had caused Isabella to feel, every tear she had shed from that day to this. And now they dared to return? Invading his home, prepared to destroy it, him, and his family?

Oh yes. They would learn a great lesson tonight.

Most of all, they would be made to understand how

much he hated the fact that he was even there. His bride's sad heart and eyes were behind his own. All of her spirit and thoughts whispered in his mind with wishes that such violence and ignorance would just go away and leave everyone to live in peace and in their own way.

The aggressors came over the cliffside in a sudden wave, the necromancers glowing head to toe in bright blue light as they levitated themselves and several hunters each with unnerving ease. Through the dark, Jacob saw the hunters holding crossbows at the ready, and the smell of rust on iron hit him tangibly. The bolts in the bows were made of iron, making the sharply pointed missiles extremely deadly. The old and heavy metal was the one true weakness of every Demon. Iron burned them, scarred them, and could quite easily kill them if it struck a mortal enough target within them. It didn't matter how powerful or how ancient they were, everyone was vulnerable.

Jacob swore under his breath but did not retreat from his position. He tried to think of how he could warn the others, who would not have the same keen sense for this earthy metal as he did. He reached out for Siena, knowing her eyesight in the darkness was unparalleled.

Siena felt the earth move beneath her hand and she withdrew with a soft gasp. The blond warrior near her shot her a look as she continued to stare at the ground. An invisible finger was drawing in the dirt. She cursed when she realized it was a word, sent to her by the Earth Demon.

"Iron," she whispered to Elijah. "All of them, I would bet."

Elijah didn't say a word, just nodded to her. He closed his eyes for a moment and then spoke the dreaded word aloud. With a skillful twist of the wind, he carried the sound away and up to the roof. The breeze moaned the warning gently to the medic and his mate.

They looked at each other, knowing it was too late for

them to warn the troops behind them. They could see the mass of flying women streaming up over the cliffside.

Jacob waited as long as he could, wanting as many of them to be caught by surprise as he could manage. The only way to do that would be to wait until they were all on the ground at his level. He was not to have the luxury of time, he realized, the stench of the black magic washing up to him with the same speed as their advance. Remaining low, he buried his fingers into the earth.

"Come, Lady, let us teach these abominations not to fool with Your children," he whispered to the loam beneath him.

With a single broad gesture, both Jacob and an enormous wall of earth rose toward the heavens. The entire area rumbled with the roar of the rising ground. The oncoming forces found themselves being washed over with a thunderous wave of dirt and rock and other natural debris.

The necromancers escaped with the most ease, soaring higher into the air and out of reach of the damaging wave; only half of the hunters found themselves being pulled in tow with them. The other half succumbed to the sheer force and weight of the attack. Yelling, shouting of commands, and wild confusion followed. Jacob did not wait long before reaching to alter the gravitational forces on the beach below his flying form.

Instantly, bodies were caught in the drag of their own weight, the force crushing enough to strike them hard upon the rocks.

Again, it was the magic-users who circumvented his attack. He was suddenly the target of brutal bolts of electricity. He was struck hard, blown back over the ridge, and driven down into the ground, the force of the strike of his body tearing up the soil in a ten-foot strip.

Elijah was the next to leap into the air, but unlike Jacob, his body was the consistency of the wind, and the electrical attacks had no effect on him. As he stirred up the ocean, bringing warm air and cold water into a mixture perfect enough to give birth to a horribly dense fog, the opposing forces found themselves blanketed with the blinding mist.

From the rooftop, Gideon and Legna had risen to their feet. As the fog advanced to a point just shy of them, they saw the bright golden hair of the Lycanthrope Queen snapping in the building wind around her, the curls of it slipping like a thousand fingers around her now-nude body. Legna watched with fascination as the hair spread out over every ounce of flesh, turning into a rich coat of fur as she dropped to all fours. With a mighty trembling of her entire body, rather like the shaking of a dog fresh out of water, she turned from a beautiful woman to a lethal mountain lion.

The scream of the cat echoed joyously in the confusing fog, rousing startled cries of fear. Forces were landing on the ground five and ten at a time, only to be lost from each other immediately. Suddenly a horrifying scream would rise out of the melee, the death cry of a human being who had met up with a rather eager huntress in the form of a great golden-eyed cat.

The Vampire joined the lion, flying into the mist with the leap of the ultimate predator. To those who became his targets, at first there was nothing but the gray dampness of fog, and then, suddenly, there was a creature so dark and fast that it was only the relief of his white fangs that gave them warning two seconds before he struck. The hunters were just humans of great prowess, so it was safe for him to pull first one, then another, under the powerful drain of his fangs.

It was the blackened blood of the necromancers he could not drink, but the humans were drained to within an inch of their lives before he dropped them carelessly away from him. There was a certain pleasure involved, as was always the case when taking female blood. Before long the fanged snarl became a smile, his dark eyes shining like onyx with the erotic high.

He caught a couple of iron crossbow bolts in nonvital areas, but the wounds only allowed him to exchange his blood supply all the faster. As he was drained, he was refilled. It was the first time in centuries that he had felt an actual pulse inside of himself. It was the artificial throb of the fresh supply forcing the existing supply out of open wounds, but it was close enough to the former workings of his still heart to give him a mighty rush.

With the troops blinded, the necromancers knew they were in trouble. Those who had mastered enslaving Demons pulled an unexpected contingent of Demons from the beach. They were Transformed, their deviant emotions striking at Legna with shock and vile clarity. She stumbled back from the force of it, and Gideon barely caught her before she went careening off the slope of the roof. Scooping her into his arms, he jumped to the ground with one great leap of empowered muscles and flexible tendons.

The minute the earth was under her feet again, Legna began to recover. Gideon knew this because her immediate rage at the abominations she was sensing washed over him like a physical force. He knew what she knew, and they both knew this was trouble. With Jacob still down and trapped in the fog with the landing force, and Isabella far away in her sickbed, they would be forced to destroy these Transformed Demons themselves.

It was understandable that they were troubled by this realization. Fighting the Transformed was the most difficult battle a Demon might ever know. And of all of them, Gideon and Noah were the only ones other than the Enforcers who had any experience with it. Even so, their experiences were at the very least a century old, and at the very most quite limited. Legna turned her attention to Noah, suddenly understanding that he could not release his assault with Jacob lying in the center of the battlefield. The Earth Demon would be just as vulnerable to fire as any of the others.

Legna disappeared with a snap of the air before Gideon could think to stop her. She felt him shout in her mind as she reappeared in the streak of torn-up soil Jacob had left behind him. She crouched low, peering through the fog for him. He would not be far, but he had to be out cold to not be giving off any emotions. And as a typical Demon, right about then he ought to have been pretty pissed off.

Suddenly someone ran out of the fog and almost tripped over her. The human hunter's eyes widened at the unexpected encounter, but she raised her crossbow and fired. Legna dodged getting the bolt in a vital body part, but as she rolled away she felt unbelievably searing pain and heat cutting through her jeans and thigh. Her mate's roar of rage drowned her cry of pain, the frightening sound of it echoing through the fog. But Legna was not the delicate, graceful flower everyone seemed to think she was. She barely hesitated in getting back to her feet. Apparently, judging by the look of confusion and shock on the hunter's face as Legna stepped with obvious menace toward her, the human had expected her to disintegrate, perhaps like the vampires did on mortal TV shows when staked through the heart.

Wait until they find out how well that *is going to work,* she thought wickedly as she lunged for her attacker. Legna tackled the woman at the midsection, disarming her as the crossbow went flying from her sweating hands. The hunter hit the ground with a grunt, echoed by an immediate second grunt when Legna bounced on her, driving her knee down into her sternum. With all of her disgust and her rage, Legna yanked the iron bolt out of her leg, screaming as the iron burned her hand and as she plunged the bolt into her victim's chest.

She left the female human gasping for breath that would not fill her collapsing lung. She stood up and turned with a wild flinging of her loosening braid, feeling the sounds and scents and sensations of the night filling her, magnifying, calling to the huntress within.

She immediately recognized that Jacob was ten feet to her right. She advanced at as fast a run as she dared in the fog. She encountered another hunter on the way, and this time she was prepared. She dove into her opponent's mind, causing a rush of fear to well in her until her heart was pounding too hard for her body to handle. It braked to a stop only a minute later; she had literally been frightened to death.

The empath dropped to her knees at Jacob's side. Her hands hit his chilled body and without a moment of hesitation she teleported them out of harm's way. Legna dropped Jacob onto the couch in his living area and teleported once more, this time popping up at her brother's side.

"Jacob is safe. Go!"

Noah nodded once and began to steal energy from the enemies before him, converting it swiftly into a rushing wall of fire. He didn't worry about Siena. He felt her heat and energy easily and was aware of her circling away from his target area. Damien was launching off the ground already to do the same.

The world went up in flames, screams of pain and death and shock filling the night air along with smoke and the scent of burning flesh. But once more it was the magic-users who managed to spare themselves. The necromancers began to land past the line of the wall of fire, facing off with Gideon, Legna, and Noah. Elijah was doubling back to call up the rear guards and the halfbreed was lying in silent wait, watching to take the Demons' cue.

Noah began to fire off little meteors of flame at the corrupted females. Gideon pulled a knife from his thigh and sent it winging into one necromancer as he reached to grasp a second around the throat. She crumpled instantly when he dove into the workings of her body and commanded her heart to stop.

Legna had reappeared at her mate's side shortly before this new onslaught had begun. She was aware of only one thing: Transformed Demons were stumbling out of the dark, most of them on fire, none of them feeling it. They would die eventually, but it could be a very long time in the making and they could still cause a great deal of harm and damage in the interim. She sent herself out, projecting her cotton-candy thoughts first into one, then another. She had them engaged in thoughts of comfort at first, but then realized it was not going to hold their attention long. If she got them to stop and sit still, the fire would consume them more quickly without giving them a chance to damage anyone.

Eventually she adjusted her visions to ones of a carnal nature. Demons Transformed had only two thoughts: freedom and lust. They had the one already, so the second was all that remained to engage them. The Transformed began to fall to the ground, flopping around with a grotesque glee and pleasure as they took hold of imaginary partners.

Weak from blood loss and all her teleporting, Legna could only engage three of them at once, leaving others to head for her brother and her beloved.

Gideon felt Legna drop to her knees. She was too close to the fighting to be left where she was, and too weak to move. But at the same time, to touch her might disrupt the tenuous control she had on the three Transformed Demons. His only choice was to battle on, to protect her by eliminating any advancing threats.

Gideon was throwing his second knife as he retrieved the first, spinning as he moved with lightning speed. He saw Noah drawing energy from one female until she collapsed and then sending a bolt of fire into the next. Many of them knew a shielding spell; some of the men's elemental attacks bounced off unharmed women.

Damien suddenly flew out of the fog and darkness from behind the attacking harpies. He had the ability to cast fear before himself, just as Siena could, though on a different, less natural level. It was a power of pure darkness, of the malevolence that inexplicably caused fear of the dark, the monsters under the bed, or the inevitability of death as that horse and rider rode across a grave. Since it was a part of every living being on the planet, no shielding could protect them from it. Shields prevented things like power and weapons from entering; the darkness Damien manipulated already existed within the shield and within the people themselves.

Magic-users were losing concentration left and right as he advanced, all safeguards and magical means destroyed along with their shattered focus. He began to seize necromancers one at a time, the quick turn of delicate necks preceding an eerily casual discarding of the remaining bodies. To Damien, it was no different than disposing of trash, and it showed. Too many of these creatures had staked out his brethren in the midday sun for the joy of watching them burn to ash, and they deserved none of his pity or his mercy.

Contrary to mythic belief, a Vampire did not conflagrate all at once when exposed to the sun. The imprisoned creature would smolder like a moss fire, for hour upon hour, no doubt screaming for mercy the entire time. And for what? For having a differing body chemistry that enhanced their mental senses, gave them the ability to fly and the need for blood to survive? The lawful majority of the race did not kill when they fed, and the idea of converting humans to Vampire was the most ridiculous in human history. Just like all species, Vampires were born to this world.

So it gave Damien no guilt, no moral dilemma to dispose of these women in this fashion. It was a far more merciful fate than they would have planned for him had they been given the chance. Even more merciful than the fates they had planned for the Enforcer female and her innocent unborn child.

Suddenly, a second wave of dirt surged up from under the feet of the front line of Demons, tumbling the fighters backward into the softened hands of Mother Earth. The wave caught up the enemy, surfing them like driftwood back to the edge of the cliff, hurling many of them off it.

There was a massive surge of power from behind the front line of battling Demons as reinforcements arrived. It was a relief to feel it. The most powerful of their species had done their worst, had destroyed the majority of the threat, but it had cost them all in energy and health. It was time for the first line to fall back and entrust others to finish the battle.

Jacob hurried forward to Legna, who lay in the soft mattress of aerated soil he had provided for her. He pulled her up into his grasp and, relieving them of the hold of gravity, used it instead to propel them skyward and behind their advancing line.

Gideon was overwhelmed with the urge to go to her but knew that she would be safe with Jacob for the moment and that he was needed to fight where he was. Elijah was lifting the fog as those who had survived the last attack sailed up over the cliffside once more. They surged up like an enraged flock of predatory birds, screeching out spells and incantations as they faced the force of Demons.

From that moment on, it was pretty much all about magic and mayhem. Natural versus unnatural. Evil versus the Just. Jacob left Legna at the paws of the mountain lion who had circled back around to get out of the line of battle. She lay down over Legna's arm, lazily licking the wounds that were scattered over her golden coat as her intelligent gold eyes reassured the Demon that she would protect Legna now.

Jacob turned back. He had some Transformed

Demons to take care of now that he was returned to his senses. He was positive that Legna's little manipulations of their warped minds could not last much longer, if indeed the barely conscious woman still had hold of them. This was his duty, to punish his own for their wrongdoings and perversions, even if it was a byproduct of being manipulated by black magic. They were beyond redemption now, beyond hope of reclamation. The only mercy he could show them would be their swift deaths. For the first time he wished Bella were there with him. This was where she excelled; this was where she would have been his relief. She was like an angel of mercy to the poor souls, and she would have swept the field with her inborn skills to bring them peace from such torment. This, he realized, would have been her best revenge: to deprive these depraved bitches of the power of the Demons they had captured, stealing away their prizes and their access to even more power names with which to make more unfortunate, deadly monsters.

Iron bolts were flying with more accuracy now that the fog had thinned, and Demons began to take both injuries and casualties. The necromancers were headed full bore into the fight, dragging fresh hunters with them. This was not the small army they had heard of in the meeting. Noah began to suspect there had been a tipped hand somewhere along the line. With so many people involved, it was always a possibility. He suspected, however, that Corrine's rescue had been the cause of the additional human influx. The Demon King believed that, when this battle ended, the Demon race would have struck a mighty blow into the ranks of necromancers. Female ones, at least. The questioned that remained was, did Mary realize she had been caught? And what of Ruth? Would they now have to hunt them both down before delivering them to the justice of the Enforcer?

The Demons followed the example of the Ancients among them, changing to hand-to-hand combat in order to dive past the magical shields meant to fend off elemental attacks. It was at this point that the Lycanthrope half-breed made her appearance. She might have been the weakest of them all in a certain sense, but she was a remarkable fighter. It was clear that, had she been a full Lycanthrope, she would have been some form of fox or vixen. She displayed sharp tearing teeth, small black claws, and a sinuous speed that left her little more than a streak of black leather clothing and auburn hair. When she stopped, victims suddenly began to fall like dominos, their throats laid open with those tiny but lethal claws. She paused to lick one of the little black blades, then smiled and was once more a blur.

The tide of battle was always meant to be in the favor of the Demons. They were the more skilled and experienced fighters. The one saving grace of all the wars they had lived through had to be the skills they had gained, now to be used in defense. It was all a tragedy of terrible proportions. The hunters thought they could win with the human version of great fighting skills, blind motivation, and following this cause whose true purpose was honestly unknown to them. No one enjoyed the idea of harming these misguided souls, but they would be foolish to let them go and survive to perpetuate more of this awful discontent.

As the humans began to fall back and retreat from the Demons' battle skills, the Demons felt little victory. As with all such clashes, there would be ramifications from this. The fighting had been cloaked from the curious mainstream human populace with the isolation of Jacob's home and the fog and storms of the Wind Demons blanketing the area. Bodies would be buried and destroyed. The field of battle would be returned to its flawless nature without so much as a speck of blood to show for the evening's work.

And yet there was a permanent stain flowing over all the surviving souls of that battle. The waste of lives, both human and Demon, all because of the need for revenge, could never be compensated for.

Finally the fighting came to an end. There was little ceremony, and less rejoicing. The only befouled humans who remained were the dead and the wounded. Very few had fled any farther than the beach below, and it was only a matter of minutes before warriors caught up with them. They began to gather prisoners. Gideon displayed his remarkable ability by casting out a powerful stasis energy across the field, helping to maintain wounded until warrior Body Demons could reach them. He held this extension of enormous energy as he turned to find his mate.

An adult Demon had aided her briefly, enough to stem the tide of blood that had gushed from her. Gideon knelt beside her pale figure, glancing at the Lycan-thropic animal beside her for only a second. He reached to stroke Legna's soil-dusted hair and a cheek streaked with blood from her own fingertips when she had scratched an itch or pushed back her hair unthinkingly. Her blood supply was dangerously low, her heart pumping valiantly to try and circulate it as fast as possible to maintain her oxygen levels.

Gideon laid a hand on her injured thigh, feeling the residual burn the fragments of iron had left behind. The adult healer had been wise to not attempt to heal this wound. It was beyond his skill and he could have done more harm than good. Gideon could heal her, working out the iron filings as he did so. She would be scarred through both sides of her thigh, but that was of little consequence considering she might have died.

He reached into her with his power, closing his eyes as he absently stroked the wound sight with incredible gen-tleness. He healed her nicked bone and proceeded out-ward. At the same time, he encircled her wrist with his other hand and fed a transfusion of his blood into her weak body. He could only give her enough to maintain her, because he was weak and still expending tremendous energy in too many directions that were required of him. He had not felt so drained in a long time. The last instance had also been during a battle of this kind. He had hoped he would never be involved in such a thing again, but it seemed the ignorant and corrupt would have their way at the expense of his wishing for a peaceful life.

She stirred, his name the first word on her lips. He smiled at that, then reached to cast a deep sleep inducement on her. He sat back, his exhaustion growing as he held the stasis field on those who had not yet received medical attention.

The Lycanthrope who had protected Legna began to shake her gleaming head, her moonstone and gold collar jingling at its links. Her hair began to peel away from her body, shaking looser and looser until it was falling in wide coils. With a majestic shudder, she went from feline sinew to human athleticism. Her hair concealed her nude figure better than a bathing suit would have, but the half-breed vixen was approaching her Queen with her clothing at that very moment. In a minute, Anya dropped a simple slip of a dress over the Queen's head. Once it settled over her curves, both women extracted her hair from beneath it.

Gideon gave little thought to the actions taking place so close to him. What he did notice, however, was Elijah watching the Queen with a dark, brooding expression. Watching the Lycanthrope change form had disturbed him. No doubt it had brought back many memories of his battles with them. They were fierce fighters; one had to respect them or find oneself quite dead. It did not surprise Gideon that Elijah remained wary of her intentions.

Elijah moved closer as he saw Gideon sway under the strain of his exertions, even though the medic was already seated. The warrior reached Gideon a moment before the paling Demon fell back into an exhausted unconsciousness. He caught him behind the head and lowered him gingerly into a supine position. The warrior was aware of the gold eyes that were fixed on him and he looked up to meet them.

"You are uncommonly gentle for a fighter," she mused softly, blinking and seemingly looking through him with those vivid eyes.

"You are uncommonly . . . peaceful, for a Lycanthrope," he returned.

"And you doubt my sincerity."

"Wouldn't you?"

"I would think you an utter fool if you did not doubt me, warrior. Instead, I am forced to respect your uncommon intelligence. Now what, do you suppose, should I do from there?"

She left him hanging on the question, rising to her feet and leaving him before he could formulate an answer. He watched her go, his gaze searching and curious as he fixed it on the feline slink that she maintained in her human form just as well as she did in her form as a lioness.

Chapter 15

All lost Demons but the Transformed would be mourned on the eve before Beltane. There would be wounded hearts, and tears to soak the timbers of the pyres. And as they burned, those fires would be tended until the Beltane torches and bonfires could be lit from them. It was the cycle of life—unfortunately not a simulated one—from death to rebirth. It was the nature of Beltane, the Rite of Spring, at its sheerest definition.

The Transformed had already been destroyed. At the moment of death, they burst into flames, pyres unto themselves. Jacob took on the task of creating a mass grave for their enemies. It was a perfunctory end to a shameful waste of life. Elijah undertook the task of organizing the prisoners for interrogation. Gideon and Legna were recovering at Gideon's manse.

As Noah expected, Mary and Ruth were nowhere to be found. It infuriated him to realize this traitorous behavior had taken place right under his nose for months. Ruth and Mary had gathered and organized these forces against them, plotted against Jacob and Bella, even as Ruth sat week by week at his Council table in her honorable seat. It pained him greatly, leaving him depressed and weary.

However, he was playing host to a Vampire Prince and

a Lycanthrope Queen. He had to push past his emotions to help prepare for the coming celebration, which had expanded from the invitation and input of the Lycanthropes to the welcoming of the same from the Vampires. Small contingents of each would be joining the Demon festival, the first such thing in known history. It was the only spirit-lifting outcome of the saddening situation. It wasn't permanent world peace or anything so grandiose, but it was a start.

When Gideon finally woke a full two nights later, he opened his eyes to see his mate sitting at her vanity, clad only in a terry towel and the wet length of her hair. She was filling the center of her palm with a scented lotion he had given her as a gift a few days ago. It had reminded him of her scent in a way, not that it could ever be truly duplicated with any perfection. He had altered it, bringing the chemistry into a satisfactory blend between her scent and the oil of her favored spices, which he had asked Jacob to retrieve for him.

She smoothed the cream over her hands and arms and Gideon was instantly riveted. Her long fingers glided over her skin, the lotion leaving a luminescent sparkle in its wake as the special healing minerals within refracted light even in their smoothly ground-down state. Watching her touch her own skin in this highly sensual manner brought every blood cell in his body to a hot attention in only a matter of seconds. Her fingers stroked over the hollow in her collarbone that always fascinated him, the curve from neck to throat that he knew the taste of so well, and desire clenched through him, his flesh solidifying into weighted granite, the ache of brutal need impossible to bear in the confines of the clothes he'd been left in as he slept.

He craved her terribly, his body feeling starved and deprived of her presence and her unique textures even though they had undoubtedly been sleeping side by side this entire time of healing. She probably had not awoken too far ahead of him. Perhaps just long enough to take her shower.

The scent of the lotion reached him in fragrant waves, but he remained still, watching her as the cream reached the expanse of her shoulders and her upper chest. She reached beneath her arm to loosen her towel, dropping it away from her body so that she sat completely nude before her mirror. Gideon felt love and fire scorching through him in inexplicable partnership. She was beautiful and desirable, gentle and sexy. She was sitting there administering care to her already perfect body, and the pose she inadvertently struck would be branded into his memory for all time. This, he realized, was the woman he had been created to love. Somehow he had been blessed with her perfection of inner and outer beauty, her pristine soul so free of the stains that he himself carried from his unforgivable past.

Unforgivable, except for by her. This beautiful creature with her generous ways would be his absolution. Every time he would take his pleasure in her welcoming and hungry body, she would be giving him a gift of peace and reconciliation, wrapping herself around him with the touch of her complementary soul, erasing sin with her soft cries and clutching hands.

Gideon felt the burn of unexpected gratitude behind his eyes, and he wished he could look away from her long enough to give himself relief from the overwhelming emotion. But he could not, and he did not. Instead he simply let it flow over him, mingling with his pulsing need for her.

Legna continued her ministrations to her body, turning a little now and again to study her features and her perfect skin. Her hands glided down over her breasts, smoothed over her stomach, and then she turned to lift her leg onto the bench she was sitting on. It was then that she noticed him watching her. She smiled, tilting her head slightly as she tried to decipher his thoughts and emotions of the moment.

Before she really had a chance, Gideon moved at last, slipping out of bed as she rested her curious gaze on his approach. The Ancient felt her knowing eyes drifting over the very blatant message of need his body was displaying so unrepentantly. The sly smile of interest and contemplation she made sliced like a knife through his already aroused body. He took her hand as he neared her, using it to guide her into turning away from the vanity, her back to the mirror as he picked up the bottle of lotion. He filled his palm with it as he knelt on both knees before her. He propped her foot on his thigh and slowly began to administer the cream to her leg with a gentle massage of both hands.

Legna sighed softly. She felt his touch like the balm it was. He had, of course, started with her injured leg. It ached badly, so she was glad of his concentrated care of it. His hands were hot over the still-raw area. He was completing the task left undone due to his weakness after the battle. He numbed the area with her natural endorphins, and she was glad of it because he extricated a few remaining iron filings before continuing to heal her. The relief was instantaneous. She exhaled happily as he bore the burn of the iron long enough to dispose of it in a nearby wastebasket.

Legna reached to run her fingers through his hair, pulling him forward so his ear was beneath her lips. She kissed him softly just below it.

"Let me finish this, love. Take a shower. Relax. I will still be here when you return," she murmured gently.

"Are you trying to tell me something?" he asked with quiet humor, kissing her nearby cheek with a brush of his lips.

"One of the perks of civilization I refuse to relinquish

to my instinctual side is the benefit of soap and water when it comes to removing the scent of battle."

"I see. For me, the rise of battle in your blood was . . . beautiful. You are one of the great creations of all time, *Nelissuna.*"

"Liar. You wanted to throttle me the moment after I first left your side."

"That, my love, is completely beside the point."

She giggled, pulling back to match silver with silver, searching his gaze for a long moment.

"You would have me bathe you myself as women once did to the males of the house when you were born. I see the thought in your mind, so do not dare to deny it. But if I start with you, should I not tend my guests as well? I am not so certain Isabella would like it if I—"

Legna gasped midsentence when he yanked her up from the bench and pulled her over his shoulder as he rose to his feet. He marched her into the connecting bath as she squealed with indignant laughter and not-so-adamant demands to put her down. He had a possessive hand on her backside as he crossed to the deep bath that had been carved out of an enormous piece of pink quartz and rubbed to a smooth shine. He set her on her feet in the center of the tub and turned on the water as she put her hands on her hips and stuck one hip out to the side in a posture that was only missing a tapping foot of impatience to complete it.

"I already took a bath," she declared, completely uncaring of the fact that she was holding the argument in the nude. "I am not the one all befouled with dirt and blood and who knows what else. That bed is going to have to be fumigated between the two of us."

"It will be replaced by midnight," he assured her as he stripped off his clothes.

Legna moved to the opposite edge of the tub from him and sat on the wide rim as she kicked the water filling it. Gideon seemed to be ignoring the fact that her kicking got stronger each time and he was beginning to get sprinkled with water as he disrobed.

At least, he ignored it until she thought to try something she had never heard of anyone doing before. She imagined a bowl in her mind in the center of the deepening water. Then she teleported the imaginary bowl and its liquid contents to a point just above his head. The water kept form for all of a second, then released in a deluge in one sudden moment.

Legna cried out, a loud cross between a victory cry and delighted laughter. Gideon shook his soaked hair back from his eyes and two seconds later was around the tub and grabbing for her. When she appeared on the opposite side of the tub with a pop, she was laughing even harder. So hard, she clutched her sides and rolled onto her back, kicking her heels against the floor with her irrepressible humor.

Undaunted, Gideon crossed through the center of the tub to grab her, and this time she was laughing too much to concentrate on a teleport. He dragged his hysterical mate into the water and dunked her head under it. She popped up spewing water and laughter, smacking him harmlessly in what he supposed was some sort of retribution for the act. It seemed more like a flirtation, however, as she moved into the circle of his arms, clinging to his shoulders as he sat back in the hot, refreshing water.

"You got water in my ears," she complained, sneezing sharply from the water that had also gone up her nose. She shook her head, spraying him with water from her hair.

Gideon frowned suddenly, noticing something was a little off. He turned her back to him, using the float of water to assist him in the task. He reached for her hair and passed it through his hand.

"You cut your hair," he said, his astonishment clear. "You have never voluntarily cut your hair. Noah always had to wait until you were sleeping before setting scissors on you. Why did you cut it now?"

She turned back toward him, moving forward to straddle his thighs and rest her hands on his shoulders as she met his perplexed gaze.

"It is nothing. If I want you to grow it for me, I know you will."

"That is not an answer to my question."

"Well, I am afraid it is the only one you will be getting. And do stay out of my head about it, if you please."

"Legna," he warned.

"Gideon," she mocked. Legna reached past his shoulders, grabbing a bar of soap and a bath sponge, holding both up with tantalizing waves and a wiggling brow. "Where should I start?"

"I will not let you change the subject," he told her. "I want to know why you—"

Legna's hands plunged beneath the water as he spoke. The sentence ended with what Legna deemed a satisfactory intake of his breath.

"Subject changed," she announced wickedly, her smile split by the appearance of a saucy little tongue touching her upper lip. "Now," she purred naughtily as her hands encircled him, stroked him, "we are going to have to discuss the concept of privacy and private thoughts. If you do not allow me to have them, I will never be able to surprise you. Now, correct me if I am mistaken, but you seem to like surprises."

She stroked him with a skillfully soapy touch to punctuate her point.

Gideon found himself nodding, completely speechless unless he counted the unstoppable groan that rose up out of him. His hands were on her thighs, flexing opened and closed rhythmically as she continued to explore him with a blind but deft underwater touch.

"You know," she mused, "I like you much better when you are like this. I think we will be doing this a little more often."

"Oh, I hope so," he said at last, dragging her forward so he could reach her giggling mouth.

He kissed the laughter right out of her, keeping his mouth locked on hers until humor was replaced by growing heat and interest. Her hands never stopped but began to skim over wider, more diverse areas. She was soon bathing him in earnest, her mouth never leaving his as she covered him with erotic swirls of soap and sponge. She relinquished both to him a while later, her chest pressed to his, her thighs bracketing his hips as she filled her hand with shampoo and began a soft, sensual cleansing of his silver hair. While the amazing feel of her fingers sent whorls of sensation down through his body, he was spreading a rich lather of soap over her back and shoulders, slipping his hands between their chests and cupping her breasts in his soapy hands.

Legna purred with soft pleasure into his mouth. She gently coaxed his head back and, using the cup of her hands, meticulously rinsed his hair even as he continued to touch her in his most arousing ways. He shook his wet head back when she finished, reaching for her hands and pulling them back beneath the water as he recaptured the lips he realized he would never grow tired of.

They traded hot, slippery caresses until they were both breathing a chain of pleasurable sounds. Legna broke away from him suddenly, her abandonment disturbing him. He reached for her, but she slid in his grasp.

Then he realized she was turning around, sliding back into his embrace and reaching to slip his hands back over her breasts, nestling her thrusting nipples into his palms with a sound of eager encouragement. His mouth was on the elegant column of her neck instantly, making her shiver as she slid back toward him. He reached for her throat, using her collarbone to steady her from floating away from him as his other hand went to her hips, moving her back into him until he was moving into her.

Legna's body arched as he began the erotic intrusion,

soapy water making them slide in incredibly stimulating ways against each other. He pulled her onto him at the same time he surged up into her, sending himself deeply into that hot haven of femininity he loved and craved.

The sound of pleasure that shuddered out of him made her smile, her eyes sliding closed as she felt him move her floating body with such ease into a second thrust.

She felt so different this way, but even better for the difference. Without her mouth to split his focus, he was left with watching her spine curve and move as she moved her silky body over him. Outside of that, he was completely fixated on the feel of her, the strange and wonderful change of temperature between her and the water, the growing friction between them as the natural lubricants of her body were washed away, replaced, and washed away again.

She clutched at him so tightly he could hardly see straight. She was lost in the creation of those sounds of pleasure he loved hearing escape her. He reached a hard crest quickly, grabbing her hips and forcing her to be still while he inhaled deeply and gritted his teeth for control over the body he should have complete mastery over.

It was astounding that she could do this to him, astounding and incredibly wonderful. She smiled, knowing his thoughts as clearly as she knew her own in that moment. She could take control of him there and then in ways he would never expect. She tested the thought, flexing her body tightly around him until she elicited the hot curse he was prone to releasing in moments of ultimate vexation. His hand wrapped around her throat, pulling her head back so her ear was against his heated mouth.

"Do not move. Do not so much as cough, Magdelegna."

"But I do not want you to stop," she said softly, her voice a coaxing, sexual stimulant. She crossed the line, clutching him once more with that dangerously skillful muscle control she had.

Before he finished the requisite swearing due the moment, she found herself out of the tub and being pushed down onto her hands and knees on the plush white carpet that covered the floor. Her hips were pulled back toward him, rejoining their bodies in one movement.

She paid a pretty price for her insolent seduction. Her mate was more animal than man in that moment, moving with hot and sure movements into her body, reaching depths she didn't realize she had. She cried out, a series of whimpers that grew in volume moment by moment, spurring him on until she felt the scrape of nails against her skin and the primal surge of his body into her, setting her on fire. He groaned one moment, then surged into her with the beginnings of a long, low growl.

The sound magnified as they reached alternating peaks of pleasure. She was the first to leap headlong off the summit of her pleasure, her wild cry drowned by his throaty vocalizations as he exploded inside of her. He threw back his head, calling out, a shout of joy, a growl of warning. She was his. *His.* If any other dared to touch her or try to take her from him, they would pay the price to the beast behind the man.

It was only a minute before he was able to relax the possessive grip he had on her, but he had bruised her nonetheless. He moved from her, turning her over in a limp movement of arms and a delightful sound of female satisfaction. He had been worried to see he had marked her pretty much all over, but that sound seemed to make everything better.

He stood up, pulling her into his arms and scooping her off the floor. She hung limply in a very theatric pose of satiation, making him laugh when she smiled and peeked at him from under her lashes. He carried her into their bedroom, dripping a trail of water the entire way. He dropped her feet, holding her against him as he secured a clean blanket from the closet and wrapped it around them both.

"What bedrooms did you give to our guests?"

"The ones all the way . . . way . . . way on the other side of the manse."

He laughed at that, hugging her tightly for giving him that ability to indulge in humor once more.

"Then I'd say the bedroom with the old armoire you like should suffice."

"Yes, master," she teased, flicking her hand and sending them there. "Oops, one sec." She winked at him and snapped her fingers, the bottle of lotion suddenly in her hand.

"Show-off. You know, you are going to have to tell me how you do that."

"Well, first you pump this little thing on top, then the lotion—"

Legna yelped when he slapped her hard on her bottom, the blanket doing little to shield her from the sting of it.

"Gideon! Do not ever do that again!" she scolded.

"Not even if you beg me to?" he countered lecherously.

Legna laughed, unable to help herself.

"I hate you!"

"No, you do not," he insisted. "How many times do I have to tell you that?"

Chapter 16

Beltane came on a moon-filled and cold night. Fire lit the horizons at every turn. The pyres of the dead had been honored the night before, and tonight the revelers threw flower wreaths on the lost ones, saying final good-byes. They had lost seven men and two women in all, nothing compared to the enemy losses, but everything to a society who valued even the weakest member as highly as any other.

These beings of the old world, be they Vampire or Demon, had known the times of matriarchal societies and worshipping, what many now called the Pagan ways or the ways of the Witches. They had never, and would never, doubt the power of females. This sad battle had been a testament to why they never should. The lost female Demons had died protecting the backs of their mates, in the way that had passed from generation to generation.

". . . and with your mate at your back, you will know that no force can ever reach you without first facing his heart and her soul," Noah said in a bold voice so all the couples being wed that night could hear him.

He never performed the yearly mass ceremony, but he was looking at his baby sister's hand, wrapped in ribbons and tied to her mate's; the hands of the Enforcers who had once been torn midceremony from each other; and the hands of Kane and Corrine, both adored family of the Enforcers, who had tolerated so much just for doing their duty for him. He owed these three couples so much, and his heart was bursting with his gratitude for being able to give them this lifelong bond.

There were four others being wed as well, and they solemnly bowed their heads at the honor of being joined by the great King of Demons. In the fire-flickered shadows stood Demons, Vampires, and Lycanthropes, all watching with avid interest.

Noah raised his hands high.

"You are all beloved of each other, beloved of your King, beloved of this generous world and all Her elements that She bestows on us. None of you shall ever know the discontentment of a lonely home or an empty heart ever again because you will be filled with all these sources of love.

"The ceremony of this night is the perpetuation of life and its circle. You will be the vessels of that continuation. You will be the keepers of the future. The witnesses at your backs hold you to this promise and you hold it to each other.

"This week, we have known great sadness and great losses. But it fades under the light of the fires that light your way tonight. Here, in her"—he gestured to Isabella and smiled—"here is our future. Bring them to me, all of you, as they come, and I will love them as I love you.

"Now, you are joined for all time." Noah nodded and the witnesses released their friends and stepped away from the couples. "Turn, now, and touch your back to your mate's. This is where they will be for all the rest of the days of their lives."

Hands joined by ribbons raised into the air as the couples turned back to back.

A cheer went up from the crowd and the newly

wedded couples laughed as they turned back to kiss their mates warmly.

Tradition now dictated that anyone could try and pull the couple apart. Whoever succeeded in separating them at their ribbons would be able to sit beside the couple as they feasted in celebration. The field became a tumble of laughing mates and contestants as males tried to remove males and females tried to remove females.

Jacob grabbed his newly healed bride and floated out of the reach of would-be renders, a cry of protest rising from below them. Gideon and Legna were left unmolested, Gideon's imposing reputation having a quelling effect on the nerves of any who might have approached.

He was kissing his bride when he felt a tap on his shoulder. He turned and saw Damien arching a challenging brow at him. Legna laughed, delighted as Gideon gave the Prince a dirty look. Her humor lasted about two seconds. That was when Damien's partner in crime tapped Legna's shoulder.

Siena gave the bride a feline grin.

"Oh, you bitch," Legna choked out, laughing in her shock at the excellent maneuver on the Queen's part.

"Uh-uh," the Queen scolded, her collar winking in the firelight. "That's not very diplomatic of you, Ambassador."

"You realize this means war," Legna said archly.

"As if I would settle for anything less," Siena returned.

Legna and Gideon sighed, looking at each other and rolling their eyes. Husband grabbed hold of wife by their joined arms and then they braced their feet. Legna felt slim, strong arms around her waist and shoulders, and Gideon was seized in a similar hold by the determined Damien.

"Darling?" Legna said.

"Yes, love."

"Yes?"

"Definitely yes."

The Vampire and Lycanthrope pulled, and immediately found themselves holding nothing but air.

They both fell over hard into the dirt, dazedly watching a pair of ribbons floating down to the ground.

"Oh look, they won," Legna remarked from her and Gideon's new position a few feet away.

"How about that," Gideon mused. "See you both at dinner. Congratulations on your victory."

The couple popped off to who knows where, leaving indignant but dubiously victorious royalty behind.

Epilogue

"*Neliss*, why is this rug wet?"

Legna peeked around the corner to glance at the rug in question, looking as if she had never seen it before.

"We have a rug there?"

"Did you or did you not promise me you were not going to practice extending how long you can hold your invisible bowls of water in the house? And what on earth is that noise?"

"Okay, I confess to the water thing, which was an honest mistake, I swear it. But as for a noise, I have no idea what you are talking about."

"You cannot hear that? It has been driving me crazy for days now. It just repeats over and over again, a sort of clicking sound."

"Well, it took a millennium, but you have finally gone completely senile. Listen, this is a house built by Lycanthropes. It is more a cave than a house, to be honest. I have yet to decorate to my satisfaction. There is probably some gizmo of some kind lying around, and I will come across it eventually or it will quit working the longer it is exposed to our influence. Even though I do not hear anything, I will start looking for it. Is this satisfactory?"

"I swear, Magdelegna, I am never letting you visit that Druid ever again."

"Oh, stop it. You do not intimidate me, as much as you would love to think you do. Now, I will come over there if you promise not to yell at me anymore. You have been quite moody lately."

"I would be a hell of a lot less moody if I could figure out what that damn noise is."

Legna came around the corner, moving into his embrace with her hands behind her back. He immediately tried to see what she had in them.

"What is that?"

"Remember when you asked me why I cut my hair?"

"Ah yes, the surprise. Took you long enough to get to it."

"If you do not stop, I am not going to give it to you."

"Okay. I am stopping. What is it?"

She held out the box tied with a ribbon to him and he accepted it with a lopsided smile.

"I do not think I even remember the last time I received a gift," he said, leaning to kiss her cheek warmly. He changed his mind, though, and opted to go for her mouth next. She smiled beneath the cling of their lips and pushed away.

"Open it."

He reached for the ribbon and soon was pulling the top off the box.

"What is this?"

"Gideon, what does it look like?"

He picked up the woven circlet with a finger and inspected it closely. It was an intricately and meticulously fashioned necklace, clearly made strand by strand from the coffee-colored locks of his mate's hair. In the center of the choker was a silver oval with the smallest writing he had ever seen filling it from top to bottom.

"What does it say?"

"It is the medics' code of ethics," she said softly, taking it from him and slipping behind him to link the piece around his neck beneath his hair. "And it fits perfectly."

She came around to look at it, smiling. "I knew it would look handsome on you."

"I do not usually wear jewelry or ornamentation, but . . . it feels nice. How on earth did they make this?"

"Well, it took forever, if you want to know why it took so long for me to make good on the surprise. But I wanted you to have something that was a little bit of me and a little bit of you."

"I already have something like that. It is you. And . . . and me, I guess," he laughed. "We are a little bit of each other for the rest of our lives."

"See, that makes this a perfect symbol of our love," she said smartly, reaching up on her toes to kiss him.

"Well, thank you, sweet. It is a great present and an excellent surprise. Now, if you really want to surprise me, help me find out what that noise is."

"Okay, okay . . . where do you hear it coming from?"

"Around here somewhere."

"Always in this spot?"

"No. Not always. You are going to think I am even more insane, but I swear it is following me around."

"Maybe it is my new powers. The power to drive you mad." She wriggled her fingers at him theatrically as if she were casting a curse on him.

"You already drive me mad," he teased, dragging her up against him and nibbling her neck with a playful growling. "Ah hell," he broke off. "I really am going mad. I cannot believe you cannot hear that. It is like a metronome set to some ridiculously fast speed."

He turned and walked into the living room, looking around at every shelf.

"The last person to own this place probably had a thing for music and left it running. Listen. Can you hear that?"

"No," she said thoughtfully, "but I can hear you hearing it if I concentrate on your thoughts. What in the world . . . ?"

Gideon turned, then turned again, concentrating on the rapid sound, following it until it led him right up to his wife.

"It is you!" he said. "No wonder it is following me around. Are you wearing a watch?" He grabbed her wrist and she rolled her eyes.

"A Demon wearing a watch? Now I have heard everything."

Suddenly Gideon went very, very still, the cold wash of chills that flooded through him so strong that she shivered with the overflow of the sensation. He abruptly dropped to his knees and framed her hips with his hands.

"Oh, Legna," he whispered, "I am such an idiot. It is a baby. It is *our* baby. I am hearing its heartbeat!"

"What?" she asked, her shock so powerful she could barely speak. "I am with child?"

"Yes. Yes, sweet, you most certainly are. A little over a month. Legna, you conceived, probably the first time we made love. My beautiful, fertile, gorgeous wife."

Gideon kissed her belly through her dress, stood up, and caught her up against him until she squeaked with the force of his hug. Legna went past shock and entered unbelievable joy. She laughed, not caring how tight he held her, feeling his joy on a thousand different levels.

"I never thought I would know this feeling," he said hoarsely. "Even when we were getting married, I never thought . . . It did not even enter my mind!" Gideon set her down on her feet, putting her at arm's length as he scanned her thoroughly from head to toe. "I cannot understand why I did not become aware of this sooner. The chemical changes, the hormone levels alone . . ."

"Never mind. We know now," she said, throwing herself back up against him and hugging him tightly. "Come, we have to tell Noah . . . and Hannah! Oh, and Bella! And Jacob, of course. And Elijah. And we should inform Siena—"

She was still rattling off names as she teleported them to the King's castle.

You will not want to miss Jacquelyn Frank's next novel
in this magical series:

Elijah: The Nightwalkers

Available in December 2007 from Zebra Books.
Here is a brief excerpt . . .

The cold of another breeze rushed up from behind her, blowing at the brief skirt of her dress and whipping through her hair. It surrounded her, engulfed her, forcing her to come to a halt just as muscled arms appeared around her waist.

Siena sucked in a startled breath as the cold vanished, replaced by the warmth, the heat, of a familiar male body. She was drawn back against his chest, his hands splaying out over her flat belly and pushing her deeper into the planes of his hard body.

"Elijah," she whispered, her eyes closing as a sensation of remarkable relief flooded through her entire body. Every nerve and hormone in her body surged to life just to be held in his embrace and she was lightheaded with the power of it all.

He put hands on her hips, using them to spin her full around to face him. The warrior dragged her back to his body, seizing her mouth with impossible hunger just as she was reaching for his kiss. She could not have helped herself. Not after the deprivation of all these days. But still, the weakness stung her painfully, leaving frustrated tears in her eyes.

It was all just as she remembered it. The vividness of the memories of their touches and kisses had never once faded to less than what it truly was. It was all heat and musk and the delicious flavor of his bold, demanding mouth. His hands were on her backside, drawing her up into his body with movement she could only label as desperation.

Elijah had not meant to attack her in this manner, but the moment he had sensed her nearness, smelled the perfume of her skin and hair, he could not do anything else. He devoured the cinnamon taste of her mouth relentlessly, groaning with relief of pleasure as her hands curled around the fabric of his shirt and her incredible body molded to his with perfection. He pulled her hips directly to his own, leaving no question about how hard and fast her effect on him was. He felt her swinging perfectly with the onslaught of his pressing body and adamant kisses.

Everything was perfection. Top to bottom, beginning to end, and he had been starving without her. He also knew she had been just as famished without him.

She was the first to put any distance between them, by breaking away from his mouth, letting her head fall back as far as it could as she drew for breath hard and quick.

"Oh, no," she groaned huskily, shaking her head so her hair brushed over the arms around her waist.

Even those strands betrayed her, reaching eagerly to coil around his wrists and forearms, trapping him around her effectively, just in case of the outrageous instance he might want to move away from her. She lifted her head and opened her eyes, their golden depths full of her desire, and her anguish.

"I did not want this," she whispered to him, her forehead dropping onto his chest when the heat in his eyes proved too intense for her to bear. "Why will you not let me go?"

"Because I can't," he said immediately, disentangling one hand from her hair so he could take her chin in hand and force her to look at him. "No more than you can."

"I hate this," she said painfully, her eyes blinking rapidly as they smarted with tears of frustration. "I hate not being able to control my own body. My own will. If this is what it means to be Imprinted, it is a weakness I will abhor with my last breath."

Then she pushed away, defying every nerve in her body that screamed at her to step back into his embrace. She could only backtrack a couple of steps however, because her hair remained locked tight around his upraised wrist, pulling him along with her . . . as if he wouldn't have followed her anyway.

When she realized her back was to a window, she felt a moment of panic. However, she realized no one was likely to see them, because they were over three stories up from the houses and people below.

"You call it weakness, and yet as affected as I am by it myself, I choose to call it strength."

His rich baritone voice echoed around, making her heart leap in alarm. She grabbed his wrist and pulled him farther down the hallway, the dark shadows enclosing them as they reduced the potential for echoes.

"Why are you here? And do not blame it on a holy day that will not arrive for two days."

"I do not intend to 'blame' anything. I don't believe I need an excuse to see you, Siena." He reached for her face, but she jerked back and dodged him. "And it is because of that holy day two nights from now that I am here. We need a little bit of resolution between us before that night comes, Siena."

"I am not in need of resolution. If you are, you must come to it on your own."

She turned to walk away from him, but she forgot he was just as quick as she was. No one could outrun the wind. His hand closed easily around her forearm, pulling her back . . . and snapping the temper and pain she had been holding in tenuous control for days.

She released the cry of a wounded animal and flew at him. He saw the flash of claws and felt the sharp sting of their cut as they scored his face. Shocked by the attack for all of a second, Elijah reacted on instinct. He had her by her hair in a heartbeat, wrapping it around his fist in a single motion, turning her around so her back was to him and her claws pointed in a safer direction. She grunted softly, and then screamed in frustration as she found herself trapped face first against the stonecutter's art.

His enormous body was immediately flush against her back, securing her to the unforgiving stone as he caught one hand and pushed it against the stone as well.

"Let go of me!" She struggled in vain, unable to move a micron in any direction. "You'll have hands full of a spitting-mad cougar if you do not release me this instant!"

"I highly doubt that," he purred easily into her ear, his mouth brushing over the lobe of it in a way that made her shiver involuntarily.

And if you didn't read

Jacob: The Nightwalkers,

the first volume of this series,
please turn the page for a sample of that terrific title.
Available now from Zebra Books.

It was daylight once more when Jacob floated down through Noah's manor until he was in the vault, one moment dust dancing through the incandescent light, the next coming to rest lightly on his feet. He looked around the well-lit catacomb, seeking his prey. He heard a rustling sound from the nearest stacks and moved toward it.

There was a soft curse, a grunt, and the sudden slam of something hitting the floor. Jacob came around just in time to find Isabella dangling from one of the many shelves, her feet swaying about ten feet above the floor as she searched with her toes for a foothold. On the ground below her was a rather ancient-looking tome, the splattered pattern of the dust that had shaken off it indicating it had been the object he had heard fall. Far to her left was the ladder she had apparently been using.

With a low sigh of exasperation, Jacob altered gravity for himself and floated himself up behind her. "You are going to break your neck."

Isabella was not expecting a voice at her ear, considering her peculiar circumstances, and she started with a little scream. One hand lost hold and she swung right into the hard wall of his chest. He gathered her up against himself, his arm slipping beneath her knees so she was safely cradled, his warmth infusing her with a sense of safety and comfort as he brought her down to the floor effortlessly. In spite of herself, she pressed her cheek to his chest.

"Must you sneak up on me in midair like that? It's very unnerving."

She had meant to sound angry, but the soft, breathless accusation was anything but. Anyway, how angry would he think her to be if she was snuggling up to him like a kitten? Damn it, Demon or not, he was still a sinfully good-looking man. Jacob was elegant to a fault, his movements and manner centered around an efficiency of actions that drew the eye. He was dressed again in well-tailored black slacks, and this time a midnight blue dress shirt with his cuffs turned back. She could feel the rich quality of the silk beneath her cheek; and when she breathed in, Jacob smelled like the rich, heady Earth from which he claimed his abilities.

Besides all the outwardly alluring physicality, Isabella knew that he was extremely sensitive about all his inter-actions with others. She could feel his moral imperatives tingling through her mind whenever he was near. His heart, she knew, was made of incredibly honorable stuff. How could she find it in herself to be afraid of that? Especially when he had never once hurt her, even though there had been plenty of influences compelling him to.

"Shall I put you back and let you plummet to your death?" he asked, releasing her legs and letting her body slide slowly down his until her feet touched the floor.

The whisper of the friction of their clothes hummed across Jacob's skin, and he felt his senses focusing in on every nuance of sensation she provided for him. The swishing silk of her hair even in its present tangled state, the sweet warmth of her breath and body, the ivory per-fection of her skin. He reached to wipe a smudge of dust from her delectable little nose. She was a mess. There was no arguing that. Head to toe covered in dust and grime, and she smelled like an old book, but those earthy scents would never be something unappealing to one of his kind. Jacob breathed deeply as the usual heat she inspired stirred in his cool blood. It was stronger with each passing moment, with each progressive day, and he never once became unaware of that fact. He tried to tell himself it was merely the effects of the growing moon, but that reasoning did not satisfy him. Hallowed madness would not allow for the unexpected compulsion toward tenderness he kept experiencing whenever he looked down into her angelic face. It would never allow him to enjoy these simple yet significant stirrings of his awareness without forcing him into overdrive. True, he was holding on to his control with a powerful leash of determination. He was tamping down the surges of want and lust that gripped him so hard sometimes it was nearly crippling, but somehow it was still different.

Then he had to also acknowledge the melding of their thoughts as something truly unique. Perhaps a human could initiate such a contact if they were a medium or psychic of noteworthy ability, but she made no claims to such special talents. Every day the images of her mind became clearer to him. She had even taken to consciously sending him visual impressions in response to some discussion they were having with Noah, Elijah, and Legna. He believed that, if things continued to progress in this manner, he and Bella would soon be engaging in actual discussions with each other without ever opening their mouths. He didn't have fact to base that assumption on, but it seemed the natural evolution to the growing silent communication between them.

He had seen Legna staring at them curiously on several occasions. Luckily, because she was a female Mind Demon, she was not a full telepath. If she had been a male she would have been privy to some pretty private exchanges between him and Isabella. Nothing racy, actually, but he found Isabella had such an irreverent sense of humor that he wasn't sure others would understand it as he seemed to.

It was a privacy of exchange he found himself coveting. It was the one way they could be together without Legna or Noah interfering. It was bad enough that the empath was constantly sniffing at his emotions, making sure he kept in careful control of his baser side. Since the King was not able to subject him to the usual punishment that was meted out for those who had crossed the line as he had with Isabella, he had been forced to be a little more creative. Setting Legna the empathic bloodhound on him had done the trick. It was also seriously pissing him off. He knew she was always there, and it burned his pride like nuclear fire.

What was more, he couldn't keep his mind away from Isabella. And since even the smallest thought of her had a way of sparking of an onslaught of fantasies that brought his body to physical readiness . . . well, it was the very last thing he wanted an audience for.

It had taken quite a bit of planning, and the deceptive use of herbal tea mixtures, in order to slip out from under Legna's observation so he could sneak away to the vault. The empath slept as soundly as the dead, and she would stay that way until this evening.

"I wouldn't have fallen to my death," Bella was arguing, her stubborn streak prickling. "At the most, I would have fallen to my broken leg or my concussion or something. Boy, you Demons have this way of making everything seem so intense and pivotal."

"We are a very intense people, Bella."

"Tell me about it." She wriggled out of his embrace, putting distance between them with a single step back. Jacob was well aware of it being a very purposeful act. "I've been reading books and scrolls as far back as seven hundred years ago. You were just a gleam in your daddy's eye then, I imagine."

"Demons may have long gestation periods for their young, but not seventy-eight years' worth."

"Yes. I read about that. Is it true it takes thirteen months for a female to carry and give birth?"

"Minimum." He said it with such casual dismissal that Bella laughed.

"That's easy for you to say. You don't have to lug the kid around inside of you all that time. You, just like your human counterparts, have the fun part over with like that." She snapped her fingers in front of his face.

His dark eyes narrowed and he reached to enclose her hand in his, pulling her wrist up to the slow, purposeful brush of his lips even as he maintained a sensual eye contact that was far too full of promises. Isabella caught her breath as an insidious sensation of heated pins and needles stitched its way up her arm.

"I promise you, Bella, a male Demon's part in a mating is never over like this." He mimicked her snap, making her jump in time to her kick-starting heartbeat.

"Well"—she cleared her throat—"I guess I'll have to take your word on that." Jacob did not respond in agreement, and that unnerved her even further. Instinctively, she changed tack. "So, what brings you down into the dusty atmosphere of the great Demon library?" she asked, knowing she sounded like a brightly animated cartoon.

"You."

Oh, how that singular word was pregnant with meaning, intent, and devastatingly blatant honesty. Isabella was forced to remind herself of the whole Demon-human mating taboo as the forbidden response of heat continued to writhe around beneath her skin, growing exponentially in intensity every moment he hovered close. She tried to picture all kinds of scary things that could happen if she did not quit egging him on like she was. How she was, she didn't know, but she was always certain she was egging him on.

"Why did you want to see me?" she asked, breaking

away from him and bending to retrieve the book she had
dropped. It was huge and heavy and she grunted softly
under the weight of it. It landed with a slam and another
puff of dust on the table she had made into her own private study station.

"Because I cannot seem to help myself, lovely little
Bella."